"A HUNDRED VIR

"No problem," Starbuck said equably. "I'm loaded and willing to pay plenty."

O'Brien eyed him craftily. "What about me? Here in Frisco, a go-between don't come cheap either."

Starbuck ventured a smile. "How does five percent strike you?"

There was a moment of weighing and deliberation. O'Brien hadn't the vaguest idea of the asking price for a hundred slave-girl virgins. Whatever the amount, it would be steep. . .too tempting to resist.

"You're on."

Starbuck flashed his gold tooth in a nutcracker grin. Today was only a first step, but his instinct hadn't played him false.

Denny O'Brien had swallowed the bait whole.

PRAISE FOR MATT BRAUN

"Matt Braun is one of the best!"
—Don Coldsmith, author of the SPANISH BIT series

"He tells it straight—and he tells it well."
—Jory Sherman, author of GRASS KINGDOM

"Matt Braun has a genius for taking real characters out of the Old West and giving them flesh-and-blood immediacy."
—Dee Brown, author of
BURY MY HEART AT WOUNDED KNEE

"Braun blends historical fact and ingenious fiction...A top-drawer Western novelist!"
—Robert L. Gale, Western biographer

THE SPOILERS

MATT BRAUN

St. Martin's Paperbacks

This novel is a work of historical fiction. Names, characters, places and incidents relating to non-historical figures are either the product of the author's imagination or are used fictitiously, and any resemblance of such non-historical figures, places or incidents to actual persons, living or dead, events or locales is entirely coincidental.

TOMBSTONE / THE SPOILERS

Tombstone copyright © 1981 by Matthew Braun.
The Spoilers copyright © 1981 by Matthew Braun.

Cover photo © Comstock Images.

ISBN: 0-312-94781-X
EAN: 978-0-312-94781-1

Printed in the United States of America

Tombstone Pocket Books edition / April 1981
Tombstone Pinnacle edition / June 1985
St. Martin's Paperbacks edition / September 2002

The Spoilers Pocket Books edition / April 1985
The Spoilers Pinnacle edition / August 1985
St. Martin's Paperbacks edition / November 2002

St. Martin's Paperbacks are published by St. Martin's Press, 175 Fifth Avenue, New York, NY 10010.

10 9 8 7 6 5 4 3 2 1

To
BETTIANE
the source of all
that matters

Author's Note

The Spoilers is for the most part a true story. In 1882, San Francisco was the wildest, the wickedest, and certainly the most dangerous city in the West. The cowtowns and mining camps, by comparison, were tame stufff. Host to the Barbary Coast and Chinatown, not to mention a waterfront steeped in infamy, the city by the bay was a cosmopolitan hellhole. In that day and time, it was considered the roughest, and by far the most depraved, metropolis on the North American Continent.

Yet, during this same era, San Francisco was the premier city of the Old West. A financial center, a place of sophistication and culture, it was already a mythical wonder famed for its natural beauty and idyllic setting. Beneath the surface, however, there was an unholy marriage between underworld vice lords and corrupt politicians. Their alliance, bolstered by savage methods and a callous disregard for human life, was to rule San Francisco for nearly a quarter-century. Their downfall, when it came, happened very much as described in the story that follows.

The characters who people *The Spoilers* are real. Their names are unchanged, and the diabolic manner in which they pillaged San Francisco required no invention. Some license has been taken with events and dates, but the spoilers themselves are, if anything, less formidable than they were in real life. Luke Starbuck represents a breed apart. A detective and manhunter, he relied on wits and guts, and when necessary, a fast gun. His assignment in *The Spoilers* borders more on fact than fiction.

CHAPTER 1

A brisk October wind swept across the bay. The ferry plowed toward San Francisco, buffeted by the choppy waters. Directly ahead lay the waterfront, a sprawling collection of wharves and warehouses below the hill-studded city.

Luke Starbuck stood alone at the railing on the bow. The other passengers, crossing on the morning ferry from Oakland, were huddled inside the warmth of the main-deck cabin. Face to the wind, Starbuck appeared heedless of the damp chill and the spray that peppered him as waves slapped against the hull. His eyes were fixed on the harbor and the city beyond. He thought it the damnedest sight he'd ever seen.

Telegraph Hill, towering prominently above the waterfront, was cloaked in fog. Around the curving shore of the bay, the terrain formed a bold amphitheater, with inland hills surrounding the center of the city. The bay itself, perhaps the finest landlocked harbor in the world, was crowded with ships. At anchor were vessels of all nations, mast upon mast, their flags fluttering in the breeze. Westward, hidden by the fog-bound peninsula, was the Golden Gate. Through its channel, and into the harbor, sailed the ships of the China trade. Their cargo holds were filled with copra and raw silk, coconut oil and sugar, and myriad imports from the exotic Orient. The trade had transformed San Francisco into one of the richest ports on earth.

To Starbuck, who was not easily impressed, it was grander than anything he'd imagined. A former cowhand and rancher, he had grown to manhood in the Texas Panhandle. Circumstance had thrust him into the role of range detective, and several years were spent in the employ of Cattlemen's Associations across the West. As his reputation grew, he'd been hired by diverse organizations, like banks and mining companies. He was known to have killed at least twenty men, and among outlaws, he was considered the deadliest of all manhunters. Yet his skill as a detective by far exceeded his renown with a gun. His services were in constant demand, and though he was something of a lone wolf, his credentials were on a level with those of the Pinkerton Agency. He was celebrated as a man who never quit, that rare blend of bulldog and bloodhound. He got results.

For all his experience, however, Starbuck was not widely traveled. His work had been confined primarily to the Rocky Mountains and the Southern Plains. To him, Denver was a metropolis, and any body of water wider than the Rio Grande was beyond his ken. The sight of the bay, with tall-masted clippers and ocean-going steamers, was therefore a marvel to command attention. San Francisco, wondrously situated in a ring of hills, and several times the size of Denver, was like a storybook come to life. A profusion of cultures, cosmopolitan and sophisticated, it was the premier city of the West.

Watching it from the bow of the ferry, Starbuck felt a keen sense of exhilaration, and a quickening excitement. He told himself he'd been wise to accept Charles Crocker's summons. Whether or not he accepted the assignment was another thing, and suddenly not too important. Simply being here—San Francisco itself—was well worth the trip. He thought he might stay a while.

Only a week before, he'd been on the verge of accepting another assignment from Wells, Fargo. Then, out of the blue, he had received a wire from Charles Crocker, president of the Central Pacific Railroad. The message was terse, lacking specifics, but urgent in tone. Crocker requested Starbuck's presence in San Francisco, stressing the need for his professional services, and offered to pay all expenses.

Headquartered in Denver, Starbuck had never been retained by a railroad, and the idea intrigued him. He wired an affirmative reply and caught the next westbound. Arriving in Oakland yesterday eve ning, he had spent the night in a lodging house. Crocker's summons had indicated no need for secrecy, but by now it was second nature. He was entering San Francisco unknown and unannounced, one of the crowd.

When the ferry docked, he was the first to step ashore. He walked along the wharf and stopped on the corner of Market Street. The main thoroughfare of the city, Market began at the waterfront and bisected the business district. He stood for a moment, feeling somewhat like a hayseed, and simply stared. There was no question that San Francisco put Denver to shame. The buildings were taller. The people were more fashionably dressed, and crowded the sidewalks in greater numbers. There was a greater profusion of carriages and hansom cabs, blocking the street as far as the eye could see. The clamor and hubbub were deafening, and the whole scene put him in mind of an ant heap busily swarming with activity. Everything was bigger and louder, and somehow larger than life. He suddenly understood why the city by the bay was spoken of in awed terms.

Still, nothing daunted Starbuck for long. He took it all in stride, and quickly decided there was no reason to gawk. People were people, and ant heaps were all much alike, some merely larger and louder than others. Stepping off the corner, he dodged in front of a carriage and hopped aboard a horse-drawn streetcar. He paid his fare, asking the conductor for directions, and found a seat in the rear. Several blocks uptown, he spotted the triangle where Montgomery and Post intersected Market, and jumped down. He joined the crowd and walked north along Montgomery.

Crossing Sutter, he saw the Wells, Fargo Building kitty-corner across the street. He was tempted to step inside and pay his respects. Only four months ago, while working undercover for the stage company, he had been instrumental in running Wyatt Earp out of Arizona. With Earp's departure, stagecoach robbery in the Tombstone district had all but ceased. The company had awarded Starbuck a generous bonus for his part in routing the gang. Now, however, he resisted the impulse to stop by Wells, Fargo. He wasn't a tactful man, but neither was he a dimdot. Having hedged on accepting a new assignment, it wouldn't do to let them know he was in town to see Crocker. Wells, Fargo could wait.

At the next corner, in the heart of the financial district, he found the Mills Building. The corporate offices of the Central Pacific Railroad occupied the entire third floor. A rickety elevator deposited him in the waiting room, and he gave his name to a man seated behind a reception desk. An office boy scurried off to announce his arrival, and he took a chair. Several minutes later, a young man with thick glasses approached, introducing himself as Crocker's secretary. He led Starbuck down a long hallway and ushered him into a corner suite.

Charles Crocker's office was lavishly appointed. Overlooking the intersection of Montgomery and Bush, it was furnished with wing chairs and a sofa crafted in lush Moroccan leather. The floor was cov-

ered by an immense Persian carpet and the walls
were lined with oil paintings of the California coast.
At the far end of the room, framed between two
windows, was a gargantuan desk that looked to be
carved from a solid piece of teak. The room seemed
somehow appropriate to the man who rose from behind the desk.

Starbuck was reminded of a whale. Charles
Crocker topped six feet and weighed not a stone less
than three hundred pounds. Age had begun to
thicken his girth, and his muttonchop beard was
flecked through with gray. Yet he moved with vigor
and held himself in a posture of ramrod self-
assurance that bordered on arrogance. His voice was
deep and resonant, with a booming, organ-like quality.

"Welcome, Mr. Starbuck!" He extended an arm
the size of a log. "Welcome to San Francisco."

"Mr. Crocker." Starbuck found his handshake
only slightly less powerful than a bear trap. "Glad
to be here."

"How was your trip?"

"No complaints. You run a pretty fair railroad."

"None better!" Crocker said affably, waving him
to a chair. "We pride ourselves on that. Indeed, we
do!"

Starbuck seated himself in one of the wing chairs.
The secretary, without being asked, took the other
chair. Adjusting his glasses, he pulled a pad and pencil from his pocket, and waited at stiff-backed atten-

tion. Crocker crossed behind the desk and lowered his bulk into a tall swivel chair.

"Well, now," he said in his orotund voice, "down to business. You haven't come all this way for chit-chat, correct, Mr. Starbuck?"

"I'm all ears, Mr. Crocker. Fire away."

"Excellent!" Crocker gestured toward his secretary. "I'll just have Higgins take notes on our discussion. For the record, so to speak."

"Why do you need a record?"

"Standard practice," Crocker explained. "I trust you have no objection?"

Starbuck looked at him without expression. "I'm not much for talking on the record."

"May I ask why?"

"Things put down on paper sometimes come back to haunt you."

"Aren't you being overly cautious, Mr. Starbuck?"

"We all protect ourselves in different ways."

"Indeed?" Crocker said gruffly. "Well, suffice it to say, I never enter into an arrangement without a written record."

"Your privilege," Starbuck remarked in a dry, cold manner. "I never make a deal in writing. A handshake does it, or it doesn't get done."

"Suppose I break my word, decide not to pay you when the assignment's completed?"

Starbuck gave him a slow, dark smile. "You won't."

Starbuck was a rock of a man. He was sledge-shouldered, with lithe catlike reflexes, and taller than he appeared. His hair was sandy colored and his pale blue eyes took another man's measure in one swift glance. His gaze, now centered on Crocker, was steady and confident. The result was striking, somehow cold and very impersonal.

Crocker met and held his gaze. He was aware he'd underestimated the younger man. From all reports, Starbuck was a crackerjack detective; but those same reports indicated he was a mankiller, devoid of compassion or mercy when pushed beyond certain limits. After a moment's reflection, he was forced to admit Starbuck had a point. Today they wouldn't be dealing in vague abstractions. Their discussion, by necessity, would touch on the subject of death. That was something better left out of the record. A handshake would do very nicely.

"That's all, Higgins." He dismissed the secretary with a curt nod. "I'll call if I need you."

Higgins rose, looking slightly bemused, and walked from the room. There was a long, strained silence until the door closed. Then Crocker leaned back in the swivel chair, which creaked ominously under his weight.

"You're a cool one, Mr. Starbuck."

"No offense," Starbuck said woodenly. "A man in my line of work can't afford to take chances."

"I daresay," Crocker agreed, quickly moving on. "Now, as to the reason I asked you here. The Central Pacific has a problem with train robbers. I want it stopped."

"How serious a problem?"

"Very close to ruinous, Mr. Starbuck. Our express cars carry gold from the San Francisco mint and currency shipments from the banks throughout California. Over the past year we've been robbed on an average of twice a month. The losses, as you may well appreciate, have been staggering."

"No idea who's behind it?"

"None."

"The same gang every time?"

"We think so, but there's no way of knowing for certain."

"Any pattern?" Starbuck ventured. "Do they favor a certain section of the line? Or maybe strike at a certain time of the month?"

"Yes to both questions. More often than not they raid the southern line, somewhere between here and San Jose. As to timing, they *always* strike when we're carrying a large shipment."

"Always?" Starbuck regarded him with impassive curiosity. "Are you saying they know exactly which trains to hit?"

"I am, indeed," Crocker said in an aggrieved tone. "That's why I summoned you, Mr. Starbuck. We have a Judas in our midst—someone who supplies them with our shipment schedules. No matter what precautions we take—despite the utmost secrecy— they always know. Always!"

Starbuck's eyes were hard, questing. "What about your own security force? With the pattern established, they could've pulled a switch and waylaid the robbers."

Crocker looked painfully embarrassed. "We tried that on two separate occasions. In both instances, the train wasn't robbed."

"Your Judas tipped them off in advance?"

"Precisely."

"So you're asking me to ferret out the Judas?"

"The Judas," Crocker said, watching him carefully, "and the gang leader. I want it stopped—permanently."

A stony look settled on Starbuck's face. He'd heard the same message many times before. Always phrased discreetly, never in the form of a direct order, it was nonetheless obvious. Someone needed to be killed, and he was being asked to do the job. He gave Crocker an evaluating glance, then shrugged.

"I work at my own speed and I do it my own way. If I take the assignment, then I'll report directly to you and no one else."

"Does that include Tom Kelly, our security chief?"

"That includes everybody and anyone. Either our meeting today stays inside these four walls or I want no part of the deal. One little hint, and your Judas would most likely punch my ticket."

"Where would you begin?"

"Where it's least expected," Starbuck said stolidly. "I'll let you know after I've had a chance to nose around."

Crocker's expression was speculative. "How would you report to me?"

"Never here," Starbuck told him firmly. "I'll figure a way to get word to you. If it's necessary that we meet, then it'll have to be somewhere else. Somewhere damn private, and always by yourself."

"In other words, you would operate independently and keep me informed as it suits your pleasure. Is that essentially correct?"

"That's the way I work," Starbuck said levelly. "So far it's kept me alive."

"An admirable record," Crocker observed with a tinge of irony. "Now, as to your fee. I presume you have a standard rate?"

Starbuck had done his homework on the Central Pacific. In 1862, two companies were awarded federal charters to build a transcontinental railroad: the Union Pacific, building westward from the Missouri River, and the Central Pacific, building eastward from California. Crocker and three business cronies—Leland Stanford, Mark Hopkins, and Collis Huntington—were the sole stockholders of the Central Pacific. Thereafter, they were known as the Big Four, and with reason. The government granted them nine million acres of land, $24,000,000 in federal bonds, and no strings attached. For four years, three thousand Irishmen and ten thousand Chinese coolies labored to build their railroad. One of the end results was San Francisco's fabled Chinatown. The other was a separate construction company, which had exclusive rights to purchase material and build the

Central Pacific. Crocker and his cohorts, once again the sole stockholders, raised $79,000,000 in bonds and cash from the government and private investors. Of that amount, $36,000,000, not counting river frontage and ocean property, was siphoned off into their own pockets. The facts had slowly come to light, and now, in 1882, the holdings of the Big Four were conservatively estimated at $100,000,000 or more.

The newspapers of the day, never overly fond of robber barons, had characterized Crocker as "ruthless as a crocodile" and a man who believed in "the brute force of money." Having briefed himself on the Big Four in general, and Crocker in particular, Starbuck saw no reason to be charitable. He had come to the meeting fully prepared to deal with a crocodile, and he hadn't been disappointed. Then, too, having heard the assignment, he now had fewer qualms about holding Crocker's feet to the fire.

"One hundred dollars a day," Starbuck said at length. "All expenses paid and a minimum guarantee of a thousand dollars. That's my standard rate."

"Awfully steep, isn't it?" Crocker complained. "The Pinkerton Agency only charges half that amount."

"The Pinkertons won't do the job you want done, otherwise you would've hired them to start with."

"I'm afraid I don't follow you."

"It's simple enough," Starbuck said in a deliberate voice. "You want your Judas and the gang leader killed. No arrest, no trial, just a couple of quick funerals and the less fanfare the better."

"I didn't say that."

"Naturally." Starbuck cracked a smile. "If you had to say it, then I'd be the wrong man for the job. Tell me it's not so and I'll head on back to Denver."

Crocker gave him a faint nod of satisfaction. "Your terms are acceptable."

"I'll be in touch."

Starbuck heaved himself to his feet. Crocker rose and they shook hands, staring gravely into each other's eyes. Then, with no parting word, Starbuck turned and walked out. He closed the door softly behind him.

Crocker slumped back into his chair. His palms were sweaty, and he breathed a heavy sigh of relief. There for a moment, looking into Starbuck's eyes, he had experienced the sensation of fear. He knew it was justified, and he felt no shame.

He had the distinct impression he'd just struck a bargain with the Devil himself.

CHAPTER 2

Starbuck arrived at the depot shortly before boarding time.

The morning train for Los Angeles departed at seven o'clock, and by his watch he had a quarter-hour to spare. He purchased a ticket for Salinas, then crossed the waiting room to the departure gate. He carried no luggage, but he was nonetheless prepared to travel. A Colt sixgun, hidden by his suit jacket, rode comfortably in a crossdraw holster.

Outside, he paused on the platform and pulled out the makings. He creased the paper, sprinkling tobacco, and rolled himself a smoke. A flick of his thumbnail struck a match and he lit the cigarette. Moving to one side, he propped himself up against a wall, quietly watchful. His eyes slowly scanned the crowded platform.

The San Francisco-to-Los Angeles run was clearly profitable. A large throng of passengers had already boarded, and others were saying their last goodbyes to family and well-wishers. Everyone looked perfectly ordinary, businessmen and drummers, working stiffs and farmers, and a dithering assortment of women and children. None of them appeared to be packing a gun, and there wasn't a suspicious face in the crowd. Insofar as he could determine, it was simply another day on the Central Pacific. Nothing out of place, no reason for alarm.

His attention moved to the train itself. There were four passenger coaches, normal for the morning run to Los Angeles. Down the line, the locomotive chuffed and belched steam. The tender was freshly loaded with coal, and directly behind, the last of the mail sacks were being loaded aboard the express car. A mail sorter and two guards, both armed with pistols, were visible through the door. Coupled to the rear of the train was a slat-sided boxcar. While unusual, for livestock was normally hauled by freight trains, its presence today was wholly unavoidable. The boxcar was part and parcel of Starbuck's plan.

On the platform, near the open door of the boxcar, a man stood smoking a pipe. He was tall and lanky, almost cadaverous in appearance, and he wore the rough-garbed clothing of a stockman. He was watching the crowd with no apparent interest, puffing cottony wads of smoke. His manner was somewhat resigned, almost bored. The look of a hired hand stuck with an unpleasant chore.

Starbuck sauntered over, the cigarette stuck in the corner of his mouth. He stopped in front of the man, nodding amiably.

"Howdy."

"Mornin'," the man replied. "Do something for you?"

"Well, neighbor, my curiosity's workin' overtime. Thought mebbe you'd oblige me by answerin' a question."

Starbuck easily slipped into the lingo of the range. His boots and wide-brimmed hat, the roll-your-own dangling from his lips, all did the trick. The man brightened and responded in the slow drawl common to south Texas.

"You're a long ways from home, ain't you?"

"For a fact," Starbuck grinned. "Hail from the Panhandle, couple of days ride north of San Angelo."

"Damnation! Ain't that one for the books! I'm from down around Laredo myself."

"Pegged you for a Texican! Yessir, I was standin' over there and I says to myself, that feller's got the look of homefolks. Figgered I'd just mosey over and see."

"Glad you did! Shore good to hear a man speak plain English again."

Starbuck held out his hand. "Name's Joe Dobbs."

"Hank Noonan." After pumping his arm, Noonan gave him a quizzical look. "What brings you out here?"

"Aww, just rubber-neckin'," Starbuck chuckled. "Fell into a little *dinero* and thought I'd take a gander at the ocean. Never seen one a'fore." He paused, took a drag on his cigarette. "What about your own-self?"

"Horse trainer." Noonan puffed importantly on his pipe. "Feller name of Crocker—owns this here very railroad—come down to the King spread a few years back and bought hisself a string of thorough-breds. I was head wrangler there at the time and he hired me to wetnurse his stock. Been out here ever since."

"Got a nice outfit, does he?"

"Fair to middlin'," Noonan allowed. "Thousand acres or so down along the coast. But he's got an eye for racehorses, and the pay's good too."

"That's what got my curiosity whetted. Wondered why they had a stockcar hooked onto a passenger train."

"Have a looksee." Noonan jerked a thumb at the boxcar. "Takin' one of Crocker's mares down to a breedin' farm in the San Joaquin Valley. Him ownin' the railroad, he can pretty damn much do what he pleases. That's how come she wasn't put on a reg-ular freight run."

Starbuck crushed his cigarette underfoot, then stuck his head through the boxcar door. A chestnut mare, haltered and tied in a stall, stood munching hay. His gaze shifted quickly around the car and abruptly stopped. He spotted an old saddle and some bridle gear piled near a water barrel. He grunted softly to himself, satisfied.

"Aboard! All aboard!"

The conductor's voice rang out in a last call to

passengers. Starbuck turned, clapping Noonan on the
shoulder, and gave him a parting handshake. Then,
as the Texan scrambled into the boxcar, he hurried
forward. Bypassing the rear coaches, he walked
along the platform. The train lurched and he swung
aboard the first coach, directly behind the express
car. The conductor gave him a dirty look and signaled the engineer. Moments later, the train gathered
speed and rolled southward out of the switching
yard.

Starbuck found a window seat toward the front of
the coach. A sundries drummer was seated beside
him, and they passed the next few minutes in idle
conversation. Presently, a candy butcher came
through hawking sweets and sandwiches. The drummer, commenting he'd missed breakfast, bought a
ham and cheese that looked stale as sawdust. Then
the conductor passed by, punching tickets, and an-
nounced an upcoming stop. Starbuck yawned a wide
jaw-cracking yawn, and settled deeper into his seat.
He pulled his hat down over his eyes, and left the
drummer to his sandwich.

Feigning sleep, he mentally reviewed all he'd
learned over the past three days. Even now, he was
looking for holes in his plan, something he might
have missed. However careful, no man was infallible. He'd made mistakes before, and he would likely
make some this trip out. But in his view, that was
no excuse for sloppy planning. He especially wanted
no miscues today.

After his meeting with Crocker, he had holed up

in a seedy Mission District hotel. There, sprawled
out on the bed, he had analyzed the various ap-
proaches he might take. On balance, he'd concluded
that the place to start was with the robbers themselves. To go undercover within Central Pacific
would have proved time-consuming, and perhaps not
all that productive. The railroad's organization—the
sheer number of people—was simply too vast and
too segmented. It would have taken him weeks,
maybe even months, to establish himself and work
his way through the organization. The time span
might have been shortened by limiting himself to
upper-echelon departments; but that approach had
serious drawbacks, as well. There were too many
people, from clerks to vice-presidents, with access
to express-car shipment schedules. And the Judas,
obviously a slippery customer, would not be caught
napping.

All in all, it seemed to Starbuck that the fastest
and most direct approach was the gang itself. Once
he identified the ringleader, and had him under surveillance, it wouldn't take long to isolate the Judas.
Barring that, he could, as a last resort, pass himself
off as a hardcase and infiltrate the gang. He'd done
it with cattle rustlers and stage robbers, and he had
no doubt it would work with train robbers. Yet that,
too, would consume time—perhaps a month or
longer—for outlaws were slow to accept a stranger
into their ranks. By far, the better plan was to let the
gang leader lay a trail to the Judas. Then, in a manner of speaking, he would kill two birds with one

stone. Or at the very least, a couple of .45 slugs.

That much decided, Starbuck had contacted Crocker the next evening, slipping unobstrusively into his mansion on Nob Hill. He obtained a map of the Central Pacific railway lines and pinpointed the exact location of all previous robberies. A detailed study of the map proved illuminating. While a few of the holdups had occurred on the run to Sacramento, the majority had taken place in the fifty-mile stretch between San Francisco and the Santa Cruz Mountains. He put himself in the robbers' boots—a feat of mental gymnastics he'd learned as a manhunter—and arrived at a gut-certain hunch. The gang was quite probably operating from a hideout within a twenty-mile radius of Los Altos, a sleepy whistlestop some thirty miles south of San Francisco. Telegraph had improved communications among law officers, and the gang leader was clearly no dimwit. After pulling a holdup, the robbers had never been sighted, much less pursued. That strongly indicated they had a hideout that was within two hours' ride of the jobs they'd pulled to date. He determined that the first step was to unearth their hideout.

The following night he had again contacted Crocker and outlined his plan. An unusually large express shipment was to be arranged two days hence, on the morning train to Los Angeles. Everything was to appear routine, and standard security measures were to be employed. Crocker had bellyached long and loud, demanding extra guards to prevent loss of

the money. Starbuck remained adamant, arguing that
the gang must be lured into a holdup and thereby
afford him the advantage of a fresh trail. In the end,
common sense prevailed and he'd got his way. His
last request, more so than the money, had brought
on a fit of near apoplexy. Using some plausible cover
story, one of Crocker's racehorses was to be shipped
south on the same train. A hot shouting match ensued, but in that, too, he had prevailed. He left
Crocker to work out the necessary subterfuge.

Now, scrunched down in his seat, he concluded
he'd left nothing undone. All was in readiness, and
it remained only for the gang to take the bait. Some
inner voice told him he wouldn't be disappointed.
He closed his eyes and almost instantly, like an animal, he was asleep.

The train passed through Los Altos an hour or so
later. Awake and watchful, Starbuck began to wonder if he'd bet a loser. The next stop was San Jose,
some twenty miles down the line. The gang, according to the information provided by Crocker, had
never robbed a train south of San Jose. Which meant
it had to happen soon or not at all.

Long ago, Starbuck had determined that outlaws
were essentially lazy. For all their cunning, those
who rode the owlhoot were unimaginative and generally possessed more balls than brains. Unlike high-
class crooks, such as con men and grifters, the
average desperado was a creature of habit. Unwittingly, because he was shiftless and indolent, he took

the path of least resistance. Once he stumbled upon a method that worked, he seemed to fall into a rut, seldom attempting anything new or novel. A pattern invariably emerged, and his actions thereafter became somewhat predictable. All of which gave Starbuck reason for concern.

Unless the gang struck soon, his plan would very likely prove a washout. There was always tomorrow, and another plan, but he much preferred today. He prided himself on outguessing crooks—the first time around.

Starbuck's judgment was vindicated some five miles south of Los Altos. On a dogleg curve, a tree had been felled across the tracks. The engineer set the brakes and the train jarred to a screeching halt. The sudden jolt caught the passengers unawares, and there was a moment of pandemonium in the coaches. Women screamed and men cursed, and luggage from the overhead racks went flying down the aisle. Untangling themselves, the passengers were dazed and not a little fearful. Their voices verged on panic.

Then, suddenly, a collective hush fell over the coaches. A gang of masked riders burst out of the woods bordering the tracks. Four men rode directly to the express car, pouring a volley of shots through the door. The three remaining men, spurring their horses hard, charged up and down the track bed. Their pistols were cocked and pointed at the passengers, who stared open-mouthed through the coach windows. No shots were fired, but the message was clear: *Stay on the train or get killed*. Which made eminent good sense to the passengers. The Central Pacific, like most railroads, was not revered by the public. A holdup, according to common wisdom, was a matter between the railroad and the bandits. Only a fool would risk his life for the likes of the Big Four. And there were no fools aboard today.

Starbuck had a ringside seat. From his position in the front of the coach, the four men outside the express car were plainly visible. Watching them, he had to admire their no-nonsense approach to train robbery. One of the riders produced a stick of dynamite and held the fuse only inches away from the tip of a lighted cigar. Another rider, his voice raised in a commanding shout, then informed the express guards that they had a choice: *Open the door or get blown to Kingdom Come!*

The guards, much like the passengers, were unwilling to die for the Central Pacific. The door slid open and the guards dutifully tossed their pistols onto the track bed. Three of the robbers dismounted and clambered inside the express car. The other three, still menacing the passengers with pointed guns, held their positions outside the coaches. The seventh man, the one with the foghorn voice, directed the operation from aboard his horse. His tone had the ring of authority, brusque and demanding. His attitude was that of a man accustomed to being obeyed.

Starbuck immediately tagged him as the gang leader. He looked to be of medium height, powerfully built, and he was dressed in the nondescript

workclothes worn by the other men. A slouch hat
covered his head, and a wide bandanna, pulled up
over his nose, effectively masked his features. Yet,
upon closer observation, Starbuck spotted something
that couldn't be hidden. A thatch of red hair, brilliant
orangey-red, spilled out from beneath the slouch hat.
Bright as a sunset, it was a head of hair that would
stand out in any crowd.

From start to finish, the holdup took less than five
minutes. The robbers inside the express car emerged
with mail sacks stuffed full of cash and quickly
mounted their horses. On signal from their leader,
the gang opened fire and raked the length of the train
with a barrage of lead. The shots were purposely
placed high, but windows shattered and wall panels
splintered and the angry snarl of bullets ripped
through the coaches. Everyone dove for the floor and
prudently stayed there. A moment later the gunfire
ceased and the thud of hoofbeats drummed the earth.

Starbuck peeked over the windowsill just as the
gang disappeared into the woods. He jumped to his
feet, hopping over the drummer, and moved through
the door. Outside, he went down the coach steps and
sprinted toward the rear of the train. Not ten seconds
elapsed from the last gunshot to the time he pulled
up in front of the boxcar. He hammered on the door
with his fist.

"Noonan! Hank Noonan! Open up!"

"Who's there?"

"Joe Dobbs! C'mon, get the lead out! It's life or
death!"

"Hold on, Joe!" The door flew open and Noonan gaped down at him with a look of fright. "Lord God A'mighty, they didn't shoot you, did—"

Starbuck showed him a cocked sixgun. "Hank, I want you to listen real close and do exactly what I say. Savvy?"

Noonan bobbed his head, eyes popped out like a pair of fried eggs. Following Starbuck's instructions, he muscled the loading ramp to the door and dropped it into place. Starbuck climbed inside, noting out of the corner of his eye that a crowd of men had gathered around the express car. He ordered Noonan to saddle the mare. The Texan suddenly pulled up, his features twisted in a mulish frown.

"No sir!" he muttered hotly. "You ain't gonna steal—"

Starbuck wagged the snout of the sixgun. "Don't play hero, *compadre*. Just get it done—*muy pronto!*"

Grumbling under his breath, Noonan went to work. He saddled the mare, afterward fitting the bit into her mouth and slipping the bridle over her head. Then he backed her out of the stall and walked her to the door. With an unpleasant grunt, he tossed the reins to Starbuck.

"I dunno your game, but you shore picked the wrong horse. Old man Crocker's gonna hang your ass a mile high."

"Obliged for the warning, Hank. Now step aside and don't make any sudden moves."

Starbuck holstered his gun and looped the reins around the mare's neck. He stepped into the saddle, tugged at the brim of his hat, and gave Noonan a sardonic smile. Then he feathered the mare in the ribs and reined her down the loading ramp. Once clear of the track bed, he gigged her hard and rode off at a gallop.

A moment later he vanished into the trees.

CHAPTER 3

The chase lasted almost three hours.

From the outset, it was apparent to Starbuck that he'd underestimated the gang leader. He had expected a furious dash, speed rather than deception. That view had been reinforced when the job was pulled scarcely five miles south of Los Altos. An hour's hard ride, on a direct beeline to the hideout, was how he had visualized it upon taking the trail. He'd never been more wrong.

Instead of a beeline, the robbers zigzagged all over the countryside. A mile or so north of the holdup scene, they suddenly changed course and circled west of Los Altos. In the process, they crisscrossed several creeks, and at one point held their horses to mid-stream for something more than a half-mile. Then they switched directions and again turned due north. Their path, however, was meandering and uncannily deceptive.

At all times, the gang warily avoided open

ground. While they never doubled back, they stuck
to redwood forests and scrub-choked hills wherever
possible. Upon encountering lowlands, they veered
off into rocky defiles latticed with brushy undergrowth. Their general direction was always north,
but the winding route followed a network of harsh
and seemingly predetermined obstacles. Quite
clearly, they knew the terrain and had developed
evasive stratagems to throw off pursuit. To all but a
skilled tracker, their trail would have been lost
within a few miles.

Starbuck's years as a manhunter served him well.
Early on in his career, he had worked solely as a
range detective. His principal targets were cattle rustlers and horse thieves, men schooled in plains lore
and the artful dodges of hiding a trail. By necessity,
he had become a tracker of surpassing skill, able to
read signs practically invisible to the naked eye. Today, those skills permitted him to follow a crazy-
quilt path that would have defeated ordinary
lawmen. Several times he lost sight of the gang, but
he never lost their trail. He stuck to their tracks like
a born Apache.

An hour into the chase Starbuck realized he had
committed another error. Having underestimated the
gang leader, he had thoughtlessly compounded the
problem by choosing the wrong mount. The thor-
oughbred mare was built for speed, not endurance.
Unlike common saddle horses, she had no bottom,
no staying power over the long haul. North of Los
Altos she began to play out, and he had no choice

but to conserve her stamina. His pace was slowed even further, and with each passing mile, he found himself falling farther behind. Once again, his ability to read sign and track on hard ground kept him in the race.

Yet, for all his skill, he barely avoided disaster in the end. Shortly after midday, he was tracking through a low range of mountains. His eyes were on broken twigs and crushed vegetation, and the sign indicated he was perhaps twenty minutes behind the gang. He topped a ridge, and spread out before him the mountains dropped off to a rolling plain. At the bottom of the ridge was a creek, bordered by trees, and on the far side was a farmhouse and a small barn. For a moment, looking down with surprise, nothing registered. Then he saw the corral, and the horses. And gathered outside the farmhouse, a group of men.

Suddenly it dawned on him that he was skylined. Wondering if he'd been seen, he sawed at the reins and whipped the mare back over the ridge. A short distance north, he dismounted and left the mare tied in a grove of trees. He walked quickly to the ridge, removing his hat, and went belly down. Below, not a hundred yards away, he had a commanding view of the farmhouse. The men were still bunched near the front door, and there was no apparent sign of alarm. He thought it was his lucky day. Goddamned lucky!

A closer look confirmed that the chase had indeed ended. He spotted the red-haired gang leader, clearly

a standout even at a distance. The men were gathered
around a water pump, taking turns sluicing off the
grime of a long and dusty ride. Apparently in good
humor, their leader was gesturing and talking in a
loud voice. The sound of laughter carried distinctly
to the ridge top.

Starbuck's attention was abruptly drawn to the
corral. He saw a man, dressed in bib overalls, fork-
ing hay to the horses. A quick count verified that he
was not one of the original seven who had robbed
the train. Upon closer inspection, Starbuck realized
there was more to the farm than he'd seen at first
glance. Beyond the house, several acres were fenced
and planted with a variety of vegetables. Off in the
distance, a herd of some twenty dairy cows grazed
placidly in the noonday sun. No hardscrabble operation, the farm had a look of substance and prosperity. The abundance of produce, and the presence of
milk cows, meant only one thing. There was a mar-
ketplace nearby, probably no more than a few hours'
ride away.

A woman suddenly stepped through the doorway
of the house and called to the men. She wore a
checkered apron, and from her scolding manner,
Starbuck sensed she was summoning the men to a
hot meal. For the first time, he noticed the mail sacks
piled beside the door. As the gang trooped inside,
the burly redhead and another man each hefted one
of the sacks. From all appearances, more than a hot
meal would be divvied up over the dinner table.

Something bothered Starbuck about the setup. A

dairy farmer and his wife seemed unlikely accomplices for a band of train robbers. Nor was the farm itself the hideout he'd expected to find. One somehow didn't dovetail with the other.

The thought prompted another question. He wondered where the hell he was. He had some general idea, for he knew the chase had carried him far north of Los Altos. But he had no notion of where it had ended, or exactly how far north.

He pulled the map from his inside coat pocket and spread it on the ground. Turning, he studied the mountain range, noting rises in elevation and dominant peaks. With one eye on the terrain, he slowly scanned the map. Suddenly he blinked and his finger jabbed at a spot that marked the flatland below. The farm was on the western slope of the San Bruno Mountains, roughly in the center of the peninsula. The hairpin bend in the creek pinpointed his precise location.

He was less than ten miles south of San Francisco.

The sheer audacity of it was stunning. No one would believe a gang of train robbers would operate that close to a major city. Nor would anyone suspect that a tranquil dairy farm was an outlaw hideout. It took the cake for nerve, and it proved that there was always an exception to any rule. The red-haired gang leader not only had a big set of balls; he had brains, as well. The whole operation had been planned with a sort of tactical genius.

On impulse, Starbuck was struck by another of his hunches. The farmhouse was a rendezvous, not a hideout. A meeting place and a way station for the horses. A stopover for the gang before they rode on to somewhere else.

He smiled, nodding to himself, and returned the map to his coat pocket. Then he settled down to wait.

A short time later Starbuck got still another surprise. The train robbers, followed by the farmer, emerged from the house. Yet they were now an altogether different group of men. Their workclothes had been exchanged for city suits and bowler hats; the transformation was startling. No longer was there any resemblance to the gang that had stopped the morning train.

The barn doors were opened and two carriages were rolled outside. A team of bays and a team of chestnuts were then led from the barn and hitched to the carriages. Four men climbed aboard the first carriage and took off along a wagon trail that snaked westward. The gang leader and the others waited, talking quietly amongst themselves, until some ten minutes had passed. Then they stepped into the second carriage, waving to the farmer, and drove off in the same direction. To all appearances, they might have been businessmen or land speculators, or even a crew of Bible salesmen canvassing the countryside. By no stretch of the imagination would anyone connect them to the train holdup.

Starbuck quickly checked his map. He located the wagon trail and saw that it intersected a main road, running north-south along the peninsula. The only other road, some miles to the west, skirted the coastline. There were fishing villages along the ocean, and a few small settlements dotted the bay side of the peninsula; all the land in between appeared to be sparsely populated, mainly farms. The relative isolation of the area merely enhanced his respect for the gang. Their rendezvous point, though close to San Francisco, was nonetheless remote. The concept was masterful and the execution flawless. The work of a man who knew his business, a professional.

Waiting until the carriage was out of sight, Starbuck mounted the mare and rode north. He forded the stream a mile or so above the farmhouse, then turned due west. Presently he crested a rise of ground and spotted the main road. He walked the mare to a grove of trees, staying hidden in the shadows, and rolled himself a smoke. Before he had time to finish his cigarette, the carriage appeared from the south. The gang's destination, much as he'd suspected, was San Francisco. Allowing them a five-minute lead, he left the trees and reined the mare toward the road.

He easily kept the carriage in sight.

Once inside the city limits, Starbuck was able to close the gap. By then it was late afternoon, and he was just another horseman on streets clogged with traffic. He had no fixed plan in mind, but he'd set himself a task that was essential to any further action. Before the night was out, he meant to establish the gang leader's identity.

The carriage led him across town, to the intersection of Jackson and Sansome. There, the team and carriage were dropped off at a livery stable. He dismounted, hitching the mare outside a saloon on the opposite corner. The four men in the first carriage were nowhere in evidence, but that gave him no reason for concern. After a robbery, very likely wearing money belts stuffed with cash, it figured they would scatter. Shortly, the thought was confirmed when the burly redhead talked with the two men a moment, then waved and walked off. He turned north on Sansome.

Starbuck followed, strolling casually along the opposite side of the street. The sidewalks were thronged with passersby, and he readily blended into the crowd. Having spent three days in San Francisco, he'd gotten his bearings, and the direction of the surveillance came as no great surprise. The gang leader was moving at a brisk pace toward the Barbary Coast.

A hellhole, infamous throughout the world, the Barbary Coast was not for those of faint heart. On the bay side, it was bounded by the waterfront and Telegraph Hill, and extended several blocks inland along Pacific and Broadway streets. A wild carnival of depravity and crime, the area was devoted to dancehalls and brothels, gambling casinos and groggeries, and sinister crimping joints where sailors were drugged and shanghaied for brutal voyages at sea. Vice and debauchery were the district's stock-in-trade.

Local legend attributed the name to the African coastline of earlier notoriety. Whatever its ancestry, the Barbary Coast transformed the dreams of sailors and landlubbers alike into wicked, and sometimes deadly, reality. On average, there were several murders a night, with seamen the most common victims. After voyages lasting two to four years, the sailors were ripe for women, alcohol, and some of the gamier pursuits known to man. The Opera Comique, a dive billing carnal entertainment, presented live shows involving feats of copulation that ranged from acrobatic couples to onstage orgies. Not to be outdone, the Boar's Head staged a show-stopper in which the buxom star was mated on alternate nights to a Shetland pony and bull mastiff. No man, however low his tastes, failed to get his money's worth on the Barbary Coast.

Starbuck trailed the gang leader to the Bella Union. A somewhat higher-class establishment, it was located at an intersection humorously dubbed Murder Corner. Offering all things to all men, it provided women, gaming tables, and risqué stage shows. A billboard out front ballyhooed the attractions inside:

PLAIN TALK AND BEAUTIFUL GIRLS!
Lovely Tresses! Lovely Lips! Buxom Forms!
At the
BELLA UNION.
And Such Fun!
If You Don't Want to Risk Both Optics
SHUT ONE EYE.

The batwing doors opened onto a large barroom and gaming parlor. Beyond the bar was a spacious theater, with an orchestra pit and a stage ablaze with footlights. The floor was jammed with tables, and a horseshoe balcony was partitioned into ornate, curtained boxes. Songs and dances were performed, pandering to the profane nature of the clientele, and the atmosphere fell somewhere between licentious and obscene. After their acts, the girls mingled with the customers in a crush of jiggling breasts and fruity buttocks. The sofas in the boxes were reserved for private entertainment, and along with the mandatory bottle of champagne, added greatly to the income of all concerned. A pretty little *danseuse* from the show went for a ten spot, and chilled bubbly doubled the tab. The girl kept half the charge for her services and the balance went to the house.

Sunset was still an hour away, but the Bella Union was already jam-packed. Starbuck shouldered a place at the bar, wedging himself in between a bow-legged sailor and a whiskery miner. He ordered rye and kept one eye on the red-haired robber, who had taken a position at the end of the bar. A close-up look revealed that the man was ugly as a toad, with pockmarked features, nut-brown eyes, and freckles almost the exact color of his hair. Starbuck committed his face to memory.

So far the gang leader had spoken to no one but the bartender. He stood with his elbows hooked over the counter and watched the show with a vacant expression. Onstage, a screeching troupe of dancers was romping through a version of the French *can-can*. Their frilly drawers and black mesh stockings exploded into view as they went into the finale and flung themselves rump first to the floor in *la split*. Then, screaming and tossing their skirts, they leaped to their feet and raced offstage as the curtain dropped. The spectators rewarded them with thunderous applause, which prompted a caterwauling curtain call. Then, awaiting the next act, everyone went back to drinking.

On his second shot of rye, Starbuck saw the gang leader straighten up and nod to someone pushing through the crowd. The man who joined him was stocky and muscular, with a square, tough face and a handlebar mustache. He was dressed like a dandy and carried himself with the cocky poise of a prizefighter. He spoke to the gang leader, who beamed a wide grin, and rapidly bobbed his head. The transformation in the train robber was immediate, and curiously out of character. He looked not just respectful, but somehow servile. A hardass bandit suddenly turned boot-licker.

Starbuck signaled for another drink. While the barkeep was pouring, he ducked his chin toward the end of the counter. "Shore wouldn't wanna tangle with that pair."

The barkeep followed his gaze, and chuckled. "You'd sure as Christ regret it if you did, cowboy."

"Why? They somebody special?"

"Well, the one with the mustache is Denny O'Brien. Owns the Bella Union and half the Coast.

The other one's Red Ned Adair, and claims he's meaner'n tiger spit. For my money, they both are."

"I don't reckon I'd care to argue it either way."

"You've got lots of company, cowboy."

The barkeep hustled off, and Starbuck silently repeated the names to himself. Then he saw the one named O'Brien turn and walk toward a staircase near the entranceway to the theater. The gang leader downed his drink and quickly followed along. Together, they mounted the stairs and disappeared from view.

Starbuck had a visceral instinct for the truth, some sixth sense for divining what lay beneath the surface. He was suddenly struck by the thought that the operation was bigger than he'd suspected. Quite probably an organized mob, with Denny O'Brien calling the shots and Red Ned Adair pulling the holdups. Something told him it was so, and he'd learned long ago never to go against his instincts.

He decided it was time to go undercover.

CHAPTER 4

Early the next morning Starbuck set out to explore San Francisco. His knowledge of the city was thus far general, and what he needed now was specifics. Every town, much like a timepiece, had inner working forever hidden to the casual observer. He meant to determine Denny O'Brien's place within the underworld mechanism.

Last night, upon leaving the Bella Union, his thoughts were disjointed and without order. He knew essentially what must be done, but he hadn't yet decided *how* it would be done. With some stealth, he had retrieved the mare and left her tied in the courtyard of Crocker's mansion. All the way back down Nob Hill, he had puzzled over the new turn of events. By the time he reached his hotel, he'd arrived at what seemed a logical first step. Before going undercover, he had to establish who was who on the Barbary Coast, and where the owner of the Bella Union fitted into the larger picture. Only then could he develop a workable approach to Denny O'Brien.

Today, like a wolf prowling unfamiliar territory, he made a personal reconnaissance of downtown San Francisco. The sporting crowd seldom awakened before noon, so he spent the morning on a sightseeing tour. He crisscrossed the Barbary Coast, gaining a sense of direction and a feel for the lay of the land. The seedier dives along the waterfront were of little interest, but the larger establishments, located primarily on Pacific and Broadway, held his attention. These were the joints that competed directly with the Bella Union, and he catalogued them for future reference. In the course of his wanderings, he gave Chinatown a brief once-over, then turned uptown. There, somewhat to his surprise, he found still another vice district. Though tightly contained, and considerably smaller than the Barbary Coast, it had the look of flourishing nightlife. He thought to himself that it merited further investigation.

By noontime, he'd seen enough to satisfy his immediate needs. The saloons were open, and he made his way back to the Barbary Coast. He picked a watering hole directly across from the Bella Union, one with a crowd of heavy drinkers and careless talkers. A schooner of beer entitled him to a free lunch, and he helped himself to cold cuts and cheese from the trencherman's counter. Then he bellied up to the bar and went to work.

A master of subtle interrogation, Starbuck had the knack of engaging total strangers in conversation. He was a good listener, and seemed raptly interested in the other man's opinion. He also played on their vanity, professing ignorance of the subject at hand, and got them to reveal more than they realized. With adroit prompting, he kept them talking and guilefully steered the conversation along the course he'd planned. When they parted, he had drained them dry of information while saying almost nothing about himself. He left them full of boozy good cheer and a profound sense of their own importance.

Before three o'clock, Starbuck had hit four saloons. At each stop he put away several schooners of beer and generously stood drinks for those he gulled into conversation. He talked with bartenders and pimps, gamblers and street-corner grifters, and one old barfly who supplied a wealth of Barbary Coast gossip. When he walked out of the fourth saloon, he had unearthed everything and more he'd hoped to learn. His view of San Francisco's underworld was by no means complete, but he knew who was who and precisely what it was they controlled. And with one possible exception, he had their names.

The city was split into three very distinct areas of vice and crime. There was a fine line of demarcation separating the areas, almost as though the boundaries had been staked and mapped. Curiously, there was no spillover of activities, even though the three areas abutted one another like wedges sliced from a pie. The city government, from the mayor's office down to the corner policeman, turned a blind eye to the whole affair. The payoffs, everyone agreed, had made rich men of those in public service.

Denny O'Brien was the acknowledged boss of the Barbary Coast. Nothing happened without his sanction, and he maintained a squad of plug-uglies to enforce his demands. He collected a percentage off the top, and no operation was too small to escape his attention. Even the lowly crib whores and crimp joints paid tribute.

His counterpart in Chinatown was Fung Jing Toy. A tong leader and supreme vice lord, he ran Chinatown with godlike impunity. His *boo how doy* hatchet men collected fees from all underworld enterprises, including gambling, opium dens, and bordellos. He also extorted protection money from legitimate businesses, using intimidation and threats of violence. Finally, with all his rivals killed or whipped into line, he controlled the market in Chinese slave girls. The trade reportedly did a brisk business with Occidental and Oriental alike.

There remained only the area Starbuck had surveyed late that morning. Known as the Uptown Tenderloin, it was a district reserved for swells and the upper strata of San Francisco society. Theaters and opulent restaurants vied with cabarets and plush gambling casinos for the gentry trade. The nightlife was almost decorous, the only exception being the high-priced parlor houses. Discreet madams and beautiful whores served the monied class with all the attention accorded the master of a harem. A parlor-house whore was the *crème de la crème* of her trade, and a bright girl occasionally snared herself a millionaire. According to those who knew, more than one matron on Nob Hill had begun her career in the Tenderloin.

Yet there was an apparent contradiction to the Uptown Tenderloin. All afternoon Starbuck had tactfully posed the same question: Who controls the Tenderloin? Each time the question was asked, he'd drawn a blank. The men in the Barbary Coast saloons had scratched their heads and appeared stumped. So far as they knew, the Tenderloin had no boss. Something of a neutral zone, it seemed to run itself. The police kept it cordoned off for the gentry, and the lowlifes avoided it on threat of a billy club upside the head and a night in jail. The playground of the rich, it was thought to be immune to the overtures of crime bosses and vice lords.

Starbuck thought otherwise. A suspicion began to form sometime that afternoon. Vague at first, it slowly blossomed, and by the time he walked from the fourth saloon, it had taken form. Despite all he'd heard, he believed there was most definitely a boss of the Tenderloin. Further, he thought it quite likely that the same man was the underworld czar of San Francisco. An overlord who dictated to both Denny O'Brien and Fung Jing Toy.

He'd seen it happen closer to home. For the past decade, a shadowy, unobtrusive man named Lou Blomger had ruled Denver from behind the scenes. It made sense that a similar situation existed in San Francisco, where the pickings were riper and vice even more prevalent. The temptation was simply too great. With the amount of money involved, someone who dealt in grand schemes would have built himself an underworld empire. That he stayed out of the limelight, operating in the dark, made it no less real. To Starbuck, it seemed undeniable, chiseled in stone. All he had to do was prove it.

However it turned out, everything he'd learned had merely reinforced his original thought. The place to start was Denny O'Brien. He even had a cover story in mind, and instinct told him the Barbary Coast boss would go for it bait and all. From there, it was simply a matter of allowing nature to take its course. Red Ned Adair had the balls, and Denny O'Brien called the shots, but they both danced to another man's tune. Time, and a bit of luck, would reveal his name.

That evening Starbuck caught the night train for Los Angeles.

The city of angels was somewhat provincial and backwoodsy compared to San Francisco. Yet, while it lacked a cosmopolitan flavor, Los Angeles was nonetheless prosperous. Certain shops in the downtown area catered to those with money to burn. However excessive the demand, a man willing to pay the price could indulge almost any whim. All within a matter of hours.

Starbuck went directly from the train station to a men's haberdashery. He knew little about Los Angeles itself, but he had developed contacts throughout the West. In his business, the tools of the trade were dictated by the nature of the case, and time was often a factor. From his contacts, he knew where to go and who to see, no matter how strange the request. While he could have satisfied the same needs in San Francisco, it might very well have compromised the case. Secrecy and a whole new identity were essential to his plan. He would depart Los Angeles a different man from the one who had arrived on the morning train. And no one in San Francisco the wiser.

At the haberdashery, Starbuck spoke privately with the proprietor. He indicated that money was no object, so long as the service met his demands. He wanted a complete wardrobe—expensive clothes with the look of hand-tailored garments—and he wanted it no later than four o'clock that afternoon. The proprietor, with a nose for profit, assured him the deadline was no problem.

A clerk materialized at Starbuck's elbow, and a tailor was summoned from the back room. Under the proprietor's watchful eye, an array of clothing was selected from the racks and paraded before Starbuck for his approval. He chose four single-breasted suits, all fashionably cut and dazzling in color, ranging from pearl-gray to lush chocolate. He next selected several brocaded vests, gaudy to the extreme and color-coordinated with the suits. Then he picked out ruffled linen shirts, cravats and string ties, and a half-dozen sets of silk underwear. A brown derby and a gray fedora, along with three pairs of kidskin boots, were added to the pile. His last purchase was a matched set of hand-rubbed leather luggage.

A meticulous fitting session followed. One at a time, Starbuck changed into the suits and stood before a full-length mirror. The tailor, his mouth stuffed full of pins, took a nip here and a tuck there. When he finished, the suit jackets and trousers draped perfectly, with the rich appearance of clothes crafted stitch by stitch. Once more in his old suit, Starbuck paid the bill and added an extra hundred for good measure. The proprietor, bowing profusely, escorted him to the door. His wardrobe would be packed and waiting at the appointed time.

On the street, Starbuck hailed a hanson cab and gave the driver the name of a local dentist. Pleased with his progress thus far, he rolled himself a smoke and settled back in the seat. He'd spent somewhat more time than intended at the haberdashery, and he quickly calculated the cash left in his money belt. He judged the amount—$3,000—adequate for what remained to be done. If not, then he would wire his bank in Denver and arrange a speedy transfer of funds. Bankers, very much like whores, would always accommodate their select clientele.

Starbuck worked at his profession by choice rather than need. He was a man of considerable means, with a portfolio of municipal bonds and commercial real estate valued in excess of $250,000 on the open market. Not quite two years ago, he had inherited the largest cattle spread in the Texas Panhandle. The owner of the ranch, who was his closest friend and something of a surrogate father, had no family and had therefore designated him sole heir. Forced to choose between ranching and the detective business, he'd found it to be no contest. He sold the ranch for $200,000 and worked out an arrangement whereby the bank would manage his holdings for a fixed fee. So far, he had no complaints. The bank had shown a respectable return on his investments, and the financial independence enabled him to accept only those cases that piqued his interest. His net worth was a matter he thought of only rarely. He considered manhunting a far more rewarding endeavor.

The dentist was a slender man, completely bald, with innocent brown eyes. After being ushered into his office, Starbuck explained precisely what he had in mind. He wanted a gold sleeve fitted over his right front tooth, and anchored securely. Once in place, he concluded, it must appear to be a genuine gold tooth.

"A fake tooth?" the dentist asked, as if he couldn't have heard correctly. "You want a fake *gold* tooth?"

"A fake tooth," Starbuck corrected, "that looks like the real article."

"Why?" the dentist said, bewildered. "To what purpose?"

Starbuck smiled. "Ask me no questions and I'll tell you no lies. Can you do it?"

"I suppose so"—the dentist shrugged, eyebrows raised—"assuming you're willing to pay the price."

"How much?"

"A hundred dollars, plus the cost of the gold."

"Done." Starbuck pulled out his wallet. "One

more thing. It has to be ready by four this afternoon."

"Impossible! I'll need at least a week."

Starbuck extracted three hundred-dollar bills from his wallet and spread them on the desk. "A day's work for a week's pay. Interested?"

The dentist pocketed the bills and pointed to a high-backed operating chair. "Have a seat. I'll have to take some measurements."

"You come highly recommended, Doc. Don't disappoint me."

"Recommended by whom?"

"Like I said, ask me no questions—"

"Very well, no more questions. Let's get on with it."

Starbuck moved to the chair and seated himself. The dentist selected several instruments from a cabinet, then pried Starbuck's mouth open and began taking measurements. Ten minutes later he walked from the office and flagged another hansom cab.

The next stop on Starbuck's itinerary was a posh jewelry store. His shopping list was itemized, though flexible, and the purchases required only a few minutes. He selected a diamond pinky ring, with a stone only slightly smaller than a sugar cube. Then he chose a garish horseshoe-shaped diamond stickpin, with matching cuff links. His last purchase was a diamond-studded pocketwatch the size of a teacup. When the lid was opened, it chimed a musical rendition of *"Darling Clementine."*

There was no haggling, and he again paid in bills

of large denominations. He stuffed the new watch into his vest pocket and threaded the heavy gold chain through a buttonhole. The old watch, along with the other items, were casually dropped into his jacket pocket. The jeweler watched the whole procedure with an expression of bemused wonder. He was still clutching a fistful of hundred-dollar bills when Starbuck hurried out the door.

One last stop completed Starbuck's shopping spree. The store was located on a sidestreet, with a small wooden sign pegged to the wall. The gunsmith's name was John Bohannon, and his work was known to lawman and outlaw alike. He was a master craftsman of the concealed weapon.

The inside of the store looked like an ordnance depot. The walls were lined with pistols of every description, and a double-shelved showcase was filled with pocket derringers and cut-down revolvers. Bohannon rose from a workbench at the rear of the store and moved to the showcase. He was a short, rotund man, with a shock of white hair and metal-framed glasses that magnified his eyes like a telescope. He greeted Starbuck genially.

"Afternoon. What can I do for you today?"

"I need a couple of guns," Starbuck told him. "One belly-gun and one hideout, the smaller the better."

"What caliber?" Bohannon asked pleasantly. "I've got everything from twenty-two to forty-five."

Starbuck's mouth curled. "Large enough to stop a man when he's centered the first shot."

Bohannon's eyes gleamed behind the bottle-thick glasses. "I take it you're an experienced shootist?"

"I generally hit the mark."

"Then something in forty-one ought to do the trick."

Bohannon bent over the showcase and took out a Colt Lightning. Only recently introduced, the revolver was double-action and fired a .41-caliber slug. The barrel and ejector rod had been trimmed to three inches. For a hideout gun, he suggested the Colt New House Model. A stubby five-shot revolver, it was chambered for .38 caliber. The birdshead grip was framed with ivory handles, and the sheathed trigger was activated by cocking the hammer. The barrel length was one and a half inches, and the entire gun could be covered by a normal handspan.

Starbuck handled the guns, testing them for balance and smoothness of action. The workmanship was flawless, and he quickly approved both selections. Bohannon outfitted him with a shoulder holster for the Lightning, and a clip-on boot holster for the hideout gun. A box of cartridges for each gun completed the deal, and Starbuck gladly forked over nearly two hundred dollars. They shook hands and parted, never once having exchanged names.

Outside, Starbuck checked his new timepiece. The watch chimed three and merrily trilled "Darling Clementine." He smiled and mentally reminded himself to wire Mattie Silks, a Denver madam who owed him a favor. Once the message was sent, all that remained was to collect his wardrobe and the gold tooth. His disguise was set and his cover story would bear scrutiny. The northbound train departed at six, and from there it was on to San Francisco and his next stop.

The Barbary Coast and Denny O'Brien.

CHAPTER 5

Starbuck arrived at the Palace Hotel late the next morning. A doorman approached, but he bounded down from the hansom cab without assistance. Slipping the man a five spot, he jerked his thumb at his luggage. Then he stepped back, craning his head upward, and ogled the architecture.

Considered San Francisco's finest, the hotel was a structure of Olympian proportions. The building occupied an entire city block, and construction costs were reported to have exceeded $5,000,000. The entrance-way was an immense courtyard, surrounded by galleries lofting seven stories high. Overhead, a domed skylight flooded the courtyard with a brilliant rainbow of colors. Already a legend to world travelers, the Palace was a home-away-from-home for visiting royalty and other people of wealth.

With the doorman at his heels, Starbuck swept into the lobby. He was attired in a getup of spectacular vulgarity. He wore a pearl-gray suit, with a sapphire-blue cravat and a brocaded vest to match. Diamonds sparkled from his ring and cuff links and stickpin with tawdry opulence. A cigar was wedged in the corner of his mouth, and his gold tooth gleamed like a lighthouse beacon.

Halfway to the front desk he suddenly stopped. The lobby floor was paved with silver dollars set in dark marble, and he gazed down on the sight with a look of pop-eyed wonder. The fashionably dressed men and women strolling through the lobby meanwhile paused and stared at him like a sideshow freak escaped from a circus. An interval of absolute silence stretched to several moments. Then, with a loud snort, he shook his head.

"Jeeezus Christ! Flat knocks your eyes out!"

Puffing clouds of smoke, he munched his cigar and proceeded across the lobby. He halted at the desk and knuckled his fedora onto the back of his head at a rakish angle. Grinning broadly, he nodded to the clerk.

"Harry Lovett's the name. I want the classiest suite you've got."

The clerk peered down his nose. "Do you have a reservation, sir?"

"Hell, no!" Starbuck trumpeted. "Harry Lovett don't need no reservation. Now hop to it, sonny! Fix me up, and none of your sass."

The clerk flushed and quickly produced a registration card. Starbuck signed his alias with a bold stroke and then dropped the pen on the desk. With obvious distaste, the clerk picked up the card and studied it at length.

"Have you stayed with us before, Mr. Lovett?"

"Nope," Starbuck said briskly. "This here's my first trip to Frisco."

The clerk flinched. Only seamen and people of low station referred to the city by the bay as "Frisco." By his expression, it was apparent he had already relegated Harry Lovett to that category. He tapped the registration card on his fingertips.

"One moment, please."

Turning away, he walked to a door at the end of the desk. A small sign identified the room beyond as the manager's office. He knocked softly and entered. Starbuck rolled the cigar to the opposite side of his mouth and looked bored. Then he noticed a stack of brochures on the counter, emblazoned with the hotel's name. He took one off the top and made a show of moving his lips while he read.

The brochure, meant to delight and inform, was a compendium of statistical trivia. Built by William Ralston, one of the city's leading industrialists, the Palace was an eclectic blend of rococo Victorian and ornate Louis XV. The hotel could accommodate twelve hundred guests and there was a fireplace in every room. A total of twenty thousand silver dollars were inset into the lobby floor, and there were nine hundred cuspidors scattered throughout the hotel. A hallmark of service, there were four hundred thirty-nine bathrooms, which provided the luxury of one bathroom for every 2.7 guests. In keeping with the overall decor, the toilet seats were specially crafted by Chippendale, that most revered of British imports. The cost of the toilet seats alone exceeded—

Starbuck stopped reading. He thought to himself he really wasn't out of place at the Palace. He was acting the part of a coarse, loud-mouthed vulgarian. The hotel, bragging about its toilet seats, was somewhat in the same league. For all their pretensions, the rich crowd wasn't above flaunting their built-for-a-king crappers.

The office door opened and the room clerk bustled forward. He stopped and carefully laid the card on the desk. His expression was dour.

"Mr. Lovett, the manager has asked me to inform you of hotel policy. A guest who hasn't stayed with us previously is required to pay at least two days in advance. As you can appreciate, our suites are commodious and therefore quite expensive. So if you would care to look elsewhere—"

"Sounds fair." Starbuck took out his wallet and fanned ten one-hundred dollars bills across the counter. "A thousand ought to do for openers. You tell me when that runs out and I'll pony up some more."

The clerk sighed and reluctantly scooped the bills into a cash drawer. Without a word, he walked to the letter boxes, fished out a room key, and returned to the desk. He snapped his fingers, signaling a bellboy.

"Bellman! Suite four-o-six for Mr. Lovett."

Starbuck started away, then turned back. "Say, almost forgot to ask. Which way's the Barbary Coast?"

The clerk looked aghast. "Simply walk in the direction of the waterfront, Mr. Lovett. I'm told it's difficult to miss."

"You mean to say you've never been there?"

"No." The clerk drew himself up stiffly. "Never."

"Damn shame," Starbuck said with a waggish grin. "You ought to turn loose and live a little. We only pass this way once, and that's a mortal fact."

Starbuck pulled out his diamond-studded watch and popped the lid. The strains of "Darling Clementine" tinkled across the lobby. Hotel guests standing nearby turned to stare and the clerk rolled his eyes toward the ceiling. Starbuck snapped the lid closed and replaced the watch in his vest pocket.

"How long does it take to walk there?"

"A matter of a few minutes, no more."

"Much obliged."

"All part of the service, Mr. Lovett."

Starbuck flipped him a salute and strode off toward the elevators. The bellboy hefted his luggage and hurried along behind. Watching them, the clerk passed his hand in front of his eyes, and slowly shook his head.

Shortly after one o'clock Starbuck pushed through the doors of the Bella Union. The noontime rush had slacked off, and there were perhaps a dozen men strung out along the bar. He hooked a heel over the brass rail and nodded pleasantly to the bartender.

"Your boss a fellow by the name of Denny O'Brien?"

"Six days a week and all day on Sunday."

"Where might I find him?"

The barkeep ducked his chin. "See that gent down there?"

Starbuck glanced toward the end of the bar. A man stood hunched over the counter, staring dully into a glass of whiskey. He was wide and tall, with brutish features and a barrel-shaped torso. His head was fixed directly upon his shoulders, and he appeared robust as an ox. Starbuck recognized him instantly as a bruiser. One of a breed, bouncers and strongarm men, who maintained order with sledgehammer fists.

"Yeah, so?" Starbuck asked. "What about him?"

"You want to see Mr. O'Brien, you start with him. His name's High Spade McQueen."

"Sounds like a gamblin' man."

The barkeep smiled. "If I was you, I wouldn't bet against him. You might try talking real polite, too."

"That tough, huh?"

"Mister, he's a cross between a buzz saw and a grizzly bear. You never seen anything like him."

"Thanks for the tip."

Starbuck shoved away from the bar and walked toward the rear of the room. He braced himself to appear bluff and hearty, a man of dazzling good humor. Working undercover, he always turned actor, assumed a role, and it wouldn't do to slip out of character. He rounded the end of the bar and halted.

Smiling affably, he showed High Spade McQueen his gold tooth.

"Mr. McQueen?"

"Who're you?"

"Name's Harry Lovett," Starbuck replied. "I've come all the way from Denver to see Denny O'Brien. The barkeep told me to check with you."

McQueen swiveled his head just far enough to look around. An ugly scar disfigured one cheek and his eyes were like ball bearings. He fixed Starbuck with a sullen stare.

"You got business with Mr. O'Brien?"

"I bear greetings from a mutual friend, Mattie Silks. She was of the opinion Mr. O'Brien and me might do one another a favor."

"Such as what?"

"I'm here to buy some whores. I need advice, and I'm willing to pay handsomely to get it."

McQueen's mouth split in a grotesque smile. His teeth were yellow as a row of old dice, and the scar distorted his features. He pushed off the bar.

"You should've said so to start with. C'mon, I'll take you up to the office."

He crossed the room and mounted the staircase. Starbuck obediently tagged along. From the rear, he was even more aware of the man's massive shoulders. He reminded himself to strike the first punch if ever he locked horns with High Spade McQueen.

Upstairs, McQueen turned into a small alcove off the central hallway. There was a door at the end of the alcove, and the balcony afforded a commanding view of both the theater and the barroom. He rapped on the door and a muffled voice from inside responded. Entering, he waved Starbuck through the door.

Denny O'Brien was stooped over a steel floor safe. He shot McQueen a look of annoyance, then quickly closed the safe door and spun the combination-knob. Before the door swung shut, Starbuck caught a glimpse of several ledgers and neatly stacked rows of cash. His expression betrayed nothing.

"Sorry, boss," McQueen apologized in a low rumble. "Thought you'd be done by now."

"You're not paid to think!" O'Brien said curtly. "What do you want?"

"This here feller's named Lovett. Says he come all the way from Denver to see you."

"Yessir, Harry Lovett." Starbuck moved forward, hand extended. "And let me say it's an honor to meet you, Mr. O'Brien! Heard lots about you, and all of it good."

O'Brien held out a square, stubby-fingered hand. He shook once, a hard up-and-down pump, then let go. He gave Starbuck's getup a swift appraisal, noting the diamonds and the dapper cut of the clothes.

"Who's been telling you all these good things?"

"Mattie Silks," Starbuck lied heartily. "She says there's only one man to grease the wheels in Frisco, and that man's your very own self."

"Did she, now?" O'Brien sounded flattered. "I

haven't laid eyes on Mattie in four, maybe five, years."

"Well you made an impression on her, Mr. O'Brien. I'm here to tell you she tagged you for a real stem-winder."

"Have a seat."

O'Brien crossed behind the desk and lowered himself into an overstuffed judge's chair. His churlish manner seemed to moderate. His ruddy features thawed slightly and his eyes were friendly but sharp. Very sharp.

Hat in hand, Starbuck took a chair directly before the desk. Once more he marked that O'Brien's whole being was charged with energy, alive and very shrewd. Up close, there was a strong sense of animal magnetism about the man. A sense of lightning intelligence and feral cunning, underscored by a sharp odor of danger. Starbuck was also aware that O'Brien's gorilla had taken a position by the door, immediately behind him. Apparently a stranger was to be trusted no further than arm's length.

O'Brien eyed him in silence for a moment. "You a friend of Mattie's?"

"Yessir, I am," Starbuck said stoutly. "Mattie and me go back a long ways."

"You're from Denver, then?"

"On again, off again." Starbuck flipped a palm back and forth. "I drift around, generally the mining camps. A man in my line's got to go where the action's the hottest."

"What line would that be, just exactly?"

"Confidence games. Leastways, it was. You might say I've retired from the profession."

"Oh?" O'Brien said lazily. "How so?"

Starbuck gave him a jolly wink. "Hooked myself the prize sucker of all time. Took him for a bundle and figured I'd make a clean break, put my flim-flam days behind me. So I decided to go legit."

"I get the feeling legit doesn't mean reformed."

"You bet your socks it don't!"

"You've got a new line in mind, is that it?"

"Yes, indeedee!" Starbuck said with great relish. "I aim to open a string of cathouses like nothing nobody's ever seen. Corner the market, in a manner of speaking."

"Corner the market where?"

"The mining camps." Starbuck lit a cigar, puffing grandly. "Leadville, Cripple Creek, four or five of the bigger camps. I'll make an absolute goddamned fortune!"

"Yeah?" O'Brien looked skeptical. "Last I heard, there wasn't any shortage of whores in the mining camps."

Starbuck woofed a bellylaugh. "Mr. O'Brien, them miners are queer birds. They'll pay double for anything that speaks foreign or looks the least bit different. So I figure to give 'em a crack at something besides white women."

"Like what?"

"China whores."

"Wait a minute!" O'Brien said bluntly. "Are you saying Mattie sent you to see me about slant-eyes?"

"She sure did," Starbuck acknowledged. "I don't know my ass from a brass bassoon about Chinamen. Never dealt with one in my life. She thought maybe you'd act as a go-between for me."

"A middleman?"

"No, not exactly. I'll make my own deal, but I need someone to open the door. Way I hear it, them Chinamen won't traffic with just anybody when it comes to slave girls."

"You plan to buy them outright, then?"

"For a fact," Starbuck said with cheery vigor. "An even hundred."

"A hundred?" O'Brien repeated, suddenly dumbstruck. "You mean to buy *one hundred* slave girls?"

"I like round numbers. Course, I'm not after just any girls." Starbuck paused, admired the tip of his cigar. "They've got to be virgins."

"Virgins!" O'Brien stared at him with a burlesque leer of disbelief. "You want a hundred *virgins?*"

Starbuck let the idea percolate a few moments. "All virgins—and the whole kit and caboodle ages twelve to sixteen."

A smile formed at the corner of O'Brien's mouth, then broke into laughter. "By God, you think big, don't you? A hundred little China dolls!" He threw back his head and roared. "With their cherries intact, for Chrissake!"

Starbuck gave him a foolish grin. "Well, don't you see, them miners will really go for little girl whores, specially the innocent kind. By kicking things off with Chinee heathen virgins, I'll put the other cathouses in the shade damn near overnight. After that, nobody'll be able to touch my operation."

"Hell, I believe you!" O'Brien shook his head with admiration. "But you're talking about a shit-pot full of money. A hundred virgins won't come cheap."

"No problem," Starbuck said equably. "I'm loaded and willing to pay plenty, just so long as I get what I want."

O'Brien eyed him craftily. "What about me? Here in Frisco, a go-between doesn't come cheap, either."

Starbuck ventured a smile. "How does five percent strike you?"

"It gets my attention." O'Brien shrugged noncommittally. "I'd listen a lot closer if you were to say ten percent."

"One of the last things Mattie told me was that you wouldn't try to stiff me. You open the right door and you've got yourself a deal."

There was a moment of weighing and deliberation. O'Brien thought it the most outlandish idea he'd ever heard. Yet that very oddity gave it a certain credibility. Nobody but a dimwitted fool would invent such a weird and grandiose story. While Harry Lovett was a smooth talker, he was clearly no simpleton, and everything about him reeked of money. O'Brien hadn't the vaguest notion of the asking price for a hundred slave-girl virgins. Whatever the amount, it would be steep, approaching the six-figure mark. A piece of any action that sweet was too tempting to resist.

"You're on," he said at length. "I'll set up a meeting with the head Chink in Chinatown. His name's Fung Jing Toy."

Starbuck flashed his gold tooth in a nutcracker grin. He looked pleased as punch and it was no act. Today was only a first step, but his instinct hadn't played him false.

Denny O'Brien had swallowed the bait whole.

CHAPTER 6

Chinatown was a world apart.

Upon crossing the intersection of Dupont and Washington, the white man's domain abruptly ended. From there, as though transported backward in time, the outsider had a sense of having entered Old Cathay. An ancient culture, unchanged for thousands of years, made only surface concessions to the blue-eyed white devils. Underneath, the old ways still existed.

In the lowering dusk, Starbuck walked along Washington Street. His appointment with Fung Jing Toy was for seven o'clock. All afternoon messages had passed back and forth between the Chinatown vice lord and Denny O'Brien. The working arrangement between them was apparently civil, but larded with distrust and an element of rivalry. Fung's initial response, relayed by High Spade McQueen, had expressed cautious interest. Then, as the negotiations progressed, further information had been requested with respect to Harry Lovett's background. Finally, with O'Brien's assurance that the slave girls were intended for Colorado brothels, the vice lord acceded. Late that afternoon, a time had been set for the meeting.

Starbuck, meanwhile, was pumping Denny O'Brien. He'd spent the afternoon with the Barbary Coast boss, still play-acting the glib and garrulous con man turned whoremaster. His questions were reasonable, and framed in a manner that made O'Brien his ally, something of a conspirator. To dicker successfully for the slave girls, he explained, he needed some general idea as to whom he was dealing with and what sort of reception he might expect. O'Brien, who evidenced no great charity toward Chinatown's vice lord, was only too happy to oblige. He spoke at length, and with considerable authority, on Fung's rise to power. What he had to say was revealing, and recounted with a certain grudging admiration. He described a man of obsessive ambition and savage methods.

Fung Jing Toy had immigrated to America at the age of five. As a child he witnessed the early tong wars on the streets of Chinatown, supporting himself as an apprentice to a shoemaker. A quick learner, ever willing to bend the rules, he displayed a compulsive drive to get ahead. At twenty-one, cloaked by a lily-white front, he began manufacturing shoes under the name of J. C. Peters & Company. The firm, however, was merely a legitimate base for criminal intrigue. He soon expanded into fan-tan parlors, opium smuggling, and prostitution. All the while, his horizons continued to broaden.

Early in 1876, Fung seized power of the Sum Yop tong. His next move, an open challenge to the other tong leaders, seemed suicidal. His gang began highjacking shipments of slave girls and assorted contraband being smuggled into San Francisco by the opposing factions. With little regard for human life, he provoked the bloodiest street war in Chinatown's history. Over a period of four years, his *boo how doy* hatchet men butchered more than a hundred of their rivals. By 1880, the other tongs were whipped into submission. A truce conference was convened, and Fung emerged the absolute ruler of Chinatown.

Since then, he had consolidated his power with ruthless efficiency. Once a week, his henchmen collected a percentage of gross receipts from all vice enterprises. Those who welched, or attempted to hold out, were swiftly raided by the police. Or in extreme circumstances, they were murdered as an object lesson. All legitimate businesses, importers and merchants alike, were required to pay weekly tribute for protection. The alternative was an unexplained fire, or a midnight visit from a squad of hatchet men. The slave girl trade, once an open market, was now Fung's province alone. Only those who obtained his sanction were allowed to traffic in human cargo.

A traditionalist, Fung still observed the old customs. He dressed like his forefathers, affected humility, and lived in a modest house on Washington

Street. He was a student of art and ancient scrolls, and his own poetry was said to contain such subtle nuances that it could not be translated into English. A playwright as well, he wrote dramas which were performed at the Chinese Theater on Jackson Street. According to rumor, he subsidized the theater and was a patron to those who displayed artistic merit.

Yet, for all his benevolent mannerisms, he had the killer instinct of a cobra and a barbaric sense of survival. Assassination by other tong leaders was an ever-present danger, and his personal living quarters were virtually impregnable. The barred steel door, leading into a suite of rooms without windows, was guarded by a pair of Tibetan mastiffs. At all times, night and day, he was also accompanied by two *boo how doy* hatchet men. Not surprisingly, his death was widely contemplated but rarely attempted.

Starbuck was intrigued by the man. From all he'd been told, Fung was an enigma, the inscrutable Oriental of legend. A vicious killer who wrote poetry and performed masterfully on the zither. A philanthropist who traded in slave girls and extorted tribute from his own countrymen. A throwback to the warlords of old, at once civilized and savage. In short, a man of many parts, and worth meeting.

Chinatown itself seemed no less a paradox. Walking along Washington, Starbuck thought to himself that it was actually a city within a city. One big tenement, it was dirty and overcrowded, squalid and diseased. The people lived in cellars and back-alley rabbit warrens, musty wooden cubicles. The women were dressed in black pantaloons and long smocks, and the men, their hair braided in pigtails, wore floppy jackets and baggy pajama pants. Most spoke only the dialect of their native land, and those who could converse with a Westerner resorted to pidgin English that was all but incomprehensible. A stranger asking directions might as well have talked to a deaf mute.

Washington Street, otherwise known as the Street of the Thousand Lanterns, teemed with people. The sweet smell of opium and the stench of sweaty bodies intermingled in an oppressive odor. The shops and stores, displaying their wares, added to the rank aroma. Dried sea horses and pickled squid were heaped in a herbalist's window. A grocer's storefront exhibited row upon row of plucked chickens and skinned ducks, dangling from overhead beams. Sidewalk bins overflowed with winter melons and rotting vegetables, and a fish peddler operated from an open cart on the corner. Amid the din of commerce, there was human barter, as well.

Crib whores, imprisoned behind barred windows, talked up their trade. The lowest form of slave girls, they wore only short blouses, naked from the waist down. Chinese men were addressed in the native tongue, and offered unknown splendors at reduced rates. White men, thought to be ignorant and lavish spenders, brought on a frantic singsong chant.

"Chinee girl velly nice! Looksee two bits, feelee floor bits. Doee only six bits!"

Hurrying past, Starbuck was reminded that the

plumbing of Oriental women was thought to be different from that of white women. To the uninitiated,
it was commonly believed that their private parts
went east-west instead of north-south. The debate,
actively fostered by the Chinese, had produced a
thriving, if somewhat bizarre, sideline to the oldest
profession. A curious customer could have a looksee
for two bits, a mere twenty-five cents. Or if he cared
to check out the plumbing personally, he could have
a feelee for four bits. That served to settle the east-
west question, and often led to an additional sale.
For another quarter, a total of six bits, he could actually doee. Quick as a wink, for the crib girls were
also velly fast, all doubt was then removed.

Starbuck was something of a novice himself. He'd
talked countless girls, from schoolmarms to saloon
tarts, out of their drawers and into bed. Yet he had
never been in the sack with an Oriental woman. He
knew the east-west question was sheer tomfoolery,
but he thought it might be worth a try while he was
in Frisco. Whichever direction the plumbing ran, it
would be worth the price of admission. A little doee
now and then kept a man from going stale.

A couple of minutes before seven, Starbuck located Fung's house. As he'd been told, it was the
only three-story building in all of Chinatown that
wasn't swarming with a hundred or more occupants.
He rapped on the door and almost instantly it swung
open. A servant bowed him inside, quickly closing
and bolting the door. Without a word, the man turned
and walked along a central hallway.

Starbuck followed. He checked left and right, naturally curious about the inside of a Chinese home. Yet there was little to see; the rooms off the corridor were dark; except for dim candles and several large vases, the hall itself was bare. He had the sense of being watched, which was reinforced by the servant's casual manner. He wondered how many hatchet men silently waited in the darkened rooms.

At the end of the hallway, the servant stopped and bowed him through a door. Stepping onto a small landing, Starbuck saw a lighted staircase leading to the cellar. He went down the stairs, which turned sharply at the bottom, and emerged in an underground chamber. One look and he understood immediately why Chinatown's vice lord still survived.

The chamber ran the width of the house. Ornate candle fixtures were attached to the walls, and a steel door stood opposite the staircase. Before the door, chained to the wall, were two beasts that vaguely resembled dogs. Huge as tigers, the mastiffs looked as though they would happily devour a man for breakfast. The dogs snarled in unison, and showed him fangs the size of tusks. He remained very still.

A Chinaman appeared in the doorway. At his command, the mastiffs dropped to the floor, silent but watchful. Another man came through the door and paused, hands stuffed up his sleeves. Tall men, muscular and hard-faced, they both wore broad-brimmed flat hats, their hair twisted in long queues. Their robes were black and their rubber-soled shoes made every movement silent as a whisper. From the look of them, there was a hatchet up every sleeve.

Starbuck thought he'd never seen men who so thoroughly fitted the part of assassins. The first one expertly patted him down, and removed the Colt Lightning from his shoulder holster. The hideout gun in his boot top went undetected, and knowing it was there gave him some degree of comfort. Still, even though he was armed, he warned himself to play it fast and loose. A bold front and quick wits were the key to leaving the chamber alive.

The hatchet man in the doorway moved aside and motioned him through. Starbuck gingerly stepped past the mastiffs and entered a spacious room. Spartan as a monk's cell, the room was furnished with floor cushions and a low teakwood table. To his immediate left was another steel door, which he assumed led to the living quarters. The hatchet men took up positions directly behind him, one on either side of the entranceway. He needed no reminder that it was also the only way out.

The side door opened and Fung Jing Toy whisked into the room. He wore a silk mandarin gown and a black skullcap. A slender man, with a long mustache and skin the texture of parchment, his bearing was that of someone who spends his life remote from the world of people. His eyes were impersonal.

"Mr. Lovett." His head dipped in a bow. "Please be seated."

"Thank you kindly."

Starbuck lowered himself onto one of the cushions. His legs were too long to fit under the table, and he awkwardly twisted around sideways. Fung moved to the opposite side of the table and took a seat, legs crossed. A moment passed; then he nodded with grave courtesy and spoke in a reedy voice.

"I am told this is your first visit to our city."

"That's a fact. Got in late this morning."

"Have your expectations been fulfilled?"

"Well . . ." Starbuck smiled lamely. "I've been pretty busy. Haven't had much time to catch the sights."

"A situation not without remedy. You must allow us to show you something of Little China during your stay."

"Little China?"

"A colloquial expression," Fung said with a patronizing smile. "Your people call it Chinatown. We find our own name more suitable."

Starbuck realized the vice lord's smile was closer to a grimace. A cold rictus that touched his lips but never his eyes. The serpentine charm and oily manner also failed to hide the hauteur in his voice, the deep arrogance. Still, there was no faulting the man's command of English. He spoke with only a slight accent, and he used three-dollar words. Starbuck thought "colloquial" was a real piss-cutter. He made a mental note to look it up in the dictionary.

"Now, as to business," Fung went on blandly. "Denny O'Brien informs me that you are interested in a purchase of some magnitude."

"All depends," Starbuck said tentatively. "The

merchandise would have to be prime stuff, pick of the litter."

"Ah, yes." Fung permitted himself an ironic glance. "Pick of the litter meaning virgin girls, is it not so?"

"Nothing less," Starbuck affirmed. "Virgins will be the come-on, if you get my drift. I'll use 'em to start the operation off in real style."

Fung gave him a thoughtful stare. "I believe you plan to open several houses, all at the same time. To one of humble aspirations, that seems a grand and daring concept."

Starbuck beamed like a trained bear. "I think big and I'm willing to put my money where my mouth is. Four or five houses—all stocked with virgins— it'll flat knock their eyes out! No way it'll fail, and there's the God's own truth."

Fung studied his nails. "An ancient proverb advises us that truth wears many faces." He suddenly looked up, eyes gleaming icons. "I understand you are a man of some influence in the Colorado mining camps?"

"Well, let's just say I've got pull with all the right people."

"Then you must know my associate, Wong Sing? He resides in the town called Leadville."

"No." Starbuck sensed danger. "Never made his acquaintance."

"How is that possible?" Fung's eyes were now veiled. "He leads the Sum Yop tong in Leadville."

"What's his front?" Starbuck asked evenly. "What's he do for a living?"

"I am told he operates a laundry."

Starbuck opened his hands, shrugged. "Not too likely we would've met. See, I don't care much for ·starch in my shirts." He paused, flashed his gold tooth in a crafty smile. "I generally find a woman willing to do my wash."

The statement was entirely plausible. In mining camps, white men were fond of saying all Chinamen looked alike. Moreover, those Chinese who owned businesses invariably ran a laundry or back-alley café. So it was understandable that the one who called himself Harry Lovett would have no knowledge of Wong Sing. Yet Fung was not wholly satisfied with the answer. He survived by trusting no man, most especially a blue-eyed devil endorsed by Denny O'Brien. He concluded the matter would bear further scrutiny.

A smile appeared at the corner of his mouth. "Upon your return, you must make yourself known to Wong Sing. He would be honored to be of service . . . should the occasion arise."

"I'll do that very thing," Starbuck said earnestly. "Who knows? Maybe we'll be able to swap favors here and there."

Fung laced his fingers together, considered a moment. "Your request is most unusual. A hundred virgins, all of such tender age, are not easily obtainable."

"No, I suppose not." Starbuck feigned a sly look.

"Course, if I made it worth your while, you likely wouldn't have any trouble, would you?"

Fung nodded wisely. "I believe it could be arranged."

"How much?"

"One thousand dollars a girl."

"Holy Christ!" Starbuck appeared shocked. "That's a little steep, isn't it?"

"Perhaps," Fung intoned. "On the other hand, where else would you turn? I alone govern the trade in slave girls."

"You've got a point." Starbuck hesitated, his features screwed up in a frown. "How would I know they're all virgins?"

"You have my word," Fung said in a voice without tone. "Or if you wish, you may have them inspected by a doctor. Such matters are readily arranged."

Starbuck pondered a moment, then laughed. "What the hell, it's only money! When can you make delivery?"

"Hmm." Fung nodded to himself as though possessed of some secret knowledge. "I will consult with my associates and advise you. These affairs must be conducted with a certain delicacy."

Starbuck found the statement too cryptic for comfort. "Don't hang me up too long. I'm already short on time."

"I beg your indulgence," Fung said politely. "In the meantime, allow us to entertain you. The treasures of Little China are many and varied . . . and quite often memorable."

Fung rose to his feet. Starbuck was assured he would be contacted, and on that note, the meeting ended. Bows were exchanged, then one of the hatchet men escorted Starbuck past the dogs and up the stairs. Once they were out of sight, Fung turned to the other guard with a look of sharp concern.

"Find May Ling!" he ordered. "Bring her to me now."

CHAPTER 7

Starbuck had no illusions about the girl. She was a gift from Fung, a young seductress meant to please and delight him. Yet she was also a spy, an enchanting interrogator with both the beauty and the thorns of a rose. He had no doubt his every word was reported directly to her master.

The invitation was extended the morning after his meeting with Fung. At first, aware of the danger, his reaction was to politely decline. Denny O'Brien had already offered him one of the Bella Union girls, and that was excuse enough to beg off. Then, wary of insulting Fung, he thought it wiser to accept. There were grave risks entailed, but he was an old hand at guarding himself in the clinches. Besides, he was horny as a billy goat and still extremely curious about Chinese women. Until he verified it for himself, the question of their east-west plumbing would always stick in his mind. He accepted, and the engagement was arranged for that evening.

Shortly after sundown, one of Fung's men met him outside the hotel. He was led to a building in the heart of Chinatown, then upstairs to an apartment on the second floor. The man knocked three times, bowed from the waist, and disappeared down the stairs. He was left alone before the door.

Whatever he expected, Starbuck was not prepared for the girl's loveliness. May Ling was tiny, with a doll-like figure and large almond-shaped eyes. Her features were exquisite, with bee-stung lips and high cheekbones, all framed by a mass of hair black as obsidian. Her voice was odd and vibrant, and there was about her an aura of innocence destroyed. She smelled sweet and alluring, and gave off a sensual radiation as palpable as musk. He judged her age at somewhere between eighteen and twenty. A child-woman of evocative beauty.

Her apartment was small but richly furnished. The walls were decorated with silk prints and the floors were lushly carpeted; the bureau and several squat chests were finished in black, heavily lacquered, and trimmed with brass fittings. A tall Oriental screen separated the living area from the bedchamber, and a miniature kitchen was partitioned off by yet another screen. A low table, used for both entertaining and dining, was surrounded by plush floor cushions.

May Ling was dressed in a milk-white kimono that seemed to mold her body in melted ivory. Her English, like Fung's, was remarkably correct, with only a trace of an accent. She greeted Starbuck with a cordial bow, and showed him to the place of honor

at the table. In deference to his Western tastes, she
served whiskey and provided a porcelain ashtray for
his cigar. She was gracious, drawing him out with
small talk, and gave no hint of embarrassment at the
arrangement. She was there for his pleasure, and
quite clearly eager to please.

Starbuck was indeed pleased. She was a creature
of surpassing beauty, and the atmosphere was con-
ducive to thoughts of erotic Oriental mysteries. The
scent of joss sticks and sandalwood was heady,
somehow intoxicating, adding to the sensation of her
nearness. When she spoke her lips moved like moth
wings, and she seemed to have an infinite variety of
smiles, all suggestive of the night ahead. He
watched, sipping whiskey, while she glided spec-
trally from the kitchen to the table. His hunger,
mounting steadily, was not for food.

Dinner was one surprise after another. She served
prawns simmered in a sticky, sweet sauce, and something that vaguely resembled pork, swimming in a
thick black gumbo. Steaming bowls of vegetables,
similar in appearance to seaweed, complimented the
meat dishes, and with each course there appeared
another mound of snow-white rice. Herbal tea and
delicate cookies, tasting faintly of ginger, finished
off the meal.

Starbuck thoroughly stuffed himself. He'd never
tasted prawns, and the other dishes, though equally
unfamiliar, were nonetheless savory. After dinner, he
loosened his belt a notch and lit a cigar. May Ling
cleared the table and poured him another whiskey.

Then she took a zither from a wall peg and seated herself across from him. Her fingers flew over the instrument like darting birds, producing a strange and haunting music. The sound was discordant to his ear, not unpleasant but seemingly without melody. To his amazement, she opened her mouth and began to sing. The words were meaningless, but the timbre of her voice was almost hypnotic, curiously intimate. Her gaze never left him, and he felt certain the song was meant to convey some seductive message. When she finished, he stuck the cigar in his mouth and applauded heartily. She blushed and modestly averted her eyes.

The evening thus far was beyond anything he had imagined. The lavish meal and the haunting song were unaccustomed preliminaries to the mating ritual he normally practiced. Yet the girl herself was by far the greatest surprise. She had asked no questions and made no reference whatever to his dealings with Fung. Nor had she displayed even passing interest in who he was or where he came from, or the nature of his business. In short, she'd made no attempt to grill him, and seemed content merely with his company. He found himself somewhat bewildered, and more than a little curious. Tactfully, choosing his words, he asked her about herself. His interest was genuine, and from the expression in her eyes, he knew it was a question she'd seldom been asked. He prompted her, gently insistent, and she slowly began to talk.

Her life, she told him simply, had been ordained

by circumstance. Her parents were poor, struggling
to eke out an existence. Like many peasant girls,
governed by a centuries old custom, she had been
sold into bondage. The contract took effect on her
tenth birthday, and by then she'd shown promise of
beauty. One of Fung's agents ultimately bought her,
and she had arrived in San Francisco not quite a year
later. Unlike ordinary slave girls, Fung had taken a
special interest in her. A tutor had been retained to
teach her English and the art of conversation, and
still another mentor had trained her in music and
song. A woman of great wisdom had instructed her
in lovemaking and the many exotic acts pleasurable
to man. At age fourteen she had been accorded a
great honor. Fung, her master and patron, had himself taken her virginity.

With a note of pride, she observed that since that
time she had lived the life of a courtesan. She entertained those men, both Chinese and American,
who were of special interest to her master. In return,
she had been given her own quarters and the free-
dom to travel Little China as she pleased. Over the
years many wealthy men had attempted to buy her,
offering thousands of dollars above the price normally paid for even the most beautiful virgin. Yet,
declaring her beyond value, her master had refused
in each instance. That refusal had bestowed great
honor on her, and wherever she went the people of
Little China treated her with the respect reserved for
one of position and rank. Few slave girls rose so
high, and she considered herself the most fortunate

of women. Not yet twenty, she had found serenity and purpose in life. She existed to serve her master, and her days were filled with happiness. She was content.

Starbuck believed her. She was a slave, and whether she called herself courtesan or whore, she would live out her days in bondage. All the same, she was happier than any white whore he'd ever known. She was at peace with herself and her world, and the serenity she spoke of was no act. Her voice, the expression in her eyes, told the story. She had found something in life that few people attain. Her mirror reflected the worth of her own esteem.

May Ling smiled and sang him another song. He lay back on the pillows, sipping whiskey and puffing his cigar. After a time, she put the zither away and held out her hand. He climbed to his feet, all but bewitched by her loveliness, and allowed himself to be led to her bedchamber. There she undressed him, and after stepping out of her kimono, she let him gaze a moment upon the golden swell of her breasts.

Then she showed him that Chinese girls were, after all, no different from white women. Some were simply better than others, and she skillfully persuaded him that she was the best.

May Ling never questioned her master's orders, or his motives. To her, a man's body was like a zither, an instrument to be strummed and caressed. Several times during the night, using her own body to strike responsive chords, she had taught Starbuck exquisite

harmonies known only to a trained courtesan. Early
the next morning, she undertook the balance of her
assignment.

After a late breakfast, she suggested a personally
conducted tour of Little China. Starbuck was feeling
a bit frazzled, his juices sapped by her arduous and
sometimes gymnastic lovemaking. Under normal circumstances he might have hesitated, but his brain
was muzzy and he suspected nothing. Chinatown
was Fung's domain, and seeing it through May
Ling's eyes seemed very much in order. He immediately approved the idea.

On the street, she took his arm and guided him
toward the center of Little China. As they walked,
she chattered on gaily, explaining that the district
was the largest Chinese settlement outside the Orient. Within a dozen square blocks, some thirty thousand people lived and worked, rarely ever setting
foot in the white sections of San Francisco.

The Chinese, May Ling noted proudly, were an
industrious people. Some twisted cigars for a living,
others worked in clothing and shoe factories, and
many served in white homes as cooks and house-
boys. For the most part, they were frugal, followed
the ancient religious rites, and kept very much to
themselves. Yet they were not the simple peasants,
ignorant and humble, so commonly portrayed by
whites. Almost all were fanatic gamblers, playing the
lottery and fan-tan, and even a variation of poker.
Opium smoking was widely practiced, and the trade
in *gow* pills, pipe-size balls of opium, had evolved

into a thriving industry. There were even exclusive establishments for white gentlemen and their ladies. Unlike common opium dens, the service there was discreet and costly, the *gow* pills of superb quality.

Still another misconception, May Ling went on, was the belief by whites that Orientals were sexually backward. To the contrary, the Chinese were a very sensual people, connoisseurs of the flesh. A Chinese man seldom limited himself to one woman, even if he was married and had a family. Nor was it considered shameful for a Chinese woman to enjoy the act, and express that joy through inventive byplay passed down from mother to daughter. In fact, the Oriental preoccupation with sex manifested itself in many forms. The most widely known was the flourishing trade in slave girls. Nowhere else on earth was the appreciation of eroticism so vividly demonstrated.

May Ling suddenly stopped. Her eyes seemed to sparkle with secret amusement. "Would you care to attend a slave-girl auction?"

"Would I!" Starbuck said, astonished. "I'd like nothing better."

"I believe one is being held this morning."

"You really think they'd let us watch? I've heard these things are sort of private, invitation only."

"Oh, yes," May Ling trilled happily. "You are with me, which means you are a very special friend of the master. We would not be turned away."

"Well, what are we waiting for? Hot damn, a real

live slave-girl auction! You're just a sackful of surprises."

"Perhaps we shouldn't." May Ling mocked him with a tiny smile. "These girls are not virgins, and much older than those you wish to purchase. You might be disappointed."

Starbuck laughed. "Don't worry your pretty head about that. C'mon, chop, chop! Let's go!"

With a minxish giggle, May Ling took his arm and led him to the corner. There they turned onto a side-street, then walked toward a warehouse halfway down the block. A squad of hatchet men, uniformed in the regulation pajama suits and black hats, stood guard outside. Approaching them, May Ling let go a volley of Chinese, her tone gracious, yet somehow imperious. The men bowed respectfully, and one of them rushed to open the door. She stepped through, followed closely by Starbuck, and directed him to a vantage point along the wall. From there, they had an unobstructed view of the entire warehouse.

Starbuck was reminded of a livestock auction. A large crowd of men, both Chinese and white, were ganged around a wooden platform. The auctioneer, a jolly-eyed Chinaman with a loud mouth and a winning smile, walked the platform like a captain commanding the bridge of a ship. Beyond the platform, huddled together in a forlorn group, were a hundred or more Chinese girls. One at a time, they were brought forward by the auctioneer's assistants and stripped naked. Shoved onto the platform, they were then forced to parade before the crowd like prize broodmares. The prospective buyers were allowed to examine each girl before the bidding began.

May Ling briefly explained the complex system underlying the slave-girl trade. Her master placed an order with procurers in China for delivery in San Francisco on a certain date. Upon arrival, the girls were secreted in padded crates, invoiced as dishware, and American customs agents were bribed to pass the bales without inspection. While special orders were often filled for wealthy whites and prosperous Chinese tradesmen, the cargo was generally sold at open auction. The choicest girls, selected for their youth and attractiveness, were auctioned off to men looking for a concubine and jobbers who resold to smaller, inland markets. Prices varied from girl to girl, but usually started with a minimum bid of $200 and climbed to $500 or higher. The refuse, those unsuitable for auction, were sold to waterfront brothelkeepers or put to work in the Chinatown cribs.

The virgin market, May Ling remarked, was conducted on a somewhat higher level. Procurers in China contracted for the girls at an early age, generally two through five. The parents then raised the girls, and the procurer meanwhile contracted to deliver virgins of a specified age group, and on a specified date, in San Francisco. Even now, her master held contracts on some four hundred virgins, ages two through sixteen, who were available for delivery on demand. Thus, there was always a plentiful stock to supply future markets.

Starbuck listened with only one ear. His attention

was fixed on the platform. Several men had stepped forward to probe and fondle a girl who looked to be no more than fourteen. She stood dull-eyed and submissive, abject in her nakedness. The auctioneer began the bidding at $200, and within minutes she was sold for $375. The man who bought her paid the auctioneer, and a bill of sale, with the girl's mark, was quickly produced. The document was legal and binding in American courts. There were quotas restricting Chinese immigration, but there were no laws forbidding the sale of Chinese girls into bondage. The young girl, now a legally bound slave, was swiftly dressed and hustled away by her new master.

"A fortunate girl," May Ling observed, noting his interest. "Had she not attracted a buyer, she might have joined those who work in the cribs."

"So young?" Starbuck said without thinking. "A girl that age in the cribs?"

"Oh, yes," May Ling replied, studying him with a half-smile. "But she would be much older tomorrow. The cribs age a girl quickly."

"How long do they last?"

"Four years, perhaps less," May Ling said in a low voice. "The work is hard, and men use them in cruel ways. Their minds go wrong, or they become diseased, and then they are no longer of value to their master."

Starbuck felt a sudden revulsion. "You mean they go crazy?"

"Some do." May Ling kept her tone casual. "For

most, it is the sailor's disease—the pox—that claims
them."

"What happens then?"

"They are sent to the hospital."

"Hospital?" Starbuck said, looking at her. "To be
cured?"

"No, to die." Her appraisal of him was deliberate,
oddly watchful. "The crib masters have a secret
place they call the hospital. When a girl outlives her
usefulness, she is taken there and given a pallet. An
attendant places beside her a cup of water and a cup
of rice, and a small oil lamp. He informs her that
she must die by the time the oil burns out. Later,
when he returns, the girl is almost always dead—
sometimes by starvation, usually by her own hand."

"Jesus Christ!" Starbuck scowled, shook his head.
"Some hospital."

"Yes." An indirection came into May Ling's eyes.
"The people of Little China call it 'the place of no
return.' "

Too late, Starbuck sensed the trap. He wiped
away the frown and quickly plastered a dopey smile
across his face. Yet he wasn't at all sure he'd fooled
May Ling. She'd brought him here, and purposely
suckered him into a conversation about crib girls, all
to get a reaction. That much was now abundantly
clear, and he realized she was swifter than she appeared. No questions, no need to interrogate him. A
night's lovemaking, and her innocent manner had
effectively lowered his guard. Then she laid the bait
and waited to see his reaction. A goddamned Orien-

tal mousetrap! And he'd gone for the cheese.

"Well, now!" He gave her a lopsided grin. "Let's hope none of my little virgins ever needs a trip to the hospital."

"Would that bother you?"

"At a thousand bucks a head!" he roared. "You bet your sweet ass that'd bother me!"

She giggled softly. "Do you truly find it sweet?"

"Sweeter than sugar, and twice as nice!"

May Ling took his arm and they turned to leave the warehouse. On the street, Starbuck gave her a squeeze and made himself a promise. One more dip of the wick, then he'd ditch her fast.

And get the hell out of Chinatown.

CHAPTER 8

The miners came in forty-nine
The whores in fifty-one.
And when they got together
They produced the Native Son.

Nell Kimball scarcely heard the lyrics. She was seated in a curtained loge with Starbuck, whose attention was directed to the stage. Covertly, out of the corner of her eye, she was watching him with a bemused look. She thought him a most unlikely whoremaster.

Onstage, a buxom songbird was belting out the tune in a loud, brassy voice. A ballad of sorts, it traced the ancestry of Nob Hill swells to the mating of whores and miners who had settled San Francisco during the Gold Rush. There was an element of truth to the ditty, and it was a favorite with audiences on the Barbary Coast. Tonight, the crowd in the Bella Union was clapping and stamping their feet, and roaring approval as the lyrics became progressively vulgar.

Starbuck looked like a peacock in full plumage. He was tricked out in diamonds and a powder-blue suit, with a paisley four-in-hand tie and a gaudy lavender shirt. The getup fitted the image of a whore-monger with grand ideas, but Nell Kimball was having second thoughts. Even the gold tooth left her unconvinced. Her whore's intuition told her Harry Lovett was something more than he appeared.

Earlier, Denny O'Brien had ordered her to enter-tain him royally. At first, she'd been a bit miffed, her vanity wounded. Harry Lovett had spent the last two days in Chinatown—doubtless getting himself screwed silly by Fung's prized hussy—and that put her in the position of playing second fiddle. Around the Bella Union she got top billing, acting as O'Brien's strong right arm. She supervised all the show girls, occasionally wooing a high roller per-sonally, and she wasn't accustomed to standing in line behind a sloe-eyed Chinese slut. Yet orders were orders, and she'd learned the hard way never to pro-voke O'Brien's temper. He considered Lovett top-drawer business, and it wouldn't do to let Fung outshine them in the entertainment department. However she managed it, Lovett was to be given ace-high treatment, and made to forget the China girl's bedroom artistry. All of which meant a long night in the saddle.

For Starbuck's part, he felt like he'd come home. Nell Kimball was his kind of woman. Unlike May

Ling's charade, there was no pretense about Nell, nothing phony. She was a saloon girl who had fought and clawed her way to the top of her profession. A tough cookie, honed by experience, she could handle a wise-ass chump or a mean-eyed drunk with equal ease. She looked to her own interests, always a step ahead of the competition, and God pity anybody who got in her way. Her counterpart was found in mining camps and cowtowns throughout the West, and she was the only kind of woman Starbuck fully understood. Moreover, he admired her for perhaps the best of reasons. Except that she wore bloomers, there wasn't a nickel's worth of difference between them. In all the things that counted, they were very much birds of a feather. Hard-headed realists, blooded but never whipped, survivors.

Then, too, Starbuck had to admit she was nothing shy in the looks department. She was compellingly attractive, tall and statuesque, with enormous hazel eyes and sumptuous figure. Her tawny hair was piled in coils and puffs atop her head, and she carried herself with assured poise. Her gaze was direct, filled with a certain bawdy wisdom, and she seemed to view the world with good-humored irony. He thought that was perhaps the one essential difference between them. He saw the world through the eyes of a confirmed cynic. She saw it through a prism that was still slightly rose-tinted, and he considered that a weakness.

By and by, perhaps later tonight, he fully intended to exploit that weakness. His visit to the slave-girl auction that morning, coupled with May Ling's boastful remarks about Fung, had merely strength- ened his original assessment. Without an overlord to keep the peace, Chinatown and the Barbary Coast could not coexist. Denny O'Brien, given the scope of his ambition, could never resist a takeover attempt in Chinatown. Someone restrained him from doing so, and that someone was the man who cracked the whip in San Francisco. Unless he missed his guess, Starbuck thought it entirely likely that Nell Kimball knew the someone's name. A gentle touch, and his softsoap routine, might very well persuade her to talk. Contrary to what people thought, the way to a whore's heart was not between her legs. Affection and kindness were what turned the trick.

The chesty songbird ended her number and the curtain rang down to wild applause. Starbuck poured champagne and lifted his glass in a toast. The eve- ning was far along, but he'd made no overtures, no suggestive remarks. He figured it was a new expe- rience for Nell, and certain to pique her interest. He wasn't far short of the mark.

"So tell me," she said with a quizzical look. "Have yourself a good time in Chinktown, did you?"

"No complaints," Starbuck allowed. "Course, I'd have to say those Chinamen take a little getting used to."

"Yeah, that Fung's a real pistol, isn't he?"

"I suppose he's all right . . . for a Chinaman."

"On the Coast, we call him Fung Long Dong."

"Oh?" Starbuck saw a glint in her eye. "Why's that?"

"Because he's got a permanent hard-on." Nell laughed at her racy admission. "Screws anything that's not nailed down. Women, girls, even little boys, so I've heard."

Her laugh was infectious, and Starbuck grinned. "Wouldn't surprise me. After seeing that three-ring circus he runs—the dogs and his hatchet men—I'd believe anything."

"Forget the dogs, honeybun! You just stay clear of Wong Yee and Sing Dock."

"His hatchet men?" Starbuck asked. "What's the story on them?"

"All bad," Nell said quietly. "When they kill someone, they tidy up the corpse's clothes, comb his hair, and press a smile on his mouth. God knows what they do before they kill him. They're both as queer as a three-dollar bill."

"No accounting for taste," Starbuck said with a crooked smile. "I've always preferred the ladies, myself."

Nell gave him a cool look. "How'd you like May Ling? Not that anybody ever called the little tramp a lady."

Starbuck mugged, hands outstretched. "A gentleman never tells. You're right about one thing, though—she's no lady!"

Nell warmed to the remark. "Well, it just bears out what I've always said. Those China girls have got no class. You're lots better off here on the Coast."

"Now that you mention it," Starbuck said casually, "I got pretty much the same story in Chinatown. The way Fung talks, there's no love lost between him and Denny."

"I guess not!" Nell tossed her head. "Denny would cut that Chink's heart out and dance on his grave."

"What stops him?"

"I don't follow you."

"What stops him from walking in there and taking over Chinatown? Hell, Fung and his hatchet men wouldn't stand a chance! If I was Denny, I'd do it in a minute."

Nell blinked and looked away. "You'd have to ask Denny about that. I keep my nose where it belongs."

"I'll bet!" Starbuck ribbed her. "Strikes me, you pretty much know what's going on around the Bella Union."

"Maybe I do," Nell observed neutrally. "But smart girls learn not to talk out of school, and I sit right up at the head of the class."

Starbuck let it drop for the moment. "Well, you're the number-one girl around here. No question about that! Wish to hell I had someone like you to run my operation. It'd sure take a load off my mind."

"Since you brought it up," Nell said slowly, "I'm curious about something. Have you ever operated a whorehouse before?"

"Nope." Starbuck's mouth widened in a devil-may-care grin. "But I'm all set to give 'er one helluva try!"

"You've got brass." Nell cocked her head in a funny little smile. "A hundred virgins and four whorehouses! How in God's name do you figure to pull it off?"

"I pray a lot," Starbuck said, deadpan. "Course, I've got a way with the ladies. So that ought to smooth things considerable."

"Now you're bragging."

"Think so?" Starbuck gave her a rougish wink. "There's one way to find out."

Nell laughed a low, throaty laugh. "Sounds like you're getting fresh, Mr. Lovett."

"The idea crossed my mind."

"Then I suppose we'll have to find out ... won't we?"

Starbuck put his arm around her, and she scooted closer on the divan. The curtain rose and a line of can-can dancers went prancing across the stage. She let her hand slip down over his thigh, and gave him a playful squeeze.

Late that night, Nell suggested they retire to her room. The Bella Union was still going strong, the barroom and the theater packed with a raucous crowd. Onstage a team of acrobats was performing to assorted hoots and jeers. The audience seemed unimpressed by gymnastic feats of daring.

Denny O'Brien and High Spade McQueen were

standing near the end of the bar. The action was
heavy at the gaming tables, and they appeared deep
in conversation. Starbuck yelled and waved, attracting their attention as Nell tugged him toward the
stairs. McQueen barely glanced around, but O'Brien
smiled knowingly and gave him the thumbs-up sign.
Starbuck responded with a jack-o'-lantern grin, and
rolled his eyes at Nell. He looked like a randy drunk,
immensely pleased with his prospects for the night.

There was little need for pretense. His head
buzzed from the effects of too much champagne, and
he was in a very mellow mood. Several bottles of
bubbly had been consumed during the evening, and
Nell, who was no slouch herself, had matched him
glass for glass. She was bright-eyed and giggly, and
led him up the staircase with a slight list to her step.
Yet, despite his muzzy look, he was reasonably sober. He kept a grin glued on his face, but reminded
himself that the night's work had really just begun.
He still had to sound Nell out, gull her into revealing
a name. And it had to be accomplished without
arousing suspicion. Wondering about the best approach, he waved one last time to O'Brien, then
trailed Nell up the stairs. The sway of her hips and
the glow of the champagne brought him to what
seemed a logical compromise. He thought perhaps
their talk might wait until after she'd shown him how
it was done on the Barbary Coast.

The rooms on the second floor of the Bella Union
were reserved for the showgirls. Most of their tricks,
ten dollars for five minutes' rutting, were turned on

the sofas in the theater boxes. A big spender, who wanted the full treatment, was brought upstairs. There, for the right price, he got to take his time. Fifty dollars bought him an hour, and a hundred purchased the whole night. The girls were versatile, willing to satisfy even the most exotic request, and the johns always got their money's worth. No one left the second floor of the Bella Union wanting more.

The third floor was occupied exclusively by the house staff. Denny O'Brien's suite consisted of a sitting room, bedroom, and private bath. Across the hall, High Spade McQueen's quarters were comparable, though somewhat smaller. Other staff members, who included the stage manager and the house manager, were assigned somewhat less spacious accommodations. Nell occupied a corner room at the end of the hall. The view overlooked the alley.

Upon entering, Starbuck was pleasantly surprised. The atmosphere was considerably more homey than he'd expected. A tall wardrobe, with a full-length mirror, was flanked by a bureau and washstand. Opposite was a grouping of two chairs and a table, upon which stood a gilt clock and a collection of porcelain figurines. The windows were draped, a hooked rug covered the floor, and a large brass bed occupied the far corner. Quite clearly, Nell had gone to great lengths to create a warm and comfortable refuge for herself. The room seemed somehow out of place in the Bella Union.

After locking the door, she turned to Starbuck.

Her hands went behind his neck, pulling his head down. Her kiss was fierce and passionate, demanding. She pressed herself against him, and he could feel her breasts and the pressure of her thighs on his loins. He stroked her back and fondled the soft curve of her buttocks, and she uttered a low moan. They parted and, in the umber glow of a lamp, hurriedly began undressing.

Her body was sculptured: high, full breasts, a stemlike waist, and long, shapely legs. She stood before him a moment, her clothes heaped at her feet. Then his arms encircled her, and she clung naked to his hard-muscled frame. Her hand went to his manhood, swollen and pulsating, and she grasped it eagerly. He kissed her lips, then the nape of her neck, felt the nipple of her breast grow erect under his touch. They caressed, played a game of tease-and-tantalize, until they were aroused and aching and the excitement became unbearable. At last, slipping out of his embrace, she pulled him down on the bed.

The hard questing part of him found her. She was ready for him, moist and yielding, and she took him deep within the core of herself. His hands clutched her flanks and they came together in an agonized clash. Her legs spidered around him, and she jolted upward, timing herself to his thrust. She clamped him viselike, her hips moving in a circle, and exhaled a hoarse gasp. He arched his back and drove himself to the molten center, probing deeper and deeper. She screamed and her nails pierced his back like talons.

Time lost meaning, and they crossed the threshold together.

A long while later Starbuck lay staring at the ceiling. Nell was snuggled close, her head nestled in the hollow of his shoulder. He felt her breath eddy through the matted curls on his chest, and sensed she was on the verge of sleep. Champagne and the afterglow of their lovemaking had left her sated, drifting lightly on a quenched flame. He thought there would never be a better time to pop the question. Yet, even with her defenses lowered, he cautioned himself to proceed slowly. He put his lips to her ear and gently stroked her hair.

"Wanna hear a secret?"

"Umm. I like secrets."

Starbuck's voice was warm and husky. "May Ling couldn't hold a candle to you. Strictly no contest, and that's a mortal fact."

"Omigod!" Nell hugged him tightly. "That's the sweetest thing anyone ever said to me in my whole life."

"I meant every word of it—cross my heart."

"Does that mean you'll stay out of Chinatown?"

"Would that make you happy?"

"Would it ever!" Nell's eyes suddenly shone, and she laughed. "Why, it would make that little pigeon-toed bitch turn pea-green with envy!"

"Consider it done," Starbuck said with a beguiling grin. "Chinatown's seen the last of Harry Lovett."

"You won't regret it." Nell squirmed around and

kissed him soundly. "I'll keep you so worn out you won't have strength enough to eat."

"Hell, why not!" Starbuck chuckled and settled back on the pillow, watching her a moment. "Now that I've told you my secret, you tell me yours."

"Ask away." Nell gave him a sassy, nose-wrinkling smile. "I've already shown you most of my secrets, anyway."

"Well—" Starbuck hesitated, his features sober. "I was wondering why you're afraid of Denny O'Brien."

"Denny?" Surprise washed over Nell's face. "What gave you the idea I'm afraid of Denny?"

"Aren't you?"

"Not on your tintype! Denny's not nearly as tough as he puts on. Besides, if he ever tried any rough stuff with me, he knows I'd take a hike. And p.d.q. too!"

"You could've fooled me."

"Honeybunch, you just lost me. Fooled you when?"

"Earlier tonight," Starbuck replied, "when I asked you why Denny hasn't taken over Chinatown. You clammed up tighter than a drum."

"So what?"

"So I'd say you're scared of him. Damn good and scared!"

"No—" Nell's voice skipped a beat. "Not Denny."

"Who, then?"

"The blind . . ."

Her words trailed away, and she stiffened in his arms. Starbuck studied her with open curiosity. "Go ahead, finish it. The blind————?"

There was an awkward pause. "Harry, take some good advice. While you're in Frisco, don't ask too many questions. What you don't know can't hurt you."

"That bad, huh?"

"You just take my word for it . . . okay?"

"Hell, forget I asked!" Starbuck laughed jovially. "No skin off my nose."

"And let's keep it that way." Nell burrowed deeper into the hollow of his shoulder. "I like your nose just the way it is."

Starbuck dropped it there. He knew he'd learned all he would for one night, and there was no need to push it further. He pulled her to him in a tight embrace, saying no more. Yet the words stuck in his mind, and he found himself genuinely baffled. He lay very still, silently repeating something that seemed to make no sense.

The blind . . .

CHAPTER 9

"Tell me about Mr. Lovett."

"I do not trust him, master."

"Please explain."

May Ling was seated across the table from Fung Jing Toy. A hatchet man had escorted her into his chambers only moments ago. Earlier that afternoon, when the one named Harry Lovett had departed her lodgings, she knew she would be summoned to the house on Washington Street. She had spent the balance of the afternoon in deep reflection, artfully phrasing the report she would deliver to her master. Now, under Fung's benign gaze, she began what seemed to her a perilous journey. She dared not to be wrong.

"I believe he is an imposter." Her voice was soft and troubled. "One who pretends to be what he is not."

Fung stared at her in a mild abstracted way. "Did he abuse you?"

"No, master," May Ling said quickly. "He was very gentle for a *fan kwei*."

"How did he differ from other white men I have sent to you?"

"He was not impatient or crude. Nor was he cruel in his demands. We joined three times during the night, and each time he took me without harshness. Today, when we returned from the auction, we joined once again. He was even more considerate . . . gentle."

Fung weighed her words a moment. The white devils, even the wealthy ones, were renowned for their coarse sexual habits and their lack of sophistication in bed. Yet, just as there were brutal Chinese, so might there be gentle white men. To think in absolutes was to cloud one's judgment.

"So then," he said quietly. "Your suspicion was aroused because he did not treat you in the manner practiced by white men?"

"I thought it strange, master. You told me his plan was to open several brothels, and such men are known for their barbaric customs. He was not what I expected."

"Very well," Fung nodded. "Mr. Lovett apparently has attributes uncommon to brothelkeepers. Is there more?"

"Yes, master," May Ling noted seriously. "His behavior at the auction was most revealing."

"You followed my instructions?"

"Oh yes! As you ordered, I asked no questions and gave him no reason for alarm. When I suggested attending the auction, he was very excited, very curious. He believed it was something I had thought of only then. A small inspiration to make his tour of Little China more enjoyable."

"What happened then?"

"At the auction, I observed him closely. His curiosity quickly turned to an attitude of disapproval. He held his tongue, but it was there to see, nonetheless. He frowned, and suddenly became very thoughtful."

"Perhaps he is a thoughtful man."

"Perhaps," May Ling said tactfully. "Quite, soon, however, a circumstance arose which allowed me to test him. I led him into a discussion of slave girls who are unsuitable for auction. His questions enabled me to speak of conditions in the cribs . . . and the hospital."

"Ah!" A pinpoint of light glittered in Fung's eyes. "You trapped him!"

"I merely deceived him, master. He betrayed himself."

"In what way?"

"He was shocked," May Ling remarked. "When I explained how the crib girls end their days, his expression was one of loathing. The very idea of the hospital was abhorrent to him."

"He told you that?"

"Not in words," May Ling said, her eyes downcast. "I sensed it, master. His reaction was that of a white devil missionary. He felt sadness and compassion for the crib girls."

"We were informed that this is his first venture as a brothelkeeper. According to O'Brien, he was what the whites call a con man. Perhaps he has not yet acquired the dispassionate nature necessary to such work."

"Certain things cannot be hidden, master. Whatever his designs are, the man named Lovett is not what he claims. He is an imposter."

"You speak now of intuition, things you divine rather than fact itself. Is it not so?"

"A woman knows," May Ling said, looking directly at him. "How she knows cannot be explained, but that makes it no less real. This man is dangerous, and I fear he will bring evil to your house. I must say what I believe to be true, master."

For a protracted interval, Fung was silent. He steepled his fingers together, considering both the girl and her statement. She was young, but wise beyond her years. Several times in the past he had used her to gain insight into men who sought to do business with him. Her intuition was a mystic thing, and a force not to be regarded lightly. Then, too, everything she'd told him merely served to reinforce his own sense of disquiet. Something about Lovett bothered him, and it was for that reason he had arranged the liaison with May Ling. He examined the alternatives, and quickly decided to heed her warning. The sale of a hundred virgins was, after all, a thing of no great consequence.

"I have learned," he said at length, "that Mr. Lovett will sleep with O'Brien's whore tonight."

"Nothing escapes you, master."

"Quite so," Fung agreed loftily. "I have eyes everywhere, even in the Bella Union."

"Will the Kimball woman also attempt deception?"

"No," Fung said without inflection. "O'Brien is blinded by greed. He suspects nothing."

"A shame," May Ling commented slyly. "But then, no *fan kwei* could be expected to have your wisdom and foresight."

A wintry smile lighted Fung's eyes. "You have performed the task well, and I am pleased."

"I live only to serve you, master."

"Leave me now. Other matters require my attention."

May Ling obediently rose, placed her hands together, and dipped low in a bow. She stepped backward to the door, then turned and walked past the dogs. Fung snapped his fingers, and one of the hatchet men appeared in the doorway. He took pen and paper off the table, and laboriously scrawled a note in English. Then he folded it and looked up at the waiting hatchet man.

"You will deliver this message to the blind white devil."

The Snug Café was located on O'Farrell Street, in the heart of the Uptown Tenderloin. Shortly before midnight, a closed carriage rolled to a halt in the alleyway behind the café. Wong Yee and Sing Dock stepped out of the carriage and inspected the alley in both directions. There was no one in sight.

The hatchet men assisted Fung down from the carriage. He walked directly to the back door of the café and knocked. He was expected, and the door swung open almost instantly. Knuckles Jackson, a pugnosed bruiser who served as bouncer, waved him through and closed the door. Wong Yee and Sing Dock exchanged a look. Only here would the master dispense with their services and enter unguarded. Neither of them thought the order odd, for only here was he safe without them. Still, it did nothing to lessen their concern.

Inside, Knuckles Jackson led Fung through a storage room and up a flight of stairs. There he stopped and rapped twice on a door. A muffled voice responded and he ushered Fung into a lavishly appointed office. The furniture was black walnut, intricately carved, and upholstered in plush velvet. Logs crackled in a black marble fireplace, and a crystal lamp bathed the room in dim light. Beyond the fireplace, cloaked in shadow, stood a massive walnut desk.

The man seated behind the desk was in his early fifties. He wore a frock coat and striped trousers, and a black cravat with a pearl stickpin. His features were lean and angular, and his gray hair was complimented by a neatly trimmed mustache. His eyes were all but invisible behind dark tinted glasses. He gestured toward a chair, and smiled.

"Do come in, Fung. Have a seat."

"Thank you, Mr. Buckley." Fung took the chair,

folding his hands in his lap. "It was kind of you to see me on such short notice."

"Not at all." Buckley dismissed Knuckles Jackson with a nod, and waited until the door closed. "Now, what can I do for you? I daresay it's nothing inconsequential at this late hour."

"That is so." Fung's tone was curiously deferential. "A problem has arisen, and I felt it should be brought to your attention immediately."

"Well, well, that does sound serious. Suppose you tell me about it."

"I regret to say it involves Denny O'Brien."

"Oh?" The smile faded and a shadow of irritation crossed Buckley's features. "I trust you and Denny aren't at one another's throats again?"

"I have not overstepped my boundaries. To my knowledge, neither has O'Brien. As you directed, we have worked together in a spirit of cooperation."

"And now?"

"There is no dispute with regard to territory. O'Brien confines himself to the Barbary Coast, and I do the same in Chinatown. In that respect, we have both honored your wishes."

"Diplomacy has its place, but let's dispense with it for the moment, shall we? Please come to the point."

"Yes, of course," Fung said promptly. "O'Brien sent a man to me three days ago on a business matter. I now have reason—"

"A white man?"

"Indeed, so," Fung said with no trace of resentment. "A white man by the name of Harry Lovett, who purports to be a whoremaster from Colorado."

"Very well. Please go on."

"I now have reason to believe Lovett is not what he claims."

"Not a whoremaster?"

"Precisely."

"What is he, then?"

"I have no idea." Fung offered an elaborate shrug. "Because the situation is confused, I thought it wise to seek your counsel."

Buckley sighed, tilting back in his chair. "In the interest of time, why not start at the beginning? And please, Fung, spare me the details. Stick to essentials, the bare bones."

The reproach was delivered in a condescending tone. Fung, who suddenly felt very Oriental and very much out of his element, evidenced no offense. Instead, he launched into a straightforward account of the past three days. He outlined O'Brien's role as intermediary, and went on to describe his meeting with Lovett. He dwelled at length on the matter of a hundred virgins, and Lovett's unusually quick acceptance of the asking price. With a certain flair for intrigue, he then recounted May Ling's role in the affair, and the sequence of events leading to the slave-girl auction. He concluded with a summation of May Ling's misgivings, adding that he, too, shared her doubts. There he paused and awaited Buckley's reaction.

"Are you telling me you're relying solely on this

girl's intuition . . . her feelings about Lovett?"

"To a large extent," Fung admitted. "She has great insight into men, and her perceptions have never failed me before."

Buckley's look was colored by skepticism. "A bit like reading tea leaves, isn't it? You really have nothing concrete to support your view."

"I am satisfied." Fung's features grew overcast. "I no longer wish to do business with this man Lovett."

"What harm could come of it? We have the fix in with immigration, so he's obviously not a government agent. I fail to see how he poses a threat."

"A threat assumes many guises. I have no way of knowing who Lovett may or may not be. On the other hand, I do know the value of caution. I would prefer to cancel the arrangement without delay."

Buckley appeared to lose interest. "Do as you please. Simply inform Lovett the deal's off."

"There are other considerations," Fung said in a musing voice. "O'Brien has quite probably charged Lovett a middleman's fee. That places me in an awkward position."

"Exactly what is it you're asking?"

"I wish you to intercede on my behalf. O'Brien will accept your judgment, and the matter will end there."

"I dislike getting involved in these petty squabbles. Good God, you and Denny are grown men! Work it out for yourselves."

Fung gave him a straight, hard look. "As you are aware, O'Brien bears me personal ill will, and he also covets Chinatown. Were I to withdraw from this arrangement—thereby causing him financial loss—he might easily use it as a pretext to start trouble. Without your intercession, our spirit of harmony may very well be jeopardized. I urge you to reconsider."

"In short," Buckley said with heavy sarcasm, "you want me to pull your chestnuts out of the fire?"

"I bow to your wisdom at all times. As you have so often reminded me—you are the boss."

Buckley gave the matter some thought. "Very well," he said finally, "I'll look into it. I want you to understand something, though. When you make your problems my problems, I begin wondering if maybe I don't need myself a new boy in Chinatown. You might reflect on that before you come begging favors again."

"I most humbly apologize." Fung rose and bowed slightly from the waist. "I wish only to maintain the peace and prosperity we enjoy under your guidance."

"Good night, Fung. I'll let you know what happens."

Buckley sat perfectly still until the door closed. Then he removed his glasses and massaged his eyes. He was tired and his head ached, and at times like tonight, he felt very much like a rooster atop a dung heap. The footing somehow never seemed all that firm. Nor had he yet accustomed himself to the smell.

*   *   *

Denny O'Brien was summoned late the next morning. The Snug Café wasn't yet open for business, but
he, too, entered through the alley door. Upstairs, he
kept his greeting short and polite, and dropped into
a chair before the desk. Buckley went straight to the
point.

"Fung paid me a visit last night. He's jumpy about
a deal you arranged with some fellow named Lovett."

"What d'you mean?" O'Brien said with an an-
noyed squint. "What's there to be jumpy about?"

"He wants out," Buckley said flatly. "He seems
to think your friend Lovett isn't on the up and up."

"That's crazy!" O'Brien burst out. "Harry Lovett's as square as they come!"

"What makes you think so?"

"Mattie Silks herself sent him to see me. She's
the biggest madam in Denver, and anyone she rec-
ommends is ace-high in my book."

Buckley looked somber. "Have you checked him
out? Wired Mattie Silks or some of our friends in
Denver?"

"No." O'Brien shook his head in exasperation.
"Why would I check him out? Jesus H. Christ, the
man's loaded! He's ready to hand Fung a hundred
thousand—for virgins, no less!"

"And I take it you've cut yourself in for a piece
of the action?"

"Why not?" O'Brien bridled. "I made the introduction, didn't I?"

"Perhaps that's the problem." Buckley's tone was

severe. "I got the distinct impression Fung suspects you slipped a ringer in on him. He's convinced Lovett is a setup of some sort."

"Goddamn him!" O'Brien roared vindictively. "That slant-eyed little son-of-a-bitch never stops! He won't be satisfied till I'm six feet under and turned into worm meat."

"Have you given him reason?"

"Hell, no! You laid out the rules and I've stayed on my side of the street. Chinatown don't mean beans to me."

"Then why would he turn leery so quickly? From what he told me, it sounds like a fairly routine deal."

"It's spite, plain and simple." O'Brien face congealed into a scowl. "He's willing to queer the deal just to give everybody a laugh at my expense. That makes him look like a big man to all his Chink pals."

"I think not." Buckley's headshake was slow and emphatic. "His concern was genuine. He believes there's something fishy, and he would sooner be safe than sorry."

"By Jesus!" O'Brien said stubbornly. "I won't hold still for it. I stood to make a cool ten thousand on this deal, and I mean to have it."

"You're wrong." Buckley's voice was suddenly edged. "You'll do exactly what I tell you to do, Denny. I won't allow you or anyone else to upset my applecart. Do I make myself clear?"

"I hear you," O'Brien said grudgingly. "But it goes down hard, you taking that slope-head's side against me."

"Wrong again," Buckley replied with weary tolerance. "I haven't ruled one way or the other, not yet."

"I don't get you."

"It occurs to me that Mr. Lovett and I should have a talk. You bring him around late this evening. I'll make my judgment then, and it won't have anything to do with you or Fung. All very impartial, based strictly on my impression of Lovett."

"Little risky, isn't it?" O'Brien looked worried. "He's no dummy, and you're not exactly somebody he'd forget real quick."

Buckley's laugh was strange and somehow cryptic. "Our talk might prove risky for Mr. Lovett. Only time and the tea leaves will tell."

O'Brien felt a tingle along his backbone. He'd heard that laugh before, and he knew precisely what it meant. Tonight there would be no quibbling, no questions left unanswered. Nor would there be anything remotely resembling a second chance.

Harry Lovett was a dead man unless he passed muster.

CHAPTER 10

It was half-past eight when Starbuck arrived at the Bella Union. He reeked of rosewood lotion and was attired in yet another of his spiffy outfits. He walked through the barroom and paused in the doorway of the theater. Thumbs hooked in his vest, he slowly scanned the crowd.

His appointment with Nell was for somewhere around nine. Their plans, with one exception, were much the same as last night. A theater box was reserved, chilled champagne was on order, and the first part of their evening would be devoted to the early show. Afterward, a late supper would be served in the privacy of Nell's room. The balance of the night, something of a return engagement, would be spent in bed. There would be lovemaking and talk, lots of talk. Tonight, he expected to learn considerably more about San Francisco's underworld. Perhaps all he needed to know.

Standing in the doorway, he thought it strange

that Nell was nowhere in sight. He glanced at the curtained box and saw that it was empty. Then, checking his watch, it occurred to him that she might still be in her room. He was about to turn when High Spade McQueen laid a hand on his shoulder. He looked around.

"The boss wants to see you." McQueen jerked his chin toward the staircase. "Now."

"Why sure thing, High Spade. Lead the way."

Something in McQueen's attitude alerted him. When they reached the staircase, any lingering doubt was dispelled. McQueen casually lagged behind and followed him, rather than leading him up the stairs. He knew then he was in trouble. He warned himself to go slow and keep a sharp lookout.

On the balcony, McQueen opened the office door and motioned him through. Denny O'Brien was seated behind the desk, his expression grim. Starbuck heard the door close, and realized he was sandwiched between them. With a jaunty air, he flipped O'Brien a salute and approached the desk.

"Evening, Denny," he said with a jocular smile. "How's tricks?"

O'Brien's hand appeared from beneath the desk, holding a pistol. "Don't make any sudden moves."

"Judas Priest!" Starbuck croaked. "What the hell's the idea?"

"Shut your trap." O'Brien looked past him. "Mac, pat him down."

McQueen expertly went over him. The Colt Lightning was discovered almost immediately, and removed from its shoulder holster. His arms were checked for a sleeve gun; then his waistband and all his pockets were thoroughly searched. He waited, certain the hideout gun in his boot top was next; but his legs weren't touched. Finally, McQueen shoved him into a chair and looked across at O'Brien.

"He's clean."

"You're sure he hasn't got a hideout?"

"One peashooter." McQueen palmed the Colt and stuck it inside his belt. "That's it, boss."

O'Brien laid his pistol on the desk. Then, with a venomous glare, his gaze shifted to Starbuck. "I oughta bust your goddamn skull wide open."

"For Chrissake!" Starbuck said, squirming around in his chair. "What's the matter? What'd I do?"

"I'll ask the questions!" O'Brien's fist slammed onto the desk. "You just gimme some straight answers, or else I'll let Mac and his sailor pals feed you to the sharks."

"Anything at all, Denny. Go ahead, ask away."

"How come you told me you're in thick with the sporting crowd in Denver?"

"I never said that," Starbuck corrected him. "I told you I mostly worked the mining camps. All I said about Denver was that me and Mattie Silks are on good terms."

"You're a liar!" O'Brien shouted. "I wired Mattie and she said she never heard of you."

"That's a crock," Starbuck said stoutly. "No way on God's green earth Mattie wouldn't vouch for me."

He saw he'd guessed right. O'Brien's eyes gave him away, and he quickly backed off from the bluff. "All right, so I wired her and just haven't got the answer yet. It amounts to the same thing. If she don't give you a clean bill of health, you'll get deep-sixed so fast you won't know what hit you."

"Denny, I'll give you odds on what her wire says."

"Don't get too cocky," O'Brien warned him. "You've still got your balls in a nutcracker."

"What's that supposed to mean?"

"Suppose you tell me about your talk with Fung."

"Fung?" Starbuck looked bewildered. "Hell, there wasn't much talk to it. He set a price, and we dickered for a while, then I finally agreed. That's the way we left it."

"You had a deal, then? You're sure of that?"

"I'm plumb sure. No two ways about it."

"When did he say he'd make delivery?"

"Well . . ." Starbuck stopped, thoughtful a moment. "He didn't say, not exactly. He allowed it would take a while to get that many virgins together, and told me he'd be in touch."

"How long? A week, two weeks?"

"He never spelled it out, and I never asked. I'd already agreed to pay top dollar, so I figured he'd hop right to it."

"Didn't it ever occur to you that you might be getting the runaround?"

"Why would he do a thing like that?"

"Forget it," O'Brien muttered. "What did he ask you about me?"

"Nothing." Starbuck shrugged, shook his head. "Near as I recollect, your name wasn't even mentioned."

O'Brien gave him a swift, intense look. "Think back on it, real hard. Maybe he asked you how long we've known each other? Whether or not we've done business before? Anything along that line?"

"Not a word," Starbuck said without hesitation. "Course, he seemed to know all about me and what it was I wanted. I just naturally assumed you'd managed to fill him in before I got there."

"You assumed right." O'Brien mulled it over briefly, then glanced up. "What about the girl, May Ling? She mention me, try to draw you out somehow?"

"Same story," Starbuck observed. "She never said boo about anything except Chinatown and the slave-girl trade."

"Yeah, that's right. She took you to the auction, didn't she? Cooked you a Chink meal and screwed your ears off—and never asked one question about me! Is that what you're saying?"

"That's the works, Denny. Start to finish."

O'Brien's voice suddenly turned querulous. "You stupid son-of-a-bitch! Do you think I'm gonna sit here and let you con me like some snot-nosed hayseed?"

"Con you?" Starbuck was genuinely surprised. "I'm telling it to you straight. Honest to Christ!"

"Bullshit!" O'Brien glowered back at him. "I happen to know you asked Nell how come I never tried to take over Chinatown."

"So?"

"So where'd you dream up that idea? I'll tell you where! Fung and that little Chinee bitch put the bee in your ear. The whole time you were with 'em, they pumped you dry about me, didn't they?"

"No, goddamnit, they didn't!" Starbuck sounded indignant. "I told it to you just the way it happened."

"Then why'd you ask Nell what you did?"

"Because any fool could see you and Fung hate each other's guts. Nobody has to say anything! It's plain as a diamond in a goat's ass."

"And you figured it out all by yourself?"

"Hell, yes!" Starbuck blustered. "Fung and his hatchet men wouldn't be any match for you and your boys. That's plain to see, too. I guess it just got my curiosity working overtime."

"Curiosity about what?"

"Well, I don't mean to insult you, Denny. But, Jesus Christ, nobody's got your arms tied, have they? The way it looks to me, you could've gobbled up Chinatown anytime you took a notion. It's like I told Nell—if it was me, there wouldn't be no way I could resist giving it a try."

O'Brien's silence was all the answer Starbuck needed. He sensed Nell had lied. She hadn't told O'Brien about his greater curiosity, the vague questions he'd asked about an underworld kingpin. Nor had she mentioned her own slip of the tongue, her unfinished statement that ended abruptly with "the blind." Quite clearly, she had lied to protect him. Whether she realized it or not, she had nudged herself a step closer to his side of the line. He now had something approaching an ally in the enemy camp. A little softsoap, with a dash of blackmail added, would soon bring her around.

O'Brien, who seemed to have recovered his humor, finally broke the silence. "Harry, I'll have to hand it to you. You're a pretty smooth article."

"Why, thank you, Denny. I'm sort of sweet on you, too."

"Don't misunderstand me," O'Brien countered. "You're not out of the woods yet."

"Oh, how so?"

"Well, as it happens, we've got a helluva problem with Fung. He wants to back out on the deal. Somehow or other, he's turned leery toward you."

"Why?" Starbuck demanded. "What's his reason?"

"I'm not altogether sure," O'Brien said, frowning. "From what I gather, he's got it in his head you're working with me—a swindle of some sort—or else you're a government agent."

"He's nuts!" Starbuck scoffed. "I don't work for you or anyone else. And that goddamned sure includes the government!"

"All the same, that's what we're up against."

"Then we'll just wait till you get Mattie's wire. Once you show him that, he'll know I'm on the level and we're back in business."

"Harry, if it was up to me, I wouldn't hesitate a minute. But it's out of my hands now."

Starbuck's pulse quickened. "I don't get your meaning."

"You've got an appointment." O'Brien rose and stuffed his pistol in the waistband of his trousers. "Tonight you're to talk with the big man himself, Mr. Frisco."

"Mr. Frisco?"

"Let's get a move on. You're expected, and I wouldn't care to keep him waiting."

With O'Brien in the lead, and McQueen bringing up the rear, they went through the door and crossed the balcony. On the way down the stairs, Starbuck was acutely aware that his gun had not been returned. He also understood, though it was left unspoken, that he had passed only Denny O'Brien's test.

Mr. Frisco, and a sterner test, was yet to come.

A gentle rain was falling as the carriage turned off O'Farrell Street. Starbuck wasn't at all surprised that their destination was located in the Uptown Tenderloin. His theory regarding the boss of San Francisco's underworld was now confirmed.

All the way uptown he had tried in vain to learn the identity of Mr. Frisco. His questions finally provoked Denny O'Brien, and he was told to drop the subject. Still, with or without a name, it was clear O'Brien and Fung answered to one man. A man who rubbed elbows with the city's social elite, the rich and the powerful. A mastermind who had created a brilliant cover, disassociating himself completely from Chinatown and the Barbary Coast. And therefore a man who was exceedingly dangerous.

The thought was foremost in Starbuck's mind as the carriage rolled to a halt in the alleyway. He knew the next few minutes would determine whether he lived or died. Mr. Frisco had gone to great lengths to conceal his identity. Yet he apparently had no qualms about exposing himself to a Colorado whoremaster. The conclusion was obvious, and the hazard involved was beyond question. Unless Mr. Frisco got all the right answers, the end result was chillingly simple to predict. One whoremaster, more or less, would never be missed.

The alley door opened and Knuckles Jackson waved them inside. Starbuck was treated to yet another search, but took scant comfort from the fact that his hideout gun once again went undetected. McQueen and Jackson, who belonged to the same brotherhood of gorillas, remained on guard in the storeroom. O'Brien escorted him up the stairs, which meant he was covered front and rear. The chances of shooting his way out weren't even worth calculating. His wits were now his only hope for survival.

The light in the office was dim, and the man behind the desk sat immobile. Starbuck had the fleeting impression of a store-window dummy propped up in a chair. Then O'Brien closed the door, removing his hat, and walked forward. Starbuck followed suit, quickly inspecting the office. The door to the store-room stairs was the only exit.

"Here he is," O'Brien said, halting in front of the desk. "Harry Lovett."

"Thank you, Denny." Buckley made a small gesture of dismissal. "Wait downstairs. I'll call if I need you."

O'Brien seemed on the verge of questioning the order. Then he bobbed his head, turning away, and crossed the office. A moment later the door closed. Starbuck grinned and stuck out his hand.

"Pleased to meet you, Mr. Frisco."

Starbuck was rocked by a sudden jolt of aware-ness. His arm extended, leaning over the desk, he got his first good look at the man. The face was a living waxwork, and behind the dark tinted glasses, the eyes were marble-like. He had the eerie sensation of gazing into the eyes of a stuffed animal, glassy and unmoving. Nell's word's flitted through his head, and abruptly it all made sense. The blind man! She'd almost blurted it out, and now he saw it for himself. The boss of San Francisco's underworld was *blind*. His mouth popped open and he slowly withdrew his hand. He stood there, too stunned to speak.

"Have a seat, Mr. Lovett." Buckley motioned him to a chair. "I presume it was Denny who referred to me as Mr. Frisco?"

"Yeah." Starbuck took a seat, rapidly collected his wits. "He said it was all the name I needed to know."

"By no means," Buckley said with a frosty smile. "My name is Buckley. Christopher Buckley."

"Well, Mr. Buckley, maybe you can explain something to me. What's all this strongarm business about? I came out here to buy myself some whores, and now I've got people sticking guns in my face."

"I'm afraid Denny overreacts at times. You see, Mr. Lovett, we have a difference of opinion with respect to the girls you wish to purchase. I've been asked to arbitrate the matter."

"You're talking about Fung trying to welch on our deal?"

"Exactly." Buckley inclined his head in a faint nod. "In Fung's words, you are not what you represent yourself to be, Mr. Lovett."

"So Denny told me." Starbuck switched to a light and mocking tone. "Dumb goddamn Chinaman! Somebody ought to tell him he's got his head screwed on backward."

"Perhaps you wouldn't mind answering a question?"

"Fire away," Starbuck said cheerfully. "I've got no secrets."

"Are you familiar with Lou Blomger?"

"Why, hell, yes! Everybody in Denver knows Lou Blomger. You name it, he runs it! The rackets, politics—the whole ball of wax."

"I wired him this morning." Buckley indicated a telegram lying open on the desk. "If you care to read his reply, he says in no uncertain terms he never heard of Harry Lovett."

"What's that prove?" Starbuck protested. "Blomger's out of my league. I work the mining camps, not Denver. He wouldn't know me from Adam's off ox."

"Come now, Mr. Lovett. A man with your connections—Mattie Silks, no less—and Blomger never heard of you. I find that difficult to believe."

Starbuck took a chance. "Tell you what, Mr. Buckley. You're so fond of sending wires, send one to Bailey Youngston in Leadville. He owns the Texas House Saloon and half the town to boot. Ask him if I didn't knock down the biggest score of my life, not two months ago, sitting right in his joint. Hell, for the right price, he'll even tell you the sucker's name!"

There was a long silence. "Very well, Mr. Lovett," Buckley said at length. "I will defer my decision for the moment—but only on three conditions. One, we will await replies from Mattie Silks and your friend, Youngston. Next, as a gesture of good faith, you will deposit one hundred thousand dollars in the bank of my choice by closing time tomorrow. Will that present any problem?"

"No problem at all," Starbuck assured him earnestly. "I came prepared to pay in cash, so you just name your bank and I'll be there johnny-on-the-spot."

"Fine," Buckley said with dungeon calm. "I feel quite certain that will go a long way toward dispelling Fung's apprehension."

"You said there were three conditions?"

"Indeed, I did." A cold smile touched the corner of Buckley's mouth. "Until the matter is resolved to my satisfaction, you will make no attempt to leave San Francisco. Need I elaborate on that condition further?"

"No, sir, no need. I get your drift completely."

Starbuck knew he'd been given a reprieve, nothing more. Bailey Youngston was the owner of the Texas House Saloon, but nobody in Leadville had ever heard of Harry Lovett. Youngston might answer a wire from a stranger, and he might not. That was a toss-up, and could go either way. The money, on the other hand, was a surefire certainty. And tomorrow at closing time was less than twenty-four hours away.

All of a sudden Starbuck felt like a juggler with one too many balls in the air. Yet there was no question which one he had to grab first, and fastest.

He wondered where the hell he could lay his hands on $100,000!

CHAPTER 11

Nell was waiting in the theater box. The Bella Union was already packed, but she easily spotted them as they moved through the crowd in the barroom. O'Brien paused near the staircase, talking with Starbuck a moment. Then, accompanied by High Spade McQueen, he mounted the stairs and disappeared into his office.

Starbuck looked toward the box and saw her. Doffing his hat, he waved, smiling broadly. She waved back, watching as he crossed the theater and went up the short flight of stairs leading to the loge. Earlier, one of the bartenders had told her he'd left the Bella Union with O'Brien and McQueen. She had no idea where they had gone or why. Nor was she about to ask. Their business dealings were none of her concern, and she preferred to keep it that way. Experience had taught her that inquisitive women often learned too much for their own good. In her view, she was paid to entertain, not ask questions.

"Sorry I'm late."

Entering the box, Starbuck tossed his hat on the sofa and took a chair beside her. Nell gave him a dazzling smile, and leaned forward to kiss him lightly on the mouth.

"No need to apologize, lover. You're here now, and that's what counts."

"We still set to have supper in your room?"

"Of course." She removed a bottle of champagne from an ice bucket and filled two glasses. "What's an hour more or less? The night's young."

"That's my girl!" Starbuck winked and lifted his glass in a toast. "Here's mud in your eye."

Nell laughed, clinking glasses. "Yours, too, honeybun."

Starbuck appraised her as she sipped champagne. He detected a false note in her voice and saw the guarded look in her eyes. He seriously doubted that O'Brien had confided in her, or told her that a meeting had been arranged with Buckley. Yet she was curious, and clearly biting her tongue not to ask questions. He thought to himself that it was a good sign. Her curiosity made her vulnerable.

Handled properly, tonight's development could accomplish two essential goals. She might easily be beguiled into revealing more about Buckley, and his place in the scheme of things. With time at a premium, any scrap of information was vital, and she represented the only dependable source. Further, the more she revealed, the simpler it would be to enlist her as an ally. By playing on her curiosity, and her fear of O'Brien, she might be forced into a conspiracy from which there was no return. A certain risk was attached, but he really had no choice. Tonight would determine whether or not he could trust her, and exactly how far she would go in the event push came to shove. All that remained was to sound her out.

Tossing off his champagne, he refilled their glasses. Then, a thumb hooked in his vest, he sat back and grinned expansively.

"So far it's been some night."

"Oh?"

"Yessir, it has for a fact. Denny introduced me to the big boy himself, in the flesh."

"The big boy?"

"The blind man." Starbuck watched her out of the corner of his eye. "Christopher Buckley."

Surprise washed over Nell's face. "Denny took you to see Buckley?"

"Sure did," Starbuck said carelessly. "Had ourselves a pretty nice chat, too."

Nell nodded, then smiled a little. "You're going up in the world. Not many people get to meet Mr. Buckley."

"You mean to say you've never met him?"

"Nooo," she said slowly. "He's out of my league."

"Then how'd you know he was blind?"

"Blind?"

"Yeah." Starbuck idly gestured with his champagne glass. "Last night you started to say something about the blind somebody or other, but you never finished it."

"I was talking out of turn. I didn't know Denny had arranged a meeting."

"Tell you the truth, I don't think Denny arranged anything."

Nell gave him a glance full of curiosity. "I'm not sure I understand."

"Well—" Starbuck took a sip of champagne, pondered a moment. "Unless I read it wrong, when Buckley say frog, Denny squats. Am I right or not?"

"You're close enough."

"Thought so." Starbuck bobbed his head sagely. "Buckley ordered him to bring me around all because of that damn fool Chinaman."

"Fung?"

"Nothing serious." Starbuck rocked his hand, fingers splayed. "Fung evidently got cold feet about our deal. Had some asinine notion that Denny and me were out to gaff him somehow."

Nell looked upset. "You mean Buckley thought you weren't on the level?"

"The way he put it, he'd been asked to arbitrate the matter. That's fancy lingo for saying it's up to him whether or not the deal goes through."

"What happened?"

"Won't know for a couple of days," Starbuck observed casually. "He wants to check out my references before he decides, and I told him that was fine by me. Harry Lovett's got nothing to hide."

"You're sure of that?" Nell asked anxiously.

"Buckley's one man you don't want for an enemy."

Starbuck uttered a low chuckle. "I got the same impression myself. Denny acted like he was in the presence of Jesus Christ and the Lord God Jehovah all rolled into one."

"You're getting warm, lover. So far as this town's concerned, anyway."

"Now that you mention it," Starbuck appeared thoughtful, "on the way uptown, Denny called him 'Mr. Frisco.' I reckon the name fits, or else Denny and Fung wouldn't report to him like good little soldiers."

"Denny told you that?"

"Told me what?"

"About reporting to Buckley?"

"Nope," Starbuck readily admitted. "But it's plain enough to see. Denny and Fung are like lieutenants; one runs the Coast and the other runs Chinatown. Buckley cracks the whip, and whatever hoop he holds up, that's the one they jump through."

"I wouldn't say that out loud too often if I were you."

. "Why?" Starbuck looked at her directly. "It's the truth, isn't it?"

Nell averted her gaze. A troupe of acrobats went tumbling across the stage, and she watched them in silence for a time. Finally, with a furtive shrug, she spoke in a low voice.

"Harry, the truth can get you hurt. Take some good advice, and don't let anybody know you've figured out how things work in Frisco."

"Yeah, I suppose you're right."

"I know I'm right."

"All the same, there's one thing that damn sure doesn't figure."

"You'll ask anyway," Nell said reluctantly, "so go ahead."

"How the hell's a blind man put the fear of God in someone like Denny O'Brien?"

"I'll give you three guesses, and the first two don't count."

"You make it sound awful simple."

"Nothing simpler, if you have the stomach for it." Starbuck smiled. "How about a clue?"

"Oh, suppose we call it the second oldest profession in the world?"

The curtain at the door opened and O'Brien stepped into the box. He nodded to Nell, his mouth split in a wide smile. Then he moved around the sofa and genially clapped Starbuck on the shoulder.

"Enjoying the show?"

"Which one?"

"Which one?" O'Brien parroted, gesturing toward the stage. "I only see one."

"Oh, that?" Starbuck rolled his eyes at Nell. "Just between you and me, Denny, I'm waiting for the finale."

"Harry, you're a sport! Goddamn me if you aren't."

"Let's just say there are other things I prefer to acrobats."

"You'll be spending the night with us, then?"

Starback looked at him, unable to guess what might be going through his mind. The question was phrased in the manner of an invitation, but there was an undertone of command in O'Brien's voice. Whether the message was meant for Starbuck or Nell seemed a moot point. The owner of the Bella Union hadn't popped into the box to make small talk. He was there for a purpose.

"Nell's the one to ask." Starbuck let go a hoot of laughter. "I can go all night and then some, but a girl needs her beauty sleep."

"Don't worry about Nell," O'Brien advised with heavy good humor. "She's lots tougher than she looks."

"I'll let you know in the morning."

"You do that, Harry."

O'Brien grinned, as if at some private joke. Then he glanced at Nell and turned away. The curtain parted and they were once more alone in the box.

Starbuck poured champagne, seemingly unperturbed by the interruption. He noted that Nell's manner was pensive and oddly taut. Her gaze was fixed on the stage. He gave her leg a squeeze and chortled softly to himself.

"That Denny's a card, isn't he? Always funning around—"

"You lied to me!"

"Lied?" Starbuck feigned astonishment. "What the hell are you talking about?"

"Stop it!" Nell said in a shaky voice. "You're trying to con me, and I don't appreciate it one damn bit."

"You got a crystal ball, or did you figure that out all by yourself?"

"I don't need a crystal ball. I know Denny like the back of my hand, and he wasn't playing patty-cake and roses. He came up here to give you a warning."

Starbuck smiled lamely and lifted his hands in a shrug. "You've got me dead to rights. I needed help and I wasn't exactly sure how to go about asking."

"What kind of help?"

"I'm caught in the middle," Starbuck lied, straightfaced. "Denny and Fung are out to axe one another, and they're using me as a stalking horse. That's what brought Buckley into it. He doesn't want any trouble, and he's willing to sacrifice me to keep the peace."

Nell looked skeptical. "Is that the truth or some more of your malarkey?"

"Buckley ordered me not to leave town, and Denny just got through warning me to stick close to the Bella Union. That pretty well tells the tale, doesn't it?"

Starbuck was improvising now. By threading a strand of truth into the web of fabrication, he hoped to draw her over to his side. She was silent for a time, her face blank, her eyes opaque. Then, finally, she sighed and her expression softened.

"Okay, lover, I'm a sucker for a sob story and you've got me hooked. How can I help?"

"First off," Starbuck said quickly, "show me how to slip out of here without being seen—maybe later, sometime after we've gone to your room. That way Denny will think I'm tucked in for the night."

"Are you planning to skip Frisco?"

"No," Starbuck said without guile. "Buckley ordered me to come up with the hundred thousand by tomorrow. I've got it stashed somewhere safe, and I want to deliver it on my own. That'll show good faith, and go a long way toward getting me out of the middle."

"All right," Nell agreed. "Denny had a dumbwaiter installed to bring meals up to the third floor. Once the kitchen closes, we'll use that to get you downstairs and then you can slip out the alley door. What's next?"

"I want the story on Buckley, the whole ball of wax. If he decides to play rough, I'll need something to trade, something he'd consider worth a standoff."

"Holy Hannah," Nell said with a theatrical shudder. "You ask a lot, don't you?"

"Only enough to keep me alive."

"Don't kid yourself." Nell looked at him with dulled eyes. "Buckley doesn't have to bargain with anybody. He has a dozen different ways to silence you, and all of them permanent."

"A man plays the cards he's dealt. It's that or run, and I've never been one to turn tail. Besides, I don't like the way Danny and Fung sandbagged me."

"What the hell? It's your funeral."

"Not yet." Starbuck grinned. "You just give me

the lowdown on Buckley, and I'll bluff him right out of his socks."

"There's not a lot to tell. I only know what I've heard when Denny goes on a toot and lets his tongue wag too much."

"How long has Buckley been top dog?"

"Long before my time. Twenty years, maybe more."

"Jesus," Starbuck marveled. "He must be tough. How'd he get his start?"

"The Tenderloin," Nell replied. "From what I gather, he killed the previous boss and just stepped into his shoes."

"You're saying a blind man was able to pull that off?"

"Well, he wasn't blind then. According to Denny, he was wounded in the shootout and lost his sight afterward. His men stuck by him and he branched out from there."

"Why would they stick by a blind man?"

"Because he's one brainy bastard! Even without eyes, he can outthink lugheads like Denny. On top of that, he's masterminded every crooked deal in this town. Nothing moves without his say-so."

"Are you talking about Chinatown and the Coast?"

"No." Nell slowly shook her head. "I'm talking about Frisco, from the bay to the Golden Gate."

"Politics!" Starbuck's eyes narrowed with sudden comprehension. "That's what you meant earlier,

wasn't it? When you said something about the second oldest profession?"

Nell bobbed her head. "Buckley *is* the Democratic Party. That's why Denny calls him Mr. Frisco. His wardheelers deliver the votes and he owns city hall like he'd foreclosed on the mortgage."

"So it's not fear—personal fear—that keeps Denny and Fung in line. They toe the mark because he's the political kingfish. Is that it?"

"No question about it," Nell affirmed. "He handpicked Denny to run the Coast, and the same with Fung in Chinatown. One word from him and they'd both be out on their ears. He made them and he can break them. It's just that simple."

"In other words," Starbuck mused thoughtfully, "Denny's plug-uglies and Fung's hatchet men couldn't save them no matter what."

"That's the setup," Nell remarked. "They've got the muscle, but Buckley's got the clout. He controls the mayor and the police department and every patronage job in the city. If he says Denny and Fung are out, then they're out. Period!"

Starbuck considered a moment. "How about payoffs? The take on the Coast alone must be worth a fortune. Is there a bagman—a go-between—or does Denny deal directly with Buckley?"

"Search me." Nell gave Starbuck a bemused look. "I only know what I hear, and nobody talks about payoffs. Even when he's drunk, Denny's not that thick."

"What about graft? Bribes? Anyone with Buckley's power has to knock down a mint with under-the-table loot."

"Oh, I imagine he robs the city like a bandit. But you couldn't prove it by me. I've never heard a rumor to that effect, much less read anything in the newspapers. He keeps a tight lid on the operation, real hush-hush. They way I get it, nobody but him knows the full score."

"How do you mean?"

"Well, it's like he wears two hats. One for politics and one for vice. He keeps them separate, never mixes one with the other. So nobody down here has any real pull with city hall or the police department. It all begins and ends with Buckley."

"Very cagey," Starbuck nodded. "One king with two kingdoms. Nobody trusts anyone else, so there's never a chance they'll join forces and kick him off the throne."

"I told you he's a brainy bastard."

"All the more reason for me to show up with the money tomorrow."

Nell smiled wanly. "You'd better think about tonight, lover. Otherwise, there won't be any tomorrow."

"As a matter of fact"—Starbuck leaned forward and poured the last of the champagne—"we're going to order another bottle of bubbly and pretend we're having ourselves a high old time. When we start up to your room, I want Denny to think we're sloshed to the gills. That way he won't get any funny notions and come tiptoeing around in the night."

"What about when we get to the room?"

"What about it?"

"Do we have to pretend then," Nell vamped him with a sultry look, "or can we play it for real?"

Starbuck laughed. "We'll play it any whichaway you like. How's that sound?"

"Love it!" Neil giggled and clapped her hands. "Simply love it, Mr. Lovett."

Starbuck wasn't sure whether she intended a pun. Nor was he curious enough to pursue it further. His thoughts turned instead to the dumbwaiter and the long night ahead.

Dawn suddenly seemed all too close for comfort.

CHAPTER 12

She had the gift of natural repose, not unlike a sleeping cat. She lay curled in the iron band of his arm, cloyed with the scent of love. Her breasts dipped and swelled with the rise and fall of his breathing.

Their lovemaking had been slow and tender. Tonight she had given herself completely, and he had brought her to full and wondrous climax. Her undulations timed to the questing thrust of his manhood, they joined in an explosive burst of sweet agony. In that final moment, her contractions had held him fast, draining him, and she discovered something she had known with no other man. She found enkindled need, and the stirring of emotion.

Now, awake and restive, Starbuck's thoughts centered on more practical matters. One step remained before they parted for the night. She had committed herself by talking openly and agreeing to assist in his escape from the Bella Union. Yet he distrusted any arrangement based solely on emotion; troublesome second thoughts might later cause her to regret the act. He felt the need to further guarantee her switch of allegiance from O'Brien. Loyalty, in his experience, was determined only in part by the degree of jeopardy one person was willing to risk for another. The greater part of loyalty was anchored to self-interest, and he saw that as an essential element yet to be realized. He wanted her obligated not to him but to herself. A commitment whereby she would lose greatly in the event she was tempted to backslide.

Starbuck patted her on the rump and gently disengaged from her close embrace. Then he stretched, yawning, and swung his legs over the side of the bed.

"Time to get a move on."

"I know, damnit." Nell sat up in bed, her breasts round and firm in the dim light. "Why is it the good things never last?"

Her words presented an opening, and Starbuck seized on the opportunity. "Funny you mentioned that. I've been lying there thinking the same thing myself."

"You have?"

"Well, not exactly the way you mean, but pretty close. I got to toying with an idea about the future."

"Whose future?"

"Yours and mine."

"Honestly?" Nell said on an indrawn breath. "You really mean it?"

"Honest Injun." Starbuck gathered his pants off a

nearby chair and began dressing. "Course, it all depends on how things turn out with Buckley."

"All what?"

"Nothing's certain, but let's play 'suppose' a minute. Suppose Buckley puts his stamp of approval on the deal. Suppose Denny and Fung salute and figure they'd be wiser to obey orders, and I end up with my hundred virgins. Suppose I take the girls back to Colorado and open a string of cathouses. In other words, suppose it all works out just the way I'd planned."

"I'll bite," Nell said, thoroughly mystified. "Suppose it does?"

"Then I'll need someone to run the operation for me. Someone like you."

"Me!" Nell squealed. "You're not serious?"

"The hell I'm not!" Starbuck began stuffing his shirt-tail into his pants, and gave her a dopey grin. "I've got big ideas and plenty of money, but I'm sort of shy on know-how. You said it yourself, when you asked me if I'd ever run a whorehouse. I guess that's what put the notion in my head."

"There's not all that much to it, not really."

"Say's you." Starbuck screwed up his face in a frown. "I don't know beans from buckshot about anything. One house would be headache enough for a tyro like me. But I aim to open four houses all at once! Think on that a minute."

"You're right," Nell conceded. "An operation that size could cause you some grief."

"Grief!" Starbuck snorted. "Christ, I'd be worse

off than a one-legged man in a kicking contest. Just for openers, I'd have to hire a madam for each house. Then I'd have to figure out a way to keep them honest and make goddamn sure their books are straight. Otherwise, they could skim off the cream and leave me wondering how I went broke so fast."

"Honey, I hate to be the one to tell you, but the madams aren't your real problem. It's the girls! When you put that many females under one roof, it turns into a slam-bang catfight, night and day. Once you lose control, the whole operation could go to hell in a handbasket."

"That's my point," Starbuck said forcefully. "I need someone to select the right madams and ride herd on all five houses. A supervisor or manager, someone who knows all the tricks of the trade. To my way of thinking, that someone is you."

"You really mean it, don't you?"

"Damn right!" Starbuck sensed it was time to dangle the carrot. "Matter of fact, I've already thought it out, and I'm willing to offer you ten percent right off the top. With four houses, I figure we'll rake in an easy million a year, maybe more. Your slice wouldn't exactly be termed chicken feed."

"Omigawd!" Nell whispered, awestruck. "A hundred thousand dollars! I'd be rich!"

"The sky's the limit," Starbuck observed grandly. "We'd make a helluva team, you and me. No telling where it would end."

Nell's head was buzzing. She suddenly saw an opportunity to put the Bella Union and the Barbary

Coast behind her. The manager of a Colorado whore-house empire was by no means a candidate for saint-hood. Still, it was the only profession she knew, and it was several rungs up the ladder from the life she'd led in Frisco. Moreover, it offered the chance for financial independence, wealth beyond anything she had ever imagined. Which meant never again having to spread her legs for whiskey-soaked highrollers and pot-gutted old men.

Then there was Harry Lovett. He evoked re-sponses in her that were all but forgotten. A sense of tenderness and affection, the deep-felt exhilaration of needing and being needed. On the surface he was glib and conniving, a grifter out to make his mark and devil take the hindmost. Yet there were quick-silver splinters of time in which she'd caught fleeting glimpses of the man beneath the rough exterior. A sensitive man with wit and understanding, even a trace of compassion. Knowing all that, she too won-dered where it might end. Other whores had married their way out of the houses, so the idea was by no means farfetched. Harry Lovett might very well be the man for her. A chance for a fresh start and a new life. Her last chance.

At length, dizzied by the thought, she realized he was waiting on an answer. Then, on the verge of replying, a shadow of anxiety clouded her features. She suddenly remembered who she was and where she was. The star whore of the Bella Union, and no less a prisoner than the slave girls of Chinatown. Denny O'Brien always collected on a debt, and she owed him . . . more than she cared to admit.

"I'm sorry, Harry." She smiled the saddest smile he'd ever seen, and shook her head. "It's a great idea, but it wouldn't work."

"Why the hell not?"

"Nobody quits Denny," she said simply. "It's a rule of the house, and he doesn't make exceptions. Especially in my case."

"Forget O'Brien," Starbuck countered. "Once Buckley gives the go-ahead, we're off and running."

"I don't understand."

"Nothing to it," Starbuck scoffed. "I'll tell Buckley that either you're included in the package or it queers the whole deal."

"Suppose he calls your bluff?"

"Not a chance in a thousand. Fung would go off like a skyrocket and accuse O'Brien of deliberately scuttling the deal. That'd give Buckley more troubles than he's got now. He just wouldn't stand for it."

"You sound awful sure of yourself."

"Why not?" Starbuck laughed. "Once I make up my mind to something, that's it! Either I get you in the bargain or the deal's off. I'll just buy myself some whores from somebody else."

"You'd do that for me?"

"Hide and watch. One way or another, you're on your way to Colorado."

Nell bounded out of bed and threw herself on him. She smothered him with kisses, her arms circled around his neck, and finally planted one soundly on his mouth. When he pried her loose, her face was lighted with an exhuberant childlike glow.

"I hope that doesn't wear off before we get to Colorado."

"Honeybun, you haven't seen anything yet. Wait till I really get warmed up!"

"Tell you what I do see." Starbuck looked her up and down. "You step out in the hall like that and we're liable to draw a crowd."

Nell laughed a bawdy little laugh. Then she turned, wigwagging her fanny, and jiggled to the wardrobe. She slipped into a housecoat and began buttoning it up. All the while, she was humming softly under her breath.

Watching her, Starbuck wasn't proud of himself. Exactly as he'd planned, he had spoon-fed her a fairy tale and she had swallowed it whole. She was now in his camp, and there was virtually no chance she would betray him to O'Brien. Yet, however much her loyalty was tested, she would come out on the short end of the stick. Her days on the Barbary Coast were numbered, and from tonight onward the future itself would prove highly uncertain. Not for the first time, it occurred to him that the detective business was a dirty game. He felt somehow soiled by what he'd done. All the more so because he'd done it before and would very likely do it again.

"I'm ready anytime you are, lover."

Starbuck nodded, watching her a moment longer. "Any idea what you'll tell O'Brien in the morning?"

"Why, I'll just bat my baby-blues and tell him

you slipped out while I was asleep. He'll never know the difference."

Starbuck smiled. "You know something? You would've made a helluva con man."

"Honey, a whore spends her whole life on the con."

She laughed softly and led the way to the door. After a quick peek outside, she signaled the all-clear. Then they stepped into the hall and walked toward the dumbwaiter.

A light fog hung over the city like gossamer curtains. Starbuck stopped at the entrance to the alleyway and checked the street in both directions. The hour was late, and he saw no one but a gang of drunken sailors weaving toward the waterfront. He crossed the street and strode off in the direction of the Palace Hotel.

The fog was an unexpected ally. Streetlamps, shrouded in a fuzzy glow, were visible half a block away. But the lampposts themselves were hidden by the swirling gray mist. He thought it unlikely that anyone could trail him in such weather. Still, all things considered, too much vigilance was better than too little. At the corner of Sutter and Montgomery, he stepped quickly into the darkened doorway of an office building. Waiting several moments, he listened intently, alert for the sound of footsteps. He heard nothing, and there were no signs of movement near the intersection. Presently, satisfied he wasn't being followed, he left the doorway and turned the corner. He reversed directions and disappeared into the fog. He walked swiftly toward Nob Hill.

Some ten minutes later, a bleary-eyed servant admitted him to the mansion of Charles Crocker. He was ushered into the study and asked to wait. Embers still simmered in the fireplace, and he soon rekindled a cheery blaze. Standing with his back to the fire, he warmed himself, slowly inspecting the room. The wooden panels were polished walnut, and one entire wall was bookshelves, stuffed from floor to ceiling with tomes bound in Moroccan leather. The books appeared untouched by human hands, and, quite probably, unread. He was examining a framed Audubon etching when the study door opened.

Charles Crocker marched into the room and slammed the door with a resounding thud. His eyes were gummed with sleep and he looked even fatter attired in a nightshirt and woolen robe. His expression was one of acute annoyance.

"What the hell do you mean coming here at this hour? Don't you realize it's after four o'clock?"

Starbuck returned his stare with sardonic amusement. "Crooks don't keep civilized hours. I operate on their timetable these days."

"Well, it better be important." Crocker flopped down in an overstuffed armchair. "I'm not accustomed to being awakened in the middle of the night."

"It's important." Starbuck took a chair across from him, lit a cigar. "Are you familiar with a man named Christopher Buckley?"

Crocker gave him a look of walleyed amazement.

"Whether I am or not has no bearing on our business. Why do you ask?"

"Because he's the man behind your train robbers."

"You're out of your mind!"

"Think so?" Starbuck blew a plume of smoke into the air. "Suppose I fill you in on the last few days. Then you can decide for yourself."

Crocker groaned and slumped deeper into his chair. Starbuck briefly outlined everything he'd un-covered since their last meeting. He established the link between the train robbers and Denny O'Brien, then went on to describe the deal he'd struck with Fung Jing Toy. From there, he recounted the con-versation with Buckley and the gist of the problems entailed. He omitted few details, and firmly dem-onstrated the chain of command in San Francisco's underworld. His report ended with a summary of his arrangement with Buckley. He stressed the time el-ement and the need for speed.

"So that's it," he concluded. "To pull it off, I'll have to produce the hundred thousand no later than noon today."

A thick silence settled over the room. Crocker, obviously disgruntled, gazed at Starbuck for a long, speculative moment. Then he shook his head in stern disapproval.

"I'm afraid you've overstepped the bounds of your assignment. I retained you to catch a band of train robbers, not organize a civic crusade. Your zeal is to be commended, Mr. Starbuck. But my only in-terest is in halting the robberies, nothing more."

"Why settle for half a loaf?" Starbuck gave him a hard, wise look. "We can capture Red Ned Adair, then offer him immunity to turn state's evidence against O'Brien. After that, we take it step by step, playing them off one against the other. When we're through, we'll have Buckley and most of his stooges behind bars. It's a perfect setup, made to order."

"No, thank you," Crocker said with an unpleasant grunt. "Your instructions are to eliminate Adair and his gang of robbers. The assignment begins and ends there. Do I make myself clear?"

All at once the truth came home to Starbuck. A practicing cynic, and something of an iconoclast, he had always viewed the world as a place of dupes and rogues. The dupes, in the natural course of things, were preyed upon by the rogues. Yet, in his absorption with the case, he'd forgotten that Charles Crocker, one of the great robber barons of the era, was essentially a rogue. Since rogues seldom locked horns with other rogues, Crocker quite naturally had no interest in exposing Christopher Buckley. The premise gained even more credence when politics were involved. A can of worms, once opened, might lead anywhere. Perhaps to the Central Pacific, and Charles Crocker himself.

"Here's the deal," Starbuck said stonily. "You have the money delivered to my hotel room before noon. I'll follow the plan I've just laid out and push it to the limit." He paused, took a long draw on his cigar. "Now, maybe you don't like the idea, but you'd like the alternative even less. Turn me down and I'll take the story to the newspapers. I've got a hunch your name would end up in big, bold headlines."

"Confound you!" Crocker's eyes were angry, reproachful. "I won't be dictated to, and I damn well won't allow you to bullyrag me. Take heed, Mr. Starbuck!"

"Save your breath," Starbuck said with a clenched smile. "When I accepted the assignment, I told you how I work. I don't take orders and I don't quit till the job's done. Buckley's a spoiler, the worst kind, and I figure he deserves to get axed. One way or another, I aim to see that it happens."

Crocker's features colored dark with blood. He rose and moved to the fireplace. Hands clasped behind his back, he stood for a long time staring into the flames. At last, he took a deep breath, blew it out heavily. When he turned around, his face was pale and there was a look of resignation in his eyes.

"Very well," he murmured in assent. "I'll go along with your request. But I warn you, Mr. Starbuck. Under no circumstances is my name to be connected with Christopher Buckley! Defy me on that and I will personally hound you out of the detective business."

"Why, hell's fire!" Starbuck laughed, a sudden harsh sound in the still room. "You just leave it to me, Mr. Crocker. I'll make you a hero! Goddamn if I won't."

"Yes, I agree." Crocker nodded gravely. "You are truly damned if you don't, Mr. Starbuck."

"Aren't we all?" Starbuck said with a cynical grin. "Have a seat, and let me tell you what I've got in mind."

Crocker walked to his chair and sat down. His expression was solemn and his mood attentive. Starbuck waited a moment, puffing quietly on his cigar. Then, with obvious relish, he began talking.

The first step, he explained, was the capture of Red Ned Adair.

CHAPTER 13

Shortly before dawn, two days later, Starbuck left the Palace Hotel by a side entrance. Once outside, he crossed the street and ducked into an alleyway. He waited several moments, until he was certain he wasn't being tailed. Then he turned and walked swiftly toward the Central Pacific train yard.

All the preparations necessary to his plan had been completed. Yesterday, at the stroke of noon, a package had been delivered to his hotel room. Inside were several packets of bills, large-denomination notes totaling $100,000, and a terse message from Charles Crocker. According to instructions, Crocker had quietly issued two orders. The first concerned today's morning train to Los Angeles: there were to be no extra guards on the express car. Crocker had announced the measure as a new gambit to deceive the robbers into believing there was nothing of value in today's shipment. At the same time, he directed that a major transfer from the San Francisco mint be put aboard the train. Starbuck had every confidence that the gang's inside man—the Judas—would leak word of this unusual operation. Red Ned Adair was virtually certain to rob the morning southbound.

Crocker's second order had been carried out in absolute secrecy. A trusted aide, less than an hour ago, had awakened Captain Tom Kelly, Chief of Security for the Central Pacific. The aide, under firm instructions never to leave Kelly's side, had then accompanied the security chief while he routed seven express guards from their beds. The men were quickly collected in the chill predawn darkness and bundled aboard waiting carriages. Once assembled, they were driven to a warehouse on the edge of the Central Pacific train yard. There, they were issued rifles and sidearms, then told to wait. Kelly's instructions, delivered by the aide, were specific and purposely vague. A man named Starbuck would arrive at the warehouse shortly before sunrise. All details regarding the mission would be explained at that time. Kelly was to follow his orders explicitly and without question.

Hurrying toward the train yard, Starbuck was satisfied that everything was now in place. Yesterday afternoon, following a meeting with Buckley, he had deposited the $100,000 in a bank selected by the political kingpin. The ploy, much as he'd expected, bought him time and got Denny O'Brien out of his hair. Within the hour, the second phase of his plan would swing into operation. Accompanied by the security force, he would travel southward from the

city. Not long after their departure, the morning
train, with an unguarded express car, would roll toward Los Angeles. The bait was laid and the trap
would be sprung somewhere around noontime. All
that remained was to ambush Red Ned Adair.

A few minutes before dawn, Starbuck stepped
through the door of the warehouse. A group of men,
jammed together in a stench of sweating bodies,
were gathered around a potbellied stove. Their faces
were grim, and most of them, still half-asleep, were
holding steaming mugs of coffee. Conversation
stopped, replaced by watchful silence, as he closed
the door and moved forward. The only sound was a
coffeepot, hissing and rattling on top the stove.

Starbuck, approaching closer, sensed the tension.
Yet nothing in his tone or manner revealed the
slightest trace of concern. He spoke with authority,
iron sureness.

"Captain Kelly?"

"That's me."

A man of formidable size, tall and massively
built, separated from the group. His hands were large
and gnarled, and his voice was a stilled rumble.
There was a heavy-lidded, lizard-like alertness to his
eyes.

"I'm Luke Starbuck."

Kelly accepted his handshake, frowning. "Pleased
to meet you."

"Has anyone left this room since you were
brought here?"

"No," Kelly acknowledged stiffly. "We've not

been here more than a few minutes ourselves."

"Good," Starbuck nodded. "Ask your men to finish their coffee and get ready to go."

"Go where?" Kelly raised an uncertain eyebrow. "I was given to understand you'd fill us in on the particulars."

"I will," Starbuck said evenly, "when the time's right."

Kelly's eyes became veiled. "Well, now, maybe you wouldn't mind explaining what all the mystery's about. We're more than a little curious, as you might well appreciate."

"Sorry," Starbuck said with an odd smile. "Where we're going—and what we've been assigned to do—will have to wait till we get there."

"Is that so?" Kelly demanded churlishly. "Then maybe you could at least tell us why we were rousted out in the middle of the night? Without so much as a by-your-leave!"

Starbuck gave him a swift, appraising glance. "Captain Kelly, you've got your orders and I've got mine. Suppose we let it go at that and get on with the job?"

"By the sweet Jesus!" Kelly said loudly. "I'm responsible for these men, and I'll not take them off to God knows where until I've had an explanation."

"For the moment, you've had all the explanation you need. We're on official business, and at the proper time, I'll lay it out for you in black and white. That's twice I've said it, so don't make me repeat myself again."

"Oh, repeat yourself, is it?" Kelly said with a sudden glare. "Well, mister-whoever-the-hell-you-are, I don't know you from Paddy's pig! You could talk yourself blue in the face and I'll not move from this spot unless I hear the reason why."

A vague disquiet settled over Starbuck. Something told him there was more to Kelly's objections than met the eye. Aside from resentment, which was natural enough at being reduced to second-in-command, there was some darker element just below the surface. The man was too antagonistic, too intractable, far more so than the situation dictated. Yet Starbuck hadn't the time nor the inclination to pursue it further. Sunrise was the deadline for their departure, and faint shafts of light were already streaming through the windows. He decided to force the issue.

"Captain Kelly," he said flatly, "the only thing you need to know is that I speak for Charles Crocker. Your instructions were to follow my orders to the letter. If that puts your nose out of joint, that's your problem. Take it up with Crocker when we get back."

"Instructions!" Kelly roared. "I've had no instructions, except from Crocker's flunky. Considering your high-handed manner, that won't do. Not for Tom Kelly, it won't!"

"Like it or lump it," Starbuck said roughly. "You're under my orders, and that's that."

"Says you." Kelly's nostrils flared. "I'll just have myself a talk with Crocker and see who's giving the orders around here. I've a strong notion there's a nigger-in-the-woodpile somewhere."

Starbuck fixed him with a pale stare. "I can't allow that."

"Blood of Christ!" Kelly said furiously. "I wasn't asking your permission. You can go or stay as you please! I mean to have a word with Charlie Crocker."

"No." Starbuck's face took on a hard cast. "You're not going anywhere except where I tell you to go."

"Out of my way!"

Kelly brushed past him and started toward the door. Starbuck struck out in a shadowy movement. He buried his fist in the big man's kidney, and Kelly's mouth opened in a great whoosh of breath. Shifting slightly, Starbuck spun him around and exploded two splintering punches flush on the jaw. Kelly went down like a pole-axed steer. He lay still a moment, then groaned and rolled heavily to his knees. He tried to rise, but his face twisted in a grimace of pain and he remained kneeling. Starbuck, scarcely winded, stood over him.

"Enough?"

"Enough," Kelly bobbed his head. "I think you busted something inside."

"You'll live."

There was a gruff buzz from the other men, and Starbuck turned. His brow seamed, and he eyed them with a steady, uncompromising gaze. When he spoke, his voice was scratchy, abrasive.

"Only one man gives the orders, and that's me. Anybody sees it otherwise, now's the time to step forward."

No one stepped forward. He waited several moments, then turned once more to face Kelly. The big man climbed slowly to his feet, and stood with a hand clutched tightly to his kidney. Starbuck gestured toward the door.

"I want everybody outside and in those carriages . . . now."

Kelly looked dazed, punchy. He stared down at the floor, tightlipped, his teeth locked against the pain. At length, he drew a deep breath and glanced up at his men.

"Let's go," he rasped hoarsely. "Everybody in the carriages."

Starbuck led the way through the door. Outside, he split the men into two groups, indicating Kelly was to ride in the lead carriage. When everyone was settled, he climbed aboard and took a seat beside the security chief. He ordered the driver to head south, and as they rolled out of the train yard the sky lightened into perfect cloudless blue. He glanced back and a slow smile creased his mouth.

The morning train stood chuffing smoke outside the terminal.

A mile or so north of the farmhouse Starbuck ordered the carriages off the road. Several hundred yards to the east, the wooded creek meandered southward. Following his directions, the carriages were driven across a grassy field and halted beneath the trees.

There he left Kelly and the men, and struck off on foot downcreek. His recollection of the gang's hideout was fairly accurate. Still, some time had passed since he'd trailed Adair and the band of robbers to the farmhouse. Leaving nothing to chance, he thought it wiser to personally scout the terrain. Today there was no margin for error.

Some while later he spotted the farmhouse through the trees. Quiet as a drifting hawk, he approached to within fifty yards, then went belly down on the ground. He crawled forward and stopped under the shelterbelt of woods. Hidden by shadow, he removed his hat and slowly scanned the layout.

Off to one side of the house, the woman was hanging a wash on a clothesline. Her husband was puttering around in a shed near the barn. The corral stood empty and the barn doors were closed. All of which confirmed his judgment about Red Ned Adair. The gang had ridden out earlier on the saddlehorses, leaving their carriages concealed in the barn. The holdup, in all likelihood, had already occurred. Without extra guards, the Central Pacific southbound was a pushover, and the express-car messenger would have offered only token resistance. Even now, the robbers were probably following the same twisting route back to the farmhouse.

Starbuck turned and studied the high ground across the creek. From the top of the knoll, he recalled, there was a clear view of the farmhouse and

the barn and the fields beyond. Outlaws were creatures of habit, and he thought it reasonable to assume
they would again approach the hideout by way of
the wooded knoll. The time to strike was when they
dismounted outside the corral. Flushed with success,
saddlebags stuffed with loot, their defenses would be
at a low ebb. Further, with the barn doors closed,
they would be caught in the open with nowhere to
run. All that, combined with the element of surprise,
should turn the trick very nicely. Barring mishap, the
robbers would never know what hit them.

Worming back to the creek, Starbuck rose and
took off at a dogtrot upstream. Several minutes later
he reached the carriages and found the men sprawled
on the ground, smoking and talking quietly amongst
themselves. Kelly stood off to one side, propped
against the base of a tree. His expression was sullen
and withdrawn.

The men scrambled to their feet as Starbuck
halted near the lead carriage. He signaled them to
gather around and waited while Kelly ambled over
to join the group. Then he went straight to the point.

"You're all aware of the train holdups that have
taken place over the past year. I was hired by the
Central Pacific to catch the robbers, and I've located
their hideout. It's a farmhouse, about a mile downstream, on the west side of the creek. Today, we're
going to lay an ambush and put an end to those
holdups."

A murmur of excitement swept over the men.
Starbuck hesitated a moment, then silenced them

with upraised palms. "Here's the way it'll work. Once we get downstream, I'll assign you to positions and point out the best fields of fire. Then we wait till the gang rides in and dismounts at the corral. That's when we hit 'em."

"A question." Kelly nailed him with a corrosive stare. "Who's their leader, and how many are there in the gang?"

"Glad you asked," Starbuck remarked. "Altogether, there'll be seven men. The leader's a gent by the name of Red Ned Adair. He's easy to spot because he's a carrot-head, bright red hair." He paused, glancing around the group. "Adair is not—I repeat—he is not to be killed. I want him taken alive."

"Are you saying," Kelly asked bluntly, "that you want the others killed?"

"When you shoot a man," Starbuck replied calmly, "I've always found it's best to kill him. Otherwise, you're liable to make him mad and then he'll kill you."

Kelly gave him a long, searching stare. "What about this fellow Adair? He'll more than likely be shooting back at us. Are you saying we're not to return his fire?"

"*Nobody,*" Starbuck underscored the word with heavy emphasis, "will fire at Adair but me. I'll either cripple him or keep him pinned down till the fight's over. So if you catch red hair in your sights, shift to another target. That's a direct order."

Kelly offered an elaborate shrug and said no more. The other men obediently bobbed their heads in affirmation. When there were no further questions, Starbuck dropped to one knee on the ground. He took a twig and sketched a crude map in the dirt.

"Here's the lay of the land. We'll go downstream and then . . ."

A brassy noonday sun stood high overhead. Squatted behind a tree, Starbuck watched as Red Ned Adair led his gang down the knoll and forded the creek. The robbers were laughing and exchanging wise-cracks, clearly in high spirits. The holdup, quite ob-viously, had come off without a hitch.

Standing, Starbuck quickly surveyed the wooded terrain. Kelly and four men were posted across the stream, on the forward slope of the knoll. Concealed by undergrowth, they were all but invisible beneath the dim shadows of the trees. The three remaining guards were flanked directly to his right, spread out along the west bank of the creek. He had assigned himself the point position, nearest the farmhouse. His shot would be the signal to open fire.

Easing around, he took a quick peek from behind the tree. The gang was aproaching the corral, and the farmer walked forward to greet them. The woman, standing at the corner of the house, looked on in silence. He thumbed the hammer on his carbine and wedged the butt into the hollow of his shoulder. He centered the sights on Red Ned Adair.

A shot cracked and bark exploded beside his head.

Cursing savagely, he crouched and swung around

as the gunfire became general. His gaze went across the creek and he saw Kelly jacking another shell into his own carbine. Without thought, operating on sheer instinct, he caught the security chief's chest in his sights and levered three quick shots. The slugs jolted Kelly backward a step at a time. The last one slammed into his brisket, splattering bone and gore, and he dropped the carbine. His hands splayed and clawed at empty air, then his legs buckled. He hit the ground and went tumbling head over heels down the knoll.

Starbuck whirled even before the body rolled to a halt. All around him the guards' rifles continued to bark, laying down a heavy volume of fire. He stepped around the tree and saw that Red Ned Adair and three of the gang were still mounted. Their horses were spooked, pitching and rearing in wild gyrations. Yet their sixguns were out, and while their aim was none too good, they were blazing away at the treeline. A quick glance confirmed that the farmer and the other robbers were down, either dead or dying.

All in an instant, Starbuck realized his only chance was to drop Adair's horse. He stepped clear of the trees, looking for an opening, and advanced toward the corral. Behind him, a staccato volley of gunfire broke loose, and the last three gang members pitched from their saddles. He saw Adair look in his direction and sensed he'd been recognized. A split-second later the outlaw leader fired, and a slug snarled past overhead. Then, before he could align his sights, Adair got control of his horse and took off down the road at a gallop. He let go a snap shot, but knew he'd missed even as he pulled the trigger. Horse and rider vanished in the next moment, blocked from view by the house.

Starbuck sprinted toward the corral. The gunfire abruptly ceased and an eerie silence descended over the farm. From behind, he heard the guards shouting to one another and vaguely noted the sound of running footsteps. The outlaws' bodies, grotesque in death, littered the ground closer to the barn. He charged past them, only to spot Adair far in the distance. He swore, skidding to a stop, and flung the carbine in the dirt. Then, almost a reflex action, he turned and caught up the reins of a loose horse. He stepped into the saddle as the guards approached and slowed to a walk. His finger stabbed out at the man in the lead.

"You!" he ordered. "Arrest the woman in the house and charge her with accessory to robbery. Then take Kelly's body to Charles Crocker. Deliver it personally! Tell him it's a present from me."

The guard gawked at him. "A present?"

"You heard right," Starbuck growled. "A present named Judas."

"What about you, Mr. Starbuck? What'll I tell him about you?"

"Tell him to look for me when he sees me."

Starbuck reined sharply around and gigged the horse in the ribs. Some distance away he saw a plume of dust drifting upward against the muslin-blue sky. He rode toward San Francisco.

CHAPTER 14

Late that afternoon, Denny O'Brien arrived at the Snug Café. After pounding on the alley door, he was admitted by a startled Chinese dishwasher. Knuckles Jackson, who doubled as one of Buckley's bodyguards, was hurriedly summoned from the front of the café.

O'Brien, whose manner was agitated and somewhat irrational, demanded to see Buckley. His appearance at the café during the daytime was unprecedented, and led to a heated argument. At last, albeit reluctantly, Jackson left him in the storeroom and went upstairs. Several moments passed; then the door opened and Jackson gave him a look reserved for fools and harebrained Irishmen.

Buckley was seated behind the desk. His composure was monumental, and his expression betrayed no hint of aggravation. Yet, when he spoke, his tone was clipped and stiff, angry.

"You were told never to come here in daylight."

"I'm sorry, but I had no choice."

"On the contrary, only an imbecile fails to exercise choice. Your presence indicates that you deliberately *chose* to ignore my wishes."

"For Chrissake, nobody saw me!"

"You miss the point," Buckley said with sudden wrath. "I will not allow anyone to override my orders." He took out a pocket watch, opened the lid, and deftly fingered the exposed hands. "Five-o-seven! Which means it will be dark in less than two hours. I presume that never occurred to you?"

"What I have to say wouldn't wait."

"Indeed?" Buckley returned the watch to his vest pocket. "Has the Bella Union burned down, or is it some lesser calamity?"

"Lots worse." O'Brien dropped into a chair before the desk. "We've got trouble! A shitpot full of trouble."

"Perhaps you could be a bit more specific?"

"It's Harry Lovett," O'Brien said, clearing his throat. "I just found out the son-of-a-bitch is a Pinkerton."

Buckley received the news with surpassing calmness. "What leads you to believe so?"

"Him and a squad of railroad bulls jumped Ned Adair and his boys this morning. Suckered them into a trap and blasted the whole gang straight to hell."

"Does that include Adair?"

"No," O'Brien said quickly. "Ned fought his way

clear. It was nip and tuck, but he came through without a scratch."

"A pity," Buckley observed dryly. "Exactly what happened?"

"Ned and his boys robbed the morning train to Los Angeles. His inside man at Central Pacific—the chief security bull—told him there wouldn't be any guards on the express car. Sure enough, there weren't, and the holdup went off slick as a whistle."

"No guards," Buckley mused to himself. "Offhand, I'd think that would have alerted Adair. It seems patently obvious."

O'Brien spread his hands in a gesture of bafflement. "None of it makes any sense. Kelly—that's the security bull—hadn't never tipped him wrong before. But goddamn if Kelly don't show up at the farmhourse—"

"Farmhouse?"

"Yeah, a farmhouse south of town. Ned used it as a cover whenever he pulled a holdup."

"Go on."

"Well, like I said, Kelly was there. Ned says he fired the first shot, evidently at someone in his own party. Then all of a sudden, Kelly goes down and the next thing you know, Lovett pops out from behind a tree. Ned thinks Kelly tried to get Lovett, and instead, Lovett got him."

"Brilliant." Buckley invested the word with scorn. "Did Adair deduce all that by himself?"

"Ned's no dimwit," O'Brien said defensively. "The way it looks, Kelly got himself boxed in and couldn't get word to Ned. Then he tried to turn it around at the last minute, and ended up dead."

"Greater love hath no man," Buckley added with satiric mockery. "Perhaps we could move on to the part about Lovett."

O'Brien hunched forward in his chair. "Ned spotted him the second he stepped out of the trees. Lovett was trying to draw a bead on him, but Ned winged a shot and took off. All his men were down, so it would've been suicide to stick around any longer."

"He's quite certain it was Lovett? In the heat of the moment, he couldn't have been mistaken?"

"No mistake," O'Brien said dourly. "It was Lovett, all right. Ned swears to it."

Buckley considered the thought. "Then we can surmise that Lovett had already identified Adair as the gang leader. Working backward, we can assume that Adair led him to you, and quite recently too. That would explain Lovett's little charade over the past week."

O'Brien looked blank. "What's a charade?"

"A deception," Buckley replied with cold hauteur. "One specifically engineered and acted out for gullible louts like yourself. It would appear our Mr. Lovett is an undercover operative for the Central Pacific."

"That's what I said!" O'Brien blurted out. "The bastard's a Pinkerton!"

"Perhaps." Buckley examined the notion a moment. "Whether he is or isn't seems a moot question at this point. What concerns me most is that you and your merry band of train robbers led him directly to me."

"The hell it did!" O'Brien denied hotly. "It was Fung! Except for him, you wouldn't have never heard of Lovett."

"You have a short memory." Buckley's voice dropped. "Fung was suspicious of him from the start. You also forget that I've warned you repeatedly about train holdups. I believe my comment was to the effect that the return in no way justified the risk."

"What's train holdups got to do with Fung?"

"Everything," Buckley said gruffly. "All of it involves greed, your greed. I gave you the Barbary Coast, but you weren't satisfied with that. You had to have something extra, smalltime side deals. Train robbery was one, and introducing Lovett to Fung was another. So you see, it's all of a piece, Denny. Bluntly put, you're too greedy for your own good . . . or mine."

"Wait a minute!" O'Brien objected. "You're not blaming me for this Lovett thing, are you? Jesus Christ, how was I to know he's a Pinkerton?"

"Again, the point eludes you." Buckley dismissed it with a brusque gesture. "Let's press on, shall we? At the moment we have a larger problem, and unless I'm mistaken, it has little to do with today's train robbery."

"Oh?" O'Brien appeared thoroughly confounded. "What problem's that?"

"Harry Lovett," Buckley told him. "If his primary target was Adair, then why did he concoct such an elaborate cover story? Why get involved with you or Fung? Why risk a hundred thousand dollars merely to gain my confidence?" He paused, reflective. "Something of an enigma, isn't it?"

"I give up," O'Brien said, attentive now. "Why?"

"Because Adair was only a means to an end. On balance, that seems the only logical conclusion. Lovett was after bigger game from the very start. Whether or not he suspected it would bring him to my door, we'll probably never know. What matters is that it did, and he capitalized on it quite cleverly. Quite cleverly, indeed."

"You think he's after you?"

"I think that's precisely what he's after."

"So what do we do now?"

"A good question."

Buckley placed his elbows on the arms of his chair, steepled his fingers. His eyes, shaded by the tinted glasses, appeared metallic, glittering yet dead. O'Brien had the strange sensation that behind those eyes was something inhuman, even demonic. An elemental force that fed itself on hate and power, and the bones of anyone who stood in its way. One thought led to another, and he dimly pondered where that left him. Then, suddenly, Buckley's voice jarred him back to the present.

"I'm afraid I have some bad news for you, Denny."

"What kind of bad news?"

"Ned Adair is expendable," Buckley said with

chilling simplicity. "I want you to get rid of him . . . today."

"Kill him?" O'Brien gave him a murky look. "What the hell for?"

"For the best of reasons." Buckley permitted himself a grim smile. "Without Adair there's no link to you, and therefore no link to me. Lovett will be left with nothing but allegations. And as we all know, allegations aren't worth a dime a dozen."

O'Brien massaged his nose, thinking. He knew, though the message was left unstated, that Ned Adair was not the subject at issue. His own knowledge of Frisco's underworld, and how the operation was structured, posed a far graver threat to Buckley. One false step and he himself would end up at the bottom of the bay. Yet, like many Irishmen, he was cursed with an obdurate nature and a volatile temper. He also possessed loyalty to those he considered friends; betrayal for the sake of expediency was to him the greatest blasphemy. His code had little to do with common standards of decency, but it was nonetheless the code by which he lived. He never welched on a deal or gaffed a friend—and he never betrayed a trust.

"I won't do it," he said stoutly. "Ned's been with me since the old days, and I've no better friend in the world. I'd sooner kill my own mother."

"An admirable sentiment," Buckley said with wintry malice. "However, in this case, we have to concern ourselves with the practical solution. If Adair were caught, and persuaded to talk, then your arrest would be a virtual certainty." He stopped, slowly shook his head. "You know I can't allow that to happen, don't you, Denny?"

"Ned won't talk," O'Brien protested. "He'd go to the gallows before he opened his mouth. As for me, I've never ratted in my life, and I've no intention to start now."

"Indeed?" Buckley's tone was icy. "Then let me put it to you this way, Denny. Are you willing to risk your neck to save Adair?"

"Look here," O'Brien said stubbornly. "Why kill Ned when there's a better way? I'll put him on a ship tonight and send him off to China. Christ, he'd be gone two years, maybe more! By then, this whole thing will've blown over and be long forgotten."

Buckley immediately thought of Fung. Once in China, Adair could be dispatched by Fung's associates with Oriental efficiency and a minimum of fuss. For the moment it would salve O'Brien's rebellious mood; later, if necessary, Fung would be delighted to dispatch the Irishman, as well. Overall, it seemed the perfect solution to an unwieldy problem.

"Very well," he conceded with a show of tolerance. "We'll strike a compromise. You put Adair aboard the first clipper bound for China. Not tomorrow or the next day, but tonight! Any delay in shipping him out and all bets are off. Fair enough?"

"Plenty fair," O'Brien agreed. "I'll handle it myself so there won't be any slipups. Before midnight, Ned will kiss Frisco goodbye, and that's a promise."

"Don't fail me," Buckley reminded him. "Otherwise, I'll be forced to call your marker. Adair or you, that's the proposition. Understood?"

"Understood," O'Brien said in a resigned voice. "One way or another, I'll have him on his way with the evening tide."

"I'm sure you will, Denny."

O'Brien looked into the dead eyes and an involuntary chill touched his backbone. Unless he delivered on the promise, there was no doubt the marker would be called. Either Ned Adair vanished tonight or his own life was forfeit. There was no third choice.

Nell sensed trouble when O'Brien hurried through the door of the Bella Union. He looked not just angry, but somehow shaken, unnerved. A moment later intuition turned to certainty. He brushed past High Spade McQueen without a word and rushed up the stairs. Something was seriously wrong, and the source of the problem was hardly in question. Somehow it involved Red Ned Adair.

Earlier that afternoon, on her way downstairs, she'd seen Ned Adair enter O'Brien's suite. Covered with sweat and grime, he had left the impression that the Devil himself was on his heels. Before she reached the stairwell, O'Brien had erupted in a burst of profanity. The sound of his curses carried clearly along the hall, and she'd thought at the time that Adair had finally pulled one boner too many. Then, dismissing it from mind, she had gone on about her business.

Now, watching O'Brien take the stairs two at a time, she was struck by a wayward thought. She wondered if it somehow involved Harry Lovett. He hadn't put in an appearance last night, and she'd heard nothing from him today. That seemed to her very strange, out of character. Knowing she expected him, he was too considerate not to have sent a message. Unless he was unable to send a message!

Stranger still was the fact that Ned Adair hadn't set foot out of O'Brien's suite since arriving. Try as she might, she couldn't imagine a connection between Adair and Harry Lovett. Yet she was no great believer in coincidence. Adair was hiding from something or somebody, and whatever he'd done, it had thrown O'Brien into a towering rage. Added to Harry Lovett's curious disappearance, it seemed altogether too timely for mere coincidence. She suddenly decided to do a little eavesdropping.

A glance toward the barroom confirmed that McQueen's attention was diverted elsewhere. She casually mounted the stairs and made her way to the third floor. As she passed O'Brien's suite, which was next to her own room, she heard loud voices from inside. Quietly, she entered her room and went directly to the washstand. Long ago, she had discovered that the wall separating her quarters from O'Brien's was wafer-thin clapboard. Further, she'd found that a girl could easily get an earful, and learn all sorts of secrets. All it required was a water glass.

She placed the open end of the glass flush against the wall. Then she pressed her right ear tightly to the bottom of the glass, and stuck her finger in her left ear. The effect was not unlike that produced by a megaphone. Sounds were amplified, and voices carried with remarkable clarity. She listened closely, and the wall seemed to evaporate. An argument was raging, and in her mind's eye, it was not difficult to imagine their faces.

"I won't go! I don't give a shit what Buckley says. I won't go, and that's that!"

Ned Adair stopped pacing, suddenly turned and glared at O'Brien. Dull despair was etched on his features, and dark bruised-looking rings circled his eyes. He sat down heavily on a sofa, his face doughy and stunned. His stomach rolled, and an unmanning sense of nausea seized him. He shook his head wildly.

"Mexico, maybe." He passed a hand across his eyes and swallowed hard. "But I'll be goddamned if I'll go to China. Not me!"

"You're damned if you don't." O'Brien's voice was firm. "Unless you sail tonight, you're a dead man. No two ways about it, Ned."

"I'll take my chances," Adair said morosely. "All I need's a fast horse and an hour's head start. Buckley wouldn't never find me! Not in a million years."

"No soap," O'Brien informed him. "I gave my word to Buckley. You take off running and it's my neck that'll get chopped. I'd have to stop you—and I would."

Adair's jaw fell open, as though hinged. "Jesus,

Mary and Joseph! Are you saying you'd kill me, Denny?"

O'Brien shrugged. "I'm saying I won't die for you. Now that you've brought the Pinkertons down on us, there's no way around it. You either sail for China or you get deep-sixed."

"You—" Adair stammered. "You're blaming me? It was you that opened the door to Lovett and took him under wing. I had nothing to do with it. Nothing!"

"No more of your guff!" O'Brien suddenly bellowed. "You're the one that robbed the train, and you're the one that led Lovett straight to the Bella Union. And to me, too! So dry up and take your medicine like a man. That's my final word on it, Ned."

Adair blinked several times. Under O'Brien's ugly stare, all his courage abruptly deserted him. He gloomily bowed his head and nodded. "Have it your way, Denny. I'd sooner sail the China Sea the rest of my life than have you down on me."

"That's the spirit!" O'Brien laughed heartily. "We'll sneak you down to Mother Bronson's joint after dark, and she'll arrange passage on the finest clipper in port. Hell, it'll be like an ocean voyage, Ned! You'll have yourself a grand time."

Adair mumbled an inaudible reply. His eyes, oddly vacant, were fixed on the floor.

On the other side of the wall, Nell numbly lowered the water glass. She paled and her cheek muscles grew taut, and her face was no longer a pleasant sight. She felt swept up in a nightmare, the flood-gates of fear suddenly opened and swirling madly about her. She crossed the room in a daze and sat down on the edge of the bed. Her ears rang with the words and she choked off a cry. She couldn't believe it, wouldn't believe it.

Harry Lovett a Pinkerton? Adair and O'Brien— even the blind man!—panicked by the dapper grifter who had shared her bed. The same devil-may-care jokester who had offered her a job and promised her a new life and sworn to take her away from the Barbary Coast. It wasn't true, none of it. For if it was, then he had lied to her, used her. She couldn't credit that, not from Harry Lovett.

Her head pulsated like a huge festering wound. She heard again the words of Denny O'Brien and she reasoned muzzily that it was a mistake. Some monstrous and terrifying mistake. She wondered what to do, and even as she asked herself the question, she knew she would do nothing. A girl had to live, and only a fool took sides when men drew the line.

She would wait and see, and do what she'd always done. She would go with the winner.

CHAPTER 15

Nell looked wretched when she opened the door. Ugly lines strained her face and her features were smudged downward. She stared at him with a mixture of dismay and surprise, momentarily dumbstruck.

With a last glance along the hall, Starbuck stepped into her room and closed the door. He twisted the key, locking the door, then turned toward her. As though expecting applause, he doffed his hat and flashed his gold tooth in a wide grin. Her face blanched, eyes round as saucers.

"How did you get in here?"

Starbuck chuckled. "I bribed the cook to send me up in the dumbwaiter."

"The cook!" she repeated sharply. "Are you crazy?"

"Like a fox," Starbuck said with a jocular wink. "I told him we had a little hanky-panky going on the side. He took to the idea right away, even wished me luck. I got the feeling he's one of your secret admirers."

"You fool!" Her voice rose suddenly. "He'll report it to McQueen. He's probably on his way out front right now."

"No chance," Starbuck assured her. "I slipped him a hundred, and told him there'd be another hundred when I come back down."

"What's to stop him from squealing to McQueen, then? Or weren't you worried about what happens to me when you leave?"

"Don't trouble yourself," Starbuck said lightly. "Silence goes to the highest bidder. I'll give him an extra hundred just to make sure he stays bought."

Nell regarded him with an odd steadfast look. "The way you bought me?"

"Bought you?" Starbuck saw anger, resentment and a trace of fear in her eyes. "I don't get your meaning."

"The hell you don't!" she said furiously. "You're a lowdown rotten bastard, Harry Lovett! You promised me the moon and I went for it like a schoolgirl with a case of the vapors."

"What in Christ's name are you talking about?"

"You're a Pinkerton!" she said loudly, staring at him through a prism of tears. "A lying, good-for-nothing snake in the grass! I know the whole story, so don't try to deny it."

"A Pinkerton?" Starbuck was genuinely astounded. "Where the deuce did you get an idea like that?"

"From Denny." She sniffed and dabbed at the tears. "I overheard him talking to Ned Adair. I know you're after Ned for robbing trains and I know—"

"Slow down," Starbuck broke in quickly. "Ned Adair's here? He's somewhere in the Bella Union?"

She motioned toward the window. "You're too late," she said, indicating the deepening indigo of nightfall. "Denny took him—got him out of here— right after it turned dark."

"You started to say O'Brien took him somewhere, didn't you?"

She tossed her head. "Wouldn't you like to know?"

"I have to know," Starbuck said urgently. "It's important, Nell. So damned important you wouldn't believe it."

"Tough tit, hotshot!" She made an agitated gesture with both hands. "I don't talk to Pinkertons."

"I'm not a Pinkerton," Starbuck said with a lame smile. "O'Brien was close, but I've never had anything to do with the Pinkertons. I work on my own."

"Your own?" she murmured uneasily. "Are you trying to tell me you're not a detective?"

"No," Starbuck confessed. "I'm a detective, but I run my own operation. I don't work for any of the big agencies."

"What's the difference?" Nell gave a dark, empty look. "You still conned me and fed me that line of hooey about Colorado."

"I'm not proud of it," Starbuck admitted. "I had a job to do and I went about it the best way I knew how. Maybe I conned you, but it wasn't like I had any real choice. It stuck in my craw the whole time."

"Go crap in your hat, buster! You wanted information, and you pumped me till the well ran dry. You got me hooked with your sweet talk and all the rest of that nonsense, and it never meant a thing to you. Nothing!"

"That's not true." Starbuck studied her downcast face. "The only lies I told you had to do with the job. Everything else was on the square." He lifted her chin, looked directly into her eyes. "The other part—what you're talking about—wasn't any lie. I meant every word of it."

"Honest to God?" She drew a deep, unsteady breath. "You're not just saying that? You really mean it?"

"Straight gospel," Starbuck said earnestly. "When I leave Frisco, you're going with me. You're through with O'Brien and the Barbary Coast and all the rest. That's a solid-gold promise."

Nell stared at him in an intense, haggard way. She was filled with conflicting emotions, and terrified that she might once again be played for a fool. Her lips trembled and she tried to smile, a tortured smile. There was a hungry, questing quality in her eyes, and she searched his face uncertainly. She wanted desperately to believe.

Then, suddenly, she stood within the circle of his arms. She shuddered convulsively against him and pressed her cheek to his chest. Her voice was muffled, almost a plea.

"I'm with you, lover. Where do we go from here?"

Starbuck took her shoulders and held her at arm's length. "You know I've got to get O'Brien and Adair, don't you?" She nodded dumbly, and he went on. "Then I want you to tell me where they've gone. Unless I'm wrong, time's running out fast."

"Once you've caught them, is it over? Will we be able to leave then, Harry?"

"You just pack your duds and wait for me. We're as good as on our way."

Nell briefly recounted everything she'd heard through the wall. Listening to her, Starbuck could generally reconstruct the sequence of events since Adair's escape at the farmhouse. It was no great surprise that everyone involved, Buckley included, now knew he was a detective. Yet one aspect of the situation left him troubled. Buckley's insistence that Adair depart San Francisco—or be killed—was ominous. The blind man quite obviously understood that the trail led to the Snug Café, and had taken measures to sever the link. Which meant there wasn't a moment to spare.

"That's all," Nell concluded. "Denny browbeat Ned into it, and I heard them leave a few minutes after it got dark."

"You mentioned Mother Bronson's joint. Who's she?"

"A witch who runs a dive on the waterfront. She shanghais sailors and sells them to captains of outbound ships. I guess Denny figured she would know which clippers are sailing tonight."

"Would O'Brien hang around until Adair ships out?"

"Probably," Nell said hesitantly. "From what I overheard, he wouldn't take any chances. Ned wasn't too keen on the idea."

"Then I reckon I'd better head for Mother Bronson's."

"Be careful," Nell cautioned. "She's tougher than most men on the Coast. And that includes Denny O'Brien."

"I'll watch myself."

Starbuck walked to the door and turned the key. With his hand on the knob, he stopped and looked around. "You be ready when I get back. Things are liable to happen fast when the fur starts to fly."

"I'll be waiting," she replied with a sudden sad grin. "I've no place to go without you, lover."

The door opened and closed, and he was gone.

A misty rain was falling, and the night was ripe with the smell of the sea. The streetlights were dim silvery globes, their lamps casting flickering shadows on the wet streets. Sailors, stumping along with the bowlegged gait peculiar to seamen, clogged the waterfront.

Starbuck walked toward Battery Point. Out in the bay, anchored away from the wharves, were hundreds of ships. Their silhouettes were fuzzy through the mist and fog, but the ghostly assemblage indicated Frisco's importance as one of the world's major ports. The lanterns of small boats bobbed like fireflies on the rolling water. Known locally as Whitehall boats, the craft ferried sailors ashore for a fee. From there, once his foot touched dry land, the seaman ventured forth at his own peril.

Oceangoing ships, not to mention the men who sailed them, were a complete mystery to Starbuck. Yet the waterfront itself was infamous, with a reputation for danger and foul play known even to landlubbers. The Barbary Coast was rough and sordid, but altogether tame compared to the waterfront. Starbuck had few illusions about the hazards that lay ahead.

All along the wharves was a seedy collection of gaming dives, whorehouses, and busthead saloons. Vice was the stock in trade, and after months at sea, the sailors were victims of their own shipboard fantasies. On reaching port, Jack Tar set off in search of women, alcohol, and gambling. The wilder the women, the better, and even popskull whiskey was none too potent for a sailor with a thirst. Whether able seaman or galley cook, he had money and was eager to blow it on a non-stop, night-and-day spree. Waiting to accommodate him was an assortment of vultures in human form.

Those who operated the waterfront dives were specialists who dealt in live bodies. Their ostensible aim was to provide the seafearer with diverse forms of entertainment. Their principal business, however, was the traffic in shanghaied sailors. The seaman's origin, whether Scandinavian or German, French or British, was of no consequence. The first step was to fleece the sailor of his wages, either at the gaming tables or at the hands of blowsy whores. Then, once he was penniless, the bartender slipped him a drink drugged with sulphate of morphine. Afterward, the warm body was delivered to a ship captain who paid cash on the spot. The sailor awoke to find himself on a voyage that lasted two to four years. Though the practice was widespread, few seamen made any effort to avoid the waterfront. The danger of being shanghaied was considered one of the lesser hazards of shore leave in Frisco.

The Whale, a sleazy dive operated by Mother Bronson, was located at Battery Point. Crude even by Frisco standards, it was a saloon with girls for rent by the trick or by the hour. The ramshackle building squatted directly on the wharf, with water lapping at the pilings below. By rowboat, the trip from The Whale to a waiting clipper was only a matter of minutes. For the shanghaied seaman, it was also a one-way trip. The next port of call was generally halfway around the world.

Starbuck drew stares the moment he stepped through the door. The patrons of The Whale were rough-garbed sailors, rank with the smell of sweat and cheap whiskey. While few of them spoke the same language, they were all dressed similarly and appeared stamped from the same mold. By contrast, Starbuck looked like a peacock among a flock of guinea fowl. His powder-blue suit and pearl-gray fedora left a buzz of conversation in his wake.

Walking to the bar, he ordered whiskey and took his time lighting a cigar. He ignored the stares and the muttered comments, idly inspecting the room. Several house girls were working the crowd, but they held his interest only briefly. On the way to the waterfront, he had formulated a loose, though somewhat credible, cover story. With a glib line of patter, and a little name dropping, he hoped to bluff his way past Mother Bronson. From there, depending on how the dice fell, he would attempt to take O'Brien and Adair without bloodshed. One elbow hooked over the bar, he sipped his drink and waited.

Presently, the door to a back room swung open. The woman who emerged was tall, with shoulders as wide as a man's, and had the stern look of a grenadier. Her hair was pulled back in a severe bun, and her drab dress somehow accentuated the massive bulk of her figure. A lead-loaded blackjack was wedged into the belt cinched around her waist. She looked entirely capable of felling man or beast with one blow.

Plowing through the crowd, she moved directly to the bar and stopped beside Starbuck. She sized him up, her beady eyes noting every detail of his gaudy attire. At last, with her hands on her hips, she rocked her head from side to side.

"Little out of your element, ain't you, sport?"

"You Mother Bronson?"

"That's the name." She gave a tight, mirthless smile. "Who's asking?"

"Johnny One-Spot." Starbuck thought the name had a certain ring. "I've got a message for Denny O'Brien."

"Oh, do you?" Her smirk widened into a smug grin. "And what makes you think you'd find him in a dump like this?"

"High Spade McQueen sent me." Starbuck knocked back his whiskey and wiped his mouth. "He said to tell you the plan's been changed. I'm to explain to O'Brien himself, and no one else."

"Are you, now?" She signaled the barkeep. "Have another drink, sport. We'll talk about it some and see where that takes us."

"What's to talk about?"

The barkeep brought another glass and the bottle. His hand passed over Starbuck's glass, deftly opening and closing, as he poured for Mother Bronson. Then he filled Starbuck's glass and casually walked away.

"Well, Johnny One-Spot"—she lifted her glass—"here's mud in your eye."

She tossed down her drink and Starbuck followed suit. He puffed importantly on his cigar and looked impatient. "I haven't got all night. You gonna take me to Mr. O'Brien or not?"

There was the merest beat of hesitation. Then her smile broadened. "Tell you the truth, you haven't got hardly any time at all, sport."

"What the hell's that supposed to mean?"

"Ask me again when you wake up."

"When I—?"

Starbuck's eyes glazed and the cigar dropped from his mouth. He slumped against the bar, then staggered sideways, and his knees suddenly turned rubbery. He pitched face down on the floor.

Mother Bronson stooped, rolling him over, and took one of his legs under each arm. Effortlessly, she dragged him toward the rear of the saloon. One of her girls rushed to open the door and she disappeared into the back room. There, waiting silently, were Denny O'Brien and Ned Adair. She let go his legs and turned to O'Brien.

"Well, dearie, there's your man. Colder'n a mackerel!"

"No," O'Brien said, staring down a moment. "I think he's Ned's man. Call it a going-away present."

"Present!" Adair repeated with a quizzical look. "You want me to take him with me?"

"Only partway." O'Brien smiled evilly. "Feed him to the sharks once you get out to sea."

Mother Bronson threw back her head and roared with laughter.

Starbuck awoke to a curious yawing motion. His vision was blurred and his head felt as though it had been cleaved down the middle. Several moments elapsed before his eyes cleared and he was able to collect himself. Sitting up, he gazed around and slowly realized he was in a cargo hold. Then, with sudden clarity, it struck him.

He was on a ship! A clipper ship bound for the Orient!

His last recollection was of Mother Bronson. Everything afterward was a blank, but not too difficult to piece together. He'd walked into a trap, with Denny O'Brien very likely watching from the back room. Then, like a prize sucker, he'd never given it a second thought when Mother Bronson called for another round of drinks. Yet he hadn't been shanghaied. Nothing so simple would satisfy O'Brien. The orders, without doubt, were to kill him and dump his body at sea.

He cursed himself for a fool. Standing, his hand went to the shoulder holster and found it empty. He lifted his pants leg and discovered they'd missed the hideout gun in his boot top. The stubby Colt was a last-ditch weapon, but deadly at short ranges. The thought occurred that it was his one hope for deliverance, and he reminded himself to make every shot count. He cocked the hammer and moved toward a ladder at the rear of the hold.

On deck, he saw that he was amidships. The rain had stopped, and stars were visible through occasional gaps in the clouds. Off the port side, far in the distance, he spotted a flashing light and the broken outline of a land mass. He realized with a start that the clipper was approaching the Golden Gate. Only minutes separated the ship from the open sea.

Crouching down, he scuttled toward the railing on the port side. Then, growing closer, he heard voices from the quarterdeck. The shadowed figures of two men appeared out of the dark. One, wearing a billed cap, was clearly a ship's officer. The other, who paused at the stairway, was Red Ned Adair. Starbuck froze, watching them intently.

"You're the captain," Adair remarked testily. "But the sooner we toss him overboard, the better I'll like it."

"I've no quarrel with that, Mr. Adair. As I told you, after we've cleared land's end, you can do as you please."

Adair grunted and started down the stairway leading to the main deck. Then, squinting hard, he suddenly saw Starbuck crouched low in the dark. His jaw popped open in a startled cry.

"Lovett—!"

The captain and Ned Adair went for their guns in the same motion. Starbuck leveled his arm and the snubby Colt spat three times. The slugs stitched an oval pattern in Adair's chest, and he tumbled down the stairway. A bullet tugged at the sleeve of Starbuck's jacket, and he saw the captain staring at him over the sights of a bulldog revolver. His arm moved and the Colt recoiled twice in quick succession. One slug punched into the captain's stomach, the other ripped through his throat and tore out the back of his skull. The impact flung him backward and he dropped raglike on the quarterdeck.

The helmsman shouted, and the thud of footsteps from below decks galvanized Starbuck to action. Working frantically, he stuffed the Colt in the waistband of his trousers and jerked off his boots. Then, in two swift strides, he crossed the deck and dove headlong over the railing. The shock of the icy water

struck him like a blow, and a moment later he knifed
cleanly to the surface. Bobbing about in the waves,
he somehow got his bearings, and saw the flash of
a beacon far astern.

A wayward thought seized him, and he vaguely
wondered if sharks attacked in the dark. Then, with
a stoic sense of fatalism, he dismissed it from mind.
He turned into the tide and swam toward the distant
light.

CHAPTER 16

The sky was like tarnished pewter, heavy with clouds. False dawn left the alleyway obscured in gloom, and a murky stillness hung over the street. Starbuck checked behind him, then rounded the corner of the Bella Union and halted at the kitchen door. He took out a pocketknife and began working on the lock.

His nerves were gritty and raw, and his head pounded with a dull, grinding weariness. The long swim, some four miles through bone-chilling seas, had sapped his strength to the very marrow. He'd come ashore at Point Lobos, and from there made his way to the Cliff House, a fashionable restaurant on the oceanfront. The manager, shaken by the sight of a waterlogged apparition, had loaned him a driver and carriage, and sent him off wrapped in a woolly blanket. Warm at last, he'd stretched out on the seat and slept during the ride back to the city. When the driver let him off at the hotel, he had felt somewhat restored, though still a bit unsteady on his feet. A hot bath and a change of clothes had improved his spirits, if not the lingering sense of exhaustion. Then, on the point of leaving the room, he'd suddenly remembered an old friend, packed away in his suitcase. He walked out of the hotel with the Colt .45 jammed in a crossdraw holster.

Now, probing at the lock, his one concern was Nell. He could only surmise that she was still in her room, waiting for him to return. She was level-headed, no stranger to tight situations, and he thought it unlikely she would have betrayed herself to O'Brien. It was reasonable to assume she had worked her normal shift, and resisted the temptation to ask questions. Yet, given the circumstances, the night would have proved an ordeal. Her position was untenable, hinging on a slip of the tongue, and by now the pressure would have taken its toll. She wouldn't be safe until he had her clear of the Bella Union, and out of harm's way. Only then would he turn his attention to Denny O'Brien.

The tumbler in the lock abruptly clicked and he eased through the door. He moved across the empty kitchen, with scarcely a glance at the dumbwaiter. He was cautious, but not overly concerned. With sunrise still an hour away, not even the swampers would have begun work. He followed a passageway toward the front of the building, and emerged through a door near the end of the bar. There he stopped, senses alert, listening.

The barroom was still as a graveyard. He waited

several moments, one ear cocked to any noise, then
walked to the staircase. On the second floor he
paused again, but saw no one and heard nothing.
Another flight up, he flattened against the wall and
edged one step at a time onto the third-floor landing.
After a while, he proceeded gingerly along the hall.
He ghosted past McQueen's room, and then, opposite the door to O'Brien's suite, he suddenly went
stock-still. From inside, he heard the low drone of
voices. Insofar as he could determine, there were
only two men, quite probably O'Brien and Mc-
Queen. He briefly considered busting through the
door and taking them prisoner. On second thought,
however, he rejected the idea. Any commotion
would arouse others, and make it impossible for him
to spirit Nell out of the Bella Union. Her safety, for
the moment, took priority over all else. Besides,
O'Brien believed he was dead, snugly tucked away
in some shark's belly. Time enough to disabuse him
of that notion later in the day. All the time in the
world, once Nell was out of danger.

On tiptoe, alert to creaky floorboards, he made his
way to the end of the hall. He paused in front of
Nell's room, debating whether to rap softly, then decided to try the doorknob. It turned, and he swiftly
ducked inside, closing the door behind him. The
latch clicked and in the same instant his guts turned
to stone.

Nell lay sprawled on the floor. Her arms were
akimbo, her hair loose and fanned darkly across her
face. The bodice of her dress was torn, exposing her

breasts, and her skirt was hitched up over her legs. She seemed too still, deathly still.

Starbuck scooped her up in his arms and carried her to the bed. Only then, with streamers of light flooding through the window, was her condition aparent. She had been beaten, expertly and brutally, with methodical savagery. Her nose was broken, her lips puffy and discolored, and her left eye was swollen shut. As he lowered her onto the bed, she groaned and her good eye slowly rolled open. Her mouth ticced upward in a ghastly smile.

"Harry."

"Don't try to talk."

"You came back for me."

"Told you I would." Starbuck forced himself to smile, leaning closer. "Now, you rest easy and let me have a look at you."

He gently brushed the hair out of her face. Unwitingly, moved by some urge to touch her, he placed his hand on her waist. She recoiled, and a sharp spasm of pain distorted her features. Her mouth opened in a wheezing moan and frothy red bubbles leaked down over her chin. She gasped, laboring desperately to get her breath.

Starbuck knew then her condition was beyond hope. Her rib cage was shattered, and the bloody froth told the tale. One lung, perhaps both, had been punctured. From the punishment she'd absorbed, blows that hard, it seemed entirely likely her insides were torn apart. A veteran of death and dying, he recognized all the signs. The life force was quickly draining out of her, and she hadn't one chance in a thousand. Which was one step removed from zero.

"Nell," Starbuck said softly. "Can you hear me?"

Her eye fluttered open. The agonized look subsided, and she struggled to bring him into focus. Her head moved in a slight nod.

"Was it O'Brien? Did he do this to you?"

"No." Her voice was weak. "He sicced McQueen on me."

"Why?"

"He knew I was"—she grimaced, caught her breath—"only one who could've told you . . . Mother Bronson's."

"He let McQueen work you over because of that?"

"Doesn't matter." She blinked, her eye suddenly brighter. "I waited, and you're here now."

"I'm sorry," Starbuck said hollowly. "I got back as fast as I could."

"Harry, do something for me?"

"Anything," Starbuck told her. "You name it, and it's yours."

"Don't leave me here."

"I won't."

"Take me with you—to Colorado—the way we . . ."

Her voice trailed off and her mouth parted in a shuddering sigh. Then her eye rolled back in her head, and she stopped breathing. She died within the space of a heartbeat.

Starbuck tenderly closed her eye and sat for a

long while holding her hand. Finally, prying her fingers loose, he stood and squared himself up. He realized he'd wanted to tell her his real name, and felt some loss that there had been no time. A slow sense of rage, fueled by his own shame, settled over him. His mouth hardened, and the rage turned to quiet steel fury. He pulled the Colt and walked quickly to the door. Without looking back, he stepped into the hall.

The murmur of voices was still audible from O'Brien's suite. Starbuck quietly tested the doorknob, then braced himself and swung the door wide. He barged into the sitting room, the Colt extended and cocked, and kicked the door shut. O'Brien was seated in an armchair, and McQueen was lounged back on a nearby sofa. A bottle, almost three-quarters empty, and a couple of glasses stood on a table between them. O'Brien's face went chalky.

"Lovett!"

"Just call me Lazarus." Starbuck's eyes were cold, impassive. "Only your boys never quite put me down for the count."

"What—" O'Brien faltered, staring at him with open disbelief. "How'd you get away from Adair?"

"Simple," Starbuck said lazily. "I killed him."

McQueen slowly rose to his feet. His jacket was splattered with flecks of blood, and the knuckles on his right hand were skinned raw. Starbuck wagged the barrel of the Colt in his direction.

"Don't get sudden."

"What the hell; you got the drop on me."

"All the same," Starbuck said shortly, "any funny moves and you'd better take a deep breath. It'll have to last a long time."

"You talk big with a gun in your hand."

"Give me an excuse and I'll fix it so you won't have to listen anymore."

"Hold off, Mac!" O'Brien interjected quickly. "He's got nothing on us."

"Think not?" Starbuck eyed him keenly. "Let's just say I've got all I need and then some."

O'Brien laughed. "With Adair dead, your case is out the window. There's no way you can tie me to those train holdups."

"I had something better in mind."

"Yeah, like what?"

Starbuck's gaze bored into him. "For openers, we'll take a walk down to your office. Then you're going to show me the ledgers you've got locked in your safe."

"Ledgers?" O'Brien went white around the mouth. "You're off your rocker! Those are my books for the Bella Union. The house accounts."

"No," Starbuck said with wry contempt. "I'd lay odds one of them is your insurance policy against Buckley. You're too slick not to keep a record of the payoffs."

"In a pig's ass!" O'Brien fixed him with a baleful look. "Even if there were payoffs, why would I keep a record?"

"A little something in reserve, something to hold over Buckley's head. The way he operates, you know you'd need it sooner or later. I figure you've got enough to convict him a dozen times over."

O'Brien peered at him, one eye sharp and gleaming. "What's your game, Lovett? Pinkertons don't get involved with political shenanigans. Maybe you're looking for a payoff yourself."

A ferocious grin suddenly lit Starbuck's face. "You'd be surprised about us Pinkertons. There's a payoff, all right, but it's not exactly what you had in mind."

"What d' you mean?"

"A rough guess would be twenty years. You and Buckley ought to make perfect cellmates. Two peas in a pod."

"Guess again!" O'Brien eyes glazed with rage. "You've got bats in the belfry if you think I'm gonna hand over those ledgers. I'll see you in hell first!"

"Don't take it so hard," Starbuck taunted. "There's lots of things worse than twenty years."

"How about me?" McQueen gave him a humorless yellow-toothed smile. "You gonna send me to the rockpile, too?"

"Nope." Starbuck's faded blue eyes narrowed. "You're something special, McQueen. You've got a date with the hangman."

"Hangman!" A sourly amused look came over McQueen's face. "Who the hell am I supposed to've murdered?"

"Nell," Starbuck said quietly. "She died a couple of minutes ago."

McQueen scowled with stuffed-animal ferocity.

He read the expression in Starbuck's eyes, and saw revealed there a cold, implacable truth. He would never live to reach the police station, much less a trial by jury. He had already been judged and sentenced. And before him stood a self-appointed executioner.

O'Brien suddenly rose from his chair. The movement momentarily distracted Starbuck, and McQueen took the only chance open to him. With an unintelligible oath, his hand snaked inside his coat and reappeared with a Sharps derringer. An instant before he could bring the gun to bear, Starbuck fired. The first round, a hurried snap-shot, caught him in the shoulder. Knocked off balance, he slammed backward and sat down heavily on the sofa. The second slug drilled through his sternum and the third struck him squarely in the heart. He sat bolt upright a moment, then the light flickered and died in his eyes. The derringer slipped from his grasp and he slumped dead on the sofa.

Starbuck crossed the room in two swift strides. He patted O'Brien down, relieving him of a belly gun, and tossed it on the chair. Then, in a quick, savage gesture, he motioned with the Colt.

"Let's get that safe open. Any tricks—anyone tries to stop us—and you'll wind up on the meatwagon. Savvy?"

O'Brien nodded sullenly. "No tricks."

"You lead the way."

Several minutes later they emerged from the Bella Union. O'Brien had the ledgers under his arm and the snout of a Colt pressed against his spine. Starbuck flagged a hansom cab and shoved him inside. After a word with the driver, Starbuck stepped into the cab and seated himself. He kept the pistol trained on O'Brien's stomach.

"What now?" O'Brien asked as the cab pulled away from the curb. "Where're you taking me?"

Starbuck's expression was sphinxlike. "You'll see when we get there."

"What's the harm in telling me? It's the police station, isn't it? You're gonna have them lock me up."

"You'd like that, wouldn't you? By suppertime, Buckley would have you sprung and on the next clipper to China."

O'Brien's jaw muscles worked. "What d'you want, Lovett? You've got the goddamned ledgers. Isn't that enough?"

"Not near enough," Starbuck said levelly. "We're headed for a warehouse, down at the train yard. We'll have it all to ourselves, just you and me. One way or another, I figure today's your day to turn songbird."

"Songbird?" A vein in O'Brien's temple stood out like twisted cord. "You want me to rat on Buckley?"

"That's the idea," Starbuck said, motioning with the Colt. "Those ledgers are only part of the story. Your testimony ought to cap it off real nice."

"It'll never happen! Denny O'Brien don't rat on nobody!"

"Wanna bet?" Starbuck regarded him evenly. "You'll talk . . . or else."

"Or else what?" O'Brien demanded. "You're not fooling anyone, Lovett. I'm no good to you dead, and we both know it."

"It's the other way round." Starbuck gave him a strange, crooked smile. "Unless you talk, you're no good to me alive. Think of it a while, and you'll see what I mean."

O'Brien saw a catlike eagerness in his eyes. Suddenly, as though his ears had come unplugged, the Barbary Coast boss got the message. Harry Lovett wanted to kill him, and would, given the slightest pretext. Which mean that his life, from that moment forward, had only one measure of value. So long as he testified, he would be allowed to go on breathing. His decision, considering the alternative, was really quite simple.

He decided to sing like a golden-throated canary.

Early that evening Starbuck walked from the train terminal and hailed a cab. Thus far, all the pieces had fallen into place, and he thought it might be wiser to quit while he was ahead. Yet one step remained, and he was determined to try. He ordered the driver to take him to Chinatown.

His day had been hectic, but rewarding. Denny O'Brien, under questioning, had proved himself a veritable gold mine of information. Once he began talking, it became apparent he had something bordering on total recall. He revealed names and dates and places, and, in most instances, tied them to events that established an unassailable time frame. Those slight lapses of memory he suffered were easily brought to light by the ledgers. There, too, the evidence was overwhelming. With meticulous care, he had entered every payoff, noting the date and the amount, along with the percentage of gross take from various Barbary Coast operations. The entries, itemized in O'Brien's laborious scrawl, covered prostitution and gambling as well as the all-pervasive protection racket. The ledgers substantiated that Christopher Buckley had shared in the proceeds to the tune of more than $1,000,000.

Late that afternoon, after taking a deposition from O'Brien, Starbuck had at last notified Charles Crocker. Shortly thereafter, a squad of Central Pacific security guards reported to the warehouse. O'Brien was sequestered in a windowless room, and men were posted both inside and outside the building. Their orders were direct and without equivocation. Anyone who attempted forcible entry to the warehouse was to be shot on the spot. When Starbuck departed the warehouse, he'd had no qualms about O'Brien's safety. Nor any concern that his songbird would try to fly away.

On the Street of a Thousand Lanterns, a crowd was gathered outside Fung Jing Toy's house. A policeman was posted at the door, and a paddy wagon stood at curbside. Starbuck paid the hansom driver, then eased through the throng of Chinese who stared silently, almost expectantly, at the front door. He approached the policeman and nodded amiably.

"What's all the commotion?"

"Oh, would you believe it?" the officer replied in a thick brogue. "The big Chink himself has done been murdered."

"Fung Jing Toy?"

"Aye, the very one," the officer observed solemnly. "God rest his heathen soul."

The door opened, and a murmur swept through the crowd. Several policemen, formed in a protective wedge, escorted two Chinese down the steps and hustled them into the paddy wagon. Starbuck instantly recognized the men, Wong Yee and Sing Dock. The last time he'd seen them they were guarding the entrance to Fung's underground chamber.

"Are those the killers?"

"Caught red-handed," the officer affirmed. "And them the Chink's own *boo how doy*. Cut him to ribbons with their hatchets, they did. Terrible sight. Terrible."

Starbuck turned and walked away. Somehow he wasn't surprised by Fung Jing Toy's death. Some dark complex of gut instinct and premonition had warned him that Buckley would move swiftly. With Denny O'Brien in custody, Mr. Frisco couldn't risk the possibility of still another turncoat. All the more imperative, Fung represented a corroborative witness, the one man who could substantiate O'Brien's testimony. Buckley, expedient to the end, had simply ordered the Chinaman's assassination.

Yet Starbuck was surprised by the choice of assassins. Wong Yee and Sing Dock were clearly the tools of Christopher Buckley. Their loyalty to a white-devil overlord, rather than Fung, confirmed Buckley's absolute domination of the Chinatown tongs. Still, while a key witness had been silenced, the blind man had no reason for celebration. He was, ironically enough, very much in the dark.

The ledgers were the one element Buckley couldn't have foreseen, and never suspected. A mute form of corroboration that spoke louder than words.

Mr. Frisco was shortly due the shock of his life.

CHAPTER 17

"Perhaps you could elaborate, Mr. Starbuck."

"Well, in a manner of speaking, you might liken it to the links in a chain. Adair led me to O'Brien, who in turn led me to Fung. From there, things led straight to Buckley. He was the last link in the chain."

"You refer to Christopher A. Buckley, proprietor of the Snug Café. Is that correct?"

"Correct."

"Now, you used the analogy—links in a chain. Would you consider it valid to broaden the analogy, and call it a chain of command?"

"Yes, I would," Starbuck agreed. "It was organized along military lines. Fung and O'Brien were like field commanders, with their own sector of operations. They were free to run things to suit themselves, but they were responsible for their actions. In other words, they reported to a higher authority."

"So Fung controlled Chinatown and O'Brien

controlled the Barbary Coast. They operated independently on day-to-day matters, but they were answerable for the overall results in their sectors. Is that essentially correct?"

"Yes."

"Would you consider it a fair statement to characterize Christopher Buckley as their commander-in-chief?"

"I would," Starbuck acknowledged. "He appointed them, and he could strip them of command any time he took a notion. His orders were the last word."

"By that, you mean there was no appeal?"

"None whatever. He was the last link in the chain, and his word was final. It all stopped there."

The Grand Jury room, located in the Hall of Justice, went silent. The jurors were attentive, listening raptly, their eyes fixed on Starbuck. They gazed at him with the look of circus spectators watching a tiger eat its keeper. From the news stories, they knew he had killed three men during the course of his assignment in San Francisco. Hushed and eager, they waited to hear more.

Edgar Caldwell, the district attorney, paused for dramatic effect. He adjusted his spectacles, and stood for a moment consulting his notes. An ambitious man, he was commonly thought to be a force in county politics. Yet his conduct of the hearing indicated he was putting distance between himself and Buckley's local machine. He was seeking an indictment, but on the man rather than the Democratic

Party. At length, he turned back to the witness chair.

"Mr. Starbuck, a minute ago you testified that—and I quote—things led straight to Buckley. What did you mean by 'things'?"

Starbuck wormed around in his chair. With a straight face, he briefly recounted his cover story, and the offer to buy one hundred Chinese slave girls. Then he told of Fung's suspicions, which led ultimately to the meeting with Buckley. He concluded with a short synopsis of the meeting, and Buckley's open admission of power.

"Let's be clear on that point," Caldwell insisted, "Buckley stated that he'd been asked to arbitrate the matter?"

"Yes."

"Then he went on to state that he would approve the deal—the sale of a hundred Chinese virgins—if your references were in order. Isn't that correct?"

"So far as it goes," Starbuck amended. "I also had to show good faith by putting up a hundred thousand in cash."

"Which you obtained from your employer, Charles Crocker?"

"That's right."

"To recap, Mr. Starbuck." Caldwell struck an elegant pose for the jurors. "Buckley dictated the terms necessary to consummate the deal, and he then imposed those terms on both Fung and O'Brien. Is that your testimony?"

"Yes, it is."

"Have you any direct knowledge of why Fung and

O'Brien would comply with his demands?"

"I do," Starbuck nodded. "O'Brien called him Mr. Frisco. He stated that Buckley could approve or disapprove the deal, and everybody would just have to live with the decision. The question at issue—and Buckley confirmed this in our meeting—was how to conclude the deal and still keep peace between Fung and O'Brien."

"If I may paraphrase," Caldwell said, one eye on the jurors. "Buckley would hand down his edict, and his henchmen, Fung and O'Brien, would have no choice but to obey. A fair summation of the facts?"

"In a nutshell, that's the way it worked."

"Very well, Mr. Starbuck. Suppose we move on. In previous testimony, one Dennis O'Brien identified a certain set of ledgers. He stated that one ledger in particular dealt with payoffs to Buckley, as regards criminal activities on the Barbary Coast. Are you familiar with the ledgers in question?"

"I personally observed O'Brien take those ledgers from his office safe in the Bella Union."

"So the ledgers were intact—all entries previously recorded—at that time?"

"Yes."

"Did O'Brien voluntarily surrender the ledgers?"

"No." Starbuck smiled. "I forced him to open the safe at gunpoint."

"Please describe the events that transpired immediately thereafter."

"I took O'Brien to a warehouse . . ."

Starbuck's testimony consumed the better part of

an hour. When he was finished, Caldwell excused
him from the witness chair and thanked him profusely. The jurors sat spellbound as he walked from
the room. Their expressions indicated they believed
the man, and the story he'd told.

Outside, moving along the corridor, he felt an
enormous sense of relief. Three weeks had elapsed
since the capture of Denny O'Brien and the death of
Fung Jing Toy. In that time, waiting for a grand jury
to be empaneled, he had worked closely with the
district attorney. His continued presence had also
worked as an influence on O'Brien. The Barbary
Coast boss had cooperated fully, and turned state's
evidence in exchange for a reduced sentence. A convincing witness, he had testified earlier in the day.
And along with his ledgers, he'd apparently made an
impression on the jurors.

There now seemed little doubt as to the outcome.
An indictment would be forthcoming, and Buckley
would stand trial on charges ranging from criminal
conspiracy to accessory to murder. Conviction would
very likely put him behind bars for the rest of his
life.

For Starbuck, it was the end to a long and trying
period. He had enjoyed the chase, and felt great personal accomplishment at having brought Mr. Frisco
to bay. Still, there were bad memories as well, and
a change of scenery seemed very much in order. His
thoughts turned to Denver.

Then, rounding the corner into the lobby, he
abruptly stopped. Christopher Buckley, being led by

another man, appeared through the front entrance and walked toward him. He recalled Buckley was scheduled to testify before the grand jury, and briefly considered not speaking. But upon second thought, he changed his mind. A last word with the blind man seemed a fitting end to the case.

"Afternoon, Mr. Buckley."

"Good afternoon." Buckley halted, his expression quizzical. "I'm afraid you have the advantage of me."

"Luke Starbuck," Starbuck replied with a ghost of a grin. "Otherwise known as Harry Lovett."

"Of course!" Buckley said, smiling faintly. "How could I ever forget that voice?"

"Yeah, I reckon a voice is pretty hard to disguise."

"Well, that's past us now, Mr. Starbuck. I understand you've even dispensed with your gold tooth."

"Oh?" Starbuck asked pleasantly. "Keeping tabs on me, are you?"

Buckley's smile turned cryptic. "You remember my associate, Knuckles Jackson? He keeps me up to date on the latest newspaper accounts of your activities. All the more so since you've become such a celebrity."

Starbuck and Jackson traded nods. A large man, Jackson had a square and pugnacious face, with cold gun-metal eyes. For a moment, Starbuck couldn't place him. Then, suddenly, he recalled the night O'Brien and McQueen had escorted him to the Snug Café. Jackson was the resident gorilla who guarded

the alley door. His presence here today spoke for
itself. He was apparently trusted to act as Buckley's
seeing-eye dog and chief bodyguard.

"Funny thing," Starbuck said, glancing back at
Buckley. "All this hoopla about me doesn't amount
to a hill of beans. I've got an idea you're the one
they'll remember."

"On the contrary!" Buckley's tone was lordly,
somehow patronizing. "You shouldn't be so modest,
Mr. Starbuck. The public loves to be titillated, and
you've certainly shown them the seamier side of San
Francisco. Small wonder it's captured their imagination."

"Here today, gone tomorrow," Starbuck said
lightly. "People forget real quick."

"True," Buckley said with an indulgent smile.
"Fame rides a fleet horse. Nonetheless, you're to be
congratulated on a splendid job. You have a few
peers in your particular line of work."

Starbuck tried to divine his mood. For a man facing prison, he was altogether too congenial, and far
too unconcerned. His excessively reasonable tone
somehow rang false. Then, too, there was something
strange about his expression. Behind the tinted
glasses, the dead eyes seemed oddly mocking, alight
with laughter. The effect was unsettling, vaguely unnatural.

"I admire the way you're taking it all in stride,
Mr. Buckley."

"Why not?" Buckley spread his hands in a bland
gesture. "Life is very much like a melodrama, Mr.

Starbuck. Look closely and you'll find that pathos and farce always merge in the end. What appears to be reality is often little more than illusion."

"I wouldn't know about that," Starbuck remarked. "Course, just from the sound of it, I get the feeling you're not losing any sleep over this grand jury business."

"You tell me," Buckley said almost idly. "Should I be losing sleep?"

"You're on your way to testify, aren't you?"

"Indeed I am."

"Then I reckon you'll be able to answer the question yourself. There's no illusion so far as the jurors are concerned. It's all hard fact."

"So I hear," Buckley said, not without bitterness. "O'Brien and his ledgers apparently make for a convincing tale."

Starbuck regarded his somberly. "You must have inside sources. Those ledgers were a pretty well-kept secret."

"People talk," Buckley replied absently. "A secret ceases to be a secret once it's known by a second party. But, of course, that's hardly news to a man in your profession."

"No, I guess not." Starbuck nodded, acknowledging the truth of the statement. "Leastways, I never had any trouble getting people to talk about you."

Buckley smiled humorlessly. "Come now, Mr. Starbuck. Denny O'Brien talked because you put a gun to his head. Except for that, you would never have gotten past the stage of speculation and conjecture."

"Maybe so," Starbuck admitted. "The way it worked out, we'll never know. He talked, and that's all that counts."

"Ah, yes," Buckley commented loftily. "The hard facts you spoke of a moment ago."

"Hard facts," Starbuck said slowly, emphatically, "and all down in black and white."

"You believe they'll indict me, then?"

"Let's just say I'd lay odds on it."

"A sporting man to the end, hmm?"

"No, I only bet on sure things."

"Touché," Buckley said equably. "And what of you, Mr. Starbuck. Where to now that your terrible swift sword has done its work?"

"Another town, another job," Starbuck countered easily. "There's so many crooks around, it keeps a fellow in my line pretty much on the go."

"Indeed?" Buckley paused as though weighing his words. "Another town, another job sounds imminently practical, Mr. Starbuck. Allow me to wish you good hunting . . . elsewhere."

"Some men might take that as a threat."

"Perhaps." Buckley smiled without warmth. "I'm sure you'll take it in the spirit in which it was intended, Mr. Starbuck."

Starbuck laughed and gave him an offhand salute. With a nod to Knuckles Jackson, he walked to the front entrance and pushed through the door. Outside, he found the way barred by a gang of reporters and several newspaper cameramen. For all the publicity surrounding the case, he had thus far avoided both interviews and photographs. Today, with the grand jury in session, the press cast aside any pretense of civility. Camera powder flashed and reporters swarmed forward, peppering him with questions.

"What's the latest, Mr. Starbuck?"

"No comment."

"Will they indict Buckley?"

"Your guess is as good as mine."

"C'mon, be a sport. Give us the lowdown!"

"I only know what I read in the papers."

"Can we quote you on that?"

"Suit yourself."

"Have a heart, Mr. Starbuck! We're only trying to do our job!"

"No comment."

To a chorus of groans and invidious remarks, Starbuck brushed past them. He hurried down the steps and walked toward Kearny Street. A moment later he disappeared around the corner.

Early the next morning Starbuck was ushered into Charles Crocker's office. The railroad tycoon greeted him with an ebullient smile and a bear-trap hand-shake. Once they were seated, Crocker tossed a newspaper across the desk.

"Have you seen that?"

"Yeah, I read it at breakfast."

Starbuck's photo stared back at him from the front page. Emblazoned across the top was a bold headline, which in itself told the story. The grand jury had indicted Christopher Buckley on all counts.

"You did it!" Crocker boomed out jovially. "By Christ, you said you would—and you did!"

"I got lucky."

"Luck, hell!" Crocker beamed. "Nobody gets his picture on every front page in town because he's lucky. You pulled off a feat of detection that's unrivaled. You're the toast of San Francisco!"

"So I read."

The irony of the moment wasn't lost on Starbuck. Crocker, not quite a month ago, had strenuously opposed the plan to expose Buckley. Yet now, basking in the reflected glory, he was something of a hero himself. His statements to the newspapers implied that the Central Pacific Railroad was in large measure responsible for Buckley's downfall. The idea struck Starbuck as amusing. All the more so since Crocker was now portraying himself as a paragon of civic virtue. He thought it a strange and unlikely role for a robber baron.

"Yessir," Crocker said with vinegary satisfaction, "you nailed Chris Buckley to the cross, and we all owe you a vote of thanks. San Francisco won't ever be the same again!"

Starbuck shrugged off the compliment. "I just did my job."

"Your job and then some!" Crocker said, jubilant. "You called Buckley and his crowd spoilers, and you were right. I'll have to admit I wasn't sold on the idea, not at first. But you turned me around, Luke.

You made me see the light!" His voice rose triumphantly. "This is a proud day for the Central Pacific. A proud day!"

"Speaking of trains," Starbuck said wryly, "I've got to get a move on. I aim to catch the eastbound out of Oakland this evening."

"Eastbound?" Crocker suddenly looked perplexed. "Where are you going?"

"Denver," Starbuck said with a tired smile. "That's my headquarters, and I've got business to look after."

Crocker pursed his lips, solemn. "The Central Pacific needs a new chief of security. Any chance you would consider it assuming I made it worth your while, stock options and that sort of thing?"

"Thanks all the same." Starbuck shook his head. "I appreciate the offer, but I'm not what you'd call a team man. I work best alone."

"I suspected as much," Crocker said with exaggerated gravity. "You will return for Buckley's trial, won't you? I understand it's been set for the spring court docket."

"Wouldn't miss it for the world."

"I should hope not!" Crocker frowned uncertainly. "O'Brien alone will never convict him. Your testimony is vital."

"I'll be here," Starbuck assured him. "You've got my word on it."

Crocker took a bank draft from inside a folder on his desk. "I intended to give you this, anyway. A bonus, so to speak." He leaned forward, extending the draft. "Perhaps it will also ensure your return for the trial."

Starbuck accepted the draft, studying it a moment. Then he looked up with some surprise. "Ten thousand is mighty generous. I would've settled for what you owed me and no bones either way."

"You earned it." Crocker laughed a short, mirthless laugh. "Ten dead men at a thousand dollars a head seems to me a rare bargain."

"Eleven." Starbuck gave him a lopsided grin. "Course, the farmer didn't rightly count. He just got in the way of a stray bullet."

"Nonetheless, he was a member of the gang. It appears I owe you another thousand, Luke."

"I'll collect when I see you in the spring."

"Done!" Crocker trumpeted. "Here's my hand on it!"

Starbuck rose and shook hands. Then, after a parting word, he walked from the office. On his way to the elevator, he stuck the bank draft in his wallet and chuckled softly to himself. A thousand dollars a head was no bargain. He'd killed men for lots less, simply because they needed killing.

And in the end, someone had to kill them.

CHAPTER 18

There was a slight chill in the air and fog obscured the waterfront. Farther away, beyond the city, a wintry sunset slowly settled into the ocean.

Starbuck stood on the fantail of the ferry. His eyes were fixed upon distance, faraway and clouded. A roll-your-own was stuck in the corner of his mouth, and he smoked without haste. San Francisco, quickly falling astern, was lost within some deeper reflection. His thoughts were on men, and events.

On the whole, he felt he'd done a creditable job. The band of train robbers and their leader had been exterminated. Fung Jing Toy was dead, leaving Chinatown in turmoil. O'Brien, who most assuredly deserved killing, would nonetheless emerge from prison an old and withered shadow of the man who had once ruled the Barbary Coast. Christopher Buckley would be convicted and die an inmate, blind and ultimately enfeebled, in some dank prison cell. So what began as a routine assignment had ended with the downfall of Frisco's underworld hierarchy. A certain pride in a job well done was by no means out of order.

Yet, with some cynicism, Starbuck saw the darker side as well. In his view, there was no logical progression in human affairs. There were merely tides of change borne on violence and an endless upheaval of political structures. The winners hung the losers— or carted them off to prison—and things went on much as they always had and always would. The evils of man, corruption and greed, were the single constant. And in one of the stranger quirks of life, a man bursting with virtue was often less esteemed than the spoilers. The voters, for all their sanctimonious tommyrot, understood greed and willfully sought those pleasures that were considered wicked and depraved. A reformer, therefore, lasted only a short while. The spoilers went on forever.

Viewed from that perspective, the only change wrought would be a change in names and faces. A new political kingpin would step into the void and quickly replace Buckley. Another thug would batter his fellow thugs into submission, and emerge the czar of the Barbary Coast. The tong wars of Chinatown would produce yet another vice lord, and the market in Oriental slave girls would continue to flourish. A whole new cast of characters would rise to ascendancy in Frisco's underworld. And soon, from the waterfront to the Uptown Tenderloin, it would return to business as usual.

Still, all things considered, those were problems

San Francisco would have to solve for itself. Starbuck saw his own role clearly, and moral judgments, while an engaging exercise, were not his bailiwick. He was a detective, not a civic crusader. He'd been hired to rout a gang of train robbers, and Red Ned Adair was dead.

Case closed.

From one standpoint, however, the case would never be closed. Over breakfast that morning, while reading the *Examiner*, he'd realized how fully the Frisco job had altered his own future. His testimony before the grand jury, and the attendant publicity, had resulted in his photo being splashed across the front pages of newspapers throughout the West. His anonymity, always an edge in past cases, was gone forever. Once a face in the crowd, he would now be known and recognized wherever he traveled. Coupled with his reputation, that loss of anonymity might shorten his life span considerably.

The upshot seemed equally clear to Starbuck. Now, more than ever, he must become a master of disguise. A man of a thousand faces, none of them his own. An undercover operative in every sense of the word. In short, a detective and a chameleon, all rolled into one.

Unbidden, the memory of Nell popped into his head. Since the night of her death, she had never been far from his thoughts. Not that he wanted to remember, or made any conscious effort to do so. Quite the contrary, the hurt and the shame were emotions yet to be reconciled. Whenever possible, he nudged all thought of her to some dark corner of his mind. Yet, despite his attempts to forget, she was always there. A vision too easily summoned, and a reminder of things lost forever.

With the clarity of hindsight, he understood he'd overplayed his hand. That night, when he'd left her alone at the Bella Union, he was supremely confident. No doubt existed that he would shortly capture Ned Adair and return to spirit her away from the Barbary Coast. He was cocky, altogether too sure of himself, and in his blind rush to get the job done, he had sadly underestimated Denny O'Brien. In effect, he had gambled Nell's life on the assumption he could outsmart a pack of cutthroats and thieves who were already wise to his game. And he'd lost.

That was the part he couldn't forget. To risk his own life was one thing. He was, after all, being paid to accept whatever risk the job entailed. To risk Nell's life was another matter entirely. Her only stake in the game was a fabrication of lies and promises. In the end, of course, he would never have welched completely on their arrangement. He fully intended to take her away from the Barbary Coast and somehow relocate her in Colorado. Perhaps set her up in a respectable business of some sort, or at the very least secure her a job a cut above the Bella Union. Yet the fairy tale about his whorehouse empire, and their partnership in the enterprise, was unadulterated poppycock. However good his intentions, he had gulled her with a pipe dream that resulted in her death.

Looking back, he saw now that he'd made a fatal error in judgment. He should have gotten her out of the Bella Union, and once she was safe—only when she was safe—should he have gone off in search of Ned Adair. At the moment, time had seemed imperative, and unwittingly or not, he had elected to jeopardize her rather than jeopardize the mission. In retrospect, it was an unconscionable decision, all the worse because he'd compounded poor judgment with dumb planning. But then, as the old-timers were fond of saying, hindsight was no better than hind tit.

The memory of Nell would never leave him. Nor would he ever wholly absolve himself of her death. With time, he might learn to live with it. One day, perhaps, he might even find justification for the act. Her death, in the larger sense, had brought about the downfall of Frisco's underworld leaders. But that, too, was more excuse than vindication, and in no way would it mitigate what he'd done. The thought of Nell Kimball would remain a burden, and one he deserved. By all rights, she belonged with him now, on her way to Colorado. He wouldn't forget why he stood alone . . . and curiously lonely.

"Hullo, Starbuck."

Knuckles Jackson halted beside him at the railing. Starbuck was instantly alert. A sudden chill settled over him, and it left a residue of uneasiness. His muscles tensed, every nerve stretched tight, yet his expression revealed nothing. He took a drag on his cigarette and tossed it over the side. Then he fixed Jackson with a stony stare.

"Let me guess," he said evenly. "You've got business in Oakland, and you just happened to board the same ferry."

"Not exactly." Jackson's mouth zigzagged in a gash-like smile. "I've got business, but not in Oakland. It's with you."

"I'm listening."

Jackson returned his gaze steadily. "Yesterday, when you had that little talk with Mr. Buckley, he was tryin' to be reasonable about things. He wanted me to make sure you got the message."

"What message was that?"

"He don't want you to show up for the trial."

Starbuck's eyes narrowed. "Guess I had wax in my ears yesterday. You're saying that without me, there's no one left but O'Brien. So you somehow manage to kill him, and when I fail to testify, there goes the prosecution's case. All charges dismissed and Buckley walks away with a clean bill of health."

Jackson gave him a wide, peg-toothed grin. "You're pretty swift. I wasn't too sure m'self, but the boss said you'd see the light. He figured a word to the wise and you wouldn't come anywhere near that trial."

"And if I do?"

"Too bad."

"Too bad if I show up?"

"No." Jackson touched the brim of his hat. "Too bad you asked the wrong question."

Out of the corner of his eye, Starbuck caught a glint of metal on the upper deck. In that split second, he realized Jackson had a confederate. The signal, touching his hat, was prearranged. A signal to end it there.

All in a motion, Starbuck pulled the Colt and dropped to one knee. A slug thunked into the wooden railing, followed an instant later by a loud report. He saw a man on the upper deck, squinting at him down the barrel of a revolver. Thumbing the hammer, he extended the Colt to arm's length and let go two rapid shots. The man stiffened, and a pair of bright red dots, centered chest high, appeared on his coat front. He stumbled, arms flapping like a scarecrow, and his legs suddenly collapsed beneath him. The gun went skittering from his hand and he keeled over backward, spread-eagled on the deck.

Starbuck twisted around. The hammer was cocked and his finger tightened on the trigger, then he stopped. Knuckles Jackson stood frozen at the rail, his hands empty and very prudently held in plain sight. His look was one of disbelief, and outright terror. The look of a vicious dog suddenly cornered by a boar grizzly.

Climbing to his feet, Starbuck's expression turned immobile and dark. His eyes flashed with a cold glitter as he took a step closer. A grim line of rage, naked and revealed, tugged at his mouth.

"You sorry sonovabitch! I ought to kill you."

"Nothin' personal," Jackson croaked. "I was just followin' orders."

"Then here's an order for you. Buckley's so keen on messages, I want you to carry one back to him."

Jackson swallowed hard. "Yeah?"

"Tell him for me that I'll see him at the trial."

"I sure will, them very words."

"One more thing," Starbuck said softly. "Tell him if anything happens to Denny O'Brien, I will personally stop his clock, tick-tock and all. You got it?"

"I got it."

"Then start swimming."

"Swimming?" Jackson's face went ashen. "What d'you mean?"

"You heard me." Starbuck commanded. "Hit the water and make like a duck."

"Jeezus Christ!" Jackson bawled. "You ain't serious! I'd drown before I got halfway to shore."

"I'm dead serious." Starbuck wiggled the Colt with a menacing gesture. "You can haul ass over the side or die where you're standing. Only make up your mind *muy* goddamn *pronto!* I'm through talking."

Jackson opted for the water. He gingerly climbed over the railing and hung there a moment, staring down with a look of queasy horror. Then he leaped, his hat drifting lazily in the air, and hit the ferry's wake with a leaden splash. An instant later he surfaced, spewing water, and bobbed about like a cork in a stormy sea. Arms flailing, he finally got himself oriented with the distant shore. He struck off at a slow crawl toward the city by the bay.

Starbuck grinned, watching from the fantail a long while. Then, not at all displeased with the outcome, he shoved the Colt in its holster and strode off in the direction of the passenger cabin. His step was jaunty, and he was quietly humming a Frisco ditty to himself.

The next time I saw darlin' Nell
She was gussied up for a spree.
She had a pistol strapped 'round herself
And a banjo draped acrost her knee!

**Before the legend,
there was the man . . .**

And a powerful destiny to fulfill.

On October 26, 1881, three outlaws lay dead in
a dusty vacant lot in Tombstone, Arizona.
Standing over them—Colts smoking—were
Wyatt Earp, his two brothers Morgan and
Virgil, and a gun-slinging gambler named
Doc Holliday. The shootout at the O.K. Corral
was over—but for Earp, the fight had just
begun . . .

THE DEVIL'S OWN...

Starbuck's anger gave way to wonderment. Never a staunch believer, he nonetheless asked himself what god watched over these men. Or perhaps it wasn't a god at all. Perhaps there was some special devil, a satanic force that protected such men from harm. Certainly no five men had ever had a closer brush with death. Within the space of three or four minutes, they had been on the receiving end of probably a hundred rifle slugs. Yet none of them had been killed, and the wounds they'd suffered were hardly worse than the nick of a dull razor. It defied understanding, and a thought occurred that left him momentarily chilled.

Perhaps, after all, Wyatt Earp wasn't meant to be killed.

Perhaps he was *unkillable*.

PRAISE FOR
SPUR AWARD-WINNING AUTHOR MATT BRAUN

"Matt Braun is head and shoulders above all the rest who would attempt to bring the gunmen of the Old West to life."
—Terry C. Johnston, author of *The Plainsman* series

"Matt Braun has a genius for taking real characters out of the Old West and giving them flesh-and-blood immediacy."
—Dee Brown, author of *Bury My Heart at Wounded Knee*

TOMBSTONE

MATT BRAUN

St. Martin's Paperbacks

This novel is a work of historical fiction. Names, characters, places and incidents relating to non-historical figures are either the product of the author's imagination or are used fictitiously, and any resemblance of such non-historical figures, places or incidents to actual persons, living or dead, events or locales is entirely coincidental.

TOMBSTONE / THE SPOILERS

Tombstone copyright © 1981 by Matthew Braun.
The Spoilers copyright © 1981 by Matthew Braun.

Cover photo © Comstock Images.

ISBN: 0-312-94781-X
EAN: 978-0-312-94781-1

Printed in the United States of America

Tombstone Pocket Books edition / April 1981
Tombstone Pinnacle edition / June 1985
St. Martin's Paperbacks edition / September 2002

The Spoilers Pocket Books edition / April 1985
The Spoilers Pinnacle edition / August 1985
St. Martin's Paperbacks edition / November 2002

St. Martin's Paperbacks are published by St. Martin's Press, 175 Fifth Avenue, New York, NY 10010.

10 9 8 7 6 5 4 3 2 1

TO THE ADAIRS

Dorothy and Harry

Eleanor and Bob

Peggy and Ham

AUTHOR'S NOTE

The gunfight at the OK Corral has become one of the more enduring myths in western folklore.

Yet, very few people realize that the OK Corral shootout was but a prelude. What occurred afterward represents one of the bloodiest chapters in the annals of the Old West.

Between October, 1881, and April, 1882, Tombstone became a battleground. A savage vendetta, triggered by the OK Corral gunfight, resulted in murder and assassination, and cold-blooded execution. There was never any question as to who did the killing, or why. There was controversy then as to Wyatt Earp's motives, and to some extent, that controversy still exists. Stripped of fabrication and myth, however, several startling truths have survived the passage of time.

The record rather conclusively demonstrates that greed and corruption, abetted by political ambition, were the root causes of the bloodletting. Stage robbery was epidemic, and Wyatt Earp was thought to be heavily involved, the mastermind behind an outlaw gang. Wells, Fargo actually sent two undercover agents into

Tombstone during this period. Their mission was to rout the gang and write an end to the bloodshed.

Luke Starbuck was uniquely qualified for such an assignment. His fame as a detective and manhunter was unrivaled in the Old West. The events depicted herein, and what he unearthed about Wyatt Earp, are for the most part documented fact. Some literary license has been taken regarding his method of operation and the actions of certain characters. All else is closer to the truth than the myth.

TOMBSTONE, through Luke Starbuck, tells the untold story.

CHAPTER 1

Starbuck angled across Larimer Street, one eye on the police station.

The Colt .45 stuffed in the waistband of his trousers gave him an uncomfortable moment. He was accustomed to enforcing the law, and the city ordinance against carrying firearms struck him as damnfool nonsense. His suit jacket concealed the gun, but he was still irked that progress had put him on the wrong side of the law.

Denver, like most western cities, considered itself a progressive metropolis. With 1881 drawing to a close, the population was approaching 100,000 and frontier customs were slowly losing ground to the civilized edicts of reformers. Not that old Denver had completely succumbed to the new cosmopolitan posture; graft and bribes still assured the discreet operation of whore-houses, gaming parlors, and busthead saloons. Yet it was now a hub of commerce, with two railroads and an expansive financial district. And a law against carrying guns.

Starbuck began wondering why he'd ever left

Texas. As he moved past the police station, it occurred to him that hindsight was the worst of all vantage points. However enlightening, it made a man feel very much the dimdot.

A brisk December wind whipped out of the northwest with biting force. He grunted, testing the wind for snow, and hurried along the street. Halfway down the block, he turned into the entrance of the Brown Palace Hotel.

In the lobby, he pulled out his pocket watch and checked the time. The letter from Vernon Whitehead had indicated ten sharp, and he still had a couple of minutes to spare. He inquired at the desk, and much as he'd expected, Whitehead's name commanded instant attention. The clerk pointed him in the right direction, all the while emphasizing that the gentleman in question occupied the hotel's finest suite. Starbuck crossed the lobby, gazing around at the ornate decor and a garish mural covering the breadth of the ceiling. He thought it beat the hell out of a bunkhouse.

Mounting the sweeping staircase, he was reminded that the whole operation had been organized on a large scale. Early next spring, the presidents of every cattlemen's association throughout the West would converge on Denver. Their purpose would be to unite in the formation of the International Cattlemen's Association. Their primary goal, aside from joining forces against homesteaders, would be an organized, farreaching campaign directed at rustlers and horse thieves. Vernon Whitehead, chairman of the Executive Committee, had extended an invitation for him to attend a preliminary planning session. He was to be considered for the position of Chief Range Detective.

John Chisum, perhaps the most respected of all western cattlemen, had recommended him for the job. Some months earlier, he had been instrumental in disbanding a gang of rustlers who were preying on Chisum's vast New Mexico spread. At the same time, he'd had a hand in tracking down Billy the Kid, and was present the night Pat Garrett killed the young outlaw. The attendant publicity had advanced his already formidable reputation as a manhunter.

Upstairs, Starbuck proceeded along the hall and stopped before the door of the suite. He removed his hat, tugged the lapels of his jacket straight, and knocked. The murmur of voices inside quickly subsided, and a moment later the door opened. An older man, with a shock of white hair like candy floss, greeted him with an outstretched hand.

"You must be Luke Starbuck?"

"Yessir, I am. And you're—?"

"Vern Whitehead." Whitehead stepped aside. "C'mon in and meet the rest of the boys."

The suite was lavishly appointed. A thick Persian carpet covered the sitting room floor and grouped before the fireplace were several chairs and a plush divan. The other committee members—Sam Urschel, Oscar Belden, and Earl Poole—rose and moved forward. After a round of introductions, Whitehead motioned everyone to chairs.

There was no attempt at smalltalk. These men were ranchers, with little polish despite their wealth, and today they were all business. From the outset, it was apparent that Whitehead would act as spokesman for the group. Moreover, it was equally clear the interview would proceed along the lines of an interrogation.

Whitehead assessed him with a shrewd glance. "You as good as John Chisum says you are?"

Starbuck wasn't impressed. They obviously meant to put him on the defensive, and the tactic didn't sit well. He let them wait while he rolled a smoke. After flicking a match on his thumbnail, he took a long drag and exhaled.

"No offense intended, but you shouldn't have sent that invite unless you'd already checked me out."

"Oh, we checked you out, Mr. Starbuck. We can't afford to go on the say-so of nobody, not even John Chisum."

"Then I reckon you got all you need."

"Well, let's see." Whitehead extracted a sheaf of papers from inside his jacket. He snapped them open and began reading. "Says here you been a range detective since the summer of '76. Headquartered at Ben Langham's LX ranch, down in the Texas Panhandle. Worked out of there for the Panhandle Cattlemen's Association."

"Close enough." Starbuck admired the tip of his cigarette. "Except for the time I was out on loan to Chisum."

"Says here you've killed fourteen men."

"I never took time out to count."

Whitehead fixed him with an inquiring gaze. "Does fourteen include the ones you hung?"

"Nope." Starbuck looked at him without expression. "That would make it considerably higher."

"Not bad for a fellow"—Whitehead consulted his

notes—"who's just pushin' thirty-four. How is it a man your age ain't never been married?"

Starbuck smiled. "I like my work."

"Do you now?" Whitehead tapped the papers with his finger. "According to this, you inherited the LX from Langham and sold out to a bunch down in the Panhandle. That must've left you sittin' on easy street."

"I got enough to see me along."

"Hold on!" Oscar Belden interrupted. "You got money to burn, and you're tryin' to tell us you aim to keep on workin' for wages. Some of us find that a mite hard to swallow."

"I told you," Starbuck said in a deliberate voice. "I like my work. How much I've got in the bank doesn't concern you or anyone else. That's my business."

The words were spoken with the iron-sureness of a man who tolerated very little from others. Starbuck was a full six feet, but built along deceptive lines. He was lithe and corded, catlike in his movements, with a square jaw and lively chestnut hair. Five years as a range detective had brutalized him, and the vestiges of a violent trade were etched around his eyes. He had the steely gaze of someone who stayed alive by making quick estimates. And now, staring at the men, he wasn't at all certain he wanted the job. They seemed far too picky to suit his style.

"Let's suppose," Whitehead resumed, "that we offered you the job. Could you recruit ten or twelve good men and teach 'em to follow orders, no questions asked? I'm talkin' about a squad of detectives that would go wherever they're needed and do whatever they're told."

"All depends."

"On what?"

"On who gives the orders," Starbuck said flatly. "I take assignments, but I don't take orders. Either I do it my own way or I don't do it at all."

"John Chisum"—Whitehead paused as though weighing his words—"told us you was strong-headed. We might be willin' to give you the leeway needed, if you was willin' to hold yourself accountable to the Executive Committee."

"I take it you mean yourself and these other gents?"

"Most likely," Whitehead acknowledged. "Course, nothin's official till the Association gets itself formed next spring. But that's the way it stacks up right now."

"Exactly what was it you had in mind that needs ten or twelve men?"

"Killin'," Whitehead said bluntly. "We wouldn't object if you brought in a few for trial, but we'd sooner see a thief hung than sent to prison."

"Sounds like you mean to form a death squad."

"Altogether I reckon ranchers lose a couple of million dollars a year in rustled stock. We aim to put a stop to it, and I don't know no better way than the gallows tree."

Starbuck unfolded slowly from the divan. There was a slight bulge over the sixgun in his waistband, and he adjusted his suit jacket. Then he looked from man to man, nodding last to Whitehead.

"I'll let you know."

Before the cattlemen quite realized his intent, he

turned and walked to the door. The interview was concluded.

On the way downstairs Starbuck made a snap judgment. The job wasn't for him. There was no denying the honor involved; as Chief Range Detective his prestige among cattlemen would be greatly enhanced. Nor were there any qualms about the killing. The past five years had hardened him to the sight of death. Hanging a man wasn't pleasant, but neither was it repugnant. It was simply a function to be performed swiftly, an object lesson for those who robbed and murdered with godlike impunity. As for shooting a man who was trying to shoot him, there was no thought, no stirring of emotion, certainly no regret. He survived by allowing no man to threaten his life.

So the job itself wasn't what bothered him. He was concerned instead about Vernon Whitehead. Some gut instinct told him the rancher had lied. He sensed that Whitehead would say anything—promise anything— to gull him into accepting the job. Further, he felt there was something of the tyrant about Whitehead. Though it hadn't surfaced during the interview, the telltale signs were there. The rancher, little by little, would begin issuing orders rather than assignments. Eventually, like a drill sergeant, he would demand blind obedience and unquestioning loyalty. All of which meant they would come to loggerheads. Somewhere down the line Whitehead would show his true colors, and there would then be no choice but to sever the arrangement. It hardly seemed worth the effort, or the aggravation.

Then, too, there was no rush to accept the first job offered. As one of the committee members had pointed out, he wasn't exactly hurting for money. Upon the death of Ben Langham, an old friend and something of a surrogate father, he had inherited the largest cattle spread in the Panhandle. Yet, even though Langham had thought to cure his wanderlust, the responsibility was ill-suited to his character. Some inner restlessness made it impossible for him to become tied down to people, or things. He traveled light and he traveled alone, obligated to no one but himself. Satisfied with his life, and under no great compulsion to change, he had sold the ranch only last month. The proceeds— some $200,000—was stashed away in a bank in Fort Worth. The interest alone was enough to cover his immediate needs, with plenty to spare for an occasional whirl at the sporting life. And that afforded him the independence to do whatever he damn well pleased. Especially where it concerned work.

By the time he reached the lobby, Starbuck had decided he wanted no part of the International Cattlemen's Association. He wasn't sure where the decision would lead, nor was he overly concerned about the future. His reputation was established, and there was work anywhere in the West for a range detective who got results. Tomorrow was time enough to ponder his next move. For the moment, he had a definite yen to sample the nightlife of Denver. He'd heard there were parlor houses that specialized in Chinese girls. Young sloe-eyed Orientals, whose plumbing was reportedly vice-versa to that of white women. The mere thought galvanized him to a quicker pace.

Approaching the hotel entrance, Starbuck noticed a man leaning against the wall. Heavyset and thick through the shoulders, he wore a bowler hat perched atop his head like a bird's nest. He smiled, flashing a gold tooth, and stepped into Starbuck's path.

"Your name Starbuck?"

"Who's asking?"

"Mr. Griffin. Horace Griffin. He'd like to see you."

Starbuck started around him. "I don't know any Horace Griffin."

"He knows you."

"Where from?"

"Why not let him tell you himself? Mr. Griffin's Division Superintendent of Wells, Fargo—and that's all I'm authorized to say."

Starbuck stared at him a moment, then shrugged. "What the hell? Won't cost me nothing to listen."

The heavyset man smiled, indicating the door. Outside, they turned onto Larimer Street and set off at a brisk walk across town. Some ten minutes later they entered the Wells, Fargo & Company express station. There, Starbuck was ushered into a private office and greeted by a man who introduced himself as Horace Griffin. Solemn as a priest, Griffin wasted no time on amenities. He offered Starbuck a chair on the opposite side of the desk, and came straight to the point.

"Mr. Starbuck, I know all about your meeting with the Cattlemen's Association. If you've accepted the position, then I won't compromise you further. If not, then I have a proposition that may very well interest you."

"How'd you get wind of the meeting?"

"One of the members on the Executive Committee is a close personal friend. Which one really has no bearing on our discussion."

Starbuck eyed him, considering. "Suppose we just say I'm at loose ends."

"Fair enough," Griffin agreed. "I presume you've heard of Tombstone?"

"Arizona?"

Griffin nodded. "In the past year, we've had fourteen stages robbed in the Tombstone district. We carry express shipments and payroll boxes for the silver mines, so the losses have been substantial. Very substantial."

"Sounds like you've got yourself a problem."

"And getting worse." Griffin leaned forward, elbows on the desk. "Ten days ago our station agent in Tombstone disappeared."

"How do you mean—disappeared?"

"Vanished, Mr. Starbuck! Without a trace."

Starbuck looked interested. "Any chance he was involved in the robberies?"

"More than a chance," Griffin replied. "Have you ever heard of Wyatt Earp? Doc Holliday?"

"Seems like I read something in the papers a while back. Near as I recall, it involved a shootout of some sort."

"The press dubbed it the OK Corral Gunfight. Of course, that's neither here nor there. What does matter is that the Tombstone sheriff believes Earp and Holliday are behind the robberies. Unofficially, he also accused our agent, Marsh Williams, of being in league with them."

"And Williams suddenly disappeared."

"Precisely!"

"Has the sheriff brought charges?"

"Last year, shortly after one of the robberies, he arrested Holliday. All indications were that he had a good case. But the court dismissed the charges, even though there was strong circumstantial evidence. Coincidently, Holliday's three alleged accomplices have since been killed in unrelated holdups."

"So where do you stand now?"

"Facing a stone wall," Griffin said dourly. "We transferred another agent into Tombstone, but he reports it's hopeless. Everyone is convinced Wyatt Earp killed Williams, and they're afraid to talk. We have no case, no evidence, and no way to stop the robberies."

"I get the feeling you're offering me a job."

"We know of your work," Griffin ventured. "Please don't misunderstand me. I'm not referring to the men you've killed, but rather your investigative work. I was particularly impressed with the way you infiltrated that gang of horse thieves some years ago. Dutch Henry Horn, wasn't that the ringleader's name?"

"For a fact," Starbuck noted. "You've got a good memory."

"I'm also an excellent judge of character, Mr. Starbuck. Quite frankly, we need an undercover operative in Tombstone. I believe you're the man for the job."

Starbuck examined the notion. "I don't know beans from buckshot about stage robbers. What makes you think I could pull it off when your own people have failed?"

"Thieves are thieves," Griffin said equably. "Their mentality differs little, whether we're talking about horse thieves or stage robbers. You've demonstrated a knack for thinking the way they do, and uncovering the evidence to expose them. In all candor, I believe you were made to order for Tombstone."

There was a moment of calculation. Then Starbuck fixed him with a stern look. "I don't work cheap and I'm plumb set in my ways. I do it at my own speed and I don't follow nobody's rules. Not even Wells, Fargo."

"Have no fear," Griffin assured him earnestly. "I'll set no rules, and you can name your own compensation. Other than that, I have only two requests."

"Oh?" Starbuck's eyebrows rose in question. "What sort of requests?"

"First, keep me informed through Fred Dodge, the station agent in Tombstone. Second, end the robberies—by whatever means you deem expedient."

"Unless I heard wrong, you're authorizing me to catch them or kill them. Whichever works best."

"I am indeed, Mr. Starbuck! And the quicker the better."

"Mr. Griffin," Starbuck grinned and stuck out his hand. "You just hired yourself a detective."

Horace Griffin heaved himself to his feet. He grasped Starbuck's hand in a firm grip, and wished him luck in Tombstone. He thought it not only the best solution, but perhaps the only solution. Indeed for Wells, Fargo & Company, it made imminent good sense.

Hire a killer to catch a killer.

CHAPTER 2

A week later Starbuck crossed the line into Arizona Territory. From there, he followed a southerly route, skirting the Dragoon Mountains through Sulphur Spring Valley. Then he turned southwest, bypassing Tombstone, and angled generally in the direction of Nogales and the Old Mexico border. On a chill morning in late December, he rode into the headquarters of the San Bernardino Ranch.

John Slaughter, who laid claim to all the land within a day's ride, operated the ranch somewhat like a feudal empire. He was a law unto himself along the border, and his JHS brand was burned on some 40,000 cattle and 5,000 horses. A former Texas Ranger, he had settled in Arizona when it was still the domain of the Apache tribes. An implacable man, he had fought the Apaches and Mexican bandidos on their own terms, and ultimately created a kingdom where no renegade dared enter. Of greater consequence to Starbuck, he was an old and trusted ally of a mutual friend, John Chisum.

The main house was an immense adobe, squatting

somewhat like a fort around an open quadrangle. A veranda, shaded by an overhead gallery, spread across the width of the front wall. Starbuck dismounted, looping the reins of his roan gelding around a hitchrack, and slapped a cloud of dust off his mackinaw. As he walked toward the porch stairs, he noted that the window shutters, constructed of thick timber, were slitted with gun ports. He smiled, certain now that he'd judged the situation correctly. John Slaughter, not Tombstone, was the place to start.

A *mestizo* servant met him at the door, taking his hat and mackinaw. Then he was led down a corridor, his spurs jangling on the tile floor, and shown into a wolf's lair of a den. Saddles and range gear were strewn about the room, and the walls were lined by an impressive array of long guns. But the whole was dominated by a battered walnut desk, and the man who sat behind it.

Starbuck was surprised. From the tales he'd heard, he had expected Slaughter to be a giant of a man, sledge-shouldered and stout as an oak. Instead, the man circling the desk was below medium height, on the sundown side of thirty, with a slight paunch. Yet his whole bearing was charged with energy, and his face looked adzed from hard darkwood. His eyes were gray and intense, and Starbuck was suddenly reminded that a man's size often counted for nothing. Determination and grit, when all else was tallied, were the measure of a man's worth.

Slaughter halted, nodding amiably. "I'm John Slaughter."

"Luke Starbuck." Starbuck extended his hand.

"John Chisum told me to look you up whenever I got over your way."

"Why, hell, yes!" Slaughter pumped his arm with sudden enthusiasm. "You're the range detective. The one that helped ol' John nail Billy Bonney and clean out Lincoln County."

"Former range detective," Starbuck told him. "I'm with Wells, Fargo now."

"Well I'll be jiggered." Slaughter indicated chairs in front of a blazing fireplace. "Take a load off your feet and tell me all about it. You takin' over the relay operation, are you?"

Starbuck saw no reason to hedge. "Mr. Slaughter, I was hired as an undercover operative. They sent me down here to investigate Tombstone."

"Call me John." Slaughter lowered himself into a chair, suddenly somber. "Luke, I'm sorry to say they didn't do you no favors with that assignment. Not by a damnsight!"

"Amen," Starbuck said without irony. "Matter of fact, that's why I've come to see you, instead of heading directly into Tombstone. I thought maybe you could give me the lowdown on things."

"What things?"

"Wyatt Earp, just for openers. Wells, Fargo says him and Doc Holliday are behind all these stage holdups."

"Yeah, them and Bill Brocius."

"Brocius?"

"Curly Bill Brocius," Slaughter elaborated. "He's leader of the gang that actually pulls the holdups. Part of his bunch are the ones Earp murdered at the OK Corral."

"Murdered?" Starbuck was astounded. "I understood it was law business of some sort."

"Christ A'mighty, no! It was a falling out amongst thieves, plain and simple."

"How so?"

"Earp had the Wells, Fargo agent in his pocket. He got all the dope on payroll shipments and fed it to Brocius through Doc Holliday. The gang robbed the stages and afterward divvied up the take with Earp. Ain't nobody yet proved it, but you can bet your boots that's the way it worked."

"So what happened?"

"Well, now, that's a tale and then some. Takes a bit of tellin'."

"Fire away," Starbuck grinned. "I've got nowhere to go."

Slaughter hauled out a pipe and tobacco pouch. After fussing around, he got it filled and puffing to suit him. Then he leaned back, the pipe jutting from his mouth like a burnt tusk, and began to talk.

Wyatt Earp, along with his four brothers and Doc Holliday, had arrived in Tombstone the latter part of 1879. An ambitious man, and quick to talk about his days as a lawman in the Kansas cowtowns, Earp sought appointment as sheriff of Cochise County. Instead, the territorial governor appointed his chief rival, John Behan. Thoroughly disgruntled, Earp threw in with a group of gamblers and gunmen. At one time or another, their number included Luke Short, Bat Masterson, and Buckskin Frank Leslie. In the meantime, one of Wyatt's brothers, Virgil Earp, was twice defeated for the office of town marshal. Yet the second election produced the very ally the Earps needed. John Clum, editor of the weekly *Epitaph*, was elected mayor. Tombstone's other newspaper, the *Nugget*, was owned by Harry Woods, who supported Sheriff Behan. Earp and Clum, cast together as members of the opposing faction, soon became close friends. And the lines were drawn.

Shortly thereafter, the stagecoach robberies began. Though no hard proof existed, word leaked out that Earp had formed an alliance with Curly Bill Brocius. Among others, the Brocius gang included the Clanton brothers, the McLowery brothers, and the most dangerous *pistolero* in Arizona Territory, Johnny Ringo. Doc Holliday, on several occasions, was linked to the outlaw gang. But no solid evidence was uncovered, and therefore no connection to Earp could be established. The Earps gained a legal front, however, when the town marshal mysteriously departed Tombstone. Mayor Clum, now considered one of the family, appointed Virgil Earp to fill the post.

Then, over a period of months, mutual distrust between the Earps and the Brocius gang ripened into open hostility. Only two months ago, on October 26, it exploded in bloodshed. The Earp brothers and Doc Holliday cornered five of the gang at the OK Corral. Only two of the outlaws were armed, but that gave the Earps no pause. Within seconds, they killed three of the men; the others survived by dodging and running, all the while being fired on by Doc Holliday. In the aftermath, with the town council in a rebellious mood,

Virgil Earp was stripped of his marshal's badge. Wyatt
and Doc Holliday were formally charged with murder,
and eye-witness testimony substantiated that the killings had been performed in cold-blood. But Justice
Wells Spicer, a political crony of the Earp-Clum faction, chose to ignore the facts. In his decision, notable
for its convoluted logic, he absolved Earp and Holliday of all blame. The charges were dismissed.

After that, an eerie lull settled over Tombstone. The
stage robberies abruptly ceased, and the Brocius gang
hadn't appeared in town for more than a month. Earp
and Holliday, conducting business as usual at the Alhambra Saloon, seemed to be biding their time. For
what, no one had the faintest inkling. But everyone in
Tombstone was convinced that Earp had yet another
card up his sleeve. Despite his unsavory reputation, he
was not noted as a quitter.

"That's the gist of it," Slaughter concluded, knock-
ing the dottle from his pipe. "Earp and his crowd lost
a little ground, but they ain't done yet. Not unless I
miss my guess."

Starbuck digested what he'd heard, silent a moment. Then he looked up. "What about Fred Dodge,
the new Wells, Fargo agent? Any chance Earp might
try to work the same deal with him?"

"I'd tend to doubt it. After what happened to Marsh
Williams—he's the one that just up and disappeared—
I suspect Dodge wouldn't much cotton to the notion
of playin' footsy with Earp."

"What're the odds on Earp making his peace with
Brocius?"

"Well . . ." Slaughter said speculatively. "I reckon

anything's possible amongst cutthroats like them. But I'd say the odds are lots better that they're sittin' around figgerin' ways to bushwhack one another."

"What makes you think so?"

"Cause Brocius has a score to settle, what with Earp havin' killed three of his men. And Earp knows he ain't never gonna be safe till he's rid of Brocius. If for no other reason, I'd imagine he's damn tetchy about the fact that Brocius could tie him to those robberies."

There was a prolonged silence. Starbuck's gaze drifted to the fire, and he appeared lost in thought. At last, watching him closely, Slaughter shifted around in his chair.

"Where do you aim to start?"

Starbuck kneaded the back of his head. "Way it looks to me, I've got to get in thick with Earp. He's covered his tracks on the outside, so I'll have to worm my way on the inside. Sooner or later he'll slip, and when he does, I'll be there to get the goods on him."

"Sounds reasonable," Slaughter nodded gravely. "Course, I don't have to tell you, you'll be walkin' into a den of vipers. One miscue and they'll kill you deader'n hell."

"I'll play it close to the vest."

"That's the ticket!" Slaughter beamed. "And by Jesus, if you need any help, all you got to do is shout. I'd jump at the chance to tangle with them sorry bastards."

"Now that you mention it, I could use some advice."

"Anything a'tall! You name it."

"I need somebody to act as a go-between with Fred Dodge. Wouldn't do for me to be seen in his company, but I've got to funnel information through him to Wells, Fargo. Anybody come to mind?"

"Harry Woods," Slaughter informed him. "That's your man."

"The newspaper editor?" Starbuck looked skeptical. "I need somebody with a permanent case of lockjaw. You think he fits the bill?"

"Godalmightybingo!" Slaughter roared. "Harry hates Wyatt Earp worse'n the devil hates holy water. You couldn't find nobody better if you searched from now till doomsday."

Starbuck smiled, rising. "I'll take your word for it, and I'm obliged."

Slaughter argued persuasively, urging him to spend the night. But Starbuck had ridden almost a thousand miles, and he was anxious now to begin the hunt. As the sun neared its midday zenith, he stepped into the saddle and rode north toward Tombstone.

In early 1878 a bedraggled, footsore prospector struggled along the jagged mountain slopes east of San Pedro Valley. His name was Ed Schieffelin, and quite literally, he stumbled upon one of the richest silver strikes in frontier history. With ore assaying at twenty thousand dollars a ton, the discovery sparked the greatest mining boom ever recorded in the southwest. Schieffelin named his strike Tombstone, and within a matter of months, the mile-high camp had mushroomed into a carnival of speculation. A stagecoach line was established across the seventy-mile stretch of desert to Tucson. Men and machinery began pouring in, followed closely by merchants and tradesmen, gamblers and saloonkeepers, and the finest assemblage of whores ever gathered in the Arizona barrens. From a few hundred whiskery desert rats, huddled in tents and squalid shacks, Tombstone burst upon the map as a rip-roaring boomtown. Within three years, the population leaped to six thousand, and still growing. A town, complete with all the civilized vices, was spawned in a land previously thought inhabitable only by Apaches and scorpions. It was a dusty helldorado, vitalized by the motherlode, and it ran wide-open day and night.

Starbuck left his horse at the livery stable early next evening. Dusk was settling over Tombstone, and he had no trouble losing himself in the crowds of miners thronging the streets. While it was approaching suppertime, saloons and gaming parlors were already doing a brisk business.

Within a half hour he had located the *Nugget* office. Outside a saloon, directly across the street, he positioned himself where he could keep a watch on it. His grimy trail clothes and bearded stubble made him all but invisible among the grubby miners. On his fourth cigarette, the wait ended. A man he assessed as the printer stepped out the front door and hurried down the street. Only moments later, another man pulled the shades on the office windows.

Grinding his cigarette underfoot, he crossed the street and entered an alleyway beside the newspaper. He located the back door and rapped softly. From in-

side, he heard the sound of footsteps, then the door
opened in a spill of light. The man who had pulled the
windowshades stood framed in the doorway.

"Harry Woods?"

"Yes?"

"I have a message from John Slaughter."

"Slaughter?" Woods appeared confused, then
quickly stepped aside. "Come in, Mr.—"

Starbuck entered, waiting until Woods shut the
door. "The name's Starbuck. Luke Starbuck."

"Are you one of Slaughter's men?"

"Not exactly." Starbuck inspected the shop, satis-
fying himself they were alone. "I need some help, and
Slaughter said you could be trusted."

Woods was a gnome of a man, with hair receding
into a widow's peak and inquisitive eyes magnified
behind thick glasses. He was slender and quick, highly
intelligent, and grasped immediately the secretive nature of his visitor. He indicated the front office.

"Come this way."

Starbuck had reconciled himself to the risks involved in revealing his identity. Seated in the office,
with Woods attentive and openly curious, he wasted
no time in sparring around. He briefly described his
mission for Wells, Fargo, stressing the fact that he
would be operating undercover. Then he related everything Slaughter had told him regarding Wyatt Earp and
Tombstone's volatile political climate. He concluded
by asking the editor to act as a go-between with Fred
Dodge. Woods, visibly caught up in the intrigue,
agreed without hesitation.

"One other thing," Starbuck added. "I'll be operating under the name of Jack Johnson. Unless it's an emergency, don't even think of contacting me. One way or another, I'll manage to stay in touch with you."

"Anything else?" Woods asked. "Anything at all. I'm willing to go the limit if it'll rid Tombstone of Earp and his crowd."

"What about Earp?" Starbuck responded. "You got anything personal on him? Habits, family, that sort of thing."

"I do indeed!" Woods laughed. "I wrote an editor friend in Kansas, and asked him to check out the newspaper files. What he turned up was enlightening, to say the least."

"Such as?"

"Oh, the fact that the Earps got their start operating a two-bit whorehouse. Court records in Wichita prove it beyond a doubt."

"I'll be damned!"

"Moreover, Wyatt and two of his brothers married some of their former whores. That too is substantiated by court records."

Starbuck appeared puzzled. "I always understood Earp was a lawman in Kansas. How does that square with what you say?"

"He was an ordinary policeman," Woods countered. "He brags about being city marshal, but that's pure tommyrot. As a matter of fact, he was fired from the Wichita police force and all but run out of town. His record in Dodge City was somewhat better, but not much. He's a four-flusher and a liar, all puff and no substance."

Starbuck decided to reserve judgment. Earp appar-

ently resorted to violence and gunplay when necessary, and that hardly indicated a man without substance. "What about his family? You mentioned wives
a minute ago."

"Sluts!" Woods invested the word with scorn.
"Common trash, and no better than the men they married." He paused, thoughtful. "Earp's sister-in-law
might be the one exception. Her name is Alice Blaylock, and from what I've seen, she's a cut above the
rest."

"She's not married?"

Woods shook his head. "She lives with Earp and
his wife. All the brothers have houses nearby, over at
the west end of Fremont Street."

Starbuck pondered a moment. "Slaughter said Earp
operates a faro game at the Alhambra. Is that it . . . no
other business interests?"

"I've heard rumors that he's involved with some of
the big mining muckamucks. Of course, considering
he's such a grifter, he might have started the rumor
himself."

"Could you nose around, see what you can turn
up?"

"Glad to." Woods hesitated, studying him closely.
"If you don't mind my asking, how do you intend to
approach Earp?"

Starbuck smiled. "I'm a pretty fair gambler myself.
Figured I'd meet him on common ground and see
where it leads."

Several minutes elapsed while they discussed
Tombstone's sporting crowd. With some revealing in-
sights into the town and its shadier element, Starbuck

finally rose to leave. Woods recommended the Occidental Hotel, commenting that the food was passable and the clientele relatively civilized for a boomtown. At the door, Woods smiled warmly, offering his hand.

"Good hunting, Luke. And a Merry Christmas."

"Christmas?"

"Why, yes." Woods gave him a quizzical look. "Tonight's Christmas Eve."

"Yeah?" Starbuck seemed somehow surprised. "Well the same to you, Harry! Hope Ol' Nick leaves you something special."

Starbuck stepped into the alley, and Woods slowly closed the door. His excitement, the sense of intrigue and danger, suddenly gave way to an infinite sadness. He thought it somehow sorrowful that anyone could lose track of Christmas. Luke Starbuck seemed to him the loneliest man he'd ever met. Lonely, and very much alone.

CHAPTER 3

Christmas Day was bleak and chilly.

Mayor John Clum trudged down Fremont Street shortly after the noon hour. His expression was distracted, and he walked with the stoop-shouldered gait of one who bears a heavy burden. Only when he met passersby was he able to present his normal air of bonhomie. Then, exchanging holiday greetings, he tipped his hat and gave them a politician's smile. The effect was forced but nonetheless convincing.

At Fremont and First, he crossed to the southwest corner. There he mounted the stairs of a modest clapboard house. A coat of whitewash had turned the color of ancient ivory, and there was a look of general disrepair about the building. On the porch, the planks underfoot creaked like a coffin lid, and he suddenly dreaded the next few minutes. Then, halting before the door, he collected himself and knocked.

A moment later the door swung open. He doffed his hat and managed a weak grin. "Afternoon, Wyatt."

With a curt nod, Earp motioned him inside. "Out makin' the rounds, are you, John?"

"I was," Clum said, moving through the door. "Until I stopped off for a drink at the Oriental."

"Yeah?" Earp closed the door and turned to face him. "Something happen to change your plans?"

"I heard something that put the damper on my Christmas spirit. Thought you ought to hear it, too."

Clum dropped into a chair, and Earp took a seat across from him. Even in repose there was something sinister about Earp. He was of medium height, powerfully built, with close-cropped hair and a brushy handle-bar mustache. His slate-colored eyes and taciturn manner were striking, yet somehow cold and dispassionate. John Clum knew him to be a man who seemed impervious to even the simplest emotion.

"From the look on your face," Earp noted dryly, "you must've heard Santy Claus died."

There was an odor of fear about Clum. His composure, already strained, suddenly deserted him. Under Earp's level gaze, his voice was shaky and his features pallid.

"You remember Dave Parker?"

"The mining engineer?"

Clum nodded. "He laid over in Benson last night. Walked into a saloon and there was Curly Bill Brocius, big as life."

Earp's face grew overcast. "Alone?"

"Ringo and some of the others were with him. Parker said he was drunk as a lord, and not even Ringo could get him to keep his mouth shut."

"About what?"

"A death list," Clum said hesitantly. "He's drawn up a death list, Wyatt. Our names are right at the top, followed by Doc and your brothers and Judge Spicer."

"That a fact?" Earp asked, open scorn in his eyes. "And the minute you heard it, you come runnin' over here like your pants was on fire."

Clum hunched forward in his chair. "I'm serious, Wyatt. Parker was right there, heard it himself."

"Maybe so," Earp said crossly. "But it's a barroom brag, whiskey talk! Nothin' to it."

"You don't understand. He had an actual list! All our names down on paper! Parker said he was waving it around, and telling everyone within earshot how we were as good as dead. To me, that sounds like Brocius talking, not whiskey."

"You're easy spooked, aren't you, John?"

Clum was a squat, fat man with sagging cheeks and heavy jowls. He lived by his wits, and because of his glib way with words, he had achieved some small success both as a newspaper editor and a politician. But he abhorred violence, and possessed almost nothing in the way of physical courage. His own fear repulsed him, and with increasing frequency, he damned himself for allowing Earp to dominate his life. Today, however, he mustered one last spark of defiance.

"I'm thinking of selling the newspaper."

"Whatever gave you a damnfool notion like that?"

"Bill Brocius," Clum confessed. "Or at least he tipped the scales. I've been considering it for some time."

"Not thinkin' of leaving Tombstone, are you?"

"Yes, I am," Clum muttered, lowering his eyes. "The Indian Agent resigned over at the San Carlos Reservation. I had an idea I might apply for the job."

"You'd have to pull some strings, wouldn't you?"

"I've still got a few connections left."

Earp rose from his chair. He stuffed his hands in his pockets and stumped to the window. He stood looking down Fremont Street toward the center of town. But his eyes were fixed upon distance, and events.

In the main, Earp relied on the flaws and frailties of other men. He was ambitious and bold, and he believed that the weakness of others forever gave him an edge. Once, in a rare moment of candor, he had remarked, "There's only two kinds of people in this world. Them that takes and them that gets took." He had lived the better part of his life by that very code. He used people to his own ends, and then discarded them.

Yet his lodestone was not power alone. It was, instead, the fruits of power. He craved respect, and he was obsessed with the need for respectability. In the cowtowns of Kansas, he had lost the struggle to achieve that goal. His brothers were notorious as whoremongers, and he himself had never risen above the status of common policeman. Uprooting the entire family, he had traveled to Tombstone, searching for a fresh start. From the onset, nothing had gone as planned, and the killings at the OK Corral had further undercut his position. Still, for all his business and political setbacks, he wasn't yet willing to call it quits in Tombstone. Nor was he ready to discard John Clum.

At length, he turned from the window. His face congealed into a scowl, and his tone was hard. "I don't

like that idea, John. I want you to stick with the newspaper till I say different."

"To what purpose?"

"The purpose we had in mind from the start. Behan
and his crowd have got the upper hand right now, but
that'll change. One way or another, I still intend to get
control of the county."

Clum shook his head doubtfully. "Wyatt, we're
through in Tombstone and we're through in Cochise
County. I saw the handwriting on the wall when the
town council overrode me and fired Virge as marshal.
I stuck by you, but now"—he faltered, toying nervously with his hat—"Brocius means to kill us, and I
haven't got the stomach for it. I just want out."

Earp dismissed his objection with a brusque gesture. "You keep thinkin' like that and you'll be
scratchin' a poor man's ass all your life."

"Better a poor man than a dead man, and that seems
to me the only choice."

"Well, by God, it's not your choice to make!
You're gutless but you're not stupid. So get the wax
out of your ears and pay attention."

Clum looked ill. "Are you threatening me, Wyatt?"

With an unpleasant grunt, Earp crossed the parlor
and resumed his chair. "I'm tellin' you I need the
mayor's office to back my play, and I need that newspaper to influence public opinion. Like it or not, that
means I need you. So let's don't hear no more talk
about you hightailin' it out of town. Savvy?"

"What happens when you don't need me any
longer?"

"Aww for chrissake!" Earp groaned. "Stop worryin'

so much. We're all gonna come out of this rich as Midas."

"I hope you're not talking about stagecoaches."

"You just tend to your knittin' and let me handle the details."

"Wyatt, listen to me, please! We can't afford any more trouble. One mistake and we'll all wind up in prison . . . or worse."

"There you go again, borrowing trouble."

"I'm simply stating a fact. Behan is watching us like a hawk, and Brocius has put our names on a death list. Good God, we're in too deep already! Why dig the hole any deeper?"

"The only holes I mean to dig are the kind with headstones. One for Brocius, and maybe even one for Behan—unless he stays clear of my business."

"No more," Clum pleaded. "I have nightmares about it, Wyatt."

"Nightmares about what?"

"Marsh Williams," Clum said hollowly. "There was no need . . . you shouldn't have—"

"Close your trap!" Earp glowered at him, motioning toward the kitchen. "The women are in there, so button up and stay buttoned up."

"Sorry. I guess I wasn't thinking."

Anger flashed in Earp's eyes, then his gaze narrowed and his look became veiled. "Don't lose your nerve on me, John. You might recall that's why Marsh Williams—disappeared."

"I know," Clum said in a resigned voice. "It won't happen again. You can depend on me, Wyatt."

"Never thought otherwise. Now, since you're here, let's talk a little business."

Earp leaned forward, elbows on his knees. The timbre of his voice dropped, and he began speaking in measured tones. John Clum listened, nodding attentively, all the while gripped by a numbing thought. He wondered if he would ever leave Tombstone alive.

In the kitchen, Alice Blaylock tried to close her mind to the drone of voices from the parlor. She had heard Earp's sudden outburst, and sensed that the mayor's visit had put her brother-in-law in one of his foul moods. Any hope for a pleasant Christmas dinner was now lost forever.

She was seated at a work table, peeling potatoes. Her sister, Mattie, stood at the sink, washing dishes left over from a late breakfast. The heat from an iron woodrange kept the kitchen toasty warm. A plump hen, already stuffed and in the oven, flooded the room with a savory aroma. It was, Alice told herself, the best of all times in the Earp household. A tranquil interlude, performing domestic chores, when she and Mattie could pretend the outside world didn't exist. Yet she knew it was only that—an interlude.

She glanced at Mattie, and a deep feeling of pity washed over her. Once attractive, Mattie was now worn and frail. Her complexion was prematurely lined by too many years in the harsh western climate. Her eyes, wrinkled at the corners by crows' feet, bore a perpetually worried expression. On her face were stamped the ravages of a cruel and unmerciful life. She was thirty years old, and looked at least forty.

Alice, who was four years younger, sometimes felt guilty about her own looks. Her black hair was drawn sleekly to the nape of her neck, accentuating the smooth contours of her face and the healthy glow of youth. Her eyes were dark and expressive, and she had a sunny, vivacious smile. She wasn't tall, but she carried herself well, dressing to compliment her slender figure. The overall effect was disarming and somehow provocative. A curious blend of innocence and minx-like worldliness.

Appearances aside, few people suspected that she was indeed an innocent. By contrast, the women of the Earp family were inured to the harsher realities of life. She had learned, much to her dismay, that vice had been their livelihood, almost a family enterprise. At times, she still had difficulty reconciling herself to the fact that Mattie was a retired prostitute.

A year ago, never once suspicioning the truth, she had come West to join her sister. Their parents, killed that spring in one of Ohio's perennial floods, had left her with meager resources. She had several suitors, hometown boys who bored her to distraction, and she briefly entertained the idea of marriage. But wedding a man for security rather than love was foreign to her character. Filled with romantic notions about the frontier, she had entrained for Arizona Territory.

Once in Tombstone, her schoolgirl illusions were quickly disabused. She found life in the mining camp coarse and uncivilized, with none of the colorful adventure she'd read about in dime novels. But her greatest letdown by far was Mattie's husband. She discovered her sister had married a monster.

By stages, a word here and a word there, she gradually learned the whole truth. Mattie, traveling the Kansas cowtowns with a troupe of entertainers, had been stranded in Wichita. Fallen on hard times, she was befriended by the Earps and lured into a life of prostitution. A year or so later, when the family departed for Dodge City, she went along as Wyatt's woman. Then, shortly before the move to Tombstone, they were married. Wyatt needed a wife to help him create a respectable front, and Mattie saw him as her last chance to outdistance the cowtowns. It was calculated and mutually advantageous. An arrangement.

Over the past year, Alice had learned all this and more. At first appalled, she slowly came to understand Mattie's reasons, and with understanding came acceptance. To her sorrow, she also came to understand that Wyatt Earp was, by nature, an insensitive brute. He was devoid of compassion, and in the privacy of his home, he sometimes displayed a sadistic streak. All the worse, he was corrupt and conniving, unscrupulous with anyone outside the immediate family. The killings last October—three men callously gunned down at the OK Corral—had left her chilled to the very marrow. She knew virtually nothing of death, and found it all but incomprehensible that she lived under the same roof with a killer. There was a sense of terror and unreality about it. The terror of awakening from a bad dream—and finding it true.

Insofar as her personal life was concerned, it had simply ceased to exist. The Earps were pariahs, and their women were the stuff of vicious gossip. In Tombstone, no decent man would tip his hat to an

Earp woman, much less pay her court or invite her to a social. Apart from Doc Holliday, and Wyatt's business cronies, few men ever came to the house anyway. She had no opportunity of meeting anyone worthwhile, and even less chance of being accepted by the respectable members of the community. Her name was Blaylock, and she'd done nothing to deserve censure. But to the townspeople, she was nonetheless one of the Earp women.

Alice often wondered how she had allowed herself to become trapped. Her own naivete was certainly one element, and her love and concern for Mattie was another. Yet she recognized all that as being more excuse than justification. On days like today, when she dwelled on it at any length, the situation seemed particularly noxious. Unless she was careful, she slipped into fits of self-loathing, and bitter regret. She searched for the strength to walk out the front door and never look back. Then, struck by the fact that she had no money and no prospects, she was reminded of a greater fear. Fallen on hard times, stranded in a remote mining camp, she too might resort to that older profession. The thought left her queasy, and desperate.

Mattie's voice intruded on her trancelike lapse. She suddenly realized she was sitting with the knife in one hand and a potato in the other, and staring blankly at the tabletop. She looked up and found Mattie watching her with a puzzled frown.

"I'm sorry," she said lightly. "I must have been star-gazing."

"We all do, honeybun. It's about the only form of entertainment the womenfolk in this family ever get."

"Did you ask me something?"

"After a fashion," Mattie observed, nodding toward the parlor. "When Wyatt and the mayor get through, I want you to be careful what you say."

"What would I say?"

"The less the better. And most especially, don't let on that we overheard what they were talking about."

Alice shuddered. "I overheard nothing. Absolutely nothing."

Mattie drew a deep, unsteady breath. "I'd give the world to say the same. Sometimes it's more than a body can stand."

"I know," Alice said darkly. "Every night I pray it just doesn't get any worse. Surely it won't, not after all this time."

"Oh Lordy!" Mattie said in a musing voice. "How I wish we'd never come to this town. I'd gladly kick it over and go back to Kansas."

"No, don't say—"

Alice stopped, glancing quickly toward the parlor. The men's voices were louder now, and the creak of floorboards filtered through the house. A few moments later the front door closed, and everything went still. Then the sound of footsteps became apparent, a measured tread growing closer. Alice began peeling potatoes, and Mattie grabbed the pump handle, jacking a rush of water into the sink. Neither of them gave any indication they heard the approaching steps.

Earp halted in the doorway. "When the hell we gonna eat? I've got business uptown."

"Damnit, Wyatt!" Mattie whirled around, hands on

her hips. "Won't your business keep till another time? It's Christmas!"

"So what?" Earp said sourly. "It's also a big gaming night, and in case you forgot, I'm a dealer."

"Well, I'd think you could take the night off. Especially Christmas night!"

"Just get it on the table and don't argue about it."

Earp turned and stalked back into the parlor. Mattie waited, listening until he had moved out of earshot. Then she winked at Alice and lowered her voice in conspiratorial whisper.

"We'll have our own Christmas! Just like old times, when we was kids and people still laughed."

"Yes." Alice smiled sadly. "Just like old times."

CHAPTER 4

Starbuck went undercover that night.

Around eight o'clock he eased through the door of the Alhambra. He was tricked out in a black broadcloth jacket, set off by a white linen shirt and a fancy string tie. On his head, cocked at a rakish angle, was a slouch hat, and on his feet he wore kidskin halfboots polished to a dazzling luster. A blind man would have spotted him as a professional gambler.

The Alhambra was one of Tombstone's finer gaming establishments. A mahogany bar ran the length of one wall. Behind it was a gaudy clutch of bottles with a gleaming mirror flanked by ubiquitous nude paintings. Along the opposite wall were keno and faro layouts, a roulette table, and a chuck-a-luck game. At the far end of the room were the poker tables, their baize covers muted by the cider glow of low-hanging lamps. The atmosphere was cordial and restrained, devoted solely to the pursuit of chance.

Halting at the bar, Starbuck ordered whiskey. After a couple of sips, he hooked one elbow over the counter and turned to survey the room. The crowd, much as

he'd expected, was a mixed lot. Tradesmen and drummers, spiffy in their townclothes, were ganged around
the tables with miners and cowhands and rough-
garbed teamsters. The action was fast and without
pause, broken only by a low murmur of conversation
and winner-loser calls by the housemen. To all appearances, the games were honest, relying on house
odds to turn a profit. The amount of money exchanging hands indicated the Alhambra was doing very well
indeed.

Starbuck's inspection was casual but nonetheless
exact. He spotted Earp at the faro layout and examined
him with the fleeting curiosity of a fellow craftsman.
His gaze drifted then to the back of the room, searching for Doc Holliday. From what Harry Woods, the
newspaper editor, had told him, Holliday was an in-
veterate poker player and a man of distinctive appearance. The information was accurate on both counts.
With no trouble, Starbuck located Holliday at the center table. Another glance confirmed that every chair at
all three tables was occupied.

Turning to the bar, he took out a silver cigar case
and selected a thin black cheroot. He struck a match,
lighting the cheroot, aware of its strange acrid taste.
As part of his disguise, he had chosen cigars over roll-
your-owns, which was more in keeping with the image
of a natty high-roller. He stuck the cheroot in the corner of his mouth, and stood for a moment reviewing
the plan he'd decided upon earlier. He saw no reason
to alter it now, for the physical layout of the Alhambra
dovetailed perfectly with what he had in mind. He

finished his drink and dropped a cartwheel on the counter.

Threading his way through the crowd, he walked toward the rear of the room. Several onlookers were clustered around the poker tables, and he casually moved through their ranks. Presently, after a brief inspection of each game, he took up a position near the center table. There were seven players, and it appeared to be a high stakes game. Out of the corner of his eye, he slowly scrutinized Doc Holliday. He was struck by the thought that here was a mankiller who looked the part.

Holliday was a tall, emaciated man, with ash-blond hair and a drooping mustache. Somewhere in his thirties, his visage was that of an undertaker; sober but not really sad. He wore a swallowtail coat and a black cravat, with a gold watch chain looped across his vest. His attitude toward the other players was an inimical union of gruff sufferance and thinly disguised contempt. Speculation had it that he had killed twenty-six men, and his manner left no question that he was equal to the task. He impressed Starbuck as someone who could walk into an empty room and start a fight.

The game was dealer's choice, restricted to stud poker and five card draw. Ante was twenty dollars, with a fifty dollar limit and three raises. Check and raise was permitted, which meant it was a cutthroat game, attracting players who took their poker seriously. The rules seemed tailor-made to Starbuck's scheme. All he had to do, he told himself, was somehow manage to beat Holliday.

That promised to be an uphill challenge. The former

dentist was a skilled gambler. He won on what appeared to be weak hands, and evidenced an uncanny knack for reading the other players. There was no pattern to his betting and raising; his erratic play made him unpredictable, and somewhat intimidating. He would bluff on a bad hand as often as he folded, and more often than not his bluff went undetected. On good hands, he would sometimes raise forcefully, allowing the money to speak for itself. At other times, when he held good cards, he would lay back and sucker his opponents into heedless raises. He was by far the best player at the table, and he won steadily.

Perhaps a half hour went past before one of the players quit the game. Starbuck jockeyed himself into position even as the man rose from his chair. Nodding around the table, he seated himself and smiled broadly. He pulled a thick wad of greenbacks from his pocket and made a show of stacking them neatly before him. Then he settled back in his chair and gave the other players a look of amiable bravado.

"Jack Johnson, at your service, gents."

Every eye at the table was on him, but no one spoke. Across from him, Holliday gathered the cards, riffled them expertly, and began dealing stud. Starbuck caught aces back to back on the first two cards, and checked. Then, on the third card, he began betting. Three players tried to draw out on him, but the aces held. He won an easy five hundred on the first hand.

Over the years, Starbuck had become something of an actor. His undercover work, by necessity, dictated that he assume various roles and disguises. Tonight, he was acting the part of a convivial smoothtalker. He was gregarious, outwardly charming, and presented himself as an affable jokester. He pulled it off with a certain panache, and he was utterly convincing. He was also lucky.

For the next few hours, the cards fell his way with consistent regularity. He won on small pairs, weak straights, and an occasional flush. More than his own luck, it seemed that fortune had deserted the other players. He was winning with hands that normally would have taken second place, and no pots. Yet, for all his luck, he was careful to establish a pattern. When he bluffed, he made a point of backing his play with unusually large bets. He used the ploy infrequently, but with jocular skill. Several times he was aware that Holliday was covertly studying him. With the trap baited, he awaited the right moment.

His chance came in the third hour of play. He opened a hand of five card draw with a fifty dollar bet. Everyone dropped out except Holliday, and he raised. Starbuck bumped it the limit and Holliday took the third raise. On the draw, Holliday took three cards and Starbuck stood pat. After another round of betting and raising, Holliday laid down two pair. Starbuck chuckled, spreading out three of a kind, and raked in the pot. He caught a tiny glint of surprise in Holliday's eyes.

A few hands later he again seized opportunity. The game was stud poker. With three cards dealt, he had a pair of tens showing, and bet fifty dollars. Holliday obviously couldn't believe he would try the same gambit twice running, and tested with a raise. Starbuck merely called, and checked the bet on the fourth card.

But on the fifth card he again bet the limit. Holliday raised, certain now he was bluffing. He bumped it fifty and waited, puffing on his cheroot. Holliday watched him narrowly a moment, then called. He flipped his hole card, revealing a third ten.

"Three tens wins! Better luck next time, mister."

Holiday grunted coarsely. "I got to admire your style, Johnson. That's twice you sandbagged me."

"Well, sir, I'd say twice is plenty for one night. I thank you kindly."

Starbuck stood, pocketing a considerably larger roll of greenbacks. He scooped up a handful of gold coins and nodded cheerily to the other players. Then he turned to leave.

Holliday fixed him with a querulous squint. "Some folks think it's not polite to win and run."

Starbuck mugged, hands outstretched. "No offense intended, but there's the other side of the coin. Some folks never learn to quit when they're ahead."

Holliday coughed, wheezing hoarsely, and pulled a handkerchief from inside his coat pocket. He covered his mouth, waiting until the wheezing subsided, then raked Starbuck with a cold glare. "A sporting man would give the losers a chance to recoup a bit before he ducks out."

"Glad to oblige!" Starbuck gave him a nutcracker grin, and clamped the cheroot between his teeth. "Another day, another time—but not tonight!"

Bowing, he flipped Holliday an offhand salute and walked away. Behind him there was a pall of silence, and he noticed some of the onlookers watching him with odd looks of disbelief. Clearly, no one had ever gaffed Holiday and lived to tell the tale. He thought he'd pulled it off rather neatly.

Drifting back to the bar, he took up a position directly in front of the mirror. He felt reasonably confident Holliday wouldn't push the matter further. Still, there were no guarantees, and he'd learned never to take undue chances with known gunmen. After ordering a drink, he leaned into the bar, casually dropping his right hand below counter level. He was now carrying the Colt in a crossdraw holster, and the butt was within an inch of his fingertips. The wide backbar mirror gave him a view of the entire room. With one eye on Holliday, he was also able to observe Wyatt Earp at work.

Faro was one of the more popular games in western cowtowns and mining camps. Its name derived from the image of an Egyptian pharaoh on the back of the cards, and the game had originated a century earlier in France.

Cards were dealt from a specially adapted box, and the player bet against the house. Every card from ace to king was painted on the cloth layout that covered the table. A player placed his money on the card of his choice, and two cards were then drawn face up from the box. The first card drawn lost and the second card won. The player could "copper" his play by betting a card to lose instead of win. There were twenty-five turns, since the first and last cards in the deck paid nothing. When the box was empty, the dealer shuffled and the game began anew.

Normally, the house hired an experienced gambler to operate the game. The dealer worked for a salary, plus a small share of the winnings. Sometimes, when a gambler had developed a reputation and a following, the house leased him the concession. Through Harry Woods, Starbuck had learned that this was the arrangement between Earp and the Alhambra. The game was Earp's and he backed the faro bank with his own money. The house received a weekly payment for the concession, plus a percentage of the winnings. With luck, and a knowledge of human nature, a faro operator could earn a handsome living. Which was one of the things that bothered Starbuck.

A handsome living hardly seemed sufficient for a man of Earp's demonstrated ambition. His activities in Tombstone left no doubt that he had raised his sights to a larger game, and much higher stakes. So far he had failed, but he was obviously undeterred. Otherwise he would have cut his losses and gone off in search of riper opportunity. The faro game, then, was merely a front. Wyatt Earp stayed on in Tombstone for reasons as yet unrevealed. Once uncovered, those reasons might very well provide the key to robbery and murder. And put a rope around Earp's neck.

Some while later, Starbuck noted a lull at the faro layout. The last player, clearly a loser, walked away and left Earp alone at the table. It was the opening Starbuck had waited for, and time to put the second stage of his plan into operation. He steeled himself to play it fast and loose—and act the part.

With a sauntering step, he moved across the room. The expression on his face was peacock proud, the look of a gambler who had found his mark for the night and scored well. He halted before the table, smiling pleasantly.

"How's tricks?"

"Tolerable." Earp's eyes were impersonal. "Care to try your luck?"

"Yessir, I do!" Starbuck said carelessly. "Got a sudden urge to buck the tiger."

"Get a hunch, bet a bunch."

Earp deftly shuffled the cards and allowed Starbuck to cut. Then he placed the deck in the dealing box and burned the top card, commonly referred to as the "soda" card. Glancing up, he nodded, indicating the game was open to play. Starbuck dug out his handful of gold coins, placing one above the ace, another between the five-six, and still another between the jack-queen. By playing several cards at once, he immediately marked himself as a professional. The system was known as "coppering the heel," and increased the chances of winning. Earp pulled two cards from the box, a king and a four.

"Close," he said in the slick cadence of a pitchman. "Give 'er another go."

"Keep dealing!" Starbuck laughed, scattering coins across the layout. "I'm on a streak tonight."

Earp was adroit and quick. His hands flashed between the box and the layout with practiced expertise. Cards popped out of the box in speedy pairs, and just as rapidly he paid the winners and collected the losers. Starbuck continued to "copper the heel," but for every bet he won, he lost double and sometimes more. He blithely tossed coins about the layout, alternately chuckling and cursing with the gusto of a man who was enjoying himself immensely. Halfway through the deck, the last of his gold coins disappeared. By the time the "hoc" card, the last card in the deck, was turned, he was deep into his wad of greenbacks. Within a matter of minutes, Earp had trimmed him for something more than a thousand dollars.

"Seems like the worm's turned."

"Damned if it don't!"

"Maybe it's just as well," Earp remarked. "Doc don't tolerate people that quit winners. He'll likely simmer down now."

"Doc?"

"Doc Holliday." Earp nodded toward the poker tables. "The fellow you snookered a while ago."

"No kiddin'!" Starbuck's eyes widened in feigned astonishment. "*The* Doc Holliday?"

"The one and only."

"Well I'll be double-dipped! I sure hope there's no hard feelings. You reckon he's still sore?"

"Don't wory about it," Earp advised wryly. "Doc wouldn't monkey with a customer of mine."

"How's that?"

"You might say we're on a first name basis."

"Wait a minute—" Words appeared to fail Starbuck. "Your name wouldn't be . . . are you Wyatt Earp?"

"Yeah, I generally answer to it."

"Judas Priest!" Starbuck grinned foolishly, and began pumping his arm. "I read all about you in the newspapers! That shootout you had with those desperadoes. It's an honor to meet you, Mr. Earp. Yessir, a puredee honor!"

Earp regarded him with impassive curiosity. "You new to Tombstone?"

"Pulled in last night," Starbuck said eagerly. "Name's Jack Johnson—my friends call me Jack."

"I take it you're a gamblin' man?"

"Poker's my game." Starbuck flicked an ash off his cheroot, and chuckled softly. "Course, I got a fatal weakness for faro. Keeps me busted most of the time."

"Johnson?" Earp eyed him thoughtfully. "Turkey Creek Jack Johnson?"

Starbuck had lifted the alias from a dead man. The risk was slight, with virtually no chance of exposure. But now, pretending wariness, he gave Earp a guarded look.

"What makes you ask?"

"Heard of you," Earp commented. "Deadwood, wasn't it?"

"You name it. Leadwood, Cripple Creek, Deadwood. I've worked all the camps."

"I was in Deadwood once't."

"Oh, when was that?"

"Back in '76."

"Before or after Hicock was killed?"

"Few months before."

Starbuck wagged his head. "You should've been there. I wasn't standing ten feet away when Jack McCall drilled him through the head."

"You saw him get it?"

"Doggone right!" Starbuck puffed importantly on his cheroot. "Saw it with my very own eyes!"

"I heard tell," Earp said in a voice without tone,

"he was holdin' aces and nines when he got it. Any truth to that?"

Starbuck sensed he was being tested. The reason was unclear, but he played along with a straightface. "You must've heard wrong. It was aces and eights. Goddamn cards had to be pried out of his hand."

"Likely you're right," Earp agreed idly. "What brings you to Tombstone?"

"Well—" Starbuck hesitated, then smiled cryptically. "You might say I came south for my health."

"Lots of folks do." Earp appeared to lose interest, indicating the layout. "Care to give it another try?"

"Not tonight!" Starbuck laughed. "I'll have to find me a poker game just to break even."

"Do yourself a favor and gaff somebody besides Doc. I'd like to keep you as a regular customer."

"Damn good advice." Starbuck bobbed his head, grinning. "See you next time I'm flush."

"Anytime, Jack. You're always welcome at my table."

Walking away, Starbuck silently congratulated himself. The next step would be easier. And the one after that, easier still.

CHAPTER 5

Early the next afternoon, Starbuck went for a stroll. Other than the hotel and the Alhambra, he'd seen little of the town since arriving. Like a wolf prowling new territory, he always felt more comfortable once he had his bearings. He reminded himself to avoid the Wells, Fargo office and the *Nugget*. Those were places to be visited only after dark.

Upon leaving the hotel, he walked west on Allen Street. Tombstone was laid out in a grid pattern, with the business district centralized in the heart of town. The main thoroughfares were Allen Street and Fremont Street, both crossing the grid east to west. North and west of downtown were the better residential areas. To the south were warehouses and the less desirable residential quarter. Vice, in the form of cribs and parlor houses, was restricted to the eastern section of the community.

Allen Street boasted most of the saloons and gambling establishments, along with three additional hotels and the Birdcage Theatre. One block north, on Fremont Street, was the main commercial district. City

Hall and a couple of banks were flanked by several blocks of cafes, shops, and general business concerns. At night, when Tombstone's sporting element awakened, Allen Street came alive. But during the day, Fremont Street was the busiest part of town. Here the hustle and bustle of everyday affairs was conducted in a more sedate atmosphere.

Starbuck was in no hurry, and he criss-crossed the town at a leisurely pace. As he walked, he gained a better perspective into Wyatt Earp's motives. Tombstone, by light of day, revealed itself as a veritable money tree. The outlying mines were processing millions of dollars of silver every year. Unlike most mining camps, the influx of people and a stable economy had created a sense of permanence. Whoever controlled the political apparatus of Cochise County would have access to a fortune in graft and taxes. Whoever wore the sheriff's badge would play a key role in the distribution of that largesse. Moreover, the sheriff's office would provide a legitimate front for other, less acceptable, forms of skullduggery. It was small wonder that Earp had twice sought the post of the county's chief lawman.

Had Earp been elected, the tin star would have made him all but invulnerable. Starbuck saw that even more clearly now; there would have been no way to infiltrate the ranks of a crooked sheriff and his henchmen. Yet a common gambler—not to mention a social leper—was an altogether different matter. Starbuck had only to prove that he and Earp were birds of a feather. He could then progress to a chummier relationship, and invent some device to make himself valuable. From there, it would require only time and guile until he wormed his way into Earp's confidence. A similar dodge had worked with all manner of horse thieves and cattle rustlers. And he had every confidence it would work with an overly ambitious faro dealer.

Around midafternoon Starbuck paused at the corner of Fifth and Fremont. His gaze fell on a general emporium, and he recalled he was almost out of cigars. He entered the store, and moved directly to the counter. A clerk hurried forward.

"Yessir, what can we do for you today?"

"Need a box of cheroots."

"Any special brand?"

"You got Varga's Deluxe?"

"Yes, indeedy." The clerk turned toward the shelves, calling back over his shoulder. "Take your time, Miss Blaylock. I'll only be a moment."

The name struck a chord. Starbuck glanced around and saw a girl one aisle over, inspecting yardgoods. She was small and compactly built, with attractive oval features. A woolen shawl was draped across her shoulders, and curls the color of sable were visible beneath her bonnet. He thought to himself she was easy on the eyes. Not a beauty, but close enough to draw second looks.

Then the name clicked, and he instantly made the connection. Harry Woods had mentioned Earp's sister-in-law. *Alice Blaylock*. And it hardly seemed possible there would be two Miss Blaylocks in a town the size of Tombstone. He felt reasonably certain this was the girl.

Before he could think it through, the clerk returned with his cigars. He paid, waiting for his change, all the while weighing the possibilities. Nothing workable occurred to him, but he resolved somehow to make her acquaintance. According to Woods, she was the only single woman in the entire Earp family. That, in itself, presented a grab bag full of options.

Outside the store, he walked upstreet a short distance. He halted in front of a mercantile, playing for time, and made a production of lighting a cheroot. Here, he told himself, was a made-to-order opportunity. If he could get close to the girl, that might very well open the door to the Earp household. Which wouldn't exactly make him one of the family, but it would be a large step in the right direction. On top of that, he'd been known to charm a few girls out of their undies and leave them begging for more. With a little romance and sweet-talk, he might easily con her into spilling all the family secrets. Certainly, he had nothing to lose by trying. The only stickler was how to approach it. He couldn't let on that he knew her name, yet he had to manage it in some offhand manner. And quickly!

Out of the corner of his eye, he saw her leave the emporium and turn in his direction. She was carrying several bundles, wrapped in brown paper, and the distance was closing rapidly. With no time to plan it out, he simply reverted to the old standby.

Puffing on his cigar, he gave every appearance of being engrossed with the mercantile's window display. As she approached, he suddenly turned and bulled directly into her path. The collision rocked her back on her heels and sent her packages flying. She gave a little yelp of fright, clutching at her bonnet.

"Pardon me, ma'am!" Starbuck grabbed her arm, supporting her. "Are you all right?"

Alice Blaylock nodded, trying to collect herself. "Yes, I think so. At least nothing seems broken."

"I'm sure sorry!" Starbuck hurried on. "No excuse for it! You're so dainty and all, I might've hurt you bad."

"No, really," Alice assured him. "I'm perfectly fine."

"Well, it was awful clumsy of me all the same. You just catch your breath and let me tend to those bundles."

Starbuck quickly gathered her packages off the boardwalk, and stuck them under one arm. Almost as an afterthought, he took the cheroot from his mouth and tossed it into the street. Then he gave her a lopsided grin, and tipped his hat.

"Jack Johnson, ma'am. And purely mortified to make your acquaintance like a runaway steam engine."

"No need to apologize, Mr. Johnson."

"Well now, that's mighty kind of you, Miss—?"

"Blaylock. Alice Blaylock."

"Miss Blaylock," Starbuck murmured pleasantly. "Here, let me carry these bundles for you aways. That's the least I can do, after nearly bowling you over."

Alice looked startled, on the verge of objecting. Then she seemed to change her mind. She smiled, turning uptown, and he fell in beside her.

"Are you new to Tombstone, Mr. Johnson?"

"I am, for a fact," Starbuck said genially. "How'd you guess?"

It was no guess. Every member of the Earp family was known on sight to the townspeople. Only a stranger would have failed to recognize her, and on sudden impulse, Alice found herself quite taken with him. He was courteous, with a certain rough charm, and rather good looking. Far and away the nicest thing that had happened to her since coming to Tombstone. She silently thanked her stars that he was indeed a stranger.

"I've lived here a while," she said casually. "I suppose you might say I'm one of Tombstone's old timers."

"Say now!" Starbuck's face split in a grin. "I reckon that makes it my lucky day."

"Oh, how so?"

"Because," Starbuck suggested, "you being familiar with the town, you might take pity on a stranger."

Alice blinked with surprise. "Excuse me?"

"I know it's bold as brass, but I was hoping you'd have dinner with me. I'd sure count it an honor, Miss Blaylock."

"Dinner?" Alice repeated the word as if she couldn't have heard correctly. "You're asking me out?"

"Yes, ma'am," Starbuck said smoothly. "I might never get another chance, and I wouldn't want to risk that."

"I—" Alice sounded uncertain. "I don't know."

"I'm a gentleman." Starbuck's square face was very earnest. "I don't take liberties with ladies, and you wouldn't have to worry a minute. You've got my word on it, and anybody will tell you—Jack Johnson's word is good as gold!"

Starbuck buttered her up all the way to the corner. By then, her head was spinning and she found herself completely captivated by his jocular manner. When they parted, he had directions to her house and an engagement for dinner. He tipped his hat, grinning, and strolled away. She felt slightly giddy, and dared not pinch herself.

Night was coming on as Starbuck approached the Earp house. To the west, under a darkening sky, low clouds scudded across the horizon. Out of habit, he tested the wind, then quickly set the thought aside. Tonight, he had only one concern, and it wasn't the weather.

Nor was it the girl. If anything, she had proved more gullible than he'd expected. She had fallen for his glib line and he felt she could be coaxed along very nicely. His major concern was Wyatt Earp. However innocent it appeared, he knew his chance meeting with the girl would draw suspicion. All afternoon he had schooled himself to give a sterling performance. Earp would be waiting when he entered the house, and at that instant, there would be no margin for error. He had to appear genuinely dumbfounded—flabbergasted!

Freshly shaved, and reeking of bayberry lotion, he mounted the porch stairs. Halting, he removed his hat and took a tight grip on his nerves. Then he knocked.

A few seconds later the door opened. Wyatt Earp, expressionless, stood framed in a glow of lamplight.

"Mr. Earp!" Starbuck gave him a walleyed look of amazement. "What are you doing here?"

"I live here."

"You—" Starbuck shook his head. "I thought this was the Blaylock house."

"C'mon in." Earp moved aside. "I'm married to Alice's sister."

"Well, I'll be damned!" Starbuck said with a dopey grin. "Don't that take the cake? You're kin!"

"After a fashion." Earp closed the door, turning to a man standing nearby. "Like you to meet one of my brothers. Virge, this here's Jack Johnson."

Virgil Earp was a lean man, with hard eyes and a slow smile. The family resemblance was immediately apparent, and like his brother, his upper lip was covered with a brushy mustache. He offered his hand to Starbuck and they shook once, a hard up-and-down pump.

"Pleased to meet you, Mr. Johnson."

"Jack," Starbuck said affably. "Folks call my pa Mr. Johnson."

"Wyatt tells me you're a gambler."

"That's my trade."

"Appears we've got lots in common, don't it?"

Starbuck played dumb. "We do?"

"Alice," Virge remarked. "First time she says boo to a stranger, and you turn out to be a gamblin' man."

"Well—" Starbuck darted a sheepish glance at Earp. "Look here, I hope there's no hard feelings about me asking her out. If I'd known she was related, I would've worked out a proper introduction. No two ways about it!"

"She's full grown," Earp informed him. "Treat her right, and you won't hear no complaints out of me."

"I appreciate it, Mr. Earp. That's mighty white of you."

"Why don't you forget that Mr. Earp stuff. The name's Wyatt."

Before Starbuck could reply, Alice entered from a hallway door. Her dress was navy serge, clearly the remnants of better days, and the same woolen shawl was thrown over her shoulders. But her hair was curled in elaborate finger-puffs and her eyes positively shone. She moved across the parlor with willowy grace.

"Good evening, Mr. Johnson."

"Ma'am." Starbuck faked a bemused smile. "I was just telling Mr. Earp—Wyatt—that I sure didn't mean any disrespect. I never had a glimmer you two was related."

"Fiddlesticks!" Alice flashed her brother-in-law a look. "He knows that very well."

Earp nodded solemnly. "I already told him he's welcome, Allie. Don't get yourself worked up."

Starbuck sensed an underlying tension, and suppressed a smile. Earp and the girl were clearly at odds, which fitted perfectly with his plan. He made a stab at polite conversation, but it went along in fits and starts, then petered out altogether. Finally, with Alice edging toward the door, he bid the Earp brothers goodnight. A wide grin plastered across his face, he waved and followed her into the night.

When the door closed, Virge muttered a low oath. "I don't like it."

"Your crystal ball workin' overtime, is it?"

"You asked me over here to size him up, and I'm tellin' you—he smells like trouble!"

"Maybe, maybe not," Earp allowed. "You didn't see his face when I opened the door. He goddamn near swallowed his tongue."

"C'mon, Wyatt," Virge scoffed. "You've conned too many people in your time to be taken in by that."

"Yeah, and I know the difference, too. I've got a hunch he's on the square."

"What happened to coincidence?" Virge reminded him. "Last night he sits down at your table out of the clear blue. Today he just accidently happens to bump into Allie on the street. You was the one that said it went against the odds."

"I've been wrong before," Earp said stubbornly. "I just don't think he could've fooled me. Nobody's that good an actor."

Virge's look was colored by skepticism. "Still seems awful damn peculiar he showed up so soon after Marsh Williams . . . disappeared."

"Soon?" Earp demanded. "Hell's fire, close to a month's passed. I don't call that soon."

"Confound it, Wyatt!" Virge said hotly. "What if he's a Wells, Fargo agent? You're stakin' a helluva lot on the fact that he didn't pee down his leg when you opened the door."

"Well, one thing's for certain," Earp said sardonically. "Whatever he is or isn't, he's got Allie in a halfway decent humor. I take my hat off to him for that."

"You're beggin' for trouble, Wyatt. And if you're not careful, you're liable to get it."

Earp frowned. "All right, if it'll ease your mind, sound him out the first chance you get. Turkey Creek Jack Johnson ought to know all there is to know about them northern mining camps."

"By God, don't worry! I'll do that very thing!"

Earp slumped down in a chair and crossed his legs. He smiled to himself, remembering the look on his sister-in-law's face. With time, and encouragement, Johnson might just take the little bitch off his hands. For good and forever.

On the walk downtown, Starbuck kept the conversation light and inconsequential. True to his word, he intended to treat her like a lady. And not a lady of negotiable virtue, like the other Earp women. Such a novelty would impress her, and bring her all the more quickly to his bed. Then the real work could commence.

With her hand tucked inside his arm, he continued to play the raffish charmer. "Did Wyatt tell you how I clipped Doc Holliday?"

"No," she said with a firmness that surprised him. "He didn't."

"Uh-oh!" Starbuck chuckled. "I hope you haven't got anything against gamblers. Wyatt must've told you that's how I make my living."

"Not gamblers," she confided, a spark of deviltry in her eyes. "Just Doc Holliday."

"Can you keep a secret?"

"Try me and see."

"I don't like him either," Starbuck said jokingly. "Never could stand a sore loser."

She cocked her head in a funny little smile. "Do you ever lose?"

"Now you're asking trade secrets."

"Tell me," she said brightly. "Do you?"

"Promise it won't go any further?"

"Cross my heart and hope to die."

"Well . . ." Starbuck lowered his voice. "I lose, but only when I want to. See what I mean?"

"You're not a cardsharp, are you?"

"No, ma'am!" Starbuck appeared wounded. "But when I set my mind to it, there's no man alive who's my equal at a poker table."

She suddenly looked quite enchanting. "Then I hope you beat them all! The sore losers most especially!"

"You know," Starbuck gently squeezed her hand. "I think I'm going to like this town."

She laughed softly. "I think you will, too."

Something in her voice startled him. Though he couldn't quite define it, he knew it wasn't to be discounted. There was more to Alice Blaylock than met the eye, something worth exploring. But for now, he played it for laughs.

"You're not making any promises, are you?"

"No." She gave him a mysterious smile. "Not yet."

CHAPTER 6

A haze of smoke hung suspended in the lamplight. The men seated around the poker table were a democratic admixture of the mining camp. There were three miners, a couple of teamsters, and a whiskey drummer. And Jack Johnson.

The hour was late and the game was slowly winding down. Starbuck, seated where he could watch the room, was the heavy winner. He lost often enough to keep the other players gaffed, but it was clearly his night. His mood was jovial, almost ingenuous, and he was at some pains to humor the losers. He was also cheating.

On the third finger of his left hand Starbuck wore a simple ring. The stone was common onyx, set in a plain gold band. It was unnoteworthy, and to all appearances of no great value. On the underside of the band, however, it was somewhat more remarkable. A small, all but invisible, needle point protruded from the bottom of the band. Among professional gamblers it was known as a "nicker" or "needle ring."

The ring provided Starbuck several advantages over

the other players. While dealing, early on in the game, he had pricked the face of key cards in the deck. This prick raised an imperceptible bump on the top of the card. Useless a man's fingertips were unusually sensitive, the bumps were virtually undetectable. Earlier, Starbuck had sandpapered the pads of his fingers, and as a result, it was somewhat like reading Braille. Simply by shuffling, he was able to identify almost half the cards in the deck.

Whenever he dealt, the coded bumps allowed him to locate key cards. Then, by dealing seconds, he was able to give himself the necessary cards for a winning hand. Since he also "read" the cards dealt to other players, he had several options. To avoid suspicion, he dealt himself a winner every fourth or fifth time around. The rest of the time, he dropped out and dealt a winning hand to a player whose luck had gone sour. With skill, and the law of averages, he also won his share of the hands dealt by others. No one suspected anything out of the ordinary, nor did they begrudge him what seemed a remarkable hot streak. It was a nifty dodge, and he worked it artfully.

Starbuck's purpose was to effect the next step in his courtship of Wyatt Earp. By establishing himself as a cardsharp—utterly lacking in honesty—he hoped to win acceptance within Earp's circle of cronies. He had selected tonight, only two days after his dinner with Alice, for the most expedient of reasons. Virgil Earp had wandered into the Alhambra shortly after the supper hour. Doc Holliday, whose own game broke up earlier than usual, had joined Virgil at the bar. As the night progressed, they had slowly, ever so gradually, worked their way to the end of the counter. From there, they had an unobstructed view of the poker table.

Starbuck scarcely glanced at them throughout the evening. Yet he was aware of their keen scrutiny whenever it came his turn to deal. Solely for their benefit, he staged a demonstration of dexterity and adroit card manipulation. Some years ago, as part of his undercover repertoire, he had taken lessons from a master cardsharp turned saloonkeeper. His performance, then, was not that of a tinhorn gambler. It was faultless, very professional, and thoroughly convincing.

Several times he saw them exchange glances with Earp. From the faro table, Earp nodded in return, and it seemed certain there was something more afoot than simple curiosity. He got the strong impression that Virgil Earp and Doc Holliday were waiting for his game to end. He had no idea what they intended, but the signals being passed were somehow ominous. Wyatt Earp, quite clearly, had rigged a surprise of his own for tonight.

Around midnight the poker game ground to a halt. Starbuck was easily a thousand dollars ahead, but no one seemed to take it personally. He told a bawdy joke—while pocketing his winnings—and left them laughing. It was the final touch, one he knew wouldn't be missed by the men at the bar. A true grifter always left his marks in a congenial frame of mind. Which made them all the easier to pluck next time around.

Walking to the bar, he was acutely aware that a new game was about to commence. He had no inkling as to its rules, nor did he know where it would lead. But he sensed it would be played in dead earnest.

"Evening, gents," he said cheerily. "Buy you a drink?"

Holliday wore his perpetually constipated expression, sour and tight-lipped. Virge's greeting was civil but cool. He nodded toward the poker table.

"How'd you come out?"

"Broke the game!" Starbuck crowed. "Damnedest run of luck you ever seen."

Holliday loosed a harsh bark of laughter. Suddenly his face reddened and he was racked by a spasm of coughing. Only after he managed to knock back a whiskey did the coughing subside. He glanced around, wiping tears from his eyes with a handkerchief.

"Some folks get shot for that kind of luck."

By now, Starbuck knew that Holliday was afflicted with consumption. Devoid of fear, since he was already on speaking terms with death, the cadaverous gambler had the edge in any fight. Whether he meant to provoke a showdown now was a moot question. Starbuck couldn't believe they had learned his true identity; but neither could he risk dropping his masquerade. He chose his words carefully.

"Outhouse luck, Doc! Here today, gone tomorrow!"

Before Holliday could respond, Virge quickly broke into the conversation. "Wyatt tells me you worked Leadville."

"A time or two," Starbuck said, wondering if he'd misread Holliday. "Not many camps I haven't worked."

"I heard Leadville's gone plumb to the dogs."

"Don't you believe it! There's easy pickings for any man that knows his way around."

"That's funny." Virge's bushy eyebrows seemed to hood his eyes. "Somebody told me Jeff Winney had folded the Texas House and gone on back to New Orleans."

Starbuck suddenly recognized the game. He was being grilled, and none too subtly. The Earps had apparently decided on one more test, with a trap thrown in for good measure. He swiftly turned it to advantage.

"That somebody," he laughed, "don't know his ass from his elbow about Leadville. First off, Bailey Youngston owns the Texas House, not Jeff Winney. And he's from down around Galveston way, not New Orleans. Hell, that's why he named his joint the Texas House!"

"Beats all!" Virge said levelly. "Fellow don't know who to believe no more."

Starbuck wedged his cheroot in the corner of his mouth. "Tell you what, Virge. It'd be like stealing money, but I'll lay you twenty to one that Jeff Winney never even set foot in the Texas House."

"No, you're likely right." Virge hesitated, then gave him a sharp sidelong look. "Wyatt says you come south for your health?"

"One of them things," Starbuck shrugged. "Some jasper went on the prod and I had to stop his clock."

"What set him off?"

"Would you believe it?" Starbuck said with mock indignity. "The sonovabitch accused me of cheating at cards!"

Holliday snorted and turned his eyes heavenward.

Virge bit down hard on a smile, seemingly stumped for another question. After a moment, he shoved away from the bar, flicking a glance in the direction of the faro table. Then he consulted his watch.

"Well, boys, time flies. I gotta be gettin' home."

"I'll walk along," Holliday added. "Got a late game waiting at the Oriental."

"Yeah?" Starbuck grinned. "Maybe I'll sit in a while. The way my luck's running tonight, I can't be beat."

Holliday examined him with a kind of cold objectivity. Then he grunted something under his breath and walked away. Virge and Starbuck fell in behind, following him toward the door. All the way along the bar, Starbuck felt a strange sensation centered between his shoulder blades. He had little doubt that Earp was zeroed on him like a watchful chickenhawk.

Outside, Virge waved and turned uptown. Holliday turned in the opposite direction, striding off toward the Oriental. Starbuck trailed alongside him, and they walked several paces in silence. Then Holliday riveted him with a sullen stare.

"None of your tricks. It might work with those bohunk miners, but I won't tolerate it in my game."

"So you caught that?" Starbuck laughed. "Christ, I must be slipping."

"No, Johnson," Holliday said cynically, "you're not slipping. You just weren't good enough to start with. A needle ring, for God's sake!"

Starbuck's reply was cut short by the hammering roar of gunfire. There were four blasts in rapid succession, and he instantly catalogued it as two men with double-barrel shotguns. All in a split-second, he and Holliday whirled, drawing pistols. The street was empty and still.

Then they spotted Virge. He lay in the gutter, where the boardwalk dropped off to the street. The dim glow of the corner streetlamp bathed him in a spectral light. He was flat on his back, spraddle-legged and unmoving.

Starbuck sprinted to the corner, cautiously checking the sidestreet. There was no one in sight, and as he turned back, Holliday dropped to one knee beside Virge. In the glow of the streetlamp, he saw that the shotguns had done a savage job. The buckshot had blown away part of Virge's coat, and what lay underneath looked like freshly butchered beef. His left arm dangled by a thread of bone flesh at the elbow.

"Get Wyatt!" Holliday thundered. "Get him quick!"

Starbuck took off running toward the Alhambra.

A stark silence permeated the house. Everyone in the parlor was immobile, their eyes fixed on the hallway door. Their mood was one of people drawn together in a deathwatch, forlorn and without hope.

The entire Earp family, all the brothers and their wives, had gathered at Virge's home. Following the shooting, Starbuck and Earp had improvised a stretcher and carried him across town. Holliday, meanwhile, had gone to fetch Tombstone's only surgeon, Dr. George Goodfellow. Now, dreading the worst, they waited for the surgeon to emerge from the bedroom. He had been operating on Virge for nearly an hour.

Starbuck stood with Alice near the front door. She gripped his hand tightly, her face pale and drawn. His presence obviously comforted her, and thus far no one had objected to him intruding on a family affair. His expression was properly solemn, but he shared none of their concern. Whether Virge lived or died was the farthest thing from his mind. He was, instead, fascinated by the tableau of the Earp family.

Until tonight he hadn't fully appreciated their numbers. Earp, his features stony and cold, dominated the group. Seated around the room were Jim, the eldest brother, and his wife. Nearby were Morg and Warren, both younger and considerably more robust in appearance. Virge's wife, whose expression was ghastly, was huddled in a corner with Mattie and the other wives. Doc Holliday, sipping from a flask, stared morosely at a spot on the wall. Their silence was palpable, and strangely unnatural.

To an outsider, their stoicism was difficult to credit. Starbuck noted that Virge's wife, despite her hollow-eyed gaze, hadn't yet shed a tear. The three brothers, like Earp, were stolid as oxen. No one spoke, and no one registered the emotion normally expected under such circumstances. It was as though any public display of sentiment had been prohibited. Whatever they felt, whatever hurt and suffering they shared, was bottled up deep inside. The effect was eerie, somehow scary. Not unlike an assemblage of brutes contemplating a bleached skull.

The spell was broken as Dr. Goodfellow appeared in the hallway door. His sleeves were rolled up and his shirtfront was speckled with blood. His expression was grim.

Earp spoke for the family. "How is he, doc?"

"Alive," Godfellow said calmly. "I got all the buckshot out of his side and back. So far as I can tell, his spine wasn't damaged."

"What else?" Earp insisted. "Let's hear it all."

Goodfellow pursed his lips. "Wyatt, I'm sorry to say it doesn't look good. I may have to amputate his arm, but he's too weak to survive major surgery. We'll just have to wait and hope his condition improves."

"Will he pull through?"

"I wouldn't hazard a guess. Quite frankly, it could go either way."

"Why now?" Earp's iron impassivity suddenly deserted him. He turned away, his eyes garnet with rage. "Goddamnit, why now?"

Virge's wife rose from the settee and crossed the parlor. Without a word, Dr. Goodfellow took her arm and escorted her down the hall. A moment later there was a faint click as the bedroom door closed.

Morg abruptly jumped to his feet. "I'll tell you why! We waited too long. We should've gone after them the minute charges was dropped against you and Doc."

"He's right!" Warren blurted out. "Brocius and them bastards figured we was runnin' scared. Otherwise they wouldn't've never done that to Virge!"

"I second the motion." Holliday saluted them with his flask. "Get them before they get us! I told Wyatt that very thing myself."

Starbuck looked from one to the other, spellbound.

He knew Morg had killed a man in the shootout at the OK Corral, and Warren was reportedly no slouch with a gun as well. Unbidden, a thought popped into his head. He realized he was listening to a brotherhood of murderers. Not just Earp and Holliday, but the entire family. All of them were cold-blooded killers.

"Take the fight to them!" Morg said vindictively. "If we don't, they're gonna pick us off one by one just as sure as hell."

Warren nodded vigorously. "The same way they did Virge!"

"Better listen, Wyatt," Holliday affirmed. "You keep trying to polish your image, and we're all liable to go up the flume."

"That'll do!" Earp said sternly. "We'll move when I say so, and not before."

"You and your damn politics!" Morg exploded. "It's not worth it, Wyatt! Not anymore."

A strained stillness settled over the room. Earp's jaw muscles knotted and a vein pulsed in his forehead. His brothers seemed to shrink back under his scowl, and he stared at them for several moments. Then, remembering himself, his gaze shuttled to Starbuck. His look once more became stolid, impenetrable.

"You boys," he admonished his brothers, "forgot we have company. Let's leave it till another time."

Starbuck took the hint. "Listen, I didn't mean to butt in on family business. I'll get on back to the hotel and catch some shut-eye."

"I'm obliged to you," Earp said quietly. "Virge and me owe you one."

"Forget it," Starbuck replied, opening the door. "I

was glad to lend a hand. Let me know how Virge gets along."

Alice walked him outside. She looked stunned. Her eyes were dulled and her features were completely drained of color. He took her hands, searching her face in the pale starlight.

"What's wrong?"

"I'm afraid," she told him. "The killing has started again, and it won't end here."

"Don't worry," Starbuck gently advised. "Wyatt and his brothers can take care of themselves."

"It's not them!" She squeezed his hands fiercely. "I'm worried about you."

"Here now," Starbuck chuckled. "You've got no call to worry about me. I'm an old hand at looking after number one."

"Get out now!" she said vehemently. "Don't let Wyatt draw you into his fight."

"All things considered, he's treated me pretty square."

"Wyatt doesn't have friends! He uses people and"— her voice became a desperate whisper—"they end up dead."

Starbuck lifted her chin, smiled. "You can ease your mind on that score. I aim to live a long time."

The door opened and Earp stepped onto the porch. As he moved down the stairs, Alice brushed past him and hurried inside the house. He glanced back at her, then halted in front of Starbuck.

"She upset?"

"Some," Starbuck admitted. "It's been a bad night."

"Bad as they come," Earp agreed. "I'm a little

touchy myself. Otherwise I wouldn't have cut you off so quick a minute ago."

"Don't give it another thought. No offense taken."

"Good." Earp paused, studying the ground. "Doc tells me you've got troubles of your own."

"Leadville?" Starbuck wagged his head. "No, that's likely water under the bridge by now."

"Wish ours were," Earp said bitterly. "Way things look, there's rough times ahead."

"Well, listen here now! You need any help, all you've got to do is holler. I mean it!"

"I appreciate the offer, Jack. And I'm not one to forget a favor."

"What the hell!" Starbuck flipped a palm back and forth. "Us gamblin' men have got to stick together."

Earp shook his hand warmly and they parted. Walking toward town, Starbuck had to restrain himself from laughing out loud. Tonight had worked out even better than he'd planned. Especially where Earp was concerned.

The sorry bastard had taken the bait, hook and all!

CHAPTER 7

For New Year's Eve, the diningroom in the hotel had been-cleared of furniture. Gaudy bunting and little Japanese lanterns festooned the ceiling, and the floor had been waxed to a mirror polish. The Volunteer Firemen's band thumped sedately over the strains of an upright piano.

Alice looked ravishing tonight. Her hair, dark as a raven's wing, was arranged in an upswept style that accentuated her oval features. Her eyes sparkled and her mouth seemed poised for laughter. She was animated and vivacious, and for one night she was clearly determined to set aside worldly troubles. She smelled sweet and alluring, and she clung joyously to Starbuck.

Holding her at arm's length, Starbuck swung her gracefully across the dance floor. For a large man, he was surprisingly light on his feet. His step was better suited to the stomping beat of a dancehall, but he managed the waltz without once stepping on her toes. It was their first dance of the evening, and already he knew he'd gauged her mood correctly. Her eyes never left his face, and her dreamy expression spoke louder than words. She was his for the asking, and he sensed she would deny him nothing. Tonight was the night all her secrets would be revealed.

When the dance ended, they walked toward a refreshment table near the front of the room. The crowd was steadily increasing, and a large throng was congregated around the punchbowl. Though other hotels were holding dances, the Occidental's gala was considered the only affair suitable for decent people. Tombstone's uppercrust, merchants and bankers and mine owners, formed a snobbish, tightly knit society all their own. So far, Starbuck and Alice had been treated with polite diffidence. A gambler and his lady weren't particularly welcome, but no one seemed inclined to make an issue of it. The general consensus was apparently one of benign tolerance.

Then, quite suddenly, the atmosphere changed. A buzz of conversation swept over the room, and Starbuck noticed that people were staring toward the entrance. Turning, he saw Morg and Warren Earp, accompanied by their wives, standing in the wide doorway leading to the lobby. As the foursome advanced into the room, the murmur from the crowd took on an ugly note. Couples near the doorway quickly moved to the opposite side of the dance floor. The Earps and their women were left in an uncomfortable vacuum.

Starbuck took Alice's hand and led her across the floor. He totally ignored the stares of onlookers and their muttered comments. With a wide grin, he greeted the Earps, shaking hands forcefully. Their wives looked painfully embarrassed, and he had no doubt the brothers had forced them to attend the dance. As usual, the women wore dresses that appeared to have been purchased at a rummage sale. The men, by comparison, were dandified fashion plates.

"Glad you folks made it," Starbuck said warmly. "I haven't seen a familiar face since we got here."

"You likely won't, either." Morg shook his head in disgust. "Our kind isn't exactly welcome at this shindig."

"Say listen, don't let this bunch of swells put your nose out of joint. It's New Year's Eve!"

"They don't seem to bother you none."

"Nosiree!" Starbuck jerked a thumb toward the crowd. "Anybody looks cross-eyed at me and I'll tell'em to stuff it where the sun don't shine."

"Jack!" Alice giggled. "They'll hear you."

"So what?" Starbuck said loudly. "Maybe an earful would do them good."

Morg burst out laughing. "You're a regular rooster, aren't you?"

"Live and let live, that's my motto."

Starbuck was mentally calculating how the moment could be turned to advantage. Thus far, he'd had no opportunity to speak with the two youngest Earp brothers. He judged Morg to be in his mid-twenties, and Warren a year or so behind. From their one meeting, he had sized them up as youthful hotheads, and therefore vulnerable. A man whose temper ruled his tongue often talked too much for his own good. What, if anything, they might reveal was sheer speculation. But it was very definitely worth a try.

"How's Virge?" Starbuck went on, suddenly sober. "Any improvement?"

"Not a whole lot," Morg said in an aggrieved tone. "He'll pull through, but it's touch and go with his arm."

"That sawbones still want to amputate?"

"Hard to say. This afternoon he told Wyatt there's no sign of gangrene. But he wouldn't commit himself one way or the other."

"Wyatt over at the Alhambra tonight?"

"No," Morg remarked. "Him and Doc are at Virge's. We're taking turns watching the house."

"You really think Brocius would try it again?"

"That crazy jaybird's liable to try anything."

Starbuck appeared thoughtful. "What's Brocius like, anyway? Crazy crazy or crazy like a fox?"

"What makes you ask?"

"Well, for one thing, he don't seem to take too many chances. He steered clear of that shootout you had with his boys, and now he ambushes Virge. Offhand, I'd say he's a pretty slick article."

"Slick, hell!" Warren struck into the conversation with an oath. "He's a dirty yellow bushwhacker! Why d'you think he got Virge in the back that way?"

"I was wondering about that," Starbuck said lazily. "What made him pick Virge? Why not Wyatt or Doc?"

"Who knows?" Warren snapped. "More'n likely he took whoever come along first."

"Queer, though, isn't it?"

"I don't follow you."

"Tell you the truth, I don't rightly follow myself. I

guess I was trying to puzzle out what's behind it."

"What's behind what?"

"Why he wants blood so bad. A man's got to hate awful strong to shoot somebody after all that time."

"Seems simple enough to me," Morg explained. "Virge was marshal the day we killed three of his men."

"But it's not just Virge," Starbuck insisted. "You said the other night he was after the whole family."

Morg's mouth hardened. "Are you sayin' he's not?"

"No, nothing like that! I'm just asking why—why he wants all of you?"

"Same reason," Morg said flatly. "We all had a hand in his men gettin' killed."

"Yeah, maybe." Starbuck looked doubtful. "But if he just wanted revenge, why did he wait so long? One dark night's as good as another."

"Tell you what." Morg's eyes suddenly became guarded. "Why don't you ask Brocius? If he's got other reasons, then he's keepin' them to himself. All I know is what I told you."

Starbuck decided to let it drop. The exchange had failed to provoke anything of value, and Morg was clearly growing suspicious. He spread his hands in an empty gesture.

"Hell, maybe he's just plain crazy after all. There's an old saying that some men will commit suicide in order to commit murder. Way it looks, he fits the ticket all the way round."

The band segued into another waltz and he held out his hand to Alice. She stepped into his arms and they joined the crowd on the dance floor. Waving to the

Earps, he grinned broadly and left them once more in their vacuum. Several minutes later he saw them turn and walk out through the lobby. He had gained nothing from the discussion, but he was in no way discouraged. The night, and Alice, still held great promise.

At midnight Tombstone's gentry lost some of their highfalutin ways. The band struck up "Auld Lang Syne," and sedate revelers were instantly transformed into riotous merrymakers. A lusty roar shook the rafters, and the prohibition not to covet thy neighbor's wife was momentarily suspended. The crowd swirled together in a mass kissing bee.

Starbuck took Alice's face in his hands and brushed her lips with a soft kiss. She regarded him a moment with an odd steadfast look. Then her arms circled his neck and she pulled his mouth to hers in a sensuous invitation. He responded, enfolding her tightly within his arms. When they parted, he gave her a suggestive smile.

"Too bad we never get any privacy."

Her voice was husky. "There's really no way . . . to be alone."

"I know a place."

"You do?"

"Upstairs." Starbuck rolled his eyes upward. "There's lots of privacy in my room."

"I—" She stopped, unable to meet his gaze. "I'm afraid, Jack. The desk clerk would see us and then . . . everyone would know."

"Not through the lobby." Starbuck nuzzled her ear,

lowering his voice. "The backstairs, behind the hotel. Nobody would see us there, especially now."

"Oh?" she said in an indrawn breath. "Are you sure?"

"Positive," Starbuck assured her. "Take a look around. They're all too busy making fools of themselves."

She darted a glance at the boisterous crowd. Then she moved closer, like a seductive butterfly. A ghost of a smile touched her lips, and she gave him a bright nod.

"I do want to be alone with you, Jack."

Their departure went unnoticed. Starbuck took her hand and they walked out through the lobby. Behind them, the revelers were still shouting and kissing and tooting paper horns. The desk clerk, stifling a bored yawn, scarcely looked at them.

Outside the hotel, Starbuck checked both ways along the street. Several drunks were gathered near a corner saloon, but the boardwalks were otherwise deserted. Walking to the side of the building, he wheeled sharply left and they vanished into the alley. Several seconds later he led her up the backstairs and through a second-floor doorway. The hall was empty and he quickly fished the room key out of his pocket. Ushering her inside, he locked the door and tossed his hat in the direction of the bureau. Then he turned and gathered her into his arms.

Whatever he expected, he was not prepared for the urgency of her embrace. Her lips were soft and moist, and her mouth parted in a hunger born of loneliness and need. She kissed him long and passionately, her body pressed fiercely against his own. He felt her breasts pushing into him and her hips moving against his loins. She moaned as he caressed her back and fondled the rounded curves of her bottom. A convulsion gripped her and her nails pierced his coat like talons.

He lifted her in his arms and carried her toward the bed.

A long while later she lay with her head nestled deep in the hollow of his shoulder. Her hair, unbound and falling loose, fanned darkly across the pillow. She slept like a naked child clutching something warm and familiar in the dark.

Starbuck was awake and thoughtful. He believed he possessed a special sixth sense. A kind of visceral instinct that cut through the tangled skein of emotion and reasoned logic. He had learned to accept it and trust it, something far more reliable than mere hunch. When it came over him, there was no blurred uncertainty, no troubling doubt. Too many times that instinct alone had saved his life. He survived because he'd always obeyed his gut, not his head.

Tonight that sense of conviction had never been stronger. But with it came something new and unsettling. He felt a stab of conscience.

The girl beside him was no virgin, but neither was she a whore. Somewhere in the midst of their lovemaking that inner certainty had washed over him. She was unlike the other Earp women, an innocent among rogues. There was nothing to substantiate the feeling, no word or act, no deductive explanation. He simply knew she was not, either in mind or spirit, a part of the Earp family. She was an outsider, alien to all with the possible exception of her sister. His instinct told him it was true.

The realization made him uncomfortable with himself. He had deceived her, strung her along, and purposedly kindled her affection. Now, under false pretenses, he had brought her to his bed and stoked that affection even higher. His conscience, which he normally kept whipped into submission, had suddenly rebelled. He wasn't at all sure that the end still justified the means.

Seldom introspective, he was a man with few illusions left intact. He saw life and people as they were, through a prism of cold reality. The dead men littering his backtrail had taught him that a cynic was rarely disappointed. Yet the girl lying peacefully in his arms deserved a better shake. Thus far he'd used her, and if his investigation was to succeed, he must continue to use her. While she might be an outsider to the Earps, she was his only inside source of information. To level with her could very well jeopardize that source. Expediency dictated that he play on her affections, and guile her into revealing whatever she knew. The idea was no longer abstract, some impersonal, though essential, part of the job. He would do it, but the thought left him troubled inside. He saw a part of himself he didn't much like.

"Penny for your thoughts."

Her voice broke into his reverie. He glanced down and found her watching him with a warm smile. Quickly, all regret shunted aside, he got on with the task. He grinned, gently stroking her hair.

"Why spoil the evening?"

"Good Lord!" She squirmed around, lifting herself on one elbow. "Now you have to tell me."

"Well—" Starbuck paused for effect, then shrugged. "I was just thinking you're not too wild about your brother-in-law."

"Wyatt?"

"Yeah, him most especially. But I get the idea you don't care much for any of that crowd."

She stared at him in silence, her dark eyes filled with some buried emotion. "What makes you say that?"

"Tricks of the trade. A gambler gets to be a pretty good judge of people."

"I suppose it's no secret," she said, not without bitterness. "For Mattie's sake, Wyatt and I tolerate each other."

Starbuck could see anger and a trace of fear in her eyes. "Why is it I get the feeling you're afraid of him?"

Her words were almost inaudible, so quiet he had to strain to hear. "Because I am."

"Afraid?"

"Scared to death."

"Why?" Starbuck inquired evenly. "Wyatt seems like a pleasant enough sort."

"You don't know him."

"I know he's got a reputation with a gun. But the way I hear it, he had cause."

"Did he?"

"Wait a minute." Starbuck looked confused. "Are

we talking about the same thing? I understood him and Doc were cleared of that shooting scrape."

"They were," she murmured uneasily. "Only there was more to it than that."

The admission startled Starbuck. He sensed she was hinting at the death of Marsh Williams, the Wells, Fargo agent. He warned himself to proceed with caution.

"You mean there was something that didn't come out in court?"

"Not something." She tossed her head. "Everything!"

"Damnation!" Starbuck chuckled lightly. "Don't tell me he gunned down somebody else!"

"Jack—" She hesitated, exploring his face. "I'm acting silly, and talking very foolish. Please forget I said anything, will you? Promise me, Jack . . . please?"

"Count it done," Starbuck nodded. "But don't wait 'til things get out of hand. If you ever need help, all you have to do is yell."

"Oh, Jack." She kissed him tenderly. "You don't know how much that means to me."

Starbuck thought he knew very well. She was quite obviously terrified of Wyatt Earp. Yet, on the other hand, her hatred for him was barely contained. At the right time, under the proper circumstances, both her terror and her hatred could be exploited to the fullest. Until then, he could afford to be patient. And sympathetic.

"One thing's for sure," Starbuck said absently. "Wyatt must have some powerful business connections."

"Business connections?"

"Why, sure. Otherwise he would've been railroaded out of town long before now."

She stared gravely into his eyes. "I know nothing about his business. And I don't want to know."

Starbuck knew he had touched another nerve. But that too could await the right moment. He cupped her chin in his hand.

"All I meant was, you don't have to worry about him or his connections. You just whistle and I'll come running."

She shifted in his arms, and he pulled her into a tight embrace. His hand covered one of her jutting breasts and the nipple swelled instantly. Then her hand touched his manhood, erect and throbbing, and she grasped it eagerly. She was ready for him, damp and yielding, and she uttered a low moan as he penetrated quickly, slipped deep within her.

He gave her salvation, and hope.

CHAPTER 8

A week later Starbuck's patience began wearing thin. His nerves were gritty and restless, and he had a sense of marking time. His investigation had gone nowhere.

The evening was crisp and chill. He paused on the hotel veranda, lighting a cheroot. For a moment, he debated calling on Alice. Her company would be far more enjoyable than spending another night watching Earp and Holliday. Still, however tedious, he wasn't one to shirk responsibility. There was a job to be done, and Alice could contribute little or nothing at this point. He walked toward the Alhambra.

On balance, Starbuck had to admit he was stymied. After the attempt on Virge's life, he had expected action of some sort. He wasn't certain what form that action would take; but he'd felt reasonably confident it would lead to a break in the case. The last thing he'd expected was what Wyatt Earp had actually done. Nothing.

To whatever purpose, Earp was playing a waiting game. Shortly after New Year's, he and Holliday had reverted to their normal routine. Every night found them at the Alhambra, business as usual. They were more cautious now, particularly on the streets after dark. But there was no mention of Curly Bill Brocius, and no hint that retaliation of any nature was in the works. To all appearances, it was as though the assassination attempt had never occurred.

Starbuck was at a loss. He needed something concrete to make a case, some tangible evidence. Yet that was heavily dependent on worming his way into Earp's confidence. So far, the ploy hadn't worked. Earp trusted him, but Earp didn't need him. And there was the crux of the matter. To become a member of the clique, it was necessary that Earp need his services, and his gun. Only then would Earp and the other members of the family speak freely around him. Equally apparent, only then would he have access to evidence linking them to robbery and murder. The fly in the butter was all too obvious. His gun simply wasn't needed.

On one side, Earp seemed content to sit on his thumb. On the other, Brocius and his gang had attempted no further treachery. The vendetta appeared to have degenerated into a stalemate, with neither side disposed to make the next move. It was a sorry mess, and getting sorrier all the time.

Entering the Alhambra, Starbuck found Holliday nursing a drink at the bar. While the evening was still early, Earp already had several players ganged around the faro layout. Starbuck waved, receiving Earp's nod in return, and moved toward the end of the counter. Halting beside Holliday, he signaled the barkeep.

"No game tonight, Doc?"

Holliday frowned. "Some of the regulars ought to drift in later."

"Maybe I'll sit in."

"We'll likely have a full table."

"Not afraid of the competition, are you, Doc?"

"There's your game." Holliday indicated a group of miners, seated at one of the poker tables. "Those boys are just about your speed."

The barkeep poured Starbuck a drink, and he took a long sip. Then he smacked his lips, grinning. "You know what your trouble is, Doc?"

"I'm fresh out of guesses."

"You're worried a smooth article like me might slip one past you."

"That'll be the day," Holliday said glumly. "I could spot you dealin' seconds with my eyes closed."

"Yeah, and I can deal'em with *my* eyes closed, too!"

"Johnson, you've got more brass than a barrel of monkeys. I'll give you that much."

Starbuck was aware that Holliday hadn't fully accepted him. There was still a tinge of skepticism in the gambler's attitude. And perhaps an element of resentment as well. Holliday was jealous of anyone who got close to Earp. His spite took the form of sarcasm and belittling remarks, and the personal rancor was openly apparent. His soliloquy on Bat Masterson was a gem of character assassination.

Pondering on it, Starbuck had concluded that Holliday had only one friend in the entire world. The greater curiosity was that he had fooled himself into believing the loyalty went both ways. In truth, Earp used him and would readily discard him if ever he became a liability. The paradox was that a cynic like Holliday deceived no one but himself. Had he asked, anyone in Tombstone could have told him he was expendable.

Holliday suddenly stiffened. Following the direction of his gaze, Starbuck saw Sheriff John Behan walking toward them. Though he knew the lawman on sight, he'd never had occasion to exchange so much as a greeting. His instinct told him that was about to change.

Behan stopped a couple of paces away. He was a stocky bulldog of a man, with a square tough face and humorless eyes. Starbuck guessed he was the type who wouldn't smile easily, if at all.

"Holliday, I'd like a word with you."

"What's on your mind, Sheriff?"

"The Benson stage."

Holliday faced him directly. "What about it?"

"A couple of hours ago," Behan said in a flinty voice, "four men robbed the stage outside Contention."

"So?"

"So I'm askin' where you were about sundown."

"Standin' right here!" Holliday bristled with indignation. "Not that it's any of your business."

"Anytime a stage gets robbed, I make it my business. Can you prove you were here?"

"I don't have to prove it."

"Yeah, you do. Unless you'd rather take a walk down to the cooler."

"Back off!" Holliday said sharply. "You've got nothing on me."

"The driver," Behan informed him, "says one of the robbers fitted your description. That'll do for openers."

Holliday fixed him with a baleful look. "I haven't set foot out of here, not once."

"He's giving it to you straight, Sheriff."

Earp halted at the lawman's elbow. Behan moved back as though he'd been stung by a wasp. His mouth set in a hard grimace.

"I don't recall askin' you, Earp."

"I'm tellin' you," Earp said tightly, "whether you ask or not. Doc's been here all evening."

"You alibied him the last time I arrested him."

"And it held up in court. You ought to know by now, Doc don't have to rob stages for a living."

"How about you?"

"Careful, Behan." There was a hard edge to Earp's tone. "Don't push your luck."

"Are you threatening an officer of the law?"

"I'm telling you not to come in here and rawhide honest citizens. If it's stage robbers you're after, why don't you take a crack at Brocius and his gang?"

Behan eyed him keenly. "You'd like that, wouldn't you?"

"Damn right!" Earp said shortly. "After the way they ambushed Virge, I don't reckon they'd be above robbin' a stage."

"Suppose we stick with you and Holliday."

"Are you accusin' me, too?"

"I'm not accusing anybody. I'm askin' you to explain your whereabouts, and I mean to have an answer."

"You've already had your answer."

"That's not good enough," Behan countered. "You and Holliday would alibi one another till hell freezes over."

"Try me, then." Starbuck's voice was firm. "I'll vouch for both of them."

Behan looked him over like a mule he was considering buying, "Johnson, isn't it?"

"Jack Johnson," Starbuck acknowledged. "I've been here since suppertime, and it's like Doc says. They haven't set foot out of the place."

"You'd swear to that, would you?"

"On a stack of bibles ten feet tall."

"You might just have to do that, Johnson."

Behan spun on his heel and stalked out. When the door closed, everyone realized the room had gone still as a church. The crowd suddenly stopped gawking and the hubbub of conversation rose to a deafening pitch. Earp shook his head in disgust, exchanging a veiled glance with Holliday. Then his gaze shifted to Starbuck.

"Wasn't no need to lie, Jack. I appreciate the gesture, but anybody could tell him you'd just walked in here."

"Hell's bells!" Starbuck laughed. "A little white lie never hurt nobody. Specially a lawdog!"

"Well, all the same, we're obliged. Aren't we, Doc?"

"Johnson," Holliday clapped him on the shoulder. "How'd you like to take a chair in my game tonight?"

"Doc, I think we'd make a puredee fortune together."

"None of your tricks! You hear me? Keep it
straight!"

Starbuck grinned. "You've got yourself a deal, Doc.
Straight as an arrow, that's me!"

Late that night Starbuck parted company with Earp
and Holliday. He mounted the stairs of the hotel veranda, watching a moment as they continued up the
street. Then he moved inside, quietly closing the door
behind him. The night clerk, dozing fitfully on one of
the couches, continued snoring. He catfooted across
the lobby.

Upstairs, he walked directly to the rear door. On
the landing outside, he paused and surveyed the darkened alley. Then, satisfied no one was around, he went
down the backstairs. He turned left and hurried to the
corner. There, he checked in both directions before
darting across the street. With utmost caution, he
worked his way from alley to alley, hugging the shadows whenever possible. His general direction was
north, toward Safford Street.

As he skulked through town, Starbuck's thoughts
were confused, speculative. There was something
strange about tonight's stage robbery. He knew Earp
and Holliday weren't involved, but the robbery
seemed somehow part of a broader pattern. Over the
past two weeks he had forged a tenuous link between
Earp and the Brocius gang. Though the proof was still
to come, the obstacles had not seemed to him insur-
mountable. Yet tonight had introduced an element that

left him baffled. The robbery had triggered the realization that a piece was missing. The sum of the known parts suddenly no longer added up to a whole. The jigsaw puzzle was incomplete.

Starbuck now considered the situation intolerable. Something was about to happen—or had already happened—and he sensed it would have a profound effect on the case. Yet he hadn't the vaguest notion of what it was, or who had done it. Nor was there any defensive measure he could take to counteract its effect. Not only was he fighting in the dark, he was grappling with an unknown, and that left him only one recourse. He had to take the offensive—and fast.

A half hour later he paused in the alleyway behind Harry Woods' home. He waited several minutes, wondering if Woods kept a yard dog, then decided there was no way to avoid the risk. He walked quickly to the back door, flattening himself in the shadows. He rapped lightly with his knuckles, listening a moment. Then he rapped harder.

The wait seemed interminable. At last, the glow of a lamp lighted the house. Through the window, he saw Woods appear in a hallway, dressed in a nightshirt. The editor entered the kitchen and hurried to the back door.

"Who is it?"

"A friend," Starbuck said in a muffled voice. "Douse the light."

The lamp went out and Woods slipped the door latch. "Come in, Luke."

"Sorry to bother you so late at night."

"It's quite all right."

Starbuck stepped into the kitchen. Woods locked the door, then moved around the room pulling windowshades. A match flared and he relit the lamp. His eyes were gummed with sleep and he peered at Starbuck like a weary gnome.

"What's wrong, Luke?"

"We've got trouble," Starbuck told him. "I need your help."

"Here, sit down." Woods pulled out a chair at the kitchen table. "What's Earp done now?"

"Harry, I wish to hell I knew."

Starbuck straddled a chair and began talking. He briefed Woods on the stage robbery and Sheriff Behan's visit to the Alhambra. Then, omitting the spicier details, he related the extent of his progress with Alice Blaylock. Finally, he gave a rundown on his dealings with Earp and Holliday, and the Earp brothers. He kept it brief, but covered all the salient points.

"That's about it," he concluded. "Or leastways as much as means anything."

Woods looked impressed. "I would say you've made excellent progress. What seems to be the problem?"

"Not *the* problem," Starbuck commenced in a sandy voice. "A whole batch of problems! Earp acts like he's waiting on an egg to hatch. I don't see any sign of him taking the trail against Brocius. And unless he does, then there's no reason for him to ask my help." He paused, slowly shook his head. "On top of all that, I've got a gut-sure hunch there's something I don't know. Something damned important."

"Oddly enough," Woods observed, "I was seriously

debating whether or not to contact you. It's just possible Earp has already hatched his egg."

"How's that?"

"Let me start at the beginning," Woods replied. "You may recall you asked me to check into Earp's business interests. With no one the wiser, I was able to gain access to both the town and county tax records. It turns out that Mr. Earp is a man of some means."

Starbuck suddenly came alert. "He owns property?"

"Several properties," Woods corrected. "Some in his own name and some in the names of various family members. Altogether, the Earp family owns eleven town lots outright. More importantly, Earp has a fifty-fifty interest in four rather substantial mining properties."

"Fifty-fifty?" Starbuck furrowed his brow. "Who owns the other half?"

"Some of the most prominent businessmen in Tombstone. Their names wouldn't mean anything to you, but they went to great pains to keep their dealings with Earp an absolute secret. Much of it was done through lawyers and paper corporations."

"Sounds like you've done a bit of detective work yourself."

"Indeed, I have," Woods admitted. "It's taken me the better part of two weeks, and led me through a maze of legal hocus-pocus. But I think it yielded some rather impressive dividends."

"Damn right!" Starbuck confirmed. "Our faro dealer turns out to be something more than he appears."

"He's a sly and devious man. I think it's fair to say

he was creating powerful alliances that would have eventually led to political control of Cochise County. After that, there would have been no stopping him."

"Lift a rock and find a scorpion." Starbuck was silent a moment, thoughtful. "You said something about him already having hatched his egg. Were you referring to this political alliance?"

"Not entirely," Woods remarked. "I'm not sure what it means, but this afternoon I happened across a curious piece of information. Within the last two weeks or so, Earp has sold his interest in three of the mining properties. He's also unloaded eight of the town lots."

"Goddamn!" Starbuck slammed his fist down on the table. "That's it!"

Woods was startled. "That's what?"

"The missing piece!" Starbuck said quickly. "He's getting ready to run."

"I fail to see the connection."

"Virge was shot on December 28. That's ten days ago, and Earp started selling off his properties right after it happened. He's just waiting around till Virge is well enough to travel. Then he's going to make dust for parts unknown."

"Hmmm?" Woods considered a moment. "You know something, Luke? It makes sense. Very good sense!"

"Maybe for Earp," Starbuck conceded. "But I don't like it one damn bit. Matter of fact, we'll have to move quicker than I thought."

"Quicker?"

"Harry, I want you to write an article about Behan

bracing Earp and Holliday. Play it up big! Tell the whole world how Earp stood right up in the Alhambra and laid the robbery off on Brocius. Tell them how he accused Brocius of ambushing Virge. Put it in big black headlines that he called Brocius a coward and a dirty yellow bushwhacker. Smear it all over the front page. No holds barred!"

Woods appeared puzzled. "To what purpose? What do you hope to accomplish?"

"I mean to push somebody into making a mistake."

"Earp?"

"Or Brocius," Starbuck nodded. "I want one of them to start shooting, and I don't much care which side kicks it off."

"Then Earp enlists your help and you become a member of the club . . . correct?"

Starbuck smiled. "That's the general idea."

"You're pretty devious yourself, Luke."

"I try," Starbuck said, grinning. "One other thing. When you get a minute, check out the dates Earp bought each of those properties."

"May I ask why?"

"So we can compare the purchase dates with a list of dates that stages were robbed. I'm betting we'll get a pretty close match."

Woods blinked. "Not even Earp would be that— arrogant."

"Harry, I've learned one thing about crooks and desperadoes. I've never yet seen it fail."

"What's that?"

"All of them," Starbuck laughed, "confuse balls with brains."

CHAPTER 9

The Clanton ranch lay in the foothills of the Whetstone Mountains. Across the vast emptiness there was a sense of desolation. The land sloped sharply downward as it stretched toward the San Pedro River, broken occasionally by buttes and treacherous arroyos.

Some miles west of Tombstone, there was no road as such leading to the ranch. Instead, a rutted trail bordered the river, eventually ending at a remote settlement called Charleston. On the afternoon of January 10 a rider appeared southward along the trail. His horse was lathered and spent, but he held it to a gallop as he rode toward the ranch headquarters. A ramshackle collection of buildings, the compound consisted of a main house, a cook shack and bunkhouse, and a log corral. No working ranch, it was a waystation for Mexican cattle rustled by the Brocius gang.

The rider slid his horse to a dust-smothered halt before the house. Vaulting from the saddle, he left the horse wheezing and near collapse. Hurrying forward, he jerked a soiled newspaper from his coat pocket and burst through the door. Inside, he slammed to a stop and waved the newspaper aloft.

"You ain't gonna believe what I got here!"

The men sprawled around the room were a rough lot. Their clothes were rank, and with the exception of one man, none of them had taken a bath since the last time it rained. The smell of unwashed bodies, stale food, and rotgut whiskey left the room permeated with a rainbow of odors. For several moments, no one spoke. They stared at the man holding the newspaper with looks of bored disinterest. Finally, he advanced toward a large man slouched down in a rickety chair. He shook the newspaper as though swatting flies.

"You made the front page, Bill! Wyatt Earp says you're—"

Bill Brocius snatched the paper out of his hand. A huge man, wide and tall, Brocius had thick curly hair and full mustaches. He snapped the paper open and began reading. His lips moved as he labored with the words, and his face slowly colored to the hairline. A leaden silence ensued while he scanned the article. Then he suddenly balled the newspaper into a wad and hurled it across the room.

"That sonovabitch!" he snarled. "Gawddamn if he couldn't lie his way out of a locked safe!"

Pete Spence, who had brought the newspaper, wisely took a chair. Frank Stilwell glanced at Johnny Ringo, who was slumped in a battered, cane-bottomed rocker. On a dilapidated sofa, Ike and Finn Clanton, owners of the ranch, exchanged a quick look. At last, Ike leaned forward and retrieved the newspaper. Unwadding it, he moved back beside his brother, and skimmed through the article. His mouth popped open in astonishment.

"Talk about the pot callin' the kettle black! The dirty scutter out and out accuses us of robbin' the Benson stage."

"That ain't no lie," Stilwell chuckled. "Unless I was dreamin', we did."

"Mebbe so," Finn Clanton allowed. "But he's still got no call to be sayin' it out loud."

"Why not?"

"Because he ain't so clean himself. That's why!"

"You'd play hell provin' it, and don't nobody know it better than him."

"Oh yeah?" Ike Clanton chimed in. "How about all them times Holliday give us the lowdown on stage shipments?"

"That was Holliday, not Earp."

"Same difference!" Finn retorted. "Earp don't itch without Holliday scratchin' his ass."

"I'm not sayin' otherwise. I just said we ain't got no proof of that."

"Johnny does!" Finn said positively. "Earp slipped up once't, and was standin' right there when Holliday gave Johnny the dope. Ain't that right, Johnny?"

Ringo lolled back in his rocker, one leg hooked over the chair arm. "You've got a big mouth, Finn."

"Awww—" Finn Clanton's wise-ass smile faded under his cold stare. "C'mon, Johnny! I didn't mean no harm."

"Then button your lip and leave my name out of it."

Ringo was swarthy man, with muddy eyes and sleek, glistening hair. He was clean-shaven, neatly dressed, and smelled like a lily compared to the others. Among all the gang members, he was the one authentic *pistolero*. Some years ago, when his brother was murdered in Texas, he had tracked down the four killers and dispatched them in *mano a mano* gunfights. When angered, his face became stern as a deacon's and his eyes turned to chilled stone. The other men saw that look now, and prudently left him to himself.

Ike Clanton, who was again perusing the newspaper article, suddenly erupted. "Dirty rotten sheep-humper! You boys wanna hear what Mr. Godalmighty Earp thinks of us?"

"Sure thing!" Stilwell cackled. "Couldn't be no worse'n what we think of him."

"He says"—Ike squinted hard at the paper—"and this here's his own words, 'Bill Brocius is a yellow-livered coward. He and his gang of penny-ante bad-men drygulched my bother with never a chance. They are nothing but bushwhackers and backshooters, the lowest form of vermin known to man.' That's what he called us! Them exact words!"

Everyone turned to look at Brocius. He glowered back at them, outrage stamped across his face. He shook a finger at Ike.

"Keep readin' and you'll find out he said all that standin' at the bar in the Alhambra. Made himself a regular gawddamn speech! Told it to the world and anybody that'd listen."

"Bastard!" Finn muttered. "He's sure got a lot of room to talk, don't he?"

Stilwell looked confused. "What d'you mean?"

"What he means," Brocius rumbled, "is that Earp and his brothers make us look like pikers. They're nothin' but common murderers, and pretty damn open about it! Ain't that right, Ike?"

Ike Clanton flushed beet red. Any mention of the OK Corral shootout brought the bright light of shame to his eyes. On that October day, less than three months past, he had shown the white feather. As the Earps and Holliday approached the livery stable, he had darted forward, screaming hysterically that he was unarmed. Then, as the shooting commenced, he had taken refuge in a nearby photographer's studio. From there, he watched the final execution of his own brother, Billy Clanton, and the two McLowery brothers. He was the lone survivor, and it was simple cowardice that had saved his life. The memory of that day had dimmed none at all. He still burned with guilt, and the other gang members held him in studied contempt.

"I'll tell you one thing," he said with false bravado, unable to meet their eyes. "Virgil Earp deserves whatever he got! That sorry asshole never even give us a chance that day."

Stilwell flashed a mouthful of brownish teeth. "Same song, second verse."

"Damn if it ain't," Brocius agreed. "Wyatt's the kingpin of that bunch, and don't you never forget it, Ike. He just used Virgil's badge to give him a license to kill."

"If that's so," Finn ventured, "then we shore as hell gunned down the wrong man."

"Quit your bellyachin'!" Brocius yelled. "We're gonna get'em all. Every last one!"

Finn hawked and spat a wad of phlegm in the direction of the stove. "How d'you figger to do that?"

"I'm thinkin' on it."

"You been thinkin' on it near about three months. So far, all we've done is wing Virgil. That ain't much to show for what's owed us."

"Why, hell, Finn," Stilwell chortled. "We stole better'n four hundred head of cows and robbed a stage. We sure as the dickens ain't done ourselves no harm."

"That's what I mean," Finn bridled. "We been runnin' around like a fart in a bottle. Half the time we're down in Mexico rustlin' cows and the other half we're in some greaser cathouse tryin' to catch a dose of clap. That ain't gettin' the Earps killed."

"We'll kill'em!" Brocius said viciously. "Wyatt Earp's on the top of my list! So don't you worry your head about it, Finn. You hear me?"

"Yeah, I hear you."

"C'mon, Finn." Ike nudged his brother in the ribs. "Don't act so down in the mouth. Bill ain't never led us wrong yet, has he? He'll get it figgered out."

"I never said he wouldn't. I'm just askin' when."

"I'll tell you when!" Brocius exploded. "When I'm gawddamn good and ready! Anybody put your brains in a jaybird and the sonovabitch would fly backwards."

"What the hell's that supposed to mean?"

"It means you're dumber'n a horseturd! Don't you think Earp's on his guard now? Christ, he probably don't stick his nose outdoors after sundown. We've got to wait till he gets over the jitters! Then we'll nail his butt once and for all."

"How long's that gonna take?"

"Till I sayso and not a minute sooner."

"Well, don't take it personal, but I sure as shit ain't gonna hold my breath waitin'."

"You keep on and you're liable to be holdin' your breath a lot longer'n you think."

Stilwell waved them apart. "Simmer down! Bill's got the right idea, and no two ways about it. We just have to wait till Earp gets careless. It'll happen, don't never believe it won't!"

"You bet'cha!" Ike slapped his knee. "Catch the bastard when he ain't lookin' and blow him to Kingdom Come. I'd give a nickel to see his face when it happens!"

"How would you manage that?"

Ringo's question took them by surprise. Everyone stared at him a moment, then turned back to Ike. He shook his head, smiling lamely.

"I don't get you, Johnny."

"It's simple enough," Ringo said mildly. "How can you see a man's face when you shoot him in the back?"

"Aw, quit your funnin', Johnny."

"I'm not funnin'," Ringo said with exaggerated gravity. "Tell you the truth, I think Earp has a point."

"A point?"

"Yeah, about you boys being bushwhackers. Course, I guess he was feeling charitable and just overlooked the fact that you're not very good at it."

Stilwell laughed uneasily. "That's a helluva thing to say, Johnny."

"Simple statement of fact," Ringo remarked. "You boys can't even backshoot a man proper. Otherwise Virgil Earp wouldn't be flyin' on one wing."

There was a moment of oppressive silence. The men looked everywhere but at Ringo, trading sheepish glances. Then Brocius wormed around in his chair, hunching forward.

"You're talkin' out of turn, Johnny."

"What's the matter, Bill?" Ringo inquired. "Your ears burning?"

"Watch yourself," Brocius said stiffly, his lips white. "I don't let no man call me yellow."

"Why, Bill, I wasn't callin' you a coward. I just said you'd sooner backshoot a man than the other way round."

"You're so gawddamn tough," Brocius challenged him. "Whyn't you go face'em down your ownself?"

Ringo regarded him without expression. The other men waited, nervously watching the test of wills. Brocius knew he'd gone a step too far. He wondered if he could outdraw the muddy-eyed gunman, and realized he might very well die trying to preserve his leadership of the gang. His pulsebeat quickened, and the palms of his hands suddenly felt sweaty. He sat perfectly still, waiting.

Then, quite casually, Ringo rose to his feet. He walked to the door and opened it. On the verge of stepping outside, he turned and looked back over his shoulder. He fixed Brocius with a gallows grin.

"I think I'll take a ride into Tombstone."

Spearing his hat off a wall peg, he laughed and jammed it on his head. The sound of his laughter still filled the room when the door closed.

CHAPTER 10

"I still say it's damn queer."

"You're too antsy." Holliday wagged his head with a wry smile. "A backshooter pays no attention to the calendar. He's got all the time in the world."

"Well, I don't," Earp reminded him. "Brocius could hold off till doomsday, and it'd suit me just fine. But he won't, and we both know it."

"I think that newspaper article impressed you more than it did him. Anyone called you those names, you'd just naturally feel bound to face him down. Brocius isn't built that way, and there's the difference. He'll swallow his pride and wait for you to drop your guard."

"I wish to hell Virge was able to travel."

"He won't mend any faster with you in an uproar all the time."

"He damn sure couldn't mend any slower! We're like ducks in a shootin' gallery, and the odds get worse the longer we wait."

"All depends," Holliday grunted. "Your number

isn't up till it shows, and every day's a new toss of the dice."

Walking along Allen Street, the men fell silent. The earth swam in a bluish dusk, and high in the sky a fiery cloud blazed in the last rays of sunset. Ahead lay the Alhambra, and for all of Holliday's philosophical tone, there was nothing leisurely about their pace. These days, neither of them trusted the streets after dark.

Yet Holliday wasn't all that displeased with the situation. The worse the odds became, the more Earp needed him. Peace and tranquility would have weakened, perhaps even eliminated, that need. He much preferred the threat of imminent bloodshed.

Their friendship, from the start, had been one of mutual dependence. Holliday, despite his sullen manner, was not altogether misanthropic. No man ever completely purges himself of the need for human contact. Several years ago, at a low point in his life, he had latched on to Wyatt Earp in the way of a drowning man grasping at flotsam. Earp had accepted him as he was, seemingly unconcerned with his racking cough or his cynical outlook. At the time, Holliday thought it was perhaps his last chance to throw in with someone worthy of his respect. He was of the same opinion even now.

In exchange, he gladly allowed Earp to trade on his reputation as a mankiller. His presence alone, particularly here in Tombstone, served to enforce Earp's will on others. While one was cunning and ambitious, the other was a perfect assassin, ever eager to pull the trigger. Still, though they worked well together, they were alike only in their willingness to resort to violence. In all other things they were quite dissimilar.

Holliday was a Southerner, a man of breeding and education. Incurable tuberculosis had brought him West, seeking a drier climate. Even on the frontier, however, there was small demand for a dentist who coughed blood. Circumstance, and physical frailty, had led him into the life of an itinerant gambler. An ungovernable temper, coupled with that same physical frailty, had transformed him into a mankiller. In the truest sense, the Colt sixgun was for him the equalizer. He killed men simply because it was his sole means of defending himself. Then, too, he enjoyed the sport of wagering life against life. It gave a certain tang to an otherwise bleak existence.

By contrast, Wyatt Earp was a Yankee whose family had joined the westward migration. An uneducated farm boy, he had become a drifter with a yearning to better himself. His upward climb had taken him from buffalo hunter to sometimes peace officer to bunco artist and mining entrepreneur. He was coarse, by no means a gentleman, but he possessed a quick mind and a near infallible insight into the weaknesses of others. He killed men not for sport or some perverted sense of contest. He killed to protect what he'd gained, and the things he yet coveted.

Holliday understood all that. In fact, he understood Earp better than Earp understood himself. Tonight, he knew full well that Earp was torn between the urge to run—thereby removing his brothers from danger—and the need to revive his political fortunes in Cochise County. Holliday, whose loyalty was unswerving, would follow either way. Given a choice, however, he would have preferred to die fighting on the streets of Tombstone rather than succumb to the ultimate ravages of lung consumption. Having killed more than a score of men, he thought it would be the supreme irony if he ended up dying in bed. By no means a brave man, he was simply a fatalist who no longer feared death. For him, the hourglass was already down to a few grains of sand.

Nearing the Alhambra, he decided there was nothing to be gained in pressing the matter further. Earp was playing for time, clearly on the defensive. He wouldn't fight unless it was forced on him, and even that prospect left him badly troubled. Weighed in the balance, the safety of his brothers had assumed greater value than personal ambition. It seemed likely he would quit and run the moment Virge was able to travel. Whether he would return to fight another day was open to speculation. With Earp, anything was possible.

From downstreet, Holliday saw Jack Johnson approaching the Alhambra. He still considered the man a smalltime grifter, but he was accommodating and always good for a few laughs. Which was more than could be said for most of the cardsharks who frequented Tombstone's gaming parlors. Johnson flipped them a salute and halted, waiting outside the front door.

"Holliday!"

The shout stopped Holliday in his tracks. He turned and saw Johnny Ringo emerge from a doorway across the street. The streetlamps were already lit and Ringo's

features were plainly visible. The corners of his mouth
were twisted in a wolfish smile.

"I got a bone to pick with you, Holliday."

"Yeah?" Holliday said tonelessly. "What's that?"

"You're a double-dipped son-of-a-bitch, and a card
cheat to boot."

Holliday's face went chalky. He was aware of Earp
at his side, but his concentration was focused on
Ringo. All in a flash, he weighed his chances and
knew he couldn't beat the younger gunman in a fair
fight. He still wasn't afraid to die, but he was reluctant
to have it happen right now. A bigger fight was brew-
ing, and he desperately wanted to stick around until
then. Besides which, he told himself, Earp still had
need of his gun. To go out now would be like leaving
a friend in the lurch.

He spread his hands in a bland gesture. "Ringo, I'm
not lookin' for trouble. Suppose we let it lay till another time?"

Ringo threw back his head and laughed. In the
lamplight, he displayed a mouthful of teeth as square
as sugar cubes. His hand hung loosely by the sixgun
holstered on his hip.

"Trouble's found you, whether you're lookin' for it
or not. I'm here to punch your ticket, Holliday!"

Starbuck remained motionless beside the door. He
saw an evil light in Ringo's eyes, a steady, confident
gaze that was at once striking and cold. Word had it
that Ringo was the deadliest gunman in Arizona, and
he could easily understand why. What he failed to understand was why Holliday would crawfish. To his

knowledge, the gambler had never declined a challenge.

Abruptly, Earp turned and strode several paces down the boardwalk. His move effectively flanked Ringo, and brought everything to a standstill. When he spoke, his jaws were clenched so tight his lips barely moved.

"Ringo, I'd advise you to let it drop."

"Stay out of this!" Ringo shouted, biting off the words. *"It's between Holliday and me!"*

Earp's face was blank, as though cast in metal. "No dice! You'll have to take both of us."

"How about it, Holliday?" Ringo taunted. "You gonna let him fight your fight for you?"

"Why fight?" Holliday stalled. "I've got nothing personal against you. Our quarrel's with your backshooter friends."

"Horseshit!" Ringo yelled in a loud hectoring voice. "We've got a score to settle and I'm callin' you out."

"Water over the dam," Holliday temporized. "Why don't I buy you a drink and let's talk about it?"

"C'mon!" Ringo said defiantly. "I always heard Doc Holliday couldn't be beat. Let's see you prove it!"

"No," Holliday slowly shook his head. "I aim to walk into the Alhambra and have that drink. You're welcome to join me."

"You four-flushin' bastard! Stand and fight!"

Starbuck saw a golden opportunity materializing before his eyes. Ringo would get Holliday, and Earp would get Ringo. One down on each side and then the killing would start in earnest. He waited, savoring the moment.

"Don't anybody move!"

Sheriff Behan and a deputy advanced along the boardwalk, guns drawn. So intent had Starbuck been on the deadly tableau before him that he hadn't seen them approaching. He cursed softly under his breath, all of his expectations suddenly spoiled. Then a random thought popped into his mind. Behan had attempted to intercede in the OK Corral shootout. Yet, despite his best efforts, three men had died that day. Perhaps tonight's opportunity wasn't lost after all.

"Drop your gunbelt!" Behan ordered. "Do it right now!"

Ringo turned his head just far enough to rivet the sheriff with a look. "Take a walk, Behan! This here's a private argument."

"Not tonight," Behan said, flicking a glance at Earp. "This time, I'm the only one wearin' a badge. You boys unload that hardware—pronto!"

Earp and Holliday were strangely silent. Watching them, Starbuck realized they would comply without protest. His hopes took another dive, then surged as his gaze shuttled to Ringo. The younger gunman's features were knotted in a brutish grimace.

"You're outta line!" he barked. "There's no law against us settlin' a personal dispute."

"Maybe not," Behan rejoined. "But there's a town ordinance against carryin' firearms. You just violated it and you're under arrest."

Holliday and Earp looked at him like he was crazy. Even his own deputy appeared somewhat uncertain.

Starbuck mentally crossed his fingers, still hoping.

"You're loco!" Ringo howled. "Everybody in this goddamn town packs a gun!"

"Tell it to the judge," Behan said bluntly. "You broke the law and that's that."

"Go to hell!" Ringo sputtered. "I don't hand over my gun to nobody!"

"I'll only warn you once more that you're under arrest."

"Stick it up your ass and sit on it!"

Behan motioned to his deputy. "Cover him! If he moves, shoot him dead."

The deputy brought his pistol to eye level, thumbing the hammer to full-cock. His arm was steady, and he centered the sights on Ringo's shirtpocket. Behan's cool stare bored into the fiery-tempered *pistolero*.

"Stubborn will get you killed! Drop that gunbelt and be mighty damn quick about it."

A taut silence fell between them. All up and down the street, miners and townspeople who had stopped to watch the affair swiftly scattered into nearby doorways. Ringo stood immobile, his eyes shifting from Behan to the snout of the deputy's pistol. At last, with a muttered curse, he unbuckled his gunbelt and let it fall to the ground.

Behan turned to Holliday. He held out a square, stubby-fingered hand. "I'll take your gun."

Holliday brushed his coat aside and unholstered an ivory-handled Colt. Extending it butt first, he jerked his chin at Earp. "Wyatt had no part in this. It was just me and Ringo."

"He's armed," Behan said deliberately. "That makes him an accessory."

"You've had your fun," Holliday warned him. "Don't get greedy."

Behan studied Earp a moment, debating with himself. Then he shrugged and glanced at Starbuck. "What about you, Johnson? Got any bright remarks tonight?"

"Nope." Starbuck squared himself up, grinning. "It's just like Doc told you, Sheriff. Wyatt and me was innocent bystanders."

"Careful, Johnson, or people will start callin' you the alibi-man."

Starbuck laughed. "Sticks and stones, Sheriff. No way to stop folks from talking."

"You still keep damn poor company."

Behan moved back a step, ordering Holliday and Ringo to precede him. Their eyes met in a hostile exchange, then they fell in alongside one another and marched off toward the jail. The deputy collected Ringo's gunbelt and hurried after Behan. A moment later, the little procession disappeared around the corner.

Starbuck looked sad. "Damn shame! Ringo's the one that started it, not Doc."

"C'mon," Earp grumbled. "I need a drink."

Starbuck followed him into the Alhambra. There was an empty space at the end of the counter, and Earp told the barkeep to leave the bottle. He knocked back a quick shot, then poured himself another round. Starbuck sipped, allowing the silence to build. His somber expression was genuine, without need of pretense. He was deeply resentful that the gunfight had been thwarted, bollixing what seemed a rare stroke of fortune. Yet he was alert to Earp's downcast mood. He thought to himself that something might still be salvaged from the night.

At last, with a violent oath, Earp slammed his glass on the bar. "Goddamn Harry Woods anyway!"

"Who?"

"Harry Woods," Earp said sharply. "That sawed-off little runt that prints the *Nugget*."

"Ooh yeah," Starbuck nodded wisely. "The one that ran that story."

"Story?" Earp rasped. "It was a death warrant! That's what brought Ringo out of his hole."

"Ringo?" Starbuck suddenly played dumb. "What's he got to do with anything?"

"Hell, he's one of the Brocius gang."

"So I've heard. But he came after Doc, not you."

"Yeah, so?" Earp conceded glumly. "What're you drivin' at?"

"Well, you said it was Woods' story that caused it. From where I stood, it sounded like Ringo's got something personal against Doc."

"Bad blood between 'em," Earp said vaguely. "Goes back a long ways."

Starbuck looked at him, unable to guess what might be going through his mind. He knew Earp was lying, and could only speculate as to the truth. An expression of idle curiosity on his face, he decided to probe a bit further.

"Must've been something mighty fierce. Took a real set of balls for him to brace both of you that way."

Earp was evasive. "I seem to recollect they had words over cards."

"Doc and Ringo?"

"You act surprised."

"I am," Starbuck deadpanned. "Doc generally plays poker with a better class of people."

"When we first got here there wasn't any better class of people. Doc used to ride over to Charleston when things got slow. That's where he met Ringo."

"Charleston?"

"Few miles west of here," Earp said woodenly. "It's a hangout for cowmen mostly. Doc could always find himself a pick-up game over there."

"Is that where your trouble with Brocius started?"

Earp stared down at his glass, tightlipped. "What makes you ask?"

"You said there was bad blood between Doc and Ringo. I just naturally figured that would get Brocius into the act."

"I suppose it did," Earp said without conviction. "I wish to hell he'd never met any of that crowd."

Watching him, Starbuck decided not to press too far too fast. Yet, even as they talked, the germ of an idea had taken root in his mind. It was an offshoot of his newspaper gambit, but he realized instantly that it had even greater potential. Somehow he had to bring the Earps and the Brocius gang together in a head-on clash. Not the hit and run tactics of bushwhackers and backshooters. An occasional assassination, even an incident such as tonight's confrontation, simply wasn't enough. It had to be total war, no quarter asked and none given. A bloodbath.

Starbuck took a chance. "I wonder if Brocius put Ringo up to making a play for Doc?"

"What gave you that idea?"

"I reckon you did. Or at least what you said about that newspaper story. It stands to reason Brocius and his boys will try to save face. So maybe Ringo was picked to get the ball rolling."

"I don't follow you."

"Seems pretty obvious," Starbuck said solemnly. "Brocius means to knock you off one at a time. Tonight was Doc's turn, only Ringo got too big for his britches."

"By God, I think you've got something there!"

"I'd bet on it," Starbuck assured him. "Course, it's none of my business, but if it was me, I'd take the play away from them."

"How would you propose to do that?"

"Simplest way on earth," Starbuck smiled. "Get them before they get you."

Earp regarded him thoughtfully a moment, then nodded. "Jack, you just gave me a helluva idea. It wasn't exactly what you intended, but it's a pip!"

"Oh, yeah? What's that?"

"I think it's time I got myself a badge." Earp's mouth curled in a sinister smile. "Way past time!"

CHAPTER 11

For the next few weeks Starbuck hung around the Alhambra like a forlorn ghost. He was moody and dispirited, and unable to come to terms with an elemental flaw in his strategy. He had once more underestimated Wyatt Earp.

Late one afternoon, he sat alone at a poker table. The lull before the evening rush had left the Alhambra virtually deserted. As he had every night for the past month, he was scheduled to take Alice to supper somewhere around six. With an hour or so to kill, and nothing better to occupy his time, he had stopped in for a couple of drinks. Now, with a hand of solitaire spread before him, he listlessly shuffled the cards. His gaze was abstracted, and almost mechanically, he laid the jack of diamonds on top of the queen of diamonds. He stared at the cards like a man peering disconsolately into an open grave.

February was half gone, and he was gripped by a leaden sense of defeat. The clarity of hindsight made his stomach churn, and the infernal waiting sawed on his nerves. He thought it one of life's greater ironies

that he had been instrumental in bringing law and order to Arizona Territory. The grandest joke of all was
that he had inadvertently transformed a shifty scoundrel into a sworn peace officer. Even now, somewhere
south of Tombstone, U.S. Deputy Marshal Wyatt Earp
led a posse in search of the Brocius gang. It boggled
the mind, and left the sour taste of bile in his throat.

A month ago, only one day after the Ringo incident,
Earp had disappeared from town. Three days later, he
had returned with a badge pinned on his chest. Somehow, though he offered no explanation, he had managed to have himself appointed U.S. Deputy Marshal
for the Tombstone District. It was all very mysterious,
and to the consternation of his political opponents, it
was also very legitimate. U.S. Marshal Crawley Dake,
headquartered in Tucson, had administered the oath
personally.

Half the town was dumbstruck, and the other half
waited with anticipatory relish for the next act in what
seemed a comedy of the bizarre. Sheriff John Behan,
now reduced to second fiddle, stomped around town
in a faunching rage. Earp's commission, being federal,
superceded both local and county authority. He was
the top lawman in all of southern Arizona. The balance
of power, virtually overnight, had changed hands.

Starbuck, no less astounded than the townspeople,
recognized it as a brilliant improvisation. For cool
nerve and audacious conniving, it was unsurpassed.
With one stroke, Earp had risen above public censure
and given himself an enormous advantage over the
Brocius gang. He loudly proclaimed that he was going
to run the outlaws out of Arizona. Privately, he let it

be known that dead or alive was not an issue. He intended to take no prisoners.

On all counts, Starbuck's plan had gone haywire. His purpose was to goad Earp into action, and thereby provoke open warfare between thieves. The upshot was that Earp had gone him one better, leapfrogging to a scheme that seemed not only outlandish but wholly improbable. Never in his wildest fancy would Starbuck have imagined such a brazen, and totally unpredictable, turn of events. Nor would he have conjured the unlikely twist that a private vendetta could so easily be spliced into a civic crusade. Even worse, he could have envisioned no outcome that would have left him sitting on his rump in Tombstone.

Yet there he sat.

Upon recovering from his initial shock, he had assumed Earp would ask him to join the posse. After all, it was his prompting that had suggested the scheme to Earp in the first place. He wasn't particularly thrilled with the idea, but as a member of the posse it would still induct him into the Earp clique. Once on the inside, he would simply adapt his plan to fit the new circumstances. Ultimately, by hook or crook, he would have emerged with Earp's scalp on his belt. It hadn't worked that way.

At no time, either by word or intimation, had he been invited to join the posse. Instead, Earp had sworn in Holliday and his younger brothers, Morg and Warren. Then, in a stunning piece of arrogance, he had imported two professional *pistoleros* from south of the border. Operating out of Nogales, Sherm McMasters and Texas Jack Vermillion were known throughout the southwest. They were hired guns, mercenaries available to the highest bidder, and their work was considered top drawer. Earp, expedient to the end, pinned federal badges on them. No mention was made of salary, but the arrangement was hardly a secret. John Clum published reports in the *Epitaph* that a "civic group" had placed a bounty of $1000 on Curly Bill Brocius.

Starbuck concluded that he'd overplayed the role of happy-go-lucky cardsharp. Earp liked him, even trusted him, but apparently considered him a lightweight when it came to gunplay. The marshal and his posse rode out of Tombstone the third week in January. Starbuck was left to contemplate the ashes of a plan gone awry.

Forced to wait it out, Starbuck had turned to Alice for comfort and diversion. His feelings about her veered wildly. He enjoyed her company and she raised his spirits, and her abandon in bed made the wait somewhat more bearable. Yet the other side of the coin disturbed him, and gave him pause. She was like a schoolgirl with her first crush, except it wasn't puppy love. She was hearing church bells and organ music. Worse, she kept dropping broad hints that clearly tagged him the bridegroom in her fantasy. He did nothing to encourage her, nor did he attempt to prick the bubble. He was genuinely fond of her, and more to the point, he couldn't afford to alienate his only potential witness. At night, when she lay snuggled in his arms, he often had difficulty reconciling one with the other.

His excuse, which he perceived as legitimate, was

the overriding goal of bringing Earp to justice. All the more so now that Earp was operating under the mantle of a badge. Through the Wells, Fargo agent in Tucson, he had learned that considerable pressure had been brought to bear on Crawley Dake, the U.S. Marshal. Apparently Earp had called in all his political markers in Tombstone. Tom Harris, one of the territory's power brokers, had pulled the necessary strings to secure Earp's appointment as Deputy Marshal. Harris, in turn, was aligned with the Tombstone businessmen who supported Earp. The link had been easily traced, and appeared to be little more than one hand washing the other. For all the quid pro quo, however, it posed a graver threat.

Brooding on it, Starbuck was of the opinion that Earp had raised his sights. Were he to rid Arizona of the Brocius gang, he would effectively kill two birds with a single stone. Foremost, and not to be discounted, was that he would eliminate the personal danger to himself and his brothers. At the same time, he would restore his own prestige, and emerge not just the man of the hour, but a lawman of imposing credentials. Using that as leverage, he could then consolidate his business alliances and move to gain control of Cochise County. It was a bold play and might very well succeed. By staking all his chips on the turn of a card, Earp could realize a complete turnabout in his political fortunes. From there, whatever venture he attempted, the sky would be the limit.

So far, Earp and his posse had produced little in the way of results. For the past three weeks they had chased around the territory without once sighting the outlaws. Clearly, Brocius and his gang had gone to ground, and were waiting for the dust to settle. There had been no more stage robberies, which pleased Wells, Fargo, and cattle rustling was reportedly at an all time low. But that in no way resolved the larger problem. Brocius and his gang, in the scheme of things, were merely a nuisance. Wyatt Earp was a dyed-in-the-wool menace.

The central question, Starbuck reflected, was how to bring the nuisance and the menace together. Slowly riffling the cards, he pondered ways to flush the gang from hiding and pit them in a bloodletting against the Earps. At this point, his options were limited and he was fresh out of ideas. He was also leery of creating any situation that might further Earp's resurgent flirtation with power. Yet anything was better than the Mexican standoff which now prevailed.

While it was no masterpiece, he still had one dodge left in his bag of tricks. Until now, he had hesitated using it simply because it was his last resort. If it failed, he would have nowhere to turn, and that prospect troubled him more than he cared to admit. Still, with the situation as it stood now, he was boxed into a corner anyway. From that viewpoint, there wasn't a hell of a lot to lose whatever he tried. Time was the enemy, and to sit on his butt any longer would be the worst mistake of all. What it boiled down to was the oldest axiom in the book. Nothing ventured, nothing gained.

He tossed the cards on the table and walked out of the Alhambra.

*   *   *

The sun dipped westward as Starbuck entered the front door of the *Epitaph*. John Clum was seated behind a desk littered with foolscap and newspaper tearsheets. His expression was somewhat harried, like a man battling several fires with only one bucket.

"Afternoon, Johnson."

"Afternoon, Mr. Mayor."

Clum brightened. He liked titles, and respect. "What can I do for you?"

"Wondered what the latest was on Wyatt. You heard anything?"

Clum's smile vanished. The sour look Starbuck received was not unexpected. It was no secret that Clum's fortunes had waned in the last six months. His association with Earp had provoked the wrath of both the town council and the voters. Barring a miracle, his political career had been consigned to the dung heap. Still worse, the *Epitaph* was steadily losing subscribers and advertisers to Harry Woods' *Nugget*. His financial position bordered on the perilous, and there were rumors he had mortgaged his home to raise operating funds for the newspaper. His frown was that of a weary and troubled man at the end of a long day.

"The last I heard of Wyatt, he was down around Bisbee somewhere. That was almost a week ago."

"If he'd caught up with Brocius, I suppose you would've got wind of it by now?"

"Probably so," Clum said dully. "News like that would travel fast."

"Bisbee?" Starbuck appeared thoughtful. "You reckon Brocius and his bunch skipped into Old Mexico?"

"I wouldn't hazard a guess."

"Seems logical, though, doesn't it?"

Clum shrugged indifferently. "Who cares where they've gone? It's hardly front page news."

Starbuck lit a cheroot and stuck it in his mouth. Then he hooked his thumbs in his vest, puffing cottony wads of smoke. "I've been thinking on that very subject, Mr. Mayor. The way it looks to me, it's high time Wyatt got the credit he deserves."

Clum looked startled. Like everyone else in town, he knew that the gambler named Johnson was practically a member of the Earp family. Alice Blaylock's visits to his hotel room, coupled with the fact he'd attached himself to Earp, had set the gossip mill churning. Yet, for all that, Clum knew he was considered something less than a mental wizard.

"Exactly what credit do you think Wyatt deserves?"

Starbuck ticked it off on his fingers. "There hasn't been a single stage robbery since he took out after Brocius. None of the mines have reported a payroll holdup. And there's talk that rustled cows are scarcer than hen's teeth. I'd say Wyatt has kept his promise, and he's done it in spades."

"You seem to forget he hasn't caught Brocius."

"Strictly beside the point," Starbuck said confidently. "He's put the Brocius gang out of business, probably scattered them to hell and gone across the border." He paused, using his cheroot like a wand, and scrolled a headline in the air. "Wyatt Earp has brought law and order to Arizona Territory!"

"You're right!" Clum marveled. "By all that's holy, he has done it, hasn't he?"

"See?" Starbuck grinned. "You hadn't thought of it that way and likely no one else has either. You stick that on your front page and they'll probably give Wyatt a medal. Might even erect a statue to him!"

Clum considered that unlikely. But the gist of the idea was sound, and anything that enhanced Earp's image would work to his own benefit as well. Elbows on the arms of his chair, he steepled his fingers and stared off into space.

"I like it." His voice was reverent, almost a benediction. "U.S. Deputy Marshal Wyatt Earp brings law and order to Arizona Territory. By the saints, that'll make them sit up and take notice! And it's true. Do you realize that, Johnson—it's indisputably true!"

"Gospel truth," Starbuck affirmed. "The town idjit could see that."

Clum grabbed a sheet of foolscap and began writing furiously. Starbuck flicked an ash with his pinky finger and crammed the cheroot back in his mouth. He looked proud as punch.

Shortly after dark, Starbuck slipped through the back door of the *Nugget*. While he waited in the print room, Harry Woods drew the shades on the front windows. Then he walked forward and took the wooden armchair beside Woods' desk.

"I just had a chat with your competition."

"Our esteemed mayor?"

"Prize sucker," Starbuck said quickly. "Nobody's easier to gaff than a man with larceny in his blood."

Woods smiled. "Tell me about it."

"I conned him into running a story on how Earp

has tied a can to Brocius' tail. He thinks he's beating the drum for Earp, but that's pure whiffledust. What it'll really do is make Brocius mad enough to chew nails."

"You are, indeed, a devious man."

Starbuck chuckled softly. "Harry, this time we'll pull out all the stops. I want you to publish those two lists, side by side. On the left side, a list of the dates the stages were robbed. On the right side, a list of the dates Earp purchased property. No editorial comment, just the lists by themselves. Let folks draw their own conclusions."

Woods studied him with admiration. "I daresay Brocius and Company will find that fascinating reading."

"I'm depending on it," Starbuck nodded. "If they're like most outlaws, they spend it as fast as they steal it. I'm betting they don't own much more than the clothes on their backs."

"Yet Earp, by contrast, is worth a fortune."

"In addition to which, he's kept them on the run for nearly a month. No holdups, no rustled cows, nothing. The way they look at it, he's taking the bread out of their mouths."

"Not to mention the fact that he's doing his level best to kill them."

"One more thing," Starbuck added. "I want you to write an editorial blasting Earp. Something to the effect that he doesn't give two hoots in hell about ridding the territory of outlaws. Charge him with using the Brocius gang to his own political ends, turning their skeletons into steppingstones. I think you get the general idea."

"Indeed, I do!" Woods laughed. "You intend to rub their noses in it. The *Epitaph* story, the lists, my editorial! Brocius and his men won't be able to ignore all that. They'll go off like skyrockets!"

"If they don't," Starbuck said ruefully, "I'll be in a helluva fix, Harry. I'm just about at the end of my string."

"Never fear, Luke! The pen is mightier than the sword . . . especially a poison pen!"

Starbuck wasn't fully convinced. But, then, as he'd told himself earlier, he had nothing whatever to lose by trying. He left Woods scribbling with a sort of mad glee over an impassioned editorial.

Starbuck knew something was wrong the moment she opened the door. Alice's smile was bleak, and she looked wretched. Stepping inside, he found Earp seated in the parlor. He stopped, genuinely surprised, then crooked his mouth in a jack-o'-lantern grin.

"Well, knock my socks off! Where'd you come from?"

"Just rode in, not more than ten minutes ago."

"You got'em!" Starbuck hopped toward him like a dancing bear. "I know you! You wouldn't have quit unless you got'em."

Earp gave him a hangdog look. "No such luck. We never even got a sniff."

"I'll be switched," Starbuck said, suddenly somber. "You mean to say they got away—clean?"

"That's about the size of it."

"So what's next? You aim to rest up a spell and then head out again?"

"Jack, I wouldn't have the least goddamn idea where to look. We've combed the territory from stem to grudgeon, and it's like they dropped through a hole in the ground."

Starbuck glanced at Alice and she ducked her head toward the door. She quite obviously wasn't pleased by her brother-in-law's return. For his own reasons, Starbuck was none too happy himself. After nearly two months of effort, he felt very much as though he'd just hop-scotched back to square one.

"Well, listen, we'll talk some more. Let me buy you a drink later and you can tell me the whole story."

"Maybe tomorrow," Earp begged off. "I'm so damn wore out my butt's draggin' the ground."

"Sure thing, Wyatt! Get yourself a good night's sleep and I'll see you tomorrow."

On the way out the door, Starbuck glanced back and got a shock. Earp looked whipped, somehow drained of resolve. Now, more than ever, the double-barrel newspaper blast represented a last ditch effort. Unless it brought Brocius into Tombstone, there would be no war. No bloodletting, and no end to the case.

A sudden black rage swept over him. He promised himself that wouldn't happen. Somehow, one way or another, it would end.

CHAPTER 12

"Ten ball in the corner pocket."

Starbuck leaned over the pool table. He stroked the cue stick with a practiced hand and cleanly sank the ten ball. The cue ball magically reversed itself, spinning backwards on the green felt, then rolled to a stop near the left hand side-pocket. The angle was perfect for his next shot, on the eleven ball.

"Would you look at that position? Talk about blind luck!"

Morg's tone was bantering, slightly envious. Standing nearby, he watched as Starbuck eyed the eleven ball. Earp and Holliday, who were seated on a bench along the far wall, exchanged a knowing glance. Spectators, and hecklers, they were having a good laugh at Morg's expense. No one spoke as Starbuck sliced the eleven into the side-pocket. Quickly, calling his shots without hesitation, he cleaned the table. When the fifteen ball dropped, he walked to the near corner pocket and extracted two ten-dollar bills. He kissed them, grinning at Morg.

"Tough break." He tucked the bills into his vest

pocket. "You had it sewed up till you missed the ten ball. Care to try another game?"

"Watch yourself, Morg," Earp ragged him. "Jack's liable to trim your wick."

Morg wasn't put out in the slightest. "Why, hell, Wyatt, don't spoil it! I'm just stringin' him along so he'll raise the stakes."

"Guess again," Holliday injected dryly. "You're the one that's being hustled."

"Oh yeah!" Morg said with a wide peg-toothed grin. "Well suppose we make it twenty a game, and see who gets stiffed. How about it, Jack?"

"Suits me." Starbuck turned his head and gave Earp a broad wink. "He thinks he's found himself a pigeon. Reckon I've got a chance?"

"What you've got," Earp smiled, "is a gift for gab."

"Amen to that," Holliday added. "Get him started and he'll talk the gold right off a man's molars."

While Morg racked the balls, Starbuck chalked his cue and prepared to break. The pool table was located in the rear of Hatch's Saloon. Benches lined the walls, and an overhead lamp bathed the table in brilliant light. A side door, with glass in the upper panel, led to an alleyway. Up front, a crowd was ranged along the bar. It was nearing midnight, and the murmur of their conversation was sportive, well laced with liquor.

Starbuck dropped the four and the nine on the break. Talking and shooting, he then ran the one through the seven. The eight ball lay flush against the rail, offering a difficult bank shot. He took a moment to study the angle, and finally addressed the cue ball with a great show of confidence. The eight ball zipped across the table, caught the corner of the pocket, and bounced erratically to the far rail. His grin faded, and he gave the eight a look of raw disbelief. Morg laughed out loud, moving into position.

"Stand back, Jack! Gimme room!"

Stepping aside, Starbuck halted beside Earp and Holliday. They immediately began razzing Morg, who returned their jibes with vulgar good humor. No slouch on a pool table, he pocketed the eight ball with a double bank shot. The cue ball rolled into perfect position, and he took a vaudevillian bow. Then, calling his shots, he began running the table with methodical precision.

Watching him, Starbuck reflected on the vagaries of the detective business. Shooting a game of pool with Morg seemed somehow emblematic of his investigation to date. By all rights, he should have had them under lock and key—or dead and buried—long ago. Instead, he was still playing games. Pool tonight, poker last night, a masquerade every night. Unproductive, and seemingly endless, games.

In a swift flight of mind, he realized a month had passed since Earp's return to Tombstone. At the time, he'd been convinced that the stories in the *Epitaph* and the *Nugget* would force someone to take action. His bet was on Brocius, but he nurtured a glimmer of hope that Earp and his posse would again resume the chase. Events of subsequent days had proved him wrong on both counts.

Brocius and his band of outlaws had seemingly vanished off the face of the earth. It was now the middle of March, and for the past month there had been no depredations of any nature. No stage holdups, no payroll robberies, no reports of rustled livestock. Nor had the gang made any attempt on the lives of Earp and his brothers. There was speculation that they had retired to less hazardous pursuits somewhere in Old Mexico. But no one knew for certain where they were. On either side of the border, all was peaceful, uncommonly quiet.

For Earp's part, he basked in the light of revitalized public esteem. Even his detractors—Harry Woods in the forefront—were forced to admit he'd routed the outlaws. Considering the number of robberies and killings in the last two years, an entire month without violence was looked upon as nothing short of miraculous. John Clum, naturally, made the most of favorable circumstances. The *Epitaph* trumpeted Earp's prowess as a lawman in every issue. According to the headlines, Arizona Territory slept better because Tombstone's noblest citizen now wore a badge.

Starbuck, observing all this with a jaundiced eye, knew his instinct hadn't played him false. Earp, like any good grifter, was quick on his feet. Having gained the upper hand, he would now milk it to the limit. If the Brocius gang reappeared, he would strike a fresh trail and resume the chase amidst great public fanfare. If the outlaws had gone on to other endeavors, he would continue to claim credit for ridding the territory of a murderous band of desperadoes. Either way, he would be a strong candidate for sheriff when election time rolled around. Earp's star was definitely in the ascendancy.

All the more apparent, Starbuck reflected, was

Earp's complete switch in attitude. He no longer spent his days, and nights, looking over his shoulder. He plainly had come to regard himself as the hunter, not the hunted. Nor was there any likelihood that he would now make a run for it. Virge was all but recuperated, and for the past several weeks, he'd been fit enough to travel. Yet there was no mention of such plans, and it seemed logical to assume the idea had been shelved. The Earp family, quite obviously, intended to remain in Tombstone.

Starbuck thought Earp's assessment of Brocius was perhaps too optimistic. An outlaw might tuck tail and run for cover, but that made him no less dangerous. In Starbuck's experience, a backshooter was the most tenacious of all mankillers. Some perverted sense of pride, harnessed with an obsession for revenge, gave them extraordinary patience. He knew of instances where such men had waited for years, nursing a long-forgotten grievance, before they struck. He considered it very probable that Curly Bill Brocius was just such a man.

Still, there was no denying that Earp had a high opinion of himself these days. The tipoff was in little things, quirks of character. Not only did he smile, which was somewhat like watching granite crack, but he occasionally attempted a joke. Tonight, with business slow, he'd even suggested they quit early and take in the town. After catching the last act at the Birdcage Theatre, they had walked over to Hatch's Saloon for a nightcap. Morg, who fancied himself a pool shark, had challenged Starbuck to a game. The stakes were friendly, but Starbuck had taken inordinate pleasure in winning the first round. Lately, he hadn't had too much success in beating the Earps at anything.

Morg dropped the fourteen ball and stood back to survey the last shot. He was directly across the table, facing them, on line with the side door. As he chalked his cue, one of the saloon regulars, George Berry, walked back to have a look. Wobbling slightly, Berry appeared to be feeling no pain. He listed to a stop beside Holliday, and focused a bloodshot gaze on the pool table.

"I got four-bits says Morg makes it."

"Four-bits!" Morg laughed. "Bet your whole bank-roll, George. It's a lead-pipe cinch!"

"No, make it four-bits," Earp said humorously. "I'll cover it, and I wouldn't want George to go away busted."

"That's a helluva note," Morg said with a mocking smile. "You mean to say you'd bet against your own brother?"

"Why not?" Earp needled him. "You're getting ready to miss that shot. I can see it in your eyes."

"He's right," Starbuck chimed in. "You choked up last game, and that was before we doubled the stakes."

"Good try, but there's no way you'll talk me out of it. I couldn't miss that shot if my hands were tied! You and Wyatt just hide and watch."

Morg chuckled and stepped in behind the cue ball. The fifteen ball was opposite him, almost directly in line with the side-pocket. He dabbed chalk on the tip of his cue stick, and checked the angle one last time. Then he leaned forward over the table.

The upper panel in the alley door suddenly erupted

in a sheet of flame and shattered glass. The roar of
gunfire swept through the room like a drum roll. Morg
screamed and dropped the cue stick. His hands clawed
at empty air, then he fell on top of the pool table and
slowly crumpled to the floor.

Shots snicked across the room in a hailstorm of
lead. Earp and Holliday, miraculously unscathed, flung
themselves off the bench. All around them slugs thunked into the walls and exploded the bench in a shower
of splinters. George Berry staggered, struck by a wayward bullet, and collapsed as though his legs had been
chopped off. In the same instant, Starbuck threw himself to the floor and rolled toward the end of the pool
table. A split-second later he rose to one knee, drawing
the Colt. He leveled his arm and thumbed three quick
shots through the alley door.

Then, as suddenly as it began, the firing ceased. A
haze of gunsmoke hung over the pool table and a
tomblike stillness descended on the room. For a moment, frozen in the eerie quiet, no one moved.

Starbuck broke the spell. Circling the pool table, he
crossed the room and flattened himself against the
wall. Then he jerked open the door and moved swiftly
into the alleyway. He crouched low, spinning in both
directions, the Colt extended and cocked. There was
nothing but darkness, and empty silence.

Turning, he stepped back through the door and
found Earp kneeling beside Morg. He glanced at Holliday, who was standing close by, and the gambler
slowly shook his head. His gaze dropped to Morg, and
he saw immediately that it was hopeless. The young-
ster had been hit several times, one of the slugs drilling

through his back and exiting high on his chest. His shirtfront was splotched with blood.

Morg groaned, his breathing rapid and uneven. His eyes focused on Earp and a trickle of blood seeped down his chin. The corners of his mouth lifted in a ghastly smile.

"Looks like my last game."

"Hang on," Earp muttered softly. "The doc's on his way."

"Funny." Morg blinked, casting his eyes about. "I can't see a damn thing."

A shudder swept over him and his mouth opened in a long sigh. One bootheel drummed the floor and his sphincter voided with a foul odor. Then he lay still.

Several moments passed in stunned silence. All the color leeched out of Earp's face and he stared stonily down at his brother. His face was blank, but his jaw muscles ticced as though he were trying to say something. At last, Holliday bent forward and placed a hand on his shoulder.

"He's gone, Wyatt."

Earp might have been deaf, for there was no response. His face became congested, and the veins in his temple knotted into purple ropes. He couldn't look away from the body.

"Wyatt." Holliday gently shook him. "It's no use. He's dead."

Earp seemed to awaken. He shrugged off Holliday's hand, took a deep breath and blew it out heavily. Almost tenderly, he reached down and closed Morg's sightless eyes. Then he climbed to his feet.

"Somebody get the undertaker. I want him looked after proper."

The night lay gripped in a mealy, weblike darkness. A clot of men stood watching from the saloon door. The undertaker and his assistant had already loaded Morg into the hearse. Now, carrying the shroud-wrapped body of George Berry, they crossed the boardwalk.

Some moments later, their task completed, they closed and latched the rear doors. Walking forward, they mounted the driver's seat from opposite sides. The undertaker gathered the reins and clucked to his team of matched coal black geldings. The hearse moved off upstreet and slowly disappeared into the night.

Under a nearby streetlamp, Earp stared after the hearse until it vanished. Then he turned to Holliday and Starbuck. His gaze shifted to the men crowded in the doorway, and he waited as they moved back inside the saloon. Finally, he glanced at Holliday.

"It's time to get Virge out of town."

Holliday nodded. "What about the women?"

"All of them except Mattie and Alice can go with Virge."

"You aim to leave them here?"

"No." Earp looked down and studied the ground a moment. "We'll find someplace to stash them in Tucson."

"Warren and Jim?"

"Jim goes with Virge and the women. Warren stays."

"It'll be tricky," Holliday said grimly. "No way to keep it a secret, and once word gets out, there's no tellin' what Brocius will try."

Earp reflected on it briefly. "We'll move 'em all at once," he said at length. "There's a westbound out of Tucson every evening. All we have to do is get them there in one piece and our worries are over."

"What then?"

Earp's eyes glazed with rage. When he spoke, the timbre of his voice was charged with malevolence. "Then we kill Brocius."

Starbuck felt his pulse skip a beat. There was a cold ferocity about Earp that he'd never seen before. The war he had tried in vain to provoke was about to start, and Earp's manner told him there would be no mercy asked nor none granted. He sensed it was time to act, or again get left behind.

"You'll need somebody to take Morg's place. I'd like the job."

Earp gave him a swift, appraising glance. "How many shots did you get off in there? Three, four?"

"Three," Starbuck said levelly. "Wish it'd done more good. By the time I got myself set, they'd already skedaddled down the alley."

"You did better than me and Doc."

"Not much," Starbuck hedged. "I didn't hit anybody."

Earp eyed him a moment. "Where'd you learn to handle a gun that way?"

"The hard way," Starbuck informed him. "The world's full of sore losers, and some of them take exception to the way I deal."

"All the same," Holliday interjected, "for a gamblin' man, you're still mighty sudden."

Starbuck smiled. "I hear you're pretty fast yourself, Doc. What makes you different from me?"

"No offense, Jack," Earp cut in quickly. "We're beholden for what you did tonight. But it's not your fight, and you'd likely be better off if we left it that way."

"Then let's just say I'm making it my fight. In case you forgot, Brocius and his boys were shooting at me too." Starbuck paused, looking from one to the other. "On top of that, I'm sort of interested in what happens to Alice. She'll tell you so herself, if you care to ask."

"Don't worry about her," Earp said with a trace of impatience. "She's family, and we take care of our own."

Starbuck played his hole card. "You haven't done so good up till now."

"What's that supposed to mean?"

"Last time out, Brocius gave you the slip six ways to Sunday. I'd say you need yourself a tracker."

Earp stared at him with puzzlement. "Are you tellin' me you're a tracker?"

"I've done my share."

"Whereabouts, just exactly?"

"Took lessons from California Joe. That was back in '67, with Custer, on the Wichita."

Holliday regarded him with squinted eyes. "You must've been the only scout in diddies."

"I'm older than I look," Starbuck said flatly. "Lots older in lots of ways."

He let the idea percolate a few moments. "What the

hell's the rub, anyway? You need another gun, and I'm willing to go along. You could damn well do lots worse!"

"Maybe so." Holliday's features were set in stubborn disapproval. "For my money, though, you're johnny-come-lately to this game."

"No, Doc, he's right," Earp said grudgingly. "Last time, Brocius ran us round and round in circles. Jack might just be the fellow we've needed all along."

"One thing's for certain," Holliday said stolidly. "He's a regular sackful of surprises."

"You tell me your secrets," Starbuck grinned, "and I'll tell you mine. Fair enough, Doc?"

"Let it lay," Earp silenced them. "Doc, get hold of McMasters and Vermillion. Tell them we ride at first light." He turned to Starbuck. "Jack, you hire a couple of buckboards from the livery. Have them at the house a little before dawn."

"Anything else?"

"Yeah," Earp said shortly. "Bring your gun. You're gonna need it."

CHAPTER 13

A streak of lightning forked the sky west of Tucson.
Within seconds, the rumble of thunder sounded in the
distance. The storm moved swiftly closer, somehow
ominous in the lowering dusk.

A rented hack rolled through one of Tucson's seedier neighborhoods. The driver, one eye on the storm,
popped his buggy whip, urging the team into a quickened pace. Up front, Warren and Mattie sat together
in strained silence. Neither of them had spoken since
the hack pulled away from the train station. No fool,
she suspicioned she was being left behind, while the
rest of the family went on to California. Earp had explained it away, telling the others he wanted her near.
But she wasn't wholly convinced, and it showed. Her
expression was one of heavy-hearted sorrow.

Starbuck, seated in the back with Alice, wasn't convinced either. Yet he thought it highly improbable that
Earp would simply dump his wife. She, along with her
sister, knew too much about his affairs in Tombstone.
Still, they were being left behind, and that in itself
raised intriguing possibilities. In the event Earp aban-

doned them, the fury of a woman scorned might very easily be turned to advantage. Wells, Fargo would then have two potential witnesses.

Alice held his hand in a death grip. She was frightened and confused, and clung to him as though terrified of the moment they must part. The news of Morg's death, he recalled, had unnerved the whole family. Their grief was heightened by the knowledge that their own lives were in jeopardy so long as they remained in Arizona. Their hasty departure from Tombstone, arranged in the dark of night, merely confirmed what no one dared say out loud. The Earp family was once more on the run. Stealing away, bag and baggage, like a caravan of gypsies.

In the early morning hours, with the sky still dark, the evacuation had gotten underway. Everyone had an assignment, and there was a sense of impending doom about the hurried preparations. Earp and Holliday, assisted by McMasters and Vermillion, had taken one of the buckboards to the funeral parlor. There, Morg's coffin was loaded aboard and lashed down with rope. Warren and Starbuck, meanwhile, got the rest of the family ready to travel. Virge and Jim, along with the six women, were dressed and waiting when Earp returned. The women were allowed only one carpetbag apiece, and even then, the buckboards were cramped and overcrowded. As false dawn lighted the horizon, the little caravan rolled north out of Tombstone.

Their immediate destination was Contention. A railway junction and freight yard, the small settlement lay some twelve miles north along the banks of the San Pedro. While the distance was not that great, it was a remote stretch of road, well suited to ambush. Earp, heedful of the danger involved, treated the operation somewhat like a military withdrawal. Outriders were assigned to the cardinal points. With himself and Holliday in the vanguard, Warren and Starbuck were posted on the flanks. The hired guns, Vermillion and McMasters, brought up the rear.

Starbuck had met the gunmen on several occasions during their stay in Tombstone. He recognized them as run-of-the-mill hardcases, a breed he held in low esteem. The border attracted many such men, quiet and cold-eyed, with little regard for the value of life. Their connection with Earp was somewhat of a mystery, never once alluded to in conversation. Yet they clearly respected Earp, and almost went out of their way to fawn over Holliday. It very much put Starbuck in mind of a wolf pack. There was a definite order of dominance, and while all were meat-eaters, those of lesser ferocity forever curried favor with the pack leader. He thought it entirely likely that they had all worked together before.

Around mid-morning, after an uneventful journey, they had arrived in Contention. From there, they caught the noon train, pulling into Tucson late that afternoon. Still under guard, the family was then herded into the depot, where they were to await the evening westbound. Warren, with Starbuck along for good measure, was assigned the task of locating a boardinghouse for Mattie and Alice. Outside the depot, Earp had handed Mattie a roll of money and allowed himself to be pecked on the cheek. Their parting was like some atavistic ritual, without emotion.

Now, less than an hour later, the hack rolled to a stop in front of a two-story structure that looked weather-beaten and in ill repair. The driver assured them it was clean and served decent meals, one of the few boardinghouses suitable for ladies. Warren jumped down and went inside to arrange accommodations. Starbuck helped the women from the hack, then unloaded the bags and carried them to the porch. On his way back to the street, Mattie passed him on the walkway. She seemed dazed, scarcely nodding when he spoke, and continued on into the house. Alice waited for him at the edge of the barren, weed-choked yard. She looked on the verge of tears.

"Cheer up!" he said lightly. "It's a little the worse for wear, but I'll bet they serve the best food in town."

Alice smiled wanly. "I wasn't thinking of that."

"Why so down in the mouth, then?"

"I was wondering—" Her eyes suddenly went misty. "Will I ever see you again, Jack?"

"Course you will," Starbuck assured her. "Once we get this business cleared up, I'll scoot on back here so fast it'll make your head swim."

"Promise?" she whispered, desperation in her voice. "I'd give anything in the world to believe you won't just . . . go away."

Starbuck was not a man who revealed his innermost thoughts. The girl was important to him, and not only as a potential witness. Over their months together he had developed a genuine affection for her, and he was concerned about her welfare. Yet old habits were hard to break, and in his business, emotions were something to be suppressed. He covered what he felt now with an offhand remark.

"Tell you what." He grinned, taking her by the shoulders. "You keep a light in your window. One of these nights I'll sneak up and blow it out, and we won't get out of bed for a whole week."

"Oh, Jack." She sniffed, blinking away tears. "You're terrible. You really are."

"Terrible good?" Starbuck cocked one eyebrow. "Or terrible bad?"

"You know very well." She bit her lower lip, silent a moment. Then she hugged him fiercely around the neck. "You will be careful, won't you? For my sake, please!"

"Why, you ought to know me better than that. Careful's my middle name! Don't worry your head on that score."

"I will," she said softly. "I'll worry every minute you're gone."

Warren appeared on the porch and came swiftly down the walkway. She pulled Starbuck's mouth to hers and kissed him soundly. Then she slipped past him, tears streaming down her face, and ran toward the house. He gave Warren a sheepish grin, lifting his shoulders in an elaborate shrug. Wordlessly, they climbed into the hack and seated themselves.

The silence lasted for several blocks. Starbuck's thoughts were on the girl, but he slowly became aware that Warren was staring vacantly into space. At length, after lighting a cheroot, he shifted around in his seat.

"Something bothering you?"

"What makes you think that?"

"For one thing, you look like you just lost your best friend."

"Maybe I did," Warren said miserably. "Mattie and me have always been pretty thick, up till now anyway. She sure gave me the dust-off back there. Wouldn't even say goodbye."

"That a fact?" Starbuck looked at him curiously. "I know she was partial to you, more so than your brothers anyhow. What's her problem?"

"Wyatt!" Warren burst out. "She's got some fool notion that Wyatt means to ditch her."

Starbuck's expression revealed nothing. "Hardly makes sense. Why would he want to get shed of Mattie?"

Warren averted his eyes, visibly troubled. "Lemme ask you something, Jack. You notice anything different about Wyatt . . . anything unusual . . . since last night?"

"I'm not exactly sure what you mean."

"I'm not either," Warren confessed. "But he's not himself. He's acting damn strange, and I can't rightly put my finger on it."

"Maybe it's Morg," Starbuck suggested. "He got hold of himself quick enough, but he took it awful hard when Morg died."

Warren shook his head. "I know Morg getting killed caused it. That's not what I'm talking about, though."

"You just lost me on the turn."

"It's—" Warren faltered, then rushed on. "Take a good look at his eyes. Maybe nobody except family

would notice it, but it's there. Something mighty goddamn queer . . . spooky."

"Hold on now! Are you trying to tell me he's
popped his cork?"

"No, I wouldn't go that far."

"Well, how far would you go?"

"I don't know, Jack. I just by God don't know!"

The storm broke shortly after nightfall. A blue-white
bolt of lightning seared the sky and an instant later a
thunderclap shook the depot. Then a torrent of rain
struck the earth in a rattling deluge.

Already an hour overdue, the westbound pulled into
town just as the storm unleashed its fury. A groaning
squeal racketed back over the coaches as the engineer
throttled down and set the brakes. The engine rolled
past the depot and ground to a halt, showering fiery
sparks in a final burst of power. The station agent,
dressed in a rain slicker, walked forward as the conductor stepped down from the lead coach.

When the train stopped alongside the platform,
Earp emerged from underneath the depot's over-
hanging roof. He carried a double-barrel shotgun, and
the shadowy figures ranged behind him were now
armed with Winchesters. He slowly inspected the platform, watching intently as several passengers alighted
from the train and hurried into the stationhouse. Then
he turned his head and nodded.

Starbuck moved forward and took a position near
the express car. A row of lanterns, strung along the
front of the stationhouse, gave him a commanding
view in either direction. Vermillion and McMasters

appeared from beneath the overhang, pulling a baggage cart which contained Morg's coffin. They trun-
dled the cart across the platform and jockeyed it into
position before the express car. A messenger threw the
door open, motioning with his hand. The gunmen
scrambled onto the cart, one on either end of the coffin, and carried it inside. Within seconds, they returned, jumping from the cart to the platform.
Collecting their Winchesters, they moved past Earp
and took up position at the far end of the depot.

Earp walked directly to the stationhouse door.
Opening it, he stuck his head inside, then turned and
moved back onto the platform. Holliday and Warren
came through the door, both of them armed with
Winchesters. Next out were Virge and his wife, trailed
closely by Jim and the other three women. They
splashed through the rain, led by Warren, and boarded
the middle passenger car. Earp took a last look around,
then followed them inside the coach.

Starbuck moved along the platform and joined Holliday. His coat was now soaked and rivulets of water
rolled off his hat as the rain continued in a steady
downpour. Through the car windows, he saw Earp and
Warren getting the family settled and stowing their
luggage in overhead racks. Watching them, he recalled
the concern expressed earlier by Warren. Since returning to the station, he'd observed Earp more closely,
and the change, though not pronounced, was evident.
Earp looked drawn, older than his years, and there was
a strange feverish cast to his eyes. Moreover, he was
quiet, uncannily quiet. All evening he had roamed the
station, avoiding conversation, curiously withdrawn.

He somehow reminded Starbuck of a mad bull hooking at cobwebs. A bull spoiling for a fight.

Some time later Earp and Warren stepped out the coach door. Their faces were somber, and it was clear their final goodbyes had been difficult. Earp glanced around the depot, then looked at Holliday.

"Everything all right out here?"

"So far." Holliday extracted a telegram from his inside coat pocket. "This came over the wire from Clum while we were in the waiting room. I figured it was best to wait till Virge and Jim were set before I showed it to you."

Earp scanned the telegram, then grunted. "Coroner's jury returned a verdict naming Pete Spence, Frank Stilwell and Florentino Cruz as Morg's killers. Wonder how they managed to overlook Brocius?"

Holliday knuckled back his mustache. "Well, at least we've got some names and a legal indictment. It's a place to start."

"Indictment, hell!" Earp tapped the marshal's star pinned on his coat. "All I need's this badge and a reasonable gun range. Let somebody else worry about the legalities."

Warren cleared his throat. "You still aim to kill 'em outright?"

"Why?" Earp asked with a clenched smile. "You got a better way?"

"Nooo," Warren said slowly. "Let's just make it look like they put up a fight. Otherwise it'll give Behan an excuse to swear out another murder warrant against us."

"Not a bad idea! Johnny Behan's one man I'd enjoy throwin' down on."

Earp's eyes strayed to the front of the train. A lightning bolt illuminated the sky and he suddenly stiffened. The figure of a man darted from behind a stack of railroad ties and ran across the tracks, disappearing around the front of the engine. Earp rapped out a sharp command.

"Doc, you and Warren stay here! Don't let anyone else on board. The rest of you come with me!"

Vermillion and McMasters rushed forward, trailing Starbuck, and they followed him down the platform. Earp led them around the caboose and across the tracks. Ahead, through the rain, they saw a man moving toward them, rising every few steps to peer in the coach windows. Then, glancing in their direction, the man spotted them and whirled to run. Earp threw the shotgun to his shoulder.

"Halt! Or you'll get it in the back!"

The man stopped and eased around with his arms in the air. As they approached him, the light from the coaches clearly outlined his features. He stared at them with a mixture of fear and bravado. Earp halted and slowly cocked both hammers on the scattergun.

"Stilwell, I know you're not alone. You've got about three seconds to tell me who's with you and where they are."

Stilwell swallowed hard. "You've got nothin' on me, Earp. There's no law against walkin' the tracks."

"Cut the bullshit! Talk quick or I'll dump both loads of this greener in your balls and let you die slow."

"Wyatt!"

Holliday rounded the caboose and hurried toward them. "We just saw Ike Clanton run around the corner of the station. Happened too fast to get a shot at him."

"That figures," Earp said over his shoulder. "Ike never was one to stick around for a fight."

Holliday halted beside him. "Who you got here?"

"Frank Stilwell." Earp grinned, turned his head slightly. "He obliged us by showin' up just when we heard he helped kill Morg."

Starbuck was startled by the expression on Earp's face. He saw there a wild homicidal rage, and deep within the ice-blue eyes, a look of feral savagery. Suddenly the engine chuffed smoke and the wheels groaned as the train got underway. Earp turned back to the outlaw, and there was a quiet steel fury in his voice.

"Stilwell, if you've got the faith, you better start prayin'. Your time's run out."

The train jolted forward and the first passenger car slowly rolled past them. Out of the corner of his eye, Starbuck saw the conductor and several passengers peering out the coach window. Then Earp triggered both barrels and the shotgun belched a yard-long streak of flame. Stilwell staggered backwards, the entire front of his coat blown apart. His knees suddenly buckled and he struck the ground hard, sprawled in a welter of blood.

The coaches gathered speed, and intermittent light from the windows framed Stilwell's face in a death-mask. Powder flash from the shotgun had set his clothes afire, but the rain quickly extinguished the flames. Wisps of smoke continued to rise from his blood-scorched body as the express car rattled past. Then the train was gone and a moment later the tail lights of the caboose were obscured by the storm.

Warren ran across the tracks. A jagged streak of lightning split the darkness, and he stopped, looking down at the body. His eyes widened, and he quickly turned away. After a moment he found his voice.

"Frank Stilwell?"

"Used to be," Holliday said without expression. "Now he's nobody."

"Better get used to it," Earp said gruffly. "You'll see lots more like him before we're through."

"Yeah," Warren mumbled. "I know."

Earp broke open the shotgun. He extracted the spent shells and contemptuously tossed them on the smoldering body. His mouth worked at the corners, and he stared down with an unsettling gaze, deep and intense. Several moments passed, then he laughed a low, gloating laugh.

"At least the sorry bastard didn't beg."

A cone of silence enveloped the men. Warren exchanged a worried glance with Starbuck, and a message passed between them. Unbidden, almost unwittingly, they were both thinking the same thing. The laugh they'd just heard was sane and yet somehow spooky. The laugh of a man skittering very near the edge of reason.

"Let's go," Earp ordered abruptly. "We've still got a long haul, and it won't all be this easy."

The men fell in behind Earp as he walked toward the depot. Lagging back, Starbuck looked at the body one last time. He smiled, telling himself it had begun and knowing in the same thought where it would end. The place where Frank Stilwell would soon take up residence.

The boneyard.

CHAPTER 14

Early the next evening Earp convened a council of war. The meeting had been called at Starbuck's suggestion, the purpose being to work out strategy for the upcoming manhunt. Apart from Holliday, no one else was asked to attend.

The others, Warren and the two hired guns, raised no objections. The previous night, after Stilwell's killing, Earp had led them on a long walk to the first flag station outside Tucson. From there, they hopped a freight train to the railway junction at Contention, and then traveled by horseback to Tombstone. The party had arrived, weary and trailworn, shortly after the noon hour. None of them had slept since day before yesterday, and the tension of the last forty-eight hours had sapped their energy. Earp took rooms at the Occidental, and the men had fallen gratefully into bed. Holliday and Starbuck were awakened before suppertime, and had joined Earp in the hotel diningroom. The others were left to their own devices for the balance of the night.

At Starbuck's request, Earp had obtained a detailed

map of Arizona Territory. Now, huddled around the
desk in Earp's room, they examined the map closely.
Starbuck, by virtue of his hitch as an army scout,
asked the questions.

"Last time out, where did you start?"

Holliday stabbed at the map with a bony finger.
"Charleston."

"Why there?"

"Because that's where Brocius and his boys hang
out."

"Any special reason?"

"There's a saloon—The Silver Dollar—that caters
to cattlemen and their hired hands. Brocius only rustles
cows down in Mexico, so the welcome mat's always
out. He sells cheap and there's plenty of ranchers that
don't mind turning a crooked dollar."

"What made you think you'd find him there?"

"That's a damnfool question!" Earp's tone was
hotly defensive. "Doc just told you why."

"I'm no lawman," Starbuck replied, suppressing a
smile, "but it never hurts to put yourself in the other
fellow's boots. Virge had just been bushwhacked, and
Brocius probably figured you'd come looking for him.
Way it worked out, he knew right where you'd start."

Earp digested the thought, nodding. "You're sayin'
we won't find them in Charleston this time either."

"That's about the size of it."

"So where do we start?"

Starbuck warded him off with upraised palms.
"Let's take it step by step. After Charleston, where did
you look next?"

"Everywhere," Earp grumbled. "We hit the Clanton

ranch that same day. Then we rode southwest." He
traced the route on the map. "The Huachuca Mountains and a swing along the border. Up to Bisbee and
across to the Dragoons and Benson. Then we circled
back to the border and kept on circlin'. Before it was
over, I felt like a dog chasin' his tail."

"All that time," Starbuck asked, "didn't you ever
once cut their sign?"

"Hell no!" Earp said bitterly. "Why do you think I
finally called it quits?"

"You have to remember," Holliday interjected,
"we're the outsiders around here. Brocius has friends
all through the southern part of the territory. Nobody
would give us the time of day, much less a tip on his
whereabouts."

Starbuck took a moment to light a cheroot. He
puffed thoughtfully, studying the map for a long while.
At last, he grunted to himself and blew a plume of
smoke into the air.

"Here's the way it looks to me. Charleston's out,
and I'd say the same thing goes for the Clanton ranch."

Earp eyed him keenly. "You don't think they'd
have gone back there after killin' Morg, is that it?"

"No, I don't," Starbuck said equably. "Even if they
had, they would've been long gone by now."

"I don't get you."

"Ike Clanton took off last night like his pants were
on fire. By now, they know Stilwell's dead and they
know you aren't."

"Aren't what?"

"Dead," Starbuck said simply. "They were after you
last night, not Virge. Probably three or four of them

spotted around the depot waiting for a clear shot. Stilwell got careless and tipped their hand. That's why Clanton lit out so fast."

A puzzled frown appeared on Holliday's face. "You've sure got the voice of experience for somebody that's no lawman."

Starbuck regarded him with an expression of amusement. "Doc, you get the same experience on the other side of the fence. Stays with you longer, too."

"How so?"

"Because you live and learn, or you don't live at all."

"Judas Priest," Holliday said scornfully. "You're a cardsharp, and you served with Custer, and now you tell us you rode the owlhoot. You're a regular jack-of-all-trades, aren't you?"

"After a fashion." Starbuck's smile broadened. "Course, that don't necessarily mean I'm the master of none."

"The way you talk, you know a damnsight more than you ever let on before."

"Hold on, Doc." Earp gave him a reproachful look. "The way he talks makes sense. Damn good sense!"

"That's my point," Holliday countered. "Ever since we met him, he's been playin' the fool. Now, all of a sudden, he's not as dumb as he acts. I don't like it."

Starbuck sensed danger. A cynic was always suspicious of change, and Holliday's skepticism might very well prove contagious. He grinned, the cheroot clamped between his teeth, and put on a bold front.

"Doc, let me tell you something, one grifter to another. I choose my friends real careful, and even then,

I wait a long time to let them know I'm swifter than I look. That's a lesson I learned the hard way, and it's brought me through many a tight scrape."

He paused, staring Holliday directly in the eye. "Now, if that rankles your fur, then it's me that misjudged you, not the other way round. You just say the word, and I'll go on about my business. Adios and no hard feelings."

The bluff worked. Earp gave Holliday the fish-eye, warning him to carry it no further. Then his glance shifted quickly to Starbuck.

"Doc didn't mean nothin', Jack. The last couple of days, you've just showed us more than we bargained for, that's all."

"No offense taken." Starbuck rocked his hand, fingers splayed. "I just tend to get serious when the killing starts."

"Who don't?" Earp said agreeably. "Now, suppose we get back on track. You never did say exactly where you figured we ought to start."

"It's all guesswork," Starbuck said earnestly, leaning over the map. "Just the same, it looks to me like there's two possibilities. First, Brocius and his boys could've made a beeline for Mexico. Offhand, though, I'd say that's the least likely."

"Why?"

"Because McMasters and Vermillion work out of Nogales. They're old timers down that way, and Brocius probably figures they'd get wind of it if he showed up below the border."

"What's your second guess?"

"I think Brocius has a hideout somewhere pretty

close to home. Matter of fact, I'd be willing to bet that's where he holed up the last time you went after him."

"So where do we start?"

"The Clanton ranch."

"Some tracker!" Holliday shouted. "You just got through tellin' us they wouldn't go anywhere near the ranch."

"They won't, but I'd be awful surprised if they just rode off and left the place to run itself."

"That's right!" Earp verified. "Last time we was by there, they'd left the cook to look after things."

"Did you question him?"

"Why hell yes! We're not that stupid, Jack."

"I take it he didn't tell you anything."

"What's there to tell?" Earp said sternly. "I damn near broke his arm off, but he didn't know nothing about nothing."

"He knows one thing."

"Yeah, what's that?"

"Unless I'm way wide of the mark, he knows which direction they rode."

"Are you sayin' you can track 'em just by knowin' which direction they took?"

"That many horses," Starbuck reminded him, "leave a ton of tracks. Ton of horseshit, too. Show me the way they went and I'll follow them clean to hell."

"By God, you're not jokin', are you?"

"I've got an idea the joke'll be on Brocius this time."

"You sound mighty—" Holliday began, but there was a knock on the door, and he stopped.

"We're busy," Earp called. "Come back later."

"Wyatt!" The voice was muffled, and the knock more insistent. "It's John Clum. I have to see you!"

Earp muttered something to himself, then nodded. Holliday rose, moving to the door, and admitted Clum. The mayor rushed into the room, scarcely glancing at Starbuck. His expression was harried and a sheen of perspiration covered his face.

"Wyatt, we've got trouble, big trouble."

Earp waved him to a chair. "What's wrong now?"

"There's a warrant out for your arrest."

Earp stared at him, dumbstruck. Clum doffed his hat, tossing it on the desk, and dropped into a chair. He took out a handkerchief and wiped his face. His hands were trembling.

"A wire just arrived authorizing Johnny Behan to arrest you on sight. Fortunately, the telegraph operator owes me a favor, and he brought the wire to me first. I got him to hold off an hour before he delivered it to Behan."

"Warrant?" Earp asked in a froggy voice. "On what charge?"

"Murder," Clum said gravely. "The sheriff in Tucson had that westbound train stopped in Prescott. He got depositions from the conductor and several passengers. They identified you and Doc."

"By God, that takes gall! I'm wearin' a badge and Frank Stilwell was a wanted man. Where the hell does anybody get off chargin' me with murder?"

"It won't wash." Clum's tone was severe. "Those people say you executed Stilwell. All of them testified that he had his hands in the air, that he'd surrendered."

"He was wanted!" Earp said angrily. "Wanted for murder!"

"Wyatt, you're the wanted man now. You killed him like a hog in a charnel house, and there are eye-witnesses that will swear to it."

"I've still got this badge, and anybody—Behan included—will think a long time before they tangle with a deputy marshal."

"You were a deputy," Clum said hesitantly. "The U.S. Marshal revoked your commission late this afternoon. That was in the wire, too."

Earp shook his head violently. "We've still got connections! There's people that owe me, owe me plenty. We'll get'em to put in the fix and have it hushed up."

"Not for murder, they won't. Face up to reality, Wyatt! Once word gets around, all of them will wash their hands of you. You won't even exist so far as they're concerned."

"They owe me!" Earp said, almost shouting. "I've been their goddamn lightning rod in this town. It was me that done the dirty work and they better not forget it!"

"For your own good," Clum persisted, "you're the one that better forget it. Politics is a rotten business, and I shouldn't have to tell you that. Killing Stilwell was the last straw, Wyatt. You're a liability to them now, and they won't lift a finger to help you."

"They're tarred with the same brush! Either they help me or I'll take'em down with me."

"It's too late for that," Clum patiently explained. "We're talking about murder, not politics. You might smear their reputations, but what would that accomplish?"

Earp's mouth hardened. "It'd blow their plans sky high! Once I got done spillin' the beans, they wouldn't be able to show their faces in Cochise County."

"On top of which," Holliday said sullenly, "I'd make it my personal business to give every one of the sonsabitches a dose of lead poisoning."

"Doc, please!" Clum sputtered. "Killing them won't solve anything. You'd only make matters worse."

"I ought to start with you," Holliday said in disgust. "Way it looks to me, you're the first rat off the ship."

Clum suddenly appeared shaken, rigid with fear. "Good God, why won't you listen? I didn't have to come here tonight, and there's nothing in it for me one way or the other. I'm trying to convince you to save yourselves."

"We beat a murder rap once before," Earp told him. "Hell, they had us up on three counts that time."

"You won't beat this one," Clum said, voice low and urgent. "In Tucson, you wouldn't have a friendly judge sitting on the bench. You wouldn't even get a fair shake, much less an under-the-table deal. The case would go to trial and you'd be convicted. You know I'm right, too."

He paused, emotionally drained, and lowered his eyes. "You're through in Arizona, Wyatt. You have to get out as fast as you can ride. Otherwise, you'll wind up at the end of a hangman's rope."

A thick silence settled in the room. Earp rose and paced to the window. He stood there a long time, staring thoughtfully down at the street. At last, with a heavy sigh, he scrubbed his face with his palms. When he turned around, he permitted himself a grim smile.

"I never much cared for Tombstone anyway."

Starbuck marked again that his smile was a strange and chilling sight. It was more on the order of a rictus, some outward grimace that creased his mouth but never touched his eyes. Watching him, Starbuck briefly considered attempting an arrest, here and now. Then he put the impulse aside. Not only was he outnumbered, but he had no real faith in a judge and jury. He told himself there was a better way. A way that might still get Earp killed.

"You fooled me," Starbuck said casually. "I never would've pegged you as a quitter."

"Quitter!" Earp flared. "What the hell you mean by that?"

"Unless I heard wrong, you just got through saying you're pulling out of Tombstone."

"So?"

"So I didn't figure you'd let Brocius off the hook, that's all."

"You figured right," Earp said firmly. "I'm callin' it a day in Tombstone, but nothing else changes."

"You're not leaving?" Clum asked anxiously. "I beg you to reconsider, Wyatt. Another day in the territory may be one day too long."

"I'll leave when my business is finished. Not before."

"Then there's a very good chance you'll get yourself killed instead of Brocius. With a warrant in his pocket, Johnny Behan has you right where he wants you. He'll deputize every two-bit gunman in town, and do his level best to bring you back draped across a horse."

"You always were a worrywart, John. Have a drink and calm your nerves. Behan's the least of my troubles."

"I hope you're right. I genuinely hope so."

Earp's gaze moved to Starbuck. "Jack, hustle on down to the livery and boot somebody in the ass. Get our horses saddled and bring'em on back here *muy pronto.*"

"We're pulling out tonight?"

"That's the general idea," Earp nodded, turning quickly to Holliday. "Doc, go roust Warren and the boys. Tell'em we ride in half an hour."

Starbuck and Holliday hurried from the room. When the door closed, John Clum was slumped in his chair, staring blankly at nothing. Earp, after folding the map into a neat square, got busy packing his saddlebags.

A short time later Earp descended the stairs to the lobby. His saddlebags were thrown over his shoulder and the sawed-off shotgun was tucked under his arm. Clum was beside him, and at the bottom of the stairs, they shook hands. Then he walked toward Holliday and the men, who were waiting near the front door.

"Everything ready?"

"All set," Holliday noted. "Horses are outside."

Earp led the way onto the veranda. The men trooped along behind him, moving in a tight phalanx to the hitch rack. There they mounted and sat watching him while he shoved the shotgun into the saddle scabbard. As he tied down his saddlebags, a voice suddenly sounded from upstreet.

"Earp! Wyatt Earp!"

Behan, flanked by a deputy, stepped off the boardwalk and rushed toward them. He halted a few paces away, darting a nervous glance at the men.

"Earp, I want to see you."

"Behan, if you're not careful, you'll see me once too often."

Behan squared himself up. "It won't do you any good to run. I've got a warrant for your arrest, and I'll be on your trail in the morning with twenty or thirty men."

"You do that." Earp's tone was icy. "We'll be lookin' for you."

Earp swung aboard his horse and reined sharply away from the hitch rack. The others brought their mounts around and rode off down the street. At the corner, where they turned west, Starbuck glanced back toward the hotel. He saw Behan throw his hat to the ground, then kick at it in an outburst of temper. Somehow, though he understood the lawman's frustration, it seemed a fitting end to his long stay in Tombstone.

He laughed and feathered his horse in the ribs.

CHAPTER 15

The dawn sky was metallic, almost colorless. The men were crouched low in an arroyo, their eyes trained on the ranch house. Behind them, the San Pedro snaked southward, and the mountains to the east were limned in the first rays of sunrise. Alert, their nerves keyed to a fight, they waited for Starbuck's signal.

Still very much in command, Earp was nonetheless relying on Starbuck for advice. Last night, shortly after departing Tombstone, he had summoned Starbuck to the front of the column. On the Charleston road, riding west toward the San Pedro, they had discussed the opening move in their search for Brocius. Starbuck had advanced the argument that a manhunt was not all that different from chasing Indians. Swift strikes, and the element of surprise, were everything to experienced Indian fighters. Their tactics were simple yet deadly effective. Hit fast, hit hard, and strike when least expected. With a poker face, he had then invented several fairy tales about his own days on the owlhoot. Hopping from lie to lie, he told Earp that he had survived only by reversing the tables on lawmen.

His service as an army scout had taught him to deny them the tactical advantage of surprise.

Earp bought the argument. By midnight, when they turned north along the San Pedro, he'd begun thinking of Starbuck as his chief tactician. An hour before dawn, when they tethered their horses downstream, he had agreed to Starbuck's plan for storming the Clanton ranch. Earp stood aside, nodding approval, while Starbuck handed out assignments. Holliday, Vermillion and McMasters would take the cook shack and the bunkhouse. Earp and Warren, along with Starbuck himself, would take the main house. The raid, Starbuck had informed them, would be carried out as though the entire Brocius gang was bedded down in the buildings. The likelihood of that was slight, but he'd warned the men to take no chances. Surprise and caution were the watchwords.

For his part, Starbuck had all he could do to keep a straight face. There was virtually no chance that Brocius would be caught napping at the gang's customary headquarters. The sole purpose of this morning's drill was to solidify his own position with Earp. That was essential to the vague plan already taking shape in his mind. Earp must not only trust him, but must become dependent on his advice. Then, somewhere down the line, the opportunity would arise for the wrong word at the right time. And Earp would go home in a box.

One eye on the ranch house, Starbuck pondered the thicket of possibilities open to him. The murder warrant, coupled with Earp's decision to remain in Arizona Territory, presented several options. The most enticing was that Brocius and Earp could be maneu-

vered into a shootout. Stymied until now, it was his
original plan and still seemed the most likely to succeed. Failing that, he would attempt to arrange a clash
between the Earps and the Behan posse. After last
night, he had every confidence the sheriff would be
gnashing his teeth for another crack at Earp. Finally,
as a last resort, there was the alternative of arresting
Earp and delivering him for trial in Tucson. Yet that
was the bottom of the barrel, the most chancey of the
lot, and Starbuck's expectations were still high. He
thought today would put them on the road to the most
satisfactory outcome. A permanent sort of good rid-
dance.

Soon after dawn the sun crested the distant mountains. Starbuck waited until the glare of the fireball
was at their backs, then he gave the signal. The men
scrambled out of the arroyo and rushed across an open
stretch of ground. Near the corral, which held fewer
than a dozen horses, they separated into two groups.
Holliday hurried toward the cook shack, while
McMasters and Vermillion burst through the door of
the bunkhouse. Starbuck, with Earp and Warren on his
heels, stormed into the main house.

Starbuck and Earp quickly checked the three bed-
rooms at the rear of the house. All were empty, and
looked as though no one had slept there in several
days. Warren came out of the kitchen as they returned
to the front room. He shook his head, indicating he'd
found nothing. Walking to a pot-bellied stove, Starbuck bent over and placed his hand on the underside
of the firebox. He straightened up, affirmation written
across his features.

"Stone cold," he said. "Hasn't been used for at least two days, maybe more."

"You called it," Earp acknowledged. "They probably cleared out the same night they shot Morg."

"Left in a hurry, too." Starbuck gestured at a disarray of clothing and gear scattered about the room. "When they missed you and Doc at the pool hall, that put a crimp in their plans. I'd judge Brocius decided it was time to pull another disappearing act."

"All I want to know—"

"Look here what we found!"

Holliday shoved a bewhiskered little man through the door. He was on the sundown side of forty, nearly bald, and stooped from a lifetime of standing over a cook stove. Barefooted, the trap door of his longjohns hanging loose, he stumbled to a halt. His eyes were wide with fear.

"Almost missed him," Holliday chuckled. "Sherm remembered to check the outhouse, and found him taking a constitutional."

Earp gave him a cool once-over. "You remember me?"

"Guess I do," the cook admitted shakily. "My arm ain't been the same since the last time you stopped by."

"You remember the question I asked you then?"

"Couldn't hardly forget. You asked me where Brocius and the boys had went to."

"I'm askin' you again."

The cook turned pallid as a gravestone. "I shore hate to tell you this, but the answer's the same. I ain't got no more idea than the man in the moon." He shot a weak glance around at the men. "It's the holy-honest-to-Christ's truth! Them boys don't never say boo to me."

"You're not deaf, are you?"

"I do my best," the cook mumbled. "What you don't hear can't hurt you."

"Wanna bet?" Earp motioned to Vermillion and McMasters. "Unplug his ears."

Vermillion, who was standing to the rear, drove his fist into the cook's kidneys. The little man doubled over, his eyes bulging with pain. His mouth popped open in a breathless whoofing sound. McMasters struck out in a fast shadowy movement. His blow connected with a mushy crack, and the cook lurched backwards, spurting blood from a broken nose. McMasters clubbed him upside the ear, then drove a whistling haymaker deep into his rib cage. The cook dropped like a wet bag of sand. He moaned, spitting frothy bubbles, and sucked great gasps of air.

Earp watched the beating with stolid indifference. But when Vermillion cocked his leg for a kick, Starbuck moved to stop it. He stepped in, shielding the cook, and waved Vermillion off.

"That's enough! He's no good to us if he can't talk."

Starbuck knelt down. "Listen to me, old man. I'll only ask once, and you'd better have an answer."

The cook stared up at him, lips puckered like a goldfish. Starbuck gave him a moment, then leaned closer. "Tell me one thing. When Brocius and his boys rode out, which direction were they headed?"

"East," the cook rasped, breathing heavily. "Acrost the river."

Starbuck climbed to his feet. "That's all we need. I checked the ground, and that thunder storm didn't get this far south. It'll be easy tracking."

Vermillion nudged the cook with his toe. "What about him?"

"Kill him," Earp said with chilling simplicity.

"No!" Starbuck turned, meeting Earp's look directly. "You start killing innocent people and we'll have to run all the way to China. I won't be a party to it."

"What's to stop me?"

"Nothing," Starbuck said evenly. "Except you'll have to find yourself another tracker."

"You've gone squeamish awful sudden."

"I've killed my share, but I never murdered anybody. I'd like to keep it that way."

"What the hell!" Earp laughed a strange, cryptic laugh. "Wouldn't want to hurt your sensitive feelings."

He stepped past the cook and walked toward the door. Starbuck, breathing an inward sigh of relief, followed him outside. The others exchanged quizzical glances, then slowly filed along behind.

Some ten minutes later McMasters and Vermillion brought the horses from downstream. Starbuck, watched closely by Earp, was walking the shoreline east of the river. Suddenly he stopped, dropping to one knee, and studied the faint imprint of tracks in the ground. He took a smidge of dirt between his fingers, nodding to himself as though the earth possessed some secret knowledge. Then he rose and walked back to Earp.

"Eight horses." He bobbed his head into a blinding sunrise. "Tracks are three days old."

"You're sure?" Earp regarded him with squinted eyes. "I wouldn't take kindly to a wild-goose-chase."

Starbuck nodded. "I'm sure."

"Then let's ride."

Florentino Cruz reminded himself to light a candle to the Virgin. A swarthy man of mixed blood, he treated religion with the superstition of one who believes that all gods are whimsical and must be constantly appeased. He thought it would be a serious error not to offer thanks for his good fortune.

A bandit, and more recently an assassin, he sometimes took refuge with his sister and her husband. Their small rancho lay on the western slope of the Dragoon Mountains. Some twenty miles northeast of Tombstone, it was off the beaten track, tucked away in a remote stretch of wilderness. Cruz's brother-in-law raised goats and pigs, and tended a vegetable garden he had scratched out of the rocky soil. In a stout log corral, he also kept an unusually large number of horses. A poor man, cursed with a barren wife, he saw no harm in supplementing his meager income. His wife's brother rode with a band of gringos, and their leader treated him with the generosity of a patron. In return, he operated a relay station for the Brocius gang.

Cruz often stopped over here when a job was completed. His sister's cooking was spicy and plentiful, and he much preferred it to the swill served at the

Clanton ranch. Furthermore, he was of the strong opinion that he was safer here. The gang's secret hideout, in his view, was not secret enough. Only this morning, following Stilwell's death last night, the gang had ridden off on fresh mounts. He had elected to remain behind, certain in the knowledge that Brocius would draw pursuit. He considered it unfortunate, almost an omen, that Earp had not been killed at the train station. He also considered himself a wise man for having separated from his gringo *compañeros*. Here, with his sister and her husband, he was out of harm's way.

In the deepening indigo of dusk, Cruz and his brother-in-law were splitting wood outside the one-room adobe. His sister appeared in the doorway and tossed a pan of dirty water into the yard. She wiped her hands on her dress, and stood for a moment watching the men. Then, on the verge of turning back into the house, she suddenly stiffened. She stared west, shielding her eyes against the dying flare of sunset. Some distance away, she saw three riders top a low rise. Their features were indistinct, but their clothing immediately identified them as gringos.

The men, following her gaze, stopped splitting wood. The riders moved toward them at a slow trot, silhouetted against the last rays of daylight. Then, emerging into the silty dusk, their features became visible. Cruz instantly recognized the two Earp brothers, and the stranger he'd seen with them at the train station. He dropped his ax, jerking a pistol from the waistband of his trousers. His eyes flicked to the adobe, then he quickly changed his mind. He ran toward the corral.

As he rounded the corner of the house, Cruz broke stride and skidded to an abrupt halt. Three more riders, one of them Doc Holliday, were circling the corral from the north. Behind him, he heard the thud of hoofbeats as the Earps spurred their horses to a gallop. Trapped and desperate, he sprinted toward a wooded outcropping east of the corral. Before he could reach the knoll, Holliday and the men he recognized as *pistoleros* cut him off. A moment later Earp and his companions closed in from the rear.

Cruz flung his sixgun on the ground and raised his hands. He watched with a doglike dumbfounded stare as the riders joined ranks in a loose, halfmoon formation. No one spoke, but he felt Earp's gaze boring into him with the intensity of fire. The horses advanced, crowding ever closer, and he scuttled backwards to avoid being trampled. Slowly, relentlessly, the riders forced him up the knoll. At the crest, still backing away, he lost his balance and tumbled head over heels down the reverse slope. The horsemen kneed their mounts into the defile and reined to a halt before him. Dazed and shaken, he hauled himself to his feet.

Earp's jaw muscles worked, and his eyes narrowed to tiny points of malevolence. He shifted in his saddle, glancing at Starbuck. A cruel smile touched his lips.

"This here's Florentino Cruz," he said without inflection. "Sometimes known as Indian Charlie."

"Wasn't he one of the men named in the indictment for killing Morg?"

Earp merely nodded, then turned to Vermillion. "Ask him if he knows who I am."

Vermillion leaned forward. *"Conoces este hombre?"*

"Sí, este hombre se llama Earp."

"Tell him"—Earp's voice dropped—"I came here to kill him for what he did to my brother."

Vermillion ducked his chin at Earp. *"Este hombre está aquí para matarte. Por la cosa tu hiciste a su hermano."*

"Madre Dios!" Cruz dropped to his knees, clasping his hands like a man offering prayer. *"Por favor yo soy innocente! Yo no quiero morir!"*

Vermillion spat tobacco juice on the ground. "Says he didn't do it."

"Gutless bastard!" Earp made a quick, savage gesture. "Tell him he's got one chance to live. I'll let him go if he tells us where to find Brocius."

"Díle a ellos donde está Brocius y este hombre no le mata."

Cruz blanched at the mention of Brocius' name. He darted an imploring look at the other men, only to be met by grim stares. After a moment, Earp pulled his sawed-off shotgun from the saddle boot and slowly cocked both hammers. Kneeing his horse to the right, he laid the shotgun over the saddle horn and lowered the muzzle until it was centered on Cruz's head. The halfbreed's eyes went round as saucers. His gaze was riveted on the shotgun, never wavering from the double black holes in the stubby muzzle.

Earp wagged the tip of the shotgun. "Tell him he's got five seconds to talk or he'll be shakin' hands with his maker."

"Usted tiene cinco segundos para hablar o usted va con Jesus Cristo muy pronto."

Cruz swallowed, his voice choked with terror. *"Brocius y siete de los hombres están en Iron Springs."*

"We got it," Vermillion said, easing back in his saddle. "He says Brocius and six or seven of the gang are holed up at Iron Springs. Near as I recollect, that's over in the Whetstone Mountains."

Starbuck, looking on, knew the halfbreed had sealed his own death warrant. But this time he raised no objections. Cruz was a murderer, one of a gang of cutthroats, and he felt not the slightest stirring of mercy. Nor was he at odds with what Earp was about to do. He himself had hung men for lesser crimes, and an execution, whatever the reason, was still an execution. Some men deserved to die.

The shotgun exploded in a double roar. Cruz's head seemed to evaporate. His skull blew apart and he was knocked kicking onto his back. A mist of bone and brain matter rained down, covering his torso with a light, blood-red spray. His legs jerked, bootheels pounding the earth in a slow dance of death. Then, with one last twitch, it stopped.

Earp reined his horse around and rode off. The others trailed him over the knoll and down past the corral. Out front of the adobe, the Mexican and the halfbreed woman were standing with their heads bowed. Earp signaled a halt, and the men reined in their mounts directly behind him. When the dust settled, he broke open the shotgun, ejecting the spent shells, and reloaded. Then he jammed it into the saddle boot, and turned his gaze on the couple. His eyes were cold and impassive, his mouth razored in a tight line. He motioned to Vermillion.

"Tell'em Cruz is dead." He dug out a gold coin and tossed it in the dirt at their feet. "Twenty dollars ought to buy a real impressive mass. Tell'em if they're smart, they'll report he got bit by a scorpion and didn't recover."

Vermillion indicated the coin. *"Su amigo está muerto. Si ustedes son listos reportarán que él fue picado por un escorpión."*

The man removed his sombrero, looking down at the coin, and bobbed his head. The woman stood stockstill, her eyes frozen on the patch of ground at her feet. Earp was silent for a time, seemingly lost in thought. Watching him, Starbuck sensed he was debating the wisdom of leaving them alive. Then, on sudden impulse, he apparently decided the gold piece would buy their silence. He brought his horse sharply around and spurred off into the gathering darkness.

The men kicked their mounts into a lope and rode after him. The thud of hoofbeats slowly diminished, and within moments the riders were lost to sight.

The sister of Florentino Cruz crossed herself and slowly collapsed in the doorway. Her husband stooped down, wiping dust off the coin, and stuck it in his pocket. He went inside the adobe, returning a moment later with a lighted lantern and a shovel. He walked in the direction of the knoll.

CHAPTER 16

"Foxy bastard!"

"Who's that?"

"Brocius," Earp said roughly. "You had him pegged all along."

"Only about halfway."

"C'mon, Jack, credit due where credit's deserved! You said he had a hideout somewhere close to home, and you hit the mark dead center. Iron Springs couldn't be no more than ten or twelve miles from the Clanton place."

"Maybe so," Starbuck said doubtfully. "Only he's lots trickier than I thought."

"So he doubled back! How the hell could you've figured that?"

"He didn't double back."

Earp gave him a swift sidelong look. "What are you gettin' at?"

"Well, I've been studying on it. Something kept me scratching my head, but it didn't rightly make sense."

"I thought you was awful quiet last night."

"Tell you the truth, it only come to me a little while ago."

The statement was a baldfaced lie. Last night, after the Cruz killing, they had camped on a small creek some miles to the west. There, following a cold supper, Starbuck had reconstructed the events of the past three days. Bit by bit, based on what he'd learned, he pieced together the movements of the Brocius gang since the night of Morg's death. Yet he'd held his silence last night, retiring early to his blankets. All day today, as they rode westerly toward the Whetstone Mountains, he had also avoided conversation with Earp. Somehow, turning it this way and that, he had searched for a means of twisting the situation to Earp's disadvantage. But now, lacking any great brainstorm, he saw nothing to lose by playing it straight. Earp would be impressed and come to rely even more heavily on his advice. Which at some point would prove vital to his overall plan.

"Yesterday morning," Starbuck said at length, "when I found the tracks at Clanton's place. You remember I said they were three days old?"

"What about it?"

"That should've tipped me off. Those tracks were made the night Morg was killed."

"So?"

"Well, the way I put it together, Brocius and his bunch swapped horses at Cruz's place the next morning. Then they rode straight to Tucson, and tried to waylay us at the train station. Afterward, they turned right around and rode back to Cruz's place."

"And swapped horses again!" Earp suddenly grasped it. "That means they were headed west toward Iron Springs at the same time we were followin' their tracks east to the Dragoons."

"We're a day late and a dollar short," Starbuck affirmed. "Lucky for us, Cruz decided to stay behind. Otherwise, I would've had to start tracking all over again. No telling how much time we would've lost."

Earp uttered a low chuckle. "I'd sooner be a day late and a dollar short than no payday at all. That's what happened the last time I took out after Brocius."

Starbuck cracked a smile. "All you needed was a hound dog. Brocius lays so many trails, it takes a damn good sniffer to pick up the scent."

"Jack, you're all right!" Earp said, with a quick nod of satisfaction. "You can scout for me six days a week and all day on Sunday. Hadn't been for you, we'd still be wonderin' which way was up."

Starbuck gave himself a pat on the back. Once more he'd euchred Earp into accepting a highly embroidered version of the facts. As the sun rose to its zenith, and they forded the San Pedro north of Contention, he felt like a cat with a mouthful of feathers. He had a hunch today was the day. The end of the line.

The sun sank lower, smothering in a bed of copper beyond the mountains. The ragged crests jutted skyward like sentinels guarding a cruel and lifeless land. Far below, bordered by a grove of trees, the springs lay hidden in purple shadow. There was no sound, only the foreboding silence of oncoming night.

The men reined to a halt on a craggy ridge overlooking the springs. A narrow trail led downward to the wooded gorge, winding around a rocky spur near the bottom. Starbuck dismounted, quickly inspecting the trail where it sloped steeply off the ridge. He grunted to himself, spotting marks left by shod horses in the hard-packed ground. After closer examination, he turned and indicated the tracks with a sweeping motion of his arm.

Earp told the other men to stay with the horses. He walked forward and joined Starbuck at the edge of the escarpment. They went belly down, removing their hats, and began a systematic inspection of the basin below. The springs was plainly visible, a cool waterhole freshened from deep within the earth's core. The shelterbelt of trees, thick with undergrowth and obscured by shadow, curved in a gentle arc beyond the springs. There was no movement, no picket line of horses, no sign of man. To all appearances, only wilderness creatures came to drink at Iron Springs.

Earp looked perplexed. "What the hell do you make of that?"

"Beats me," Starbuck said, studying the springs intently. "Looks dead as a doornail down there."

"No way they could've known we're on their trail."

"You reckon they're camped back in those trees?"

"I dunno," Earp confessed. "If they are, why don't we see smoke from a fire? They'd have no reason to pitch a cold camp."

"Well, I know one thing," Starbuck said with conviction. "Those tracks were made yesterday. Somebody went down that trail before nightfall."

"Then where the Jesus are they?"

"Is there another way out of here?"

"Could be," Earp allowed, pointing south along the gorge. "The ground seems to drop off in that direction. Maybe something spooked them and they've done hightailed it."

"I guess there's only one way to find out."

"What's that?"

"Somebody has to go down there and have a look-see."

Earp glanced sidewise. "You volunteerin' for the job?"

"Got no choice." Starbuck grinned shallowly. "I'm the dumbbell that signed on as scout with this outfit."

"All right, but you take it slow and easy. We'll cover you from up here just in case things aren't as peaceful as they look. Any sign of trouble, you hump your butt out of there muy damn pronto."

"Don't worry! I'm a regular streak of lightning when I put my mind to it."

Starbuck was playing a longshot. He recalled the last words out of Florentino Cruz's mouth, and he couldn't believe the halfbreed had lied. He thought there was at least a fifty-fifty chance that Brocius had posted a lookout here on the ridge. If true, that meant the gang had been alerted, and was now waiting in the copse of trees below. Somehow, without getting himself killed, he had to lure Earp down to the springs. He was betting that Brocius wouldn't betray his position merely to kill one man. He took cold comfort from the thought that Brocius had only one known obsession, Wyatt Earp. He hoped, at last, to bring them together.

Without a word to the others, he went back to his horse and mounted. As he rode down the trail, he saw Earp positioning them along the rim of the cliff. Then he turned his attention to the dusky basin. Daylight was fading rapidly, and he knew he hadn't a moment to spare. Even Brocius and his bushwhackers needed enough light to see their sights.

At the bottom of the trail, he rode straight toward the springs. Holding his horse to a steady walk, he circled the waterhole and reined to a halt on the far side. He was within ten yards of the treeline, and a perfect target. He twisted around in the saddle, slowly scanning the shadowed thickets. He saw nothing and heard nothing. Yet an odd shiver went up his backbone, as though he'd caught a whisper of wind whistling through the eyesockets of a skull. His instinct, strong enough to set his skin tingling, told him they were there. He knew they were watching him, trigger fingers tensed and ready, waiting for him to sound the alarm. He let his eyes rove through the trees a moment longer, then he kneed his horse into a walk. All the way around the springs, the hair on the back of his neck was stiff as broomstraw. He told himself with mute wonder that he'd been a damn fool. But he sensed he had won the gamble. There would be no shots. Not yet.

His horse took the steep grade in a series of bounding lurches. Once more on top, he stepped from the saddle and calmly lit a cheroot. His guts were quivering, but he struck and doused the match with a steady hand.

"Well talk up!" Earp demanded, hurrying forward. "What'd you see?"

"Quiet as a church," Starbuck said, exhaling smoke. "I think you hit the nail on the head. Brocius and his boys must've spooked and took off for parts unknown."

The other men collected around Earp, their faces expectant and sober. A moment slipped past, then Holliday let go a muttered curse. He regarded Starbuck with narrow suspicion.

"I don't like it! Something don't smell right."

"Tell you what, Doc." Starbuck inspected the tip of his cigar. "If you're not satisfied, why don't you ride on down there and check it out for yourself?"

"No need." Earp waved them apart. "I'm satisfied, and that's all that counts. We'll just have to pick up their trail come first light and see where it leads."

"What about tonight?" Holliday persisted. "I don't much like the idea of campin' at the springs."

"Quit borrowin' trouble," Earp admonished him. "Nobody shot Jack! Besides, the horses need water, and we could all use a decent night's sleep. Let's get mounted."

In the deepening twilight, the men gathered their horses. Earp led the way, followed by Holliday and Warren. Starbuck managed to position himself in the center, with Vermillion and McMasters bringing up the rear. They went down the narrow trail single-file, the jangle of saddle gear chiming musically in the stillness. No one spoke, and Starbuck took that as a good sign. The men were weary, their senses dulled after nearly four days in the saddle. Except for Holliday, none of them had shown any concern about camping at the springs. They had come here prepared for a fight, and there was a natural letdown upon learning that Brocius had once again eluded their grasp. Starbuck thought it was near-perfect, their mood tailor-made for an ambush. His single qualm was not for his own safety, but rather that one of the outlaws would suddenly turn trigger-happy. Timing was essential, and he worried that the trap might yet be spoiled.

The trail bottomed out and Earp reined toward the springs. One by one, the men rode forward, loosely grouped behind him. The gorge was rapidly turning dark, and ahead, the grove of trees was cloaked in inky shadow. Then, like blinking fireflies, a row of guns spat flame all along the treeline.

Earp's saddle horn disintegrated and his hat flew off his head. He kicked free of the stirrups, grabbing his shotgun, and dove headlong from the saddle. He landed on his side and rolled over, thumbing back the hammer as he came to rest on his stomach. Across the waterhole, the trees were now alive with the fiery blast of gunshots. He slammed the scattergun into his shoulder and centered on a muzzle flash. When he pulled the trigger, a man screamed and stumbled out of the underbrush. He fired the second barrel and saw the man go down. Then he tossed the shotgun aside and jerked his pistol.

Behind him, the men had quit their horses and hit the ground. With the exception of Warren's horse, they had survived the first volley unscathed. Veterans of countless shootouts, they reacted almost instinctively after the initial shock of the ambush. The gunfire became general as they quickly joined the fight. Bellied down, they made poor targets despite the storm of lead whistling across the waterhole. The crack of the outlaws' rifles was punctuated by the dull boom of their own sixguns. Unlike the outlaws, however, they were not scattering their shots in a random barrage. Instead, making each bullet count, they fixed on a muzzle flash and aimed slightly to the right. Accuracy under darkened conditions was difficult, but their fire had a telling effect. A howl indicated that at least one of the gang had been wounded, and another fell thrashing at the edge of the treeline. Yet the fight quickened in tempo, and the sound of gunfire rose to a staccato roar. A patchwork of snarling lead hissed back and forth across the springs.

From his position in the center, Starbuck hugged the ground and poured a steady fire into the trees. He was aware of Warren, who was shooting from behind the fallen horse, and he heard the bark of guns off to one side. But he was too busy to count, and he had no idea who might have been wounded or killed. When he emptied the Colt, he rolled to a new position and reloaded all six chambers. His next shot drew return fire, two quick rounds. One slug kicked dirt in his face and the other fried the air around his ears. Beside a tree, momentarily revealed in the muzzle flash, he saw the bare outlines of a man's face. He dropped his sights a notch and thumbed off three shots, rapid fire. Almost instantly there was a downward flash as the rifle fired into the ground, and the man pitched sideways into the undergrowth. Then, too suddenly to

comprehend, all firing from the treeline abruptly
ceased.

Several more shots were fired by the Earp party
before they realized the fight was over. A stillness settled across the spring, and moments later the rumble
of hooves filtered through the trees. A blur of horses,
almost invisible in the darkness, suddenly bolted from
the far end of the grove. The riders whipped their
mounts into a gallop and were quickly gone, clattering
south through the gorge. Within seconds, even the
thud of hoofbeats faded to nothing.

Starbuck stood, holstering his gun, and went slack-
jawed. He saw Earp not twenty feet in front of him,
and for an instant, he couldn't credit his own eyes. He
recalled hearing the shotgun, but he'd assumed that
Earp, who was in the vanguard, had taken the brunt
of the gang's fire. Now, stunned speechless, a sullen
coal of rage exploded in his chest. All the conniving
and trickery had come to nothing. The ambush, en-
dangering his own life to force a showdown, all for
nothing. Earp, seemingly immune to death, had
emerged without a scratch.

His fists balled into hard knots, and he uttered a
low brutish curse.

Starbuck's sense of outrage and disgust was quickly
compounded. Earp ordered a fire built, and it soon
became clear that Warren's horse was the only casu-
alty. Holliday had been grazed along the cheekbone,
and Vermillion had suffered a flesh wound, but the
others were untouched. By the light of the fire, it was
also apparent that Earp enjoyed a state of grace almost
beyond belief. His clothes hung in tatters. There were

three holes through his coat, another drilled through
his hat, and a slug was imbedded in the heel of his
boot. Not one had drawn blood.

Starbuck's anger slowly gave way to bemused wonderment. Never a staunch believer, he nonetheless
asked himself what god it was that watched over these
men. Or perhaps it wasn't a god at all. Perhaps there
was some special devil, a satanic force that protected
such men from harm. Certainly no five men had ever
had a closer brush with death. Within the space of
three or four minutes, these men had been on the receiving end of probably a hundred rifle slugs. Yet none
of them had been killed, and the wounds they'd suffered were hardly worse than the nick of a dull razor.
It defied understanding, and a thought occurred that
left him momentarily chilled. Perhaps, after all, Wyatt
Earp wasn't meant to be killed. Perhaps he was *unkillable*.

The idea was foreign to Starbuck's character. No
man, himself included, led a charmed life. Nor was
there any great mystery that he too had come through
tonight unscathed. There was a time and place for
every man to die, and when a man's number was
called, he answered. Earp wasn't unkillable. Tonight
simply hadn't been his night. Starbuck vowed to himself he would cancel that reprieve, at the right time
and the right place. However long it took.

In the light of the fire, it was revealed that three
outlaws had answered the call. One of them was the
man Starbuck had shot, three neat holes stitched beneath his breastbone. Another, whose identity was un-

known, had been dusted front and back by several pistol slugs. The third man, however, was instantly recognizable. Curly Bill Brocius had taken a double load of buckshot directly above his beltbuckle. His shirtfront was a plate-sized starburst of blood and gore. He was eviscerated, quite literally blown to bits.

Earp seemed to derive no satisfaction from the outlaw leader's death. There was no question his shotgun had done the job, but his expression betrayed no hint of vindication. Staring down at the body, he appeared curiously disgruntled, somehow unappeased. After a long while, he looked up, his features set in a tight scowl. His gaze settled on McMasters.

"Sherm, get a rope."

"A rope?"

"String him up in the tallest tree you can find."

McMasters looked startled. "You mean hang him?"

"That's exactly what I mean."

"Why hell, Wyatt, he's already dead."

"Do it!" Earp commanded. "Before the buzzards pick his bones, I want every backshooter in the territory to get the message. So hang him high."

Starbuck watched the hanging with a sense of the unreal. McMasters and Vermillion dragged the body under a tree and tossed the rope over a stout limb. Then they hoisted the body high in the air and snubbed the rope tight around the base of the tree. The job finished, they walked away as though they had taken part in something unnormal, not altogether human. The dead man overhead seemed to mock them all.

Earp turned and walked to the fire. He held out his

hands to the flames, and a sudden tremor rippled along his jawbone. Looking on, Starbuck was reminded of a man he'd seen in a courtroom long ago. A man on his way to the madhouse.

CHAPTER 17

In the darkness, the campfire was a small island of light. The men, after wolfing down their supper, were seated on the ground. No one spoke, and the cheery blaze did nothing to dispel a sense of gloom.

Vermillion and McMasters, assigned the first guard shift, were posted along the south end of the grove. Holliday, immediately after the hanging, had insisted on mounting a watch. None of them believed the gang would return, but they all felt more comfortable with someone standing guard. Their horses, picketed at the edge of the treeline, were also kept near at hand. Standing hipshot and drowsy, the animals were visible in the flickering glow of the fire.

Over the crackle of flames, the only sound was the measured creak of a rope. The body, little more than a dim shape in the erratic light, was pushed gently to and fro by an evening breeze. Earp, who hadn't spoken in the last hour, stared at the hanged man with a vacant expression. His eyes had a faraway look, as if he was gazing at something obscured by distance. He sat perfectly still, legs crossed and hands dangling over his knees. The sawed-off shotgun was cradled in his lap.

The long, stony silence was at last broken by Holliday. His tone was caustic, laced with hostility. His remark was addressed directly to Starbuck.

"You're one piss-poor scout, Johnson."

Starbuck was hard put to suppress a smile, but he managed an offhand answer. "All's well that ends well."

"Like hell!" Holliday said furiously. "You come pretty goddamn close to gettin' us killed."

"Easy to say when you've got hindsight on your side."

After the fight, Holliday had taken a torch and walked off into the trees. Halfway through the grove, he'd found a camp site, the fire hastily extinguished and still smoldering. On the far side of the wooded thicket, he had stumbled upon a picket line, with the horses of the three dead outlaws standing walleyed in the night. Since then, he had kept to himself, sullen and withdrawn. Now, in a burst of temper, his anger spilled out.

"Hindsight's got nothin' to do with it! Anybody with a lick of sense would've spotted something fishy. You'd have to be blind to miss it!"

"The way it worked out," Starbuck said lightly, "there wasn't anything to miss. Brocius must've had a lookout posted up there on the ridge. He had plenty of warning, all the time he needed."

"Don't change the subject," Holliday grated. "We're talkin' about you, not Brocius."

"What I'm saying," Starbuck explained, "is that

Brocius probably had a good half hour to make his move. He could've cut and run long before we got here. Instead, he used that time to fix up a real fine ambush."

"That's right!" Warren put in. "You saw it your ownself, Doc. The way they'd doused the fire, and had their horses picketed on the back side of the trees. Brocius was cagey as hell! He rigged a trap and just waited for us to ride into it."

"And we did!" Holliday said sharply. "With Johnson's help, it worked slick as a whistle."

"Help?" Starbuck looked offended. "You're off your rocker, Doc! It was me that rode down here and took a chance on getting ventilated. Or maybe you forgot that?"

"You'd like me to forget, wouldn't you?"

"What the devil's that supposed to mean?"

"You led us in here like a goddamn Judas goat and got us drygulched. That's what it means—plain and simple."

"Doc, you've got a mighty short memory."

"Oh yeah?" Holliday bridled. "What'd I forget now?"

"Couple of things," Starbuck said lazily. "Just for openers, I was getting shot at, too. So it's not like you were all by your lonesome. On top of that, out of the three we killed, I cooled one of them myself. If you care to count the holes, they're dead center through the brisket. All in all, I'd say I carried my share of the load and then some."

"Damn good thing," Holliday grumbled sourly. "If you hadn't, I would've put out your lights myself."

"C'mon, Doc!" Warren laughed uneasily. "Christ, nobody's perfect. Brocius and his boys were hid so well anybody could've missed spottin' them. Isn't that right, Jack?"

"Well—" Starbuck gave him a jolly wink. "Doc might've tumbled to them, but then we'll never know, will we? He seemed real happy to stay up on the ridge and let me come down here for a looksee."

Holliday skewered him with a glare. "You've already pushed your luck enough for one night."

"Who, me?" Starbuck opened his hands, shrugged. "I was just funning you, Doc. No harm in that."

"You're liable to fun yourself—"

"Quit your squabblin'!"

Earp's voice brought them around. His spell appeared broken, and it seemed some cord of sanity had kept him from slipping over the edge. His face was drawn and solemn, and his tone was irritable.

"You want to fight amongst yourselves, save it till another time. We've got plans to make."

Holliday was watching him carefully. "What sort of plans?"

"Johnny Ringo."

"What about him?"

"I'll tell you what about him," Earp said harshly. "He's the only one that ever saw us together. We've got to run him down."

"Be a waste of time," Holliday observed. "I know that bunch. None of them could hardly take a leak without instructions from Brocius. With him dead, they'll scatter all over hell and half of Mexico."

"You're not listenin'," Earp said with strained patience. "Until Ringo's dead and buried, I'll always be lookin' over my shoulder. He's the only one that knows—*the only one!*"

"Give it up, Wyatt." Holliday's tone softened, turned persuasive. "It's time we started worryin' about murder, not robbery. The way things stand, Ringo's the least of our troubles."

Starbuck felt a jolt of excitement. The link he'd sought all these months had just been revealed. He had no idea of the circumstances involved, no hint as to when it had occurred. Yet there was no question as to its meaning. Johnny Ringo could tie Earp to the stage robberies!

"Doc's right." Warren placed a hand on his brother's shoulder, reassuring him. "We've evened the score for Morg, but we can't afford to stay in the territory much longer. If we try chasin' Ringo down, it's us that's liable to get caught. And you'd never get off, not for murder."

"Frank Stilwell," Earp said quietly, "was a good-for-nothin' backshooter. Him and Cruz both deserved to die."

"Maybe they did," Holliday agreed. "But that don't change the shape of things. Behan's on our trail, and sooner or later, he's bound to get us cornered. Once he does, he'll move heaven and earth to put us on the gallows. You know it for a fact, too."

"So you're sayin' we should run, is that it?"

Holliday nodded. "We've played out our string. No sense bettin' into a cold deck when there's always a new game somewhere else."

"I suppose," Earp said in a resigned voice. "You got any place special in mind?"

"Colorado," Holliday replied quickly. "Behan wouldn't never figure us to head north. That's why we haven't run across him up till now. He's probably got the whole Mexican border covered like a mustard plaster."

A tight fist of apprehension suddenly gripped Starbuck. With Earp in Arizona, there were several options open to him. At least two murder charges were outstanding, which made every lawman in the territory Starbuck's ally. There was, moreover, the new possibility presented by Johnny Ringo. He had no idea where it would lead, or even how it might be turned to advantage. Yet it would be of no advantage whatever in Colorado. He had the sinking feeling that everything was suddenly falling apart.

"Doc's on the right track," Warren said earnestly. "Once we're across the line into Colorado, they couldn't touch us in a month of Sundays. It'd be a whole new ball of wax. A fresh start!"

"A fresh start." Earp's voice was abstracted. "How many times would that make?"

"How many times what?"

"Three, four," Earp mumbled to himself. "We've started over so many times I've lost count."

"One thing about it," Holliday said morosely. "It beats the hell out of having your neck stretched."

Earp inclined his head in a faint nod. "No argument there. I just don't like the idea of leavin' loose ends."

"You talkin' about Ringo?"

"He's about the only loose end left."

"You think about a hangin' rope," Holliday advised him. "That'll take your mind off Ringo."

Earp's gaze drifted to the body swaying overhead. He permitted himself a single ironic glance, and his eyes shuttled away. He turned slowly to look at Holliday.

"We'll pull out at sunrise."

Starbuck felt like he'd been punched in the mouth. All his plans were out the window, and there seemed no alternative to tagging along. His thoughts turned north, to Colorado. He considered a last desperate gamble, a way to end it. Perhaps the only way.

A week later the Earp party rode into Trinidad. They were bone-weary, with the look of men who had ridden hard and traveled light. At one of the town's sleazier hotels, rooms were engaged for the night. There, with plans to meet for breakfast, they separated. Tomorrow seemed time enough to discuss the future.

In his room, Starbuck stripped and poured a pitcher of water into the washbasin. He took a bird-bath, sponging away layers of grime, then used the dirty water to shave. From his saddlebags, he laid out a fresh shirt and a clean pair of trousers. Padding around the room in his undershorts, he lit a cheroot and turned down the bed covers. The bath had refreshed him, but he was hollow-eyed with fatigue and needed sleep. He stretched out on the bed, placing a stone ashtray on his stomach. He blew a slow, thoughtful smoke ring at the ceiling.

Trinidad, he told himself, was a shrewd choice on Earp's part. By rail, it lay some two hundred miles south of Denver. Of greater significance, from a strategic standpoint, it was perfectly situated for a man on the run. Only ten or twelve miles south of town, at the state boundary, Raton Pass provided a gateway into the wilds of northern New Mexico. To the east, perhaps a day's ride away, was No Man's Land, a lawless sanctuary for outlaws and killers. To the southeast, bordering New Mexico and No Man's Land, was the Texas Panhandle, equally remote and bereft of peace officers. Within that unholy trinity, a man could lose himself forever. In the event Earp had to run, there was no better jumping off point than Trinidad. But then, having escaped Arizona, why would it be necessary to run?

The question summoned a thought from some dark corner of Starbuck's mind. For the past few days he'd been toying with a new, and not altogether improbable, idea. The details were still fuzzy, and it was another in a string of longshots he had played so unsuccessfully over the past four months. Yet it was entirely legal, and unlike killing Earp outright, it would boost his stock as a detective. Not that he flinched from killing, but he'd undertaken the assignment with the thought of adding a feather to his cap rather than a notch on his gun. All the same, the critical factor was Earp himself.

Nothing had been said openly, but Starbuck sensed that Trinidad was the end of the line. Tomorrow, Earp would cut the cord and send his band of gunmen their separate ways. Their usefulness to him had ended the day he fled Arizona. Like ragtag soldiers, recruited for the duration of hostilities, they had served their pur-

pose. The war was lost, the last battle fought, and tomorrow they would be mustered out. Their leader,
simply put, no longer needed them.

Vermillion and McMasters doubtless expected to be
sent packing. They were, after all, professionals who
formed alliances rather than personal bonds. As for
Holliday, Starbuck suspected he was in for a surprise,
perhaps the shock of his life. He was about to discover
that all men are expendable. Loyalty was a fragile currency, and even those who risk death in the name of
friendship ultimately outlive their usefulness. Holliday, so long an asset, had now become a liability. He
was a notorious gunman and certain to attract attention
wherever he might go. All of which meant his time
had come and gone. The man he'd faithfully served
now sought obscurity, not headlines.

Starbuck's decision, then, boiled down to a single
element. If Earp stayed put, then legal means might
yet deliver him into the hands of the hangman. If he
tried to run, assuming a new identity, then he would
have to be killed swiftly, using whatever pretext presented itself. Tomorrow would tell the tale.

Starbuck stubbed out his cheroot and set the ashtray
on the floor. He turned down the lamp, easing back
on the pillow, and closed his eyes. He was asleep almost instantly.

After a late breakfast, Earp led the men to a saloon
across from the hotel. The noontime rush was still an
hour away, and the place was empty except for a few
loafers. He signaled the barkeep, and walked toward
a table at the rear of the room.

Over breakfast, Starbuck had detected traces of the man he'd first met in Tombstone. Apparently a night's sleep had restored Earp's vitality. Of greater consequence, the relative haven of Colorado had quite clearly restored his spirits. He exuded confidence, once more in command of himself and events. The thin cord of sanity was on the mend.

The barkeep brought a bottle and glasses. Earp poured for himself, then passed the bottle around the table. When everyone had a drink, he raised his glass in salute.

"You're as good a bunch as a man ever rode with. Here's mud in your eye!"

The men nodded, pleased by the compliment, and drained their glasses. The bottle once more circled the table, but this time there was no toast. Everyone sensed Earp had something on his mind, and they dutifully waited for him to speak. He took a slow sip of whiskey and set his glass on the table. Then his eyes moved from face to face. He smiled.

"Well, boys, I guess it's time for adios and goodbye. Like the man said, all good things come to an end."

Vermillion bobbed his head agreeably. "Where to from here, Wyatt? Any ideas?"

"Now that you mention it," Earp said briskly, "I was talkin' with the desk clerk before you boys came down this morning. He tells me they've struck it big over at Gunnison."

"Gunnison?" Vermillion repeated blankly. "Never heard of it."

"New silver camp," Earp informed them. "Hundred

miles or so west of Colorado Springs. Way it sounds, it'll make Tombstone look like small potatoes."

McMasters chuckled. "You sound like you got the itch again. Figure Gunnison needs a head dog, do you?"

"Aim high, that's my motto! Nobody ever caught the brass ring with his eyes on the ground."

"Damned if that ain't the truth."

"How about you, Sherm?" Earp inquired. "Headed back to Nogales?"

"Not right off," McMasters said vaguely. "Thought I'd take a little sashay down through Texas."

"Don't say?" Earp glanced at Vermillion. "You boys aren't breakin' up the team, are you?"

Vermillion grinned. "I reckon we'll stick together. Folks always figure they're gettin' two for the price of one."

Earp sipped, quiet a moment. Then his gaze swung to Holliday. "How about you, Doc?"

Holliday looked startled. "What d'you mean?"

"Where're you headed? I'd ask you to come along with me and Warren, but Gunnison's just startin' up. Wouldn't be enough action to suit your style."

There was a long silence. Holliday eyed him with a steady, uncompromising stare. No one, least of all Holliday, had missed the point. Dodge City and Tombstone, all the years in between, were of another time. The slate had been wiped clean, and this time he wasn't being invited along. At length, collecting himself, he gave Earp an ashen grin.

"It's Denver for me," he said casually. "I've got a

taste for bright lights and easy livin'. Tombstone pretty
well cured me of mining camps."

"Know what you mean," Earp remarked with false
cordiality. "Course, you're always welcome, Doc.
Anytime you get the urge, why pop on over and see
us." He paused, glancing at Starbuck without much
interest. "What about yourself, Jack?"

Starbuck made a spur of the moment decision. His
gut-instinct told him Earp was actually headed for
Gunnison. That allowed a little leeway in his own
plans. A trip to Denver, and a conference with the
Wells, Fargo superintendent, suddenly seemed very
much in order.

"I'll tag along with Doc," he said in high good humor. "Bright lights and fancy sportin' houses sound
awful tempting right about now."

"Christ!" Holliday muttered aloud. "Don't get any
fool notions. I play a lone hand, no partners!"

"Wouldn't have you anyway," Starbuck ribbed him.
"You're too honest for a grifter like me. Strictly along
for the ride, Doc! Good company makes the time fly."

"You just remember that when we get to Denver."

"Say now!" Starbuck said abruptly, turning to Earp.
"Just thought of something. When you bring the
women up from Tucson, be sure and tell Alice goodbye for me. It's not likely I'll get over Gunnison way."

"I'll do it," Earp said a little too hastily. "She'll be
sorry she missed you."

Starbuck heard the lie in his voice. Suddenly it was
all the more important that he get to Denver. There

were things to be done, and no time to spare. With a broad smile, he raised his glass and looked around the table.

"Here's to you, gents! Better days ahead!"

CHAPTER 18

Alice's hair was loose and unbound. She was still wearing her nightgown and her expression was dreamy. Sitting up in the bed, her legs were drawn up and her chin rested on her knees. She was watching Starbuck dress.

His morning ritual seldom varied. By now, she could anticipate every move, step by step. A short, vigorous scrubbing of teeth and a quick splash in the washbasin. A methodical shave, the razor gliding along his jaw bone with deliberate strokes, followed by a few haphazard rakes of a comb through the sandy thatch of hair. Then he selected one of two suits hanging in the wardrobe and began dressing. His final act, which seemed to require the utmost concentration, was knotting his four-in-hand tie. He stood now before the mirror, adjusting the tie with one last tug.

Today, though, her thoughts were not on the morning ritual. Her eyes followed his every movement but her mind was fastened upon the man himself. She marveled that she could love him so completely. With utter candor, she also considered the fact that he did not love her.

A month ago, at the boardinghouse in Tucson, she had received a wire. His request was simple and straightforward: he asked that she and Mattie join him in Denver. He alluded as well to the fact that they were now on their own and had no compelling reason to remain in Tucson. By then, of course, they knew Earp had departed Arizona one jump ahead of a murder warrant. His exact whereabouts were unknown, and since dumping them at the boardinghouse, he had never once attempted to communicate with Mattie. The conclusion, after all those weeks of silence, was inescapable. They could wait until doomsday and there would be no letter, no message of any kind. He had deserted Mattie.

Jack Johnson's wire had seemed a godsend. They were without funds and without prospects. A woman stranded in Tucson and seeking a livelihood was faced with hard times. Her choices were limited to laundress, cafe waitress, or dancehall girl. Or in the extremity, she could join the girls on crib row, selling herself for whatever the traffic would bear. Alice, her heart thumping wildly, chose instead to join Jack Johnson.

All her arguments directed to Mattie were to no avail. Despondent, drinking heavily, Mattie would listen to no slander aimed at her husband. While she wallowed in self-pity, she still loved him and she was almost irrational in her belief that he would one day send for her. After a night of fruitless wrangling, Alice realized it was hopeless. She could stay, knowing full well Mattie was destined for crib row, or she could take a chance on happiness. She wired Jack Johnson to meet her train in Denver.

There, after a warm and passionate reunion, she learned the truth. With shock and dismay, she sat round-eyed while Jack Johnson slowly revealed himself as Luke Starbuck. He told her the whole story, omitting nothing. He made no excuses, openly admitting that he had used her to cultivate Earp's trust. He went on to explain he'd planned to use her as a witness with regard to Earp's involvement in the Tombstone stage robberies. Holding nothing back, he then related he was working secretly to have Earp and Holliday extradited to Arizona on murder charges. In the event that scheme was successful, her testimony would still prove invaluable. She could corroborate, through personal knowledge, a conspiracy that had ultimately led to cold-blooded murder. At the same time, she could avenge her sister, who was no less a victim of Earp's brutality. At last, looking her straight in the eye, Starbuck had told her of his own feelings. He made no promises, but he clearly cared for her and he was deeply concerned with her welfare. She was free to go or stay as she chose. He hoped she would stay.

She stayed. Nothing he'd told her had changed the way she felt toward him. She was there because he wanted her there. He could just as easily have left her in Tucson and called her to testify at the appropriate time. His interest in her, though he dwelled on her importance to the investigation, was clearly personal. She believed that the night he'd taken her into his confidence, and she still believed it. A month with the man she now knew as Luke Starbuck had only served to heighten her emotional attachment.

Underneath the hard exterior, she had discovered that he was not only gentle but delighted in spoiling her. Their suite in the Brown Palace was small but well appointed, far more luxurious than anything she'd ever known. He insisted on outfitting her in stylish gowns, took her to the theater and the finest restaurants, and lavished her with thoughtful gifts. Even more revealing, he was an attentive lover and seemed never to tire of their madcap romps in bed. She had only one complaint. He was still operating under his alias, and the hotel staff always addressed her as Mrs. Johnson. She would have much preferred Mrs. Starbuck.

Yet marriage, under any name, was a remote possibility. She daydreamed a great deal, but she never deceived herself. For all his gentleness and concern, she understood that the man who shared her bed was wary of any permanent bond. He was drawn by wanderlust and his lodestone was some inner vision of distant places he'd not yet seen. She thought there was little likelihood he would ever marry her. She contented herself with the man and the moment, asking nothing more. It was enough for now, perhaps forever. A treasured time of joy and immense happiness.

Starbuck turned from the mirror, smiling. "How do I look?"

"Very spiffy," she said pertly. "What's the occasion?"

"Today's the day we put Holliday on ice."

Her voice went husky and something odd happened to her face. "Will there be trouble?"

"Let's hope so!" he said with great relish. "I'd welcome the chance to put Holliday away for keeps."

"You—" She hesitated, looking at him seriously. "You'll be careful, won't you?"

He made a small gesture of dismissal. "It's in the bag! You get yourself gussied up and we'll go out on the town tonight."

She smiled uncertainly. "I'll be ready."

"Why don't you write Mattie another letter? Tell her Holliday's in the cooler and her no-account husband is next on the list. Maybe that'll bring her around."

"It's no use," she admitted unhappily. "Mattie won't change. She'll destroy herself before she would betray him."

"Damn shame." He met her eyes, but the words came hard. "She's too good a woman to waste herself in the cribs. Wish she'd listen to reason."

Her lips trembled. "I'm worried about you, not Mattie. It frightens me . . . what you're doing . . . all of it."

"Hey, none of that!"

He walked to the bed and took her chin in his hand. He kissed her softly on the mouth, looked deep into her eyes. "Come on, now, no tears allowed! Let me see a smile."

"Yes, sir." She smiled a sad clown smile. "But don't you dare give him an even break."

"That's the ticket!"

He grinned and quickly crossed the room. At the door, he jammed his hat on his head and gave her a reassuring wink. After he'd gone, she sat for a long while with her hands folded in her lap. Her eyes were veined with fear.

Outside the hotel Starbuck turned onto Larimer Street. It was a sunny morning with a hint of spring in the air. The fine weather made his mood all the more chipper, and he stepped along at a brisk pace. He was whistling softly under his breath.

The long wait, like Denver's prolonged winter storms, had at last drawn to a close. Six weeks ago, upon arriving from Trinidad, he had parted with Holliday at the train station. Since then, though they had seen each other only rarely, he had managed to keep tabs on the lean gambler. The Wells, Fargo agent at Gunnison, sworn to secrecy, also kept him posted on Earp. Time had vindicated his hunch, and it soon became apparent he had no reason for concern. True to form, Earp had designs on Gunnison. He was operating a faro game and slowly forming political alliances.

Starbuck, meanwhile, had set the wheels in motion on his latest plan. Arizona authorities were informed of Earp's whereabouts, and it was suggested that Colorado would act favorably on extradition papers. The plan was well received, but very quickly developed into a political tug-of-war. Sheriff John Behan of Tombstone and Sheriff Bob Paul of Tucson were both determined to be the man who returned Wyatt Earp to Arizona. The battlelines were drawn at the territorial capital, and shortly degenerated into a stalemate. The credit for capturing Earp seemed somehow more important than the act itself.

Only last night word had arrived that a solution was near at hand. The details were as yet unknown, but Starbuck took it as a positive sign. Working with Wells, Fargo, he had concocted an elaborate scheme to jail Holliday. With that done, he would then travel to Gunnison and maintain a close surveillance on Earp. Once the extradition papers were served, the net would close and the law would take its course. Earp and Holliday would rapidly, if reluctantly, he hustled aboard a train bound for Arizona.

On the stroke of ten, Starbuck entered the Slaughterhouse Saloon. Always punctual, Perry Mallan was waiting at a table in the rear. An ox of a man, Mallan was heavyset, with shoulders like a singletree. He looked tough as nails, and perfectly suited to the Slaughterhouse, the rawest busthead dive in all of Denver.

In truth, Mallan was a gentle soul, a frustrated actor, with a secret yearning to tread the boards. Lacking the stature to play Hamlet, he practiced instead the ancient art of chicanery. He was a swindler and confidence man nonpareil, and his performances had drawn rave reviews from every police department throughout the midwest. Starbuck had imported him from Chicago early last week.

Mallan was nursing a warm beer. Starbuck ordered one of the same, and waited until the bartender returned to his station behind the counter. Then he smiled, searching Mallan's face.

"All set for the big day?"

"You bet'cha," Mallan blustered. "It'll be a piece of cake."

"Got your papers?"

Mallan patted his coat pocket. He had a forged document, provided by Starbuck, which identified him as a Utah peace officer. He also had an outstanding murder warrant for one John H. "Doc" Holliday. There was a slight hitch in his voice when he spoke.

"You're sure the bulls won't tumble?"

"Dead sure," Starbuck affirmed. "Holliday's like a black-eye to Denver. The police will jump at the chance to put him behind bars."

Mallan looked worried. "I'm still not too keen on the next part. What if they release him to me? I'd play billy-hell taking him back to Utah."

"I've told you a dozen times. Holliday will hire himself a lawyer, and the whole thing's certain to get bogged down in the courts. You just stick to your story and tell everyone you've requested extradition papers."

"That's what bothers me. Somebody could get nosy and check with the Utah authorities. Then I'd be left holding the bag."

"No chance," Starbuck assured him. "It'll take weeks, maybe even a month, before anyone gets wise. By then, you'll be long gone and a helluva lot richer."

"I'll drink to that."

Mallan took a long draught from his beer stein. Starbuck leaned back in his chair, his legs stretched out before him. A moment passed while he studied the con man with an appraising look. For the past week they had rehearsed until Mallan had the story letter perfect. But now he seemed to have developed a case of the last minute jitters. At length, Starbuck leaned forward, elbows on the table.

"You got your pitch down pat?"

"Oh, sure," Mallan said hoarsely. "I could spiel it off backwards."

"Anything left to iron out? Now's the time to do it."

"No." Mallan sounded uncertain. "I'm as ready as I'll ever be."

"How ready is that?" Starbuck asked in a low voice. "You're not getting cold feet on me, are you?"

"Not on your tintype!" Mallan said indignantly. "I'm too old a hand for that. Nerves like a rock!"

"Cut the crap!" Starbuck said curtly. "Something's bothering you. Let's hear it, and don't give me any song and dance!"

"Well—" Mallan shrugged, his mouth downturned in a grimace. "All right, I'll be square with you, Luke. I'm a grifter, not a gunman! I've got the sweats about Holliday."

Starbuck waved the objection aside. "For Chrissake, you'll have the drop on him! What could go wrong?"

"Good question." Mallan gave him a hangdog look. "What if he decides to make a fight of it? I've never shot a gun in my life, much less a man. It's not my style!"

"Leave that to me," Starbuck said calmly. "I'll back your play straight down the line, and I don't miss. If he even looks cross-eyed, he's a dead man."

"I get the feeling you'd like that."

"Let's just say I wouldn't lose any sleep over it."

"Fair enough," Mallan said with a lame smile. "I'll be there on the dot of six. You just keep your eyes peeled in case he gets testy."

"Like you said," Starbuck noted dryly. "It's a piece of cake."

His beer untouched, Starbuck rose and walked toward the door. Mallan watched him a moment, wondering vaguely how the night would end. Then, with an unsteady hand, he quaffed the mug of beer in a single gulp.

Shortly before six, Perry Mallan stepped through the door of the Criterion. One of the Denver's plusher establishments, the Criterion was a high-class saloon and gambling casino. The front of the room was devoted to assorted games of chance, and several poker tables were ranged along the rear wall. Doc Holliday was seated at the center table.

Mallan exchanged a glance with Starbuck, who was standing idly at the end of the bar. Then he moved through the crowd and walked directly to the poker table. He halted on an angle that gave Starbuck a clear field of fire. Without hesitation, he pulled a bulldog pistol from inside his coat and leveled it on Holliday. The other players froze, their eyes glued on the gun.

"John H. Holliday!" Mallan said forcefully. "I have a warrant for your arrest."

"Arrest!" Holliday croaked, like a whorehouse parrot learning a new obscenity. "On what charge?"

"The murder of Charles Dunwood."

"Who?" Holliday glared at him in baffled fury. "I don't know anybody named Dunwood."

"You should," Mallan countered. "You murdered him in Provo, Utah, on August 8, 1878."

"Utah!" Holliday's eyes held a wicked glint. "I've never set foot in Utah! And who the hell are you, anyway?"

"Deputy Sheriff Mallan." Mallan cocked the bulldog pistol. "I'd advise you to come along peaceable."

"Come along where?"

"To the police station, where formal charges will be lodged awaiting extradition to Utah."

"You're crazy." Holliday went white around the mouth. "I'm not going anywhere, especially Utah."

"Be warned!" Mallan boomed. "If you resist, I will be forced to shoot you dead where you sit."

Holliday hesitated, eyeing the snout of the pistol. Then, with an unintelligible oath, he drew himself up stiffly, hands raised. Mallan patted him down, tossing a Colt sixgun and a hideout stiletto on the table. All business, Mallan next spun him around like a top and shoved him hard.

"March! And no tricks if you value your life!"

Holliday marched. On the way past the bar, he gave Starbuck a look of muddled outrage. Starbuck lifted his hands in an elaborate shrug, and looked equally dumbfounded. Then the crowd parted and Mallan hustled his prisoner toward the door.

Outwardly sober, Starbuck gritted his teeth to keep from laughing. He thought to himself that Mallan had missed his calling. The man was a born stage actor, and a ham to boot. A regular goddamn Edwin Booth!

*   *   *

"When do you leave?"

"Tomorrow morning."

Horace Griffin pursed his lips and nodded solemnly. "Any chance Earp will run?"

Starbuck had gone directly from the Criterion to the Wells, Fargo office. He was seated now beside the superintendent's desk. He pondered the question a moment, then wormed around in his chair and flexed his shoulders.

"Always a chance," he conceded. "I'm counting on him to stay put once he hears it's a Utah warrant. Not very likely he'd connect that to the Arizona business."

"And if he does?"

"Then I'll stop him," Starbuck said evenly. "That's why I'm going to Gunnison."

Griffin gave the matter some thought. "There's still no indication," he said finally, "as to when we'll receive the extradition papers from Arizona. It could be tomorrow or it could be a month from now."

"I'll wait," Starbuck observed stoically. "Holliday's on ice, and Earp might as well be. Even if he spooks, he won't get very far."

"At this point," Griffin remarked, watching him closely, "the company would much prefer to see Earp stand trial. The publicity would serve as an excellent object lesson for stage robbers." He paused, weighing his words. "Don't kill him unless it's unavoidable."

"That's the only reason I ever killed anybody."

Starbuck rose and the superintendent gravely shook his hand. As he went out the door, Griffin frowned and settled back in his chair. A thought persisted, and he found himself unable to shake it off. He wondered how long Wyatt Earp had to live.

CHAPTER 19

The sun was a swollen ball of orange on the western horizon. The evening train from Denver chuffed into the Gunnison station and ground to a halt. The passengers, as usual, were a motley assortment drawn to Colorado's latest boomtown.

Starbuck was standing near the depot door. His wait in Gunnison had stretched to almost two weeks, and he was still operating undercover. Coded telegrams from Horace Griffin kept him advised of events at the state capital. Until yesterday, there had been little or no progress. Then a wire notified him that the extradition papers had been delivered to the governor in Denver. Another wire, arriving late this morning, instructed him to meet the evening train. The deciphered message gave him a description, and more importantly, a name. Sheriff Bob Paul of Tucson, Arizona.

Starbuck waited now under the overhang of the depot roof. The stationmaster was a nodding acquaintance, but he saw no one else who might recognize him. His eyes scanned the passengers debarking the train. Gunnison was growing rapidly, and every train was packed with new arrivals. The mix was generally split between workingmen and rogues. Tonight's lot was sprinkled with miners and drummers, but the sporting crowd, especially fancy ladies, was well represented. Like every boomtown, the lure was strongest for the most disreputable element. Vice was already the backbone of Gunnison's commerce.

One of the last passengers off the train brought Starbuck alert. The man stepped onto the platform and stood looking around. He was of medium height, solidly built, with angular features and a neatly trimmed mustache. He wore a broadcloth coat and a high-crowned Stetson, and he was carrying a battered warbag. Under his coat the bulge of a sixgun was plainly visible. He fitted the description in the telegram perfectly.

With a casual air, Starbuck moved from underneath the overhang and lit a cheroot. He glanced at the lawman over the flare of the match, and their eyes met. He ducked his chin, indicating Paul was to follow him. Then he turned and walked toward the end of the platform.

The main street of Gunnison was lined with saloons and stores and several greasy-spoon cafes. The evening crowds were already out in force, and the town hummed with activity. Halfway up the street was the Olympic House, one of three hotels already in operation. Starbuck sauntered along at an unhurried pace, weaving in and out of the throngs jamming the boardwalk. He felt certain Paul would keep him in sight, and he paused only when he reached the hotel. There, he glanced back and saw the lawman a few steps behind. A quick look was exchanged, then he entered the hotel.

Crossing the lobby, he mounted the stairs to the second floor. A central hallway ran the length of the hotel, and he moved rapidly to his room. He unlocked the door, stepping inside, and waited. The sound of footsteps grew louder, and a moment later Paul entered the room. Starbuck closed the door, locking it with a twist of the key. When he turned, the lawman was watching him with a fixed smile.

"No offense," Starbuck told him, "but I'd like to hear your name."

"Bob Paul," Paul said, hand outthrust. "If you're not Luke Starbuck, we're both in a lot of trouble."

Starbuck shook his hand warmly. "I'm damn glad to meet you. It's been a long wait."

"So I'm told." Paul tossed his hat and warbag on the bed. "Horace Griffin filled me in on the whole story. He says you've been doggin' Earp since last December."

"That's the way it worked out."

"Then you were with him the night he killed Frank Stilwell."

"It was more like an execution. Earp never gave him a chance, just cut loose with that shotgun."

"He's bound to hang, then! With you on the witness stand, we'll have an airtight case."

Starbuck waved him to a chair. "What's the latest on the extradition?"

"Looks good," Paul said, seating himself. "I left the papers with the governor's office yesterday. Griffin said he'd wire us the minute they're signed."

"Why didn't you wait and bring 'em along?"

"Politicians aren't much at keepin' secrets. Figured I'd come on here, just in case word leaked out to Earp."

"Sounds reasonable." Starbuck straddled a chair. "Speaking of politicians, how'd you leave things in Arizona? We heard you and Behan locked horns over who had first dibs on Earp."

Paul chuckled softly. "I finally convinced the territorial governor that I had the best case. Behan damn near tore Tombstone apart when he got the word."

"Wouldn't be surprised," Starbuck noted. "Earp made a fool out of him more times than you could count."

"Tell me about Earp," Paul said with a quizzical frown. "What's his game here in Gunnison?"

Starbuck gave him a slow, dark smile. "Leopards don't change their spots. He's got himself a faro concession at the Tivoli Saloon, and from what I gather, he's buying property hand over fist. Give him a little time, and he'll end up the town's leading citizen."

"How about politics?"

"Same as Tombstone." Starbuck shook his head ruefully. "Course, you've got to give him credit. He sizes things up and then he moves fast. No flies on him!"

"And folks buy it?" Paul said, troubled. "Don't they know all the stuff he pulled in Arizona?"

"Earp's a smooth article," Starbuck replied. "He gets close to the right people, and keeps telling them he was framed by Behan because he tried to run the criminal element out of Tombstone. Pretty soon they start believing it."

"What do you mean—the right people?"

"Well, for one thing, he's already in thick with a couple of the big mine owners. That's what I mean about a leopard. He's working the same dodge, damn near step-for-step, that he used in Tombstone."

"I hope to Christ—"

There was a knock at the door. Hitching back his chair, Starbuck motioned the lawman to the far side of the room. Then he walked to the door and opened it. A bellman handed him a telegram and accepted a dollar tip in return. Closing the door, he tore open the envelope.

"It's from Griffin."

While Paul watched, he took a pencil and slowly decoded the message. His expression turned grim, then gradually dissolved into a look of thunderstruck rage. At last, cold fury written across his features, he glanced up at the lawman.

"The governor refused to sign the extradition papers."

"On what grounds?"

"Legal technicalities." Starbuck studied the telegram a moment. "Griffin doesn't spell that out, but he says there was pressure brought to bear on the governor. Pressure not to extradite."

"Pressure!" Paul repeated. "Pressure from where?"

"Gunnison," Starbuck said in disgust. "Earp's evidently in thicker than I thought with the mine owners."

"But it's a murder charge!" Paul's eyes were rimmed with dull despair. "The evidence was all laid out, depositions and everything. How the hell could he refuse to extradite?"

"Who knows," Starbuck said woodenly. "Where politics are concerned, it don't pay to underestimate Earp. I should've learned that in Tombstone."

The truth suddenly came home to him. There was no way to touch Earp. Working within the law was a waste of time. With bleak irony, he asked himself why he'd even tried. Some men, using politics to insulate themselves, were above the law. Even in Arizona, had Earp been brought to trial, it very likely would have resulted in acquittal. There were too many skeletons that couldn't bear the light of day. Too many men of wealth and power who, as a last resort, would have called all their political markers in his defense. Only outside the law could Wyatt Earp be stopped. There was no legal way.

"How bad do you want Earp?"

"Pretty bad," Paul said slowly. "Why?"

"Because I'm fixing to handle this thing the way I should've handled it a long time ago."

"How's that?"

"Feet first." Starbuck's voice was edged. "You got any objections?"

"Objections!" Paul's laugh was a harsh sound in the cramped room. "Hell, I'll back your play!"

"It might cost you your badge."

"Would it get Earp killed?"

"If I can force him to draw," Starbuck said with surpassing calm, "he'll be dead before he gets the message."

"How d'you figure to do that?"

"He's got a weak spot. I aim to gig it till he sees red."

"When?"

"Tonight," Starbuck said, rising to his feet. "Let's go."

"Where to?"

"The Tivoli."

Upstreet from the hotel, the Tivoli Saloon was wedged between a dancehall and a two-bit a night flophouse.

By comparison with Denver gaming parlors, the Tivoli was crude and barnlike in appearance. Coal oil lamps hung bare from the rafters and the back bar mirror was webbed with cracks. The ubiquitous nude paintings were conspicuous by their absence, and the bar, though mahogany, looked as if it had been purchased at a bankruptcy auction. Spittoons were much in evidence, and sawdust covered the floor to absorb blood from the nightly slugfests.

While miners were not partial to guns, they took queer delight in maiming one another in no-holds-barred rough and tumble brawls. A bullet-headed bouncer, wearing an eye-patch and an evil grin, refereed the bouts with a lead-loaded bungstarter. He allowed the fights to go no more than a couple of rounds before he waded in and began splitting skulls. An ivory tickler, generally souped on rotgut whiskey, accompanied the thunk of his bungstarter on a rinky-dink piano. Such as it was, the bouncer and his musical colleague were the only entertainment in the Tivoli. The gaming tables, thought to be rigged, were considered more challenge than amusement. The miners spent their evenings trying to outguess quick-fingered dealers.

The bouncer was dragging a limp gladiator through the door as Starbuck and Paul entered the saloon. A raucous crowd already jammed the room, and the gaming tables were under siege by miners as yet unconvinced that the hand was quicker than the eye. Starbuck led the way to the bar, and bulled a spot for himself and the lawman amongst the serious drinkers. He chose a position directly across from Earp's faro layout.

Sipping whiskey, Starbuck turned his back to the bar, one heel hooked over the brass rail. Several minutes passed before Earp happened to glance in his direction. A ferocious grin lit his face and he rolled his eyes toward Bob Paul.

Earp followed his gaze and abruptly stopped dealing. From past meetings, he knew the Arizona lawman on sight. Once, during his brief tenure as a U.S. Deputy Marshal, they had even worked together in an effort to trap the Brocius gang. The faro game forgotten, his eyes hooded and his look suddenly became veiled.

"Wyatt Earp!"

Starbuck shouted the name. His abrasive tone claimed the crowd's attention like a clap of thunder. All eyes turned toward him and the buzz of conversation faded to watchful stillness. The men ganged around the faro layout slowly edged away. He pointed a finger directly at Earp.

"You're wanted for murder!"

Earp's expression was sphinxlike. He stared at Starbuck with eyes slitted against the smoky haze separating them. His voice was clipped, without inflection.

"What's your game, Johnson?"

"No game," Starbuck said, jerking a thumb at the lawman. "You know my friend here?"

"I know him."

"Course you do." Starbuck looked around at the crowd, grinning. "All the same, he ought to have a proper introduction. Gents, I'd like you to meet Sheriff Bob Paul, Pima County, Arizona. He's got a murder warrant for Earp's arrest."

"That's old news," Earp said tightly. "Everybody knows I was railroaded out of Arizona."

"So you say!" Starbuck's face took on a sudden hard cast. "What they don't know is that you're a garden-variety murderer. Common as dirt!"

"That's a goddamn lie!"

"No, it's the truth. You're no gunman, Earp! You've got everyone believing it, but that's the lie. You don't have the guts to meet a man face to face!"

"Watch your mouth, Johnson."

"Why? You aim to do something about it?"

Warren Earp, who was working the roulette wheel, stepped clear of the table. Countering his move, Bob Paul eased away from the bar, fixing him with a warning look. Silence thickened in the room. Open hostility was stamped on the Earp brothers' features, and a gunfight seemed inevitable. Then, at length, Earp shook his head.

"Something stinks here," he said gruffly. "Johnson, how come you're sidin' with a lawdog?"

Starbuck shoved off the bar. He crossed the room,

halting directly before the faro layout. There was a catlike eagerness in his eyes.

"I am a lawdog," he said with a cynical smile. "I work for Wells, Fargo."

Earp's composure slipped. His face became a mask of black and angry bafflement. "You no-good sonovabitch. You suckered me!"

"It was easy as pie," Starbuck taunted. "You're a tinhorn chiseler! Strictly smalltime."

No response.

Starbuck goaded him viciously. "Your whole family's smalltime. Your brothers are whoremongers! Your own wife's a whore. You're nothing but a bunch of penny-ante pimps! All of you!"

Earp's face was arrested in brute outrage. So complete was his shock that he appeared dazed, punchy. Yet he saw something in Starbuck's eyes that cut through his numbed senses. He knew his life was forfeit if he moved. The man standing before him was prodding him to draw, and be killed. He kept his hands plainly visible on the table.

Starbuck backhanded him across the mouth. His lip split, spurting blood, and a dread humiliation swept over him. But still he refused the challenge.

"Christ!" Starbuck said coarsely. "You've lost your balls, haven't you? You want to live so bad you'd take anything."

Earp merely stared at him, saying nothing. A moment passed, the crowd frozen in a spellbound tableau, watching them. Then Starbuck wagged his head back and forth.

"All right," he grunted. "Here's the way we'll play

it. You be on the morning train out of town. Otherwise I'll kill you and take my chances with a jury."

Wheeling around, Starbuck pushed through the crowd and walked toward the door. Bob Paul backed along the bar, his eyes guarded, then turned and hurried outside. The miners looked stunned, like spectators at a public witch burning. They slowly moved away from the faro layout, and Wyatt Earp.

The Tivoli closed early that night.

The sky lightened into cloudless dawn. The train stood puffing steam and smoke before the platform. An eerie quiet hung over the depot, and the passengers boarding the train seemed strangely subdued. Once in their seats, they crowded the windows, gawking at the two men near the stationhouse door.

Starbuck took out the makings and built himself a smoke. He lit the cigarette, inhaling deeply, savoring the taste. Last night he'd thrown away the cheroots and gone back to roll-your-owns. The act was a token gesture, but nonetheless symbolic. He had laid Jack Johnson to rest. Today, like slipping into an old shoe, he was himself again. He thought it a damned comfortable feeling.

Bob Paul, standing beside him, stiffened as the stationhouse door opened. Earp, trailed closely by Warren, emerged and started across the platform. Starbuck quickly moved forward and blocked their path. Without a word, he took the train ticket from Earp's hand. Unfolding it, he studied the schedule a moment, then looked up.

"California," he said, not asking a question. "I hear

there's ships there that go all the way to China."

Earp's expression was dour. "I reckon California's far enough."

"Think so?" Starbuck blew smoke in his face. "You just keep looking over your shoulder, Wyatt. One of these days you'll see me."

"What's your name?" Earp spoke through clenched teeth. "Who the hell are you, anyway?"

Starbuck grinned. "Death don't have a name. Now run along and catch your train before I change my mind."

Earp stepped around him and led Warren aboard the nearest passenger coach. The conductor signaled the engineer, and the locomotive chuffed a great cloud of steam. Wheels groaned and couplings cracked, and the train slowly got underway. As the caboose rolled past, Paul walked forward, halting at Starbuck's elbow. They watched, preoccupied with their own thoughts, until the train disappeared down the tracks. Then the lawman let out a heavy sigh.

"Too bad," he said glumly. "About Earp, I mean."

"Oh?" Starbuck's eyes were fixed upon distance. "What about him?"

"That he got away, beat the hangman."

"Maybe he only thinks he got away."

"What d'you mean by that?"

A cryptic smile touched one side of Starbuck's mouth. "Let's just say it's not over yet."

CHAPTER 20

Eagle City lay in the shadow of the Bitterroot Mountains. The town, not yet one year old, was the heart and hub of the Coeur d'Alene goldfields. The discovery had set off a mad stampede, and the small Idaho community quickly became the latest in a long string of western mining camps. Gold, the eternal magnet, drew adventurers by the thousands.

On a brisk autumn afternoon, Starbuck rode into Eagle City. His reputation as a detective was now legend throughout the West. Only last year, in perhaps his most celebrated case, he had broken a ring of train robbers in northern California. The reverberations shook the very power structure of San Francisco, involving political kingpins and warring Chinese tongs. The attendant publicity, with Starbuck's photograph splashed across dozens of newspapers, had robbed him forever of his anonymity. His face was known wherever he traveled, and he no longer undertook an assignment as himself. He was instead a master of disguise. A man of a thousand faces, none of them his own.

Today, like a chameleon, he blended perfectly with his surroundings. His appearance was that of a scruffy miner, a common day laborer. He wore a threadbare mackinaw, soiled trousers stuffed into mule-eared boots, and a woolen duckbill cap. His features were concealed beneath a wild shrub of a beard, and his hair sprouted down over his ears. He smelled rank as a billygoat and his jaw was ballooned by a wad of Red Devil chewing tobacco. His own mother would have disclaimed him.

His mission in Eagle City lacked official sanction. His disguise was not meant for payroll robbers or holdup men who plundered bullion shipments. Nor was he drawn by the lure of gold itself. He was there on personal business.

Starbuck was not a vengeful man. Yet he was proud, and by his own measure, he considered himself a man of character and worth. His reputation as a detective was the single most compelling force in his life. Once he accepted an assignment, he went about it with bulldog tenacity and an obsessive drive to emerge the victor. Failure was a word foreign to his lexicon, and defeat was anathema to his temperament. A deep and overwhelming sense of integrity dictated that once a job was undertaken he would see it through. He imposed no time limit on himself, and short of a complete reckoning, the case was never closed. However long it took, he earned his pay.

For eight years, he had served western business interests as a detective and professional manhunter. In all that time, despite the magnitude of the assignment, he had failed only once to deliver as promised. It was

a singular loss of prestige, and the one black mark on
an otherwise unblemished record. Today, he meant to
wipe the slate clean.

An item in the *Denver Post* had alerted him to old
and unfinished business. Not particularly newsworthy
in itself, the story carried a dateline of Eagle City,
Idaho. What made it of interest to Denver readers was
that it involved a man who, albeit briefly, was once
one of Colorado's more notorious citizens. The story
related that Wyatt Earp and three associates had recently been convicted of claim jumping in the Coeur
d'Alene goldfields. Tongue in cheek, the story went
on to state that Earp, at one time considered the terror
of Arizona, had now been reduced to petty misde-
meanors. The concluding paragraph posed something
of a question. Wondering aloud in print, it asked where
Earp had been keeping himself since his short, and
abruptly terminated, stopover in Gunnison.

Starbuck, in idle moments, had often pondered that
very question. Upon departing Gunnison, some two
years ago, Earp had simply dropped out of sight. Except for a fleeting sojourn to Dodge City, duly reported
by the Kansas papers, he had studiously avoided the
limelight. The reason was no great mystery to Starbuck. That last morning in Gunnison, at the train depot, he had warned Earp that the matter was by no
means settled. Earp, first and foremost a survivor, had
taken the threat seriously. Vanishing into nowhere, his
name had been all but forgotten by press and public
alike.

Yet now, the subject of an obscure news item, Earp
had surfaced once more. And Starbuck, unlike the

public, hadn't forgotten. The case was still open, and the duebill was collectable on demand. In strictest confidence, he fired off a query to an old and trusted colleague in Idaho.

The reply, based on a week's investigation, was much as he'd expected. Earp had arrived in Eagle City shortly after New Year's. The gold camp was remote and lawless, and he was soon up to his old tricks. Forming a combine, he and three other men had begun a campaign of outright intimidation. Some claim holders were persuaded to sell; those who refused found their claims jumped and the property thereafter held at gunpoint. Even when suit was brought, and the combine was fined for claim jumping, the net effect was unaltered. Earp, who apparently had no interest in working the claims, sold out his interest. With a substantial stake, he then bought the White Elephant Saloon & Gaming Parlor. Ever the grifter, it was the kind of goldmine Earp understood best. He relieved the suckers of their poke over the gaming tables, and according to the report, he was doing very well indeed. All in a matter of months, he had gone from claim jumper to proprietor of the largest gambling dive in Eagle City.

On the train ride north from Denver, Starbuck found himself reflecting on the vagaries of time. Some men's lives were touched by it, others were not. Doc Holliday was now in a tubercular sanitarium, wasted by disease and dying a lingering death. Warren Earp, perhaps the best of all the brothers, had been killed in a saloon shootout. But the head of the Earp clan, by all accounts, had been affected little by the passage of time. In some ways, Starbuck thought to himself, Wyatt Earp was like a pestilence. He infected those around him, then moved on. He flourished while they died.

Only Alice had escaped. Upon returning from Gunnison the summer of '82, Starbuck had set her up in a millinery and dress shop. She proved a level-headed businesswoman, repaying the loan with interest, and they had kept company for nearly a year. When it finally became apparent he would never settle down, she proved equally realistic about her personal life. After the long assignment in California, he returned to Denver and found her engaged to a prominent attorney. He wished her well, aware that she needed the security of home and family, and even attended the wedding. On occasion, when he was in Denver, he still dropped by for a visit. She was radiantly happy, heavy now with child, and time had done nothing to dim their closeness. The memory of her often came to him in strange places, when he was alone and without friends. He cherished it in the way of a lonely man compelled to travel a solitary road. Not with regret, but with the warm remembrance of things past.

A week ago, before departing Denver, he had called on her one last time. He told her nothing of his plan to kill Earp. Any number of things might go wrong, and he saw no reason to worry her needlessly. He had every confidence he could outdraw Earp, but there was always the chance he would himself die in the effort. Bracing a man in his own saloon, where he was surrounded by henchmen, entailed a high degree of risk. Moreover, if his own identity was somehow discovered, there was a good chance he would be charged with premeditated murder. For with some care, he had indeed calculated the death of Wyatt Earp.

Three days on the train, rattling northward, had done nothing to alter his resolve. Some men deserved to die, and Earp, more deserving than most, had been living on borrowed time. He thought it reasonable that he had appointed himself the instrument of Earp's death. By all rights, he should have ended it long before now.

Spokane, situated on the Washington-Idaho border, was the nearest train terminal to the Coeur d'Alene goldfields. There, at a livery stable, he had hired a horse and ridden toward the Bitterroots. His disguise was complete, and the plan, thoroughly rehearsed in his mind, was worked out to the last detail. Camped that night beside the trail, he slept the sound sleep of a man at peace with himself. He was ready.

Today, as he rode into Eagle City, his thoughts went no farther ahead than the next hour. He steeled himself to end it swiftly, without revealing either his identity or his purpose. The White Elephant, a clapboard building liberally doused with whitewash, was located in the center of town. He dismounted a couple of stores downstreet, and looped the reins around a hitch rack. Dusting himself off, he checked the Colt sixgun, snug against his belly in a crossdraw holster. Then he walked toward the White Elephant.

The layout in the gaming parlor was little different than he'd expected. A long bar fronted one wall. Keno, Chuck-a-luck, faro and roulette were ranked along the opposite wall. Poker tables, with baize-covered tops, were grouped at the rear of the room. The bar was crowded and the games were doing a brisk business. Several miners, dressed in rough garb similar to his own, were collected around the faro layout. He thought it entirely in character that Earp was dealing. He'd planned on it, and he hadn't been wrong.

Without pause, he moved straight to the faro table. He brusquely elbowed a place between two players standing directly across from Earp. Jostled aside, the miners cursed, on the verge of protesting. His pugnacious scowl seemed to invite trouble, and the men quickly decided to let it drop. He pulled a handful of gold coins from his pocket and looked over at Earp. His appearance was that of a grubby miner, and by pushing in at the table, he gave the impression of a short-tempered bully with an even shorter fuse. He saw no sign of recognition in Earp's eyes. To complete the ruse, he changed the timbre and inflection of his voice.

"This here game got a limit?"

"Fifty dollars," Earp replied calmly. "Bet'em any way you choose."

"Aim to," Starbuck growled. "Gonna bust your bank, mister! Today's my day to howl!"

"Get a hunch, bet a bunch."

Earp indicated the table was open to play. Starbuck leaned across the layout and placed fifty dollars on the ace. When the other players had their bets down Earp dealt two cards, queen and deuce. He called the turn in a sing-song chant.

"The queen lays and the two spot pays."

"C'mon, deal!" Starbuck grunted testily. "Gimme an ace!"

Earp flashed him a look, but said nothing. The play continued, and Starbuck's luck, as though ordained, dovetailed perfectly with his plan. Always betting the ace, he lost one hundred fifty dollars within the space of eight turns. He fumed and cursed, one eye cocked askew each time an ace came up loser. On the eighth turn, watching his money disappear across the table, he fixed Earp with a sullen glare.

"You ain't listenin', dealer," he said hotly. "Ace to win, that's my play! Not the other way around."

"The cards talk," Earp said with a trace of irritation. "Place your bets, gents."

Starbuck slammed the last of his coins down on the ace. "Lemme see it! Gotta show this time!"

Earp dealt the cards. The case ace, the last in the deck, appeared first, a loser. Before the second card could be turned, Starbuck bristled and crashed his fist onto the table, scattering bets.

"Gawddamnit!" he roared. "I caught you!"

Earp's gaze narrowed. "Caught me what?"

"Caught you red-handed, you buttermouthed piss-ant! You're dealin' from a rigged box!"

"I run an honest game. I'd advise you to button up and back off."

"Honest, my ass!" Starbuck exploded. "You're slick, but you ain't that slick. I saw you kick out that ace!"

Earp appraised him at a glance. He saw no threat, merely a hotheaded trouble-maker spoiling for a fight. On sudden impulse, he decided to push it to the limit.

A sore loser, killed in a fair gunfight, would serve as a warning. A reminder that the White Elephant's square-deal policy was never to be questioned.

"One last chance," Earp said coldly. "Walk away or get carried away."

"You'd like that wouldn't you? Lemme go for my gun and your boys would backshoot me 'fore I even got started."

"We'll keep it private." Earp signaled the housemen to stay clear, then nodded to Starbuck. "All right, squarehead, just you and me."

"Wooeee! Let'er rip!"

Starbuck's hand snaked inside his mackinaw. The miner next to him, at that very instant, ducked and jarred his arm. He saw Earp's gun clearing the leather and he snapped off a hurried shot. Even as he pulled the trigger, he knew he'd missed the mark.

A splotch of blood blossomed on Earp's right coat sleeve, and his Colt clattered to the floor. He slammed backwards into the wall, arm hanging limp, his eyes bulging with shock. He stared across the table with a look of ashen terror.

There was a split-second when Earp's life hung in the balance. Starbuck wanted to kill him, felt some deep visceral need to kill him. But rational thought, not conscience, stayed his finger on the trigger. To kill a wounded man, standing helpless and disarmed, would make him fair game for the mob. Mining camps were infamous for their kangaroo courts and vigilante justice. Kill Earp and he would swing from a tree within the hour. There was no appeal, no court of last resort, in Eagle City.

Starbuck slowly lowered the hammer of his sixgun. He holstered it in a practiced motion, showing empty hands to the housemen. Then he leaned across the table, looking Earp straight in the eye.

"You don't remember me, do you?"

"I—" Earp shook his head, clutched painfully at his arm. "I don't know you."

"Yeah, you do," Starbuck said in his normal voice. "Think back, and it'll come to you. Gunnison, a couple of years ago, the train station."

"Johnson!" Earp croaked, his face a living wax-work. "Jack Johnson."

Starbuck gave him a strange crooked grin. One side of his mouth curled upward while the other remained set in a grim line. His eyes were cold as stone.

"Keep looking over your shoulder. We'll meet again."

Earp fainted. His eyes rolled back in his head and he toppled to the floor like a felled tree. Starbuck uttered a harsh bark of laughter. The housemen stared at him as though he were crazy, and the miners nearest the table seemed to shrink back in dread fear. A moment passed, then he turned and waded through the crowd. No one spoke and no one made a move to stop him. Halfway through the door, he suddenly wheeled around and fixed the room with a wintry smile.

"When he wakes up, tell him to sell out and take off running. I won't be far behind."

His laugh still lingered when the door swung closed. Later, men would say it was the laughter of death itself. The thought gained credence when Wyatt Earp sold the White Elephant to the first bidder. On

September 26, only ten days after being shot, he fled Eagle City. His time in the western mining camps ended there.

Outside town, Starbuck gigged his horse into a lope. His smile vanished like a shutter being closed. He'd put on a bold front in the White Elephant, but he felt no elation now. He was wrestling instead with one of life's great imponderables. A question that had dogged him since his earliest days as a manhunter.

Today's shootout was no feather in his cap. No one would record that his arm had been jostled, spoiling his aim, and thereby sparing Earp's life. On the contrary, the incident would be twisted out of proportion, facts interlaced with fiction, until it became scarcely more than a pretzel of reality. Were Earp to live long enough, the line separating truth from myth would slowly diminish, ultimately disappear. That he had been outdrawn and wounded, very nearly killed, would be lost in the shuffle. He would emerge cloaked in an aura of invincibility. A gunfighter who in the end had proved unkillable.

Starbuck knew, from bitter experience, that truth counted for little. His years as a manhunter had taught him that people much preferred a candy-coated fairy tale to the wormwood of cold facts. The public exhibited some bizarre need for legends larger than life, readily accepting the invention of dime novels as the stuff of truth. Outlaws such as Jesse James and the Youngers, portrayed as victims of injustice, were transformed into folk heroes. Three years ago, when he'd witnessed the death of Billy the Kid, he had seen the process snowball with incredible speed. Virtually overnight, a mad dog killer had been canonized with all the attributes of an avenging angel. Once again, folklore and truth had joined hands in a fantasy concocted as a sugar-tit for the public.

Where Earp was concerned, the process assumed an added dimension. Truly great villains, who practiced murder and corruption on a wholesale level, were often remembered with more affection than dime-a-dozen outlaws. A dab of hypocrisy mixed with a dab of self-delusion very neatly whitewashed reality. Evil fascinated people, and they were prone to attach cardboard virtues to a scoundrel who dared greatly. With time, the murders at the OK Corral, the brutal executions of Frank Stilwell and Florentino Cruz, would be immortalized by penny-a-word hacks grinding out yet another potboiler. Wyatt Earp would emerge from the printed page a man of determination and grit, ever-ready to enter where angels feared to tread. A frontiersman and gunfighter with all the mythical qualities of the breed.

Yet sainthood was rarely conferred on the living. There were exceptions, but more often than not a man was dead and buried long before the legend took form. Always the pragmatist, Starbuck thought the tradeoff was distasteful but nonetheless acceptable. He lived in the present, and events of some distant time were wholly beyond his control. For now, it was enough that Wyatt Earp died. He reaffirmed his vow that it would happen, and soon. He even took ironic amusement from the fact that he would hasten the legend.

In his own way, he would earn a niche in the dime novels.

The man who killed Wyatt Earp.

Westward lay the sunset of another day. He rode there, whistling softly to himself. All the yesterdays were behind him, and his thoughts turned toward tomorrow. Time meant nothing to the hunter, for time alone was his unalterable edge over the hunted. He idly wondered where they would next meet.

Starbuck and Wyatt Earp never again crossed paths.

Upon departing the Coeur d'Alene goldfields, Earp kept on the move. For the next thirteen years, seemingly always on the run, he roamed the West like a nomadic vagabond. He appeared briefly in Kansas, Texas, and Wyoming, never staying long in any one spot. Off and on, he returned to California, but only for short periods of time.

Then, in 1897, he joined the Alaska gold rush. He opened a saloon in Nome, and remained there for four years. Once more on the move, he spent the next half-decade wandering California and Nevada. Finally, in 1906, he settled in Los Angeles. He was fifty-eight years old, and living from hand to mouth. Police records indicate he was arrested at least once on a charge of vagrancy.

All these years Starbuck served in one capacity or another as a free-lance detective. Usually operating undercover, his assignments took him the length and breadth of the West. Yet chance, or what some men call fate, never brought him in contact with Earp. He kept an eye on the newspapers, and an ear to the grapevine, constantly seeking word as to Earp's whereabouts. His search was relentless, but in the end to no avail. Several times he narrowly missed his man, arriving in Tonopah or Goldfield, and twice in San Francisco, only days after Earp pulled still another vanishing act. At last, in 1911, he called off the manhunt.

True to form, Earp was arrested in July of that year on a bunco charge. A brief news item related that he and two confederates were charged with conspiracy to fleece a Los Angeles businessman out of $25,000. Starbuck, who was in California at the time, read the account with grim satisfaction. His search, after twenty-seven years, seemed finally to have ended.

Upon investigating, however, Starbuck lost his taste for the kill. Earp was now an old man, pushing sixty-four, and living a precarious existence. Under constant scrutiny by the police, he was out on bail on another charge when arrested for complicity in the bunco swindle. Starbuck felt nothing akin to compassion. Nor had he mellowed after all that time, even though Tombstone lay a quarter-century and more in the past. He simply couldn't bring himself to kill a toothless old grifter. The act seemed somehow beneath his personal sense of dignity, and he left Los Angeles before the conspiracy trial began. He would, in later years, deeply regret the decision to let it end there.

Wyatt Earp lived to be an octogenarian. He died at age eighty-one on January 3, 1929. To the last, he maintained that he had served law and order as a frontier marshal in Tombstone and the Kansas cow-towns.

By the late 1920s, hucksterism was part of the American scene, and there were many people willing to exploit the windy pipe-dreams of a doddering old man. Exactly as Starbuck had foreseen, the myth-makers ultimately convinced the public that Wyatt Earp was a noble lawman, a gunfighter of legendary proportions. Earp went to his grave with the sly satisfaction of a grifter who has played the big con, and won. The public swallowed the fairy tale whole, sinker and all.

Starbuck knew the truth. Yet he was a manhunter, with no great urge to justify himself or leave testament to his work. Thus he never committed his thoughts to paper and spoke no word of those long ago days in Tombstone. He tried instead to kill Wyatt Earp.

The day they laid Earp to rest he still carried the scar of Starbuck's bullet. He lived out his life thinking the name of the man who shot him was Jack Johnson.

Starbuck always thought it a damn fine joke.

**Before the legend,
there was the man . . .**

And a powerful destiny to fulfill.

On October 26, 1881, three outlaws lay dead in
a dusty vacant lot in Tombstone, Arizona.
Standing over them—Colts smoking—were
Wyatt Earp, his two brothers Morgan and
Virgil, and a gun-slinging gambler named
Doc Holliday. The shootout at the O.K. Corral
was over—but for Earp, the fight had just
begun . . .

**AVAILABLE WHEREVER BOOKS ARE SOLD
FROM ST. MARTIN'S PAPERBACKS**

WE 7/98

IN 1889, Bill Tilghman joined the historic land rush that transformed a raw frontier into Oklahoma Territory. A lawman by trade, he set aside his badge to make his fortune in the boom-towns. Yet Tilghman was called into service once more, on a bold, relentless journey that would make his name a legend for all time—in an epic confrontation with outlaw Bill Doolin.

OUTLAW KINGDOM

MATT BRAUN

AVAILABLE WHEREVER BOOKS ARE SOLD FROM ST. MARTIN'S PAPERBACKS